"Take them!" Decker yelled as he dove behind the desk.

Boomer fired once, then hit the deck as the pair of men who had followed Decker opened fire with submachine guns. The glass that had separated Colonel Coulder's office from the rest of the tunnel exploded inward.

Boomer stuck his hand up over the three-feet-high wall and fired blindly. He heard the roar of Skibicki's gun a few feet to the other side and glanced over. The sergeant major was hunched behind the wall, also firing blindly to keep them from getting closer . . .

"They aren't asking us to surrender," Boomer hissed to Skibicki.

"I noticed," Skibicki replied.

THE LINE

BOB McGUIRE

St. Martin's Paperbacks

THE LINE

ISBN: 0-312-95874-9

Printed in the United States of America

St. Martin's Paperbacks edition/December 1996

10 9 8 7 6 5 4 3 2 1

THE LINE

☆ PROLOGUE

ALEXANDRIA, VIRGINIA
25 NOVEMBER
1:00 P.M. LOCAL/ 1800 ZULU

The man in the high-backed chair was hidden in the shadows cast by the halogen desk lamp. A thin sheaf of laser-printed pages was the only object on the desk in front of him. A hand, the skin withered with age, slowly reached out and angled the first page so it could be read.

11 JUNE 1930
U.S. MILITARY ACADEMY,
WEST POINT, NEW YORK

The smooth marble felt cool to Cadet Benjamin Hooker's hand. He gazed up the shaft of Battle Monument to the stars overhead, then up the Hudson River where the hulking presence of Storm King Mountain loomed to the left, a darker presence against the night sky. It was a view that never failed to raise a strong feeling of attachment and sentiment in Hooker's heart.

That feeling was immediately followed with an uncertainty that had two causes. The first was that tomorrow he would graduate and be leaving his home for the last four years. The second was the written message he'd been given by a plebe earlier in the day. The words had been simple and direct: "TROPHY POINT. 2130 HOURS." There had been no signature, but the paper was written on stationery from the office of the Commandant of Cadets.

Hooker momentarily played with the notion that the note

1

was an elaborate prank set up by his classmates; but he knew he dared not be here, on the chance that the message was legitimate. Although why the commandant would want to see him at such a strange place and time left him at a loss.

Hooker knew he held a special place in his class of 241 cadets. He was ranked second in academic standing and was the fifth recipient of a Rhodes Scholarship in the history of the Academy. Tall and thin, with an angular face that most of the women coming to the Academy for hops found appealing, there was about him a sense of intellectual reserve and emotional distance from others that counteracted his physical attraction. He had straight brown hair that was at the very limit the regulations would allow—unusual for a man who otherwise followed every rule and regulation to the letter. His eyes were black, and when they focused on an individual they had the ability to make that person feel that they had 100 percent of Hooker's attention. Many a long-suffering plebe had felt the power of that gaze during a hazing session in Hooker's room.

Those same eyes flickered across the Plain to the barracks where his classmates were spending their last night as cadets. There was a distinct feeling of excitement and anticipation in the air. Although Hooker shared in it, he had different expectations for the immediate future. While his classmates would go to various officer courses and then report to regular Army units scattered all over the world, Hooker was heading to England for two years of study at Oxford before becoming part of the "real" Army. Although the prestige of the scholarship was great, he was concerned about the possible negative effect those two years out of the active Army loop might have on his career.

"Good evening, Mr. Hooker."

The voice caught Hooker off-guard, his thoughts already halfway across the ocean. He stiffened as he recognized the figure silhouetted in the glow of lights around the Plain. "Good evening, sir," he automatically responded.

Colonel William B. Kimbell's physical appearance was in accordance with his martial reputation. West Point, class of '14, Kimbell had been blooded on the fields of Europe in the Great War, earning a Silver Star for gallantry. The colonel had been wounded three times, but each time had returned to the fight until peace had arrived before a fatal wound. As commandant, Kimbell was in charge of the welfare of the Corps of Cadets, and because of that, ran every aspect of their lives outside the classroom.

"Beautiful, isn't it?" Kimbell said.

Hooker automatically knew that Kimbell was referring to the overall view—regardless of direction. To the north, the Hudson and Storm King framed a scene many artists had captured on canvas. To the east, across the river, lay Constitution Island, the far anchor point for the Great Chain that had been stretched across the river during the Revolution to stop the British from moving on it. To the west, at Plain-level, stood the cadet gym and above it and to the left, loomed the impressive edifice of the cadet chapel, overlooking the main Academy grounds, a slight concession by the planners that there might possibly be an institution more powerful than the Academy. To the immediate south was the billiards-table green surface of the Plain where Hooker had sweated through four years of innumerable parades. Beyond the grass were the barracks where the comraderie of four years of suffering had forged unbreakable bonds among the members of the class of '30.

"Yes, sir, it is."

The commandant turned and started walking, Hooker immediately fell in step, half a pace to the rear as required by etiquette. They passed the links of the Great Chain that were displayed and halted behind a collection of old cannon barrels. "Looking forward to Oxford, Mr. Hooker?"

"Yes, sir."

Kimbell glanced at him in the darkness. "It is an honor for the Academy to have had you selected for the scholarship."

Hooker let that pass without comment. He reined in his emotions and focused on the present. There was a sense of something important about to happen—something beyond graduation and the beginning of a new life.

"Are you worried about missing two years of time in the field?" Kimbell asked.

Hooker wasn't surprised that the commandant could

guess his worry. Any officer would feel the same. "Somewhat, sir."

"Somewhat?" Kimbell snapped. "What does that mean?"

Equivocal answers were not acceptable at West Point. Hooker had had that lesson beat into him from the first moment he'd disembarked the train four years ago. There he had been given the four answers a new cadet was allowed: "Yes, sir; no, sir; no excuse, sir; sir, I do not understand!"

Hooker hastened to amend his mistake. "Yes, sir, I am concerned. While Oxford is certainly an excellent opportunity, nothing can replace spending two years with troops."

"Hmmph," Kimbell snorted. He reached into his dress uniform coat and pulled out a pipe and started filling it. "I've watched you, Hooker. I've looked through your records and talked to your instructors and tactical officer. They say you like working alone. That you possess a mind of the highest caliber, but that your leadership ability might leave something to be desired."

Hooker stiffened at the implied rebuke, because he knew it was true. He had a hard time dealing with subordinates who couldn't keep up with his thinking. He had little patience for those who could not meet his high standards.

"Major Whittaker in Engineering says that you are the type of person who would rather deal with conceptual problems than with people," Kimbell continued. "Is that true?"

Hooker had already been chastised once for a vague answer. "Yes, sir, it's true."

"Then two years away from troops won't make much difference, will it?"

Hooker felt himself being controlled into a position, although he didn't know what it was. "No, sir."

Kimbell's voice softened. "You know, Mr. Hooker, we all can't be at the head of regiments and divisions. The Army has other needs."

"Yes, sir."

"Especially in these hard times with all the cutbacks. There are dark clouds on the horizon. Not many see them, but I think you do, don't you?"

"Yes, sir." Hooker was surprised. Kimbell must have

read his paper on German rearmament, otherwise why would he have made that comment? But why would the commandant be interested in a senior cadet's history theme paper?

"When do you leave for England?"

Hooker wondered about the change in direction of the questioning but promptly answered. "The tenth of July, sir."

"Where are you sailing out of?"

"New York, sir."

"Change it. Sail out of Savannah. I want you to go to Fort Benning before you leave."

Hooker remained silent, waiting for the commandant to clarify his command.

"Do you know Colonel Marshall, the deputy commander of the Infantry School at Benning?" Kimbell asked.

"I heard him speak in March when he came up here, sir. The topic was—"

"Yes, yes," Kimbell interrupted. "I was at the lecture too. Marshall is a most fascinating man. He has some interesting ideas," he added cryptically. "And he's not even a graduate, did you know that?"

"I understand he graduated from the Virginia Military Institute, sir."

"That's correct. Not quite the same thing as the Academy but they do an adequate job with what they have," Kimbell conceded. "Indeed, it's to our advantage that Marshall's not a Graduate."

Our advantage? Hooker thought. He felt a slight trickle of sweat run down the back of his stiff dress gray uniform coat.

Kimbell was looking up the river. "Marshall's got vision, Hooker. He's no fool. He was in the war with me and he saw what happened afterwards. Even with two years to prepare, we weren't ready for France. We lacked the proper training, and we most certainly did not have the proper equipment. Many good men died because of that. And then we came back, and the first thing they did was gut the Army. And we're back where we were before the war, even worse in many ways.

"This Briand-Kellogg Act," Kimbell shook his head. "As

*if by signing a piece of paper they can outlaw war. Hell,
Hooker, I don't like war but my job is to be prepared to
fight and to win. Now the President signs this treaty and
seems to think everyone else in the world is going to abide
by it. Well, you and I know they will not. So it is our job
to be prepared, no matter what those damn civilians in
Washington think.*

"They use the state of the economy as an excuse to justify
what cannot be justified. The national defense must always
be the number one priority. It cannot be tied to the vagaries
of those fools on Wall Street. We must be beyond that."

Colonel Kimbell let loose a few puffs from his pipe.
"What do you think, Hooker?"

Hooker didn't have to think about his answer. "I agree,
sir. It's our duty to defend our country and that means being
as well prepared as possible in peacetime, as well as being
ready to give our lives in war if that is required."

Kimbell nodded. "Yes, but that first task is difficult, given
the short memories of most of our politicians." He reached
out and tapped Hooker on the shoulder. "Colonel Marshall
and I talked for a long time in March. He's in a very good
position at Benning. He's in charge of all tactics instruction
and not only does he see the students who go through the
Infantry School, he also gets to know all the instructors."

Kimbell turned back and faced Hooker. "Every few years
we are going to select someone—someone special—among
the Corps. Someone to do a different sort of job that will
be very important." Kimbell paused and Hooker felt his
heartbeat slow down and time seem to stand still. He felt
on the verge of a great destiny. One that had been written
just for him.

"I told you that not all of us can be at the front of the
troops. That's why I want you to see Colonel Marshall. Why
I've chosen you to be the first one. Colonel Marshall will
tell you what is expected of you. What your country expects
of you. Do you understand?"

"Yes, sir."

Kimbell slapped Hooker on the shoulder. "Good. Good.
Well, you need to go back to the barracks and get some
sleep. You've got a big day tomorrow. The biggest day of
your life so far, if I remember my graduation correctly."

"Yes, sir." Hooker watched as the commandant walked off toward the officer quarters on the northwest side of the Plain. Alone again with his thoughts, he realized that the past four years had prepared him for this moment. The rigorous academics, the physical conditioning, the hazing, the forge of high demands that had made him what he was. And now the future beckoned for him to serve his country—his army—in the way his abilities were best suited.

He didn't know what Colonel Marshall would ask of him, but Hooker knew he was prepared to give all just as the 2,230 names inscribed on Battle Monument—the name of every officer and enlisted man of the Regular Army killed in the Civil War—had given all. He also understood from the recent conversation that the statue at the top of the monument, representing Fame, was not to be his lot. He was going to be asked to serve in another capacity and, while it brought a momentary rush of regret, he also accepted it with the same fortitude that had served four hard years on the Plain.

Hooker used his right hand to remove his class ring from his left ring finger. West Point was the first school in the country to adopt the use of class rings, beginning with the class of 1835. The Academy tradition was that while still a cadet, the ring was worn with the class crest turned toward the heart. After graduation, the ring is turned and the Academy crest is closest to the heart. Hooker turned the ring in the moonlight, watching the stars reflect off the black onyx stone, then he slipped it back on, the Academy crest turned in toward his heart.

"Fanciful but dangerous," the old man muttered, removing his reading glasses. "We have all copies?" he asked in a louder voice from the shadows, holding the pages up.

The aide had stood silently on the other side of the large wooden desk, unmoving while the pages had been read. "We have all that were sent out, sir. The author still has the original."

"Is this all of it?"

"That's all that was sent, sir."

"And this is being submitted as fiction?"

"Yes, sir. It's just a book proposal right now. We believe that's all that is written."

The gnarled fingers crumpled the pages. "You were right. This must be stopped." As the old man threw the wad of paper toward the trash can, the light glinted off the black onyx set in the large ring on his left hand. "We need to know where she got this information. Then take care of it and the author."

"Yes, sir."

CHAPTER ☆ 1

"One minute! Lock and load!"

In the glow of his night vision goggles, Major "Boomer" Watson could see the hand gestures reinforcing the words of his executive officer, Captain Martin—one finger up, then palm slapping the magazine well of the AK-74.

The Soviet-made Mi-24 Hind-D shuddered as the pilots reduced airspeed and crept even lower to the heavily wooded Ukrainian countryside, until they were flying less than twenty feet above the highest treetops. Boomer reached up and slightly adjusted the focus on his AN-PVS-7 night vision goggles, using the forward bulkhead separating the eight Delta Force troopers from the pilots up front as his reference point. In the green glow of the inner eyepieces, the other occupants of the blacked-out cabin showed up clearly, the men similarly outfitted in long Soviet-style overcoats, night vision goggles, AK-74s, and combat vests bristling with the tools of death.

Boomer knew the pilots were wearing their own goggles up front in order to fly the Russian aircraft well below minimum safety zones. He wasn't overly worried. The pilots were from the top-secret 4th Battalion of Task Force 160—the Nightstalkers—and were more than proficient in their job of flying captured and "appropriated" foreign aircraft.

Instinctively, Boomer slid a thirty-round plastic maga-

9

zine out of a side pocket of his load bearing vest, slipped
the back lip into the magazine well, then levered it forward,
locking it in place. He smoothly slid back the charging
handle on the right side, chambering a 5.45mm round. His
thumb flicked over the safety, ensuring the weapon was still
on safe.

"Ten seconds!" Martin yelled from the right door.

Boomer stood, letting the folding-stock AK dangle on its
sling and grabbed both sides of the open left door. He
peered out, ignoring the chill night air blown down by the
rotor wash. Getting oriented, he recognized the landing
zone from the satellite imagery they'd hurriedly been fed
minutes before loading at their base in northern Turkey. On
time and on target.

The LZ was on a mountainside and the only way the
pilots could get in close without having the tips of their
blades hit dirt, was to put the nose in, touching the front
wheels, while keeping the tail up in the air. As soon as the
wheels touched, Boomer jumped out, landing in waist-high
grass. He ran to the side ten paces and hit the ground,
weapon pointing into the darkness. As soon as the last man
was out, the sound of the turbines increased and the helicopter lifted and was gone, leaving a deep silence.

Boomer got to his knees and pulled a global positioning
receiver (GPR) out of the top flap of his backpack. He
popped up the small integrated antenna and twisted the ac-
tivating key on the side. No larger than a portable phone,
the GPR fit in the palm of his hand. The small screen
quickly glowed with data received from the network of satellites the Department of Defense had blanketing the planet.
By finding the best four satellites in the night sky, the GPR
could pinpoint their location to within ten meters. Boomer
punched the POS key and was rewarded with grid coordinates confirming that they were exactly where they were
supposed to be.

Despite the visual confirmation prior to landing—and
trust in the pilot's navigating skill along with the chopper's
own GPR—Boomer had long ago learned the importance
of double-checking. "Assume means make an ass of you
and me!" Boomer had heard more than once in his twelve
years in the Special Forces and Delta Force, and he'd had

those words confirmed on several missions. He punched the NAV button and the route information he had memorized was displayed:

235 D MAG. 2.3 KM

2.1 HOURS TOT

EL +256M

STEER RIGHT

Boomer stood and turned clockwise until the bottom line changed to read ON COURSE. He glanced over his shoulder to make sure the other members of his team were all accounted for, and then he moved off in the indicated direction. They had slightly over two hours to get to their target, and it was downhill most of the way.

The team had been dropped off along a mountainous ridge line in the southern Ukraine that ran parallel to a two-lane asphalt road between the town of Senzhary and the province capital at Barvenkovo. The road was their goal. Their target would be traveling this road between 0430 and 0530. Or at least that's what the Intelligence dinks doing the mission briefing had assured Boomer. He himself had little trust in the wisdom of those who kept their rear end comfortably ensconced in chairs and didn't have to live— or die—based on the accuracy of their information.

That was left to Boomer and his team. He grimaced slightly as he remembered the colonel from the Joint Chiefs of Staff office, his nametag identifying him as Decker, who'd given them the mission briefing. Decker assured them that their target would be traveling along this road. In Boomer's opinion, the man would have been more comfortable in a three-piece suit on Wall Street than wearing camouflage fatigues at a secret forward staging area in the mountains of northern Turkey.

Boomer especially remembered the flash of the large diamond set against black hematite in Decker's West Point ring as he slapped the pointer on the satellite photo of the ambush area. Boomer couldn't remember the last time he'd worn his own West Point ring. As a matter of fact, he couldn't quite remember where the ring was. Hopefully it was somewhere in the one-room apartment he kept back at

Fayetteville, North Carolina, for the few weeks in the year
he was actually back at his home base.

The terrain steepened. Boomer could see the dark snake
of the road ahead and below. He halted briefly, the team
mimicking his actions, and did another GPR check. Check-
point One. On course and ahead of schedule. Less than a
thousand meters from the road.

"Let's split," Boomer whispered, the acoustic mike built
into the transceiver clamped on his head transmitting the
message on low power FM to the other seven men. The
whisper did little justice to his normally deep voice. It was
a voice that instilled confidence in listeners. An advantage
for a man who led others into death and destruction.

Boomer and his commo and security men—Headquarters
Element—moved to the left, the two men falling in place
and covering his flanks. Captain Martin, the team executive
officer, went off to the right with the remaining four team
members to set up the kill zone.

The Headquarters Element scrambled down the hillside,
staying hidden under the pines that covered the rock-strewn
ground, until they reached a small knoll overlooking the
road. Boomer crouched behind the trunk of a tree, one of
his men going off to the left to provide far left flank security, the other settling next to the team leader. Boomer
scanned the deserted stretch of road fifty meters away and
ten meters below.

"Bronco, are you in position? Over." He asked over the
FM radio.

"Roger, Mustang," Martin replied. "In position. At my
mark, I'll turn IR on for your identification."

Boomer peered off to his right.

"Mark. Over."

Boomer spotted the brief glow as Captain Martin illuminated an infrared flashlight—invisible to anyone not
wearing goggles—then just as quickly turned it off.
"Roger, Bronco. I've got you. How's it look? Over."

"Good field of fire. Good cover. Palamino Element is at
the road installing their toys. Over."

"Roger. We'll keep an eye open for the target. Mustang
out."

Boomer lay down on his stomach in the pine needles at

the base of the tree, pulling the Russian overcoat in tight around his neck. It was cold, somewhere in the low thirties. He looked to his lower right along the road and spotted the silhouettes of the demolitions men, Palamino Element, at work. He checked the time on the GPR: 0413. Seventeen minutes before the estimated target window. Boomer tapped the shoulder of the man lying next to him. "Are we up on Satcom, Pete?"

Staff Sergeant Peter Lanscom nodded. "Five by." He handed over the small handset for the satellite communications radio.

Boomer pressed the send button on the handset. "Thunder Point, this is Mustang. Over."

The reply from Turkey was immediate. "Mustang, this is Thunder Point. Go ahead. Over." Boomer recognized Colonel Decker's voice.

"We're in position. What's the latest from the eye in the sky? Over."

"We're getting live downlink from an Intelsat on your target, Mustang. You've got two vehicles en route your location. A car in the lead and a bus following. Just as briefed," Colonel Decker couldn't help adding. "They're approximately twenty-two klicks from your position, moving at about sixty kilometers per hour. Over."

"Roger. Out." Boomer replied. He returned the handset to Lanscom. The math was easy: twenty-two minutes, give or take a couple. Nothing to do but wait. He glanced down the road. The demo men were done.

Boomer hissed in a lungful of cold air, trying to still the churning in his stomach. The flash of white teeth was framed in the moonlight by his naturally dark skin, an inheritance from a grandmother on his father's side who had been a full-blooded Cherokee. His black hair, a few inches longer than allowed by regulations, had just the slightest tinge of grey at the temples. His eyes were so dark as to appear black, but more unusual was the warmth they emanated regardless of Boomer's mood. While Boomer's overall reputation as a calm, likable individual was valued by friends and acquaintances, it mattered little to the organization that received the bulk of his time and attention.

Boomer was a long way from home. He'd grown up on

the Upper West Side of Manhattan, where the George
Washington Bridge touched New York City. Boomer's ear-
liest memories were of his mother taking him on walks in
Fort Washington Park along the banks of the Hudson beneath the high arch of the bridge. She'd taken him there
when he was ten years old after receiving the telegram that
his father had been killed in action in Vietnam. That was
in 1969, prior to the Army instituting the policy of having
notification officers deliver the grim news. At that time, the
Army had simply sent telegrams and had them delivered
by cab drivers.

Virginia Watson had had the driver take them down to
the park and drop them off, the piece of yellow paper
gripped tightly between her clenched fingers. The news of
Michael Watson's Medal of Honor for actions on the last
day of his life would come many months later, but on that
bright fall day nothing had mattered other than the intense
grief Boomer could feel and see in his mother. Boomer's
emotions were more complex. His father had been gone for
eight of the first ten years of his life and Boomer's memories of him were blurry images of a large man dressed in
a uniform with a strange green beret that he wore cocked
at an angle.·

Just as Boomer had sensed the grief that day, seven years
later, he had sensed his mother's disapproval of his decision
to accept the automatic offer of an appointment to West
Point that every child of a Medal of Honor winner was
given. Boomer's attitude had been that at least something
good had come from his father's death. Besides, he had
rationalized, she couldn't really afford to send him to college anywhere else. The idea of a free education *and* pay
more than satisfied his seventeen-year-old mind.

His mother had already gone into debt to send him to
Cardinal Spellman Catholic High School in the Bronx. And
though she would have preferred more bills rather than give
another man to the Army, Boomer was not to be swayed.
His easygoing attitude was blunted in this regard, and she
accepted his decision.

She'd seen this tenacity on the basketball court at Spellman. Despite his—by basketball standards—relatively
short height of six feet, he'd earned a starting slot on the

Spellman varsity team by outworking all the other players on the team and impressing the coach with his hustle.

What had really caught the coach's eye thought, was Boomer's actions as a sophomore in a game against perennial New York basketball mecca Power High School, alma mater of Kareem Abdul-Jabbar. Boomer had been sent in after the starting backcourt had fouled out trying to guard Power's all-city forward, later an NBA player. The coach had told Boomer to let the Power forward have no free shots. Boomer had promptly stuck to the more talented player like glue, hacking him severely every time he handled the ball, to the point where the Power player had lost his temper and took a swing at Boomer. The fight that erupted had cleared both benches and half the stands and resulted in Boomer and the Power player being ejected, but not before Boomer had returned the swing and decked the other player. The action had surprised the coach, but not Boomer's mother in the stands. She knew that, like his father, her son had a hard streak in him.

The years had passed and now Boomer was lying in wait, a familiar but always nerve-wracking position as far as he was concerned. As the countdown to action continued, Boomer was shifting to his action mode, his nerves freezing over and a wary calmness settling in. He grabbed the handset for the Satcom radio again. "Angel, this is Mustang. Over."

The reply from the pilot of the MI-25 was instantaneous. "This is Angel. Over."

"Status? Over."

The pilot's laconic southern drawl was reassuring. "At hold position. All clear. We can be there in a jiffy to pick ya'll up. Over."

"Roger." Boomer checked the time display on the GPR. "We're probably going hot here in five mikes. We're going to need you real quick then. Over."

The Russian-made aircraft, appropriated from Saddam Hussein's air force during the Gulf War years previously, and the Soviet made weapons and uniforms, were a subterfuge to influence any possible survivors of the ambush—or anyone who might be in the area—that the events that were about to occur were the work of a renegade

Ukrainian militia group of which there certainly were many. The only pieces of equipment that were not endemic to the area were the GPR, night vision goggles, and satellite radios, but if any of them were captured, there would most certainly be a body captured also, at which time the foreign origin of the equipment would no longer matter and diplomatic denial would take over.

The muted roar of the helicopter blades sounded behind the pilot's voice. "No sweat. Over."

"Mustang, out." Boomer glanced down the road, trying to catch the glow of the oncoming vehicles headlights in his goggles, where they would show up like brilliant spotlights. Nothing yet.

Boomer spoke into his FM radio. "Bronco, this is Mustang. Status? Over."

Martin's reply was swift. "All set. Over."

That meant Martin's team had the Soviet made PK machine gun set up and their RPG rocket launchers ready. Contrary to the movies, Boomer knew a good ambush consisted of setting up the kill zone, then backing off so that the weapons can effectively cover the killing ground which must be too far from the ambushers for the victims to overrun. In this case, Boomer was satisfied his men had all the little checkmarks in the manual of efficient killing ticked off.

A faint glow appeared in the hills to the south: the reflection of the headlights. Boomer picked up the handset for the Satcom. "Thunder Point, this is Mustang. Over."

"This is Thunder Point. Over."

"Request final mission authorization. Over."

"Your mission is a go, Mustang," Decker said. "Authorization code Victor Romeo Two Four. I say again, your mission is a go. Code Victor Romeo Two Four. Out." The radio went dead.

"There's gonna be some hurting puppies in a few minutes," Lanscom whispered, the snout of his NVG pointed down the road, picking up the glow, as he fingered his AK-74. This was Lanscom's first live mission, and Boomer could understand the younger man's nervousness. He himself had been on several, but that didn't necessarily make it any easier. In fact, having witnessed the effects of modern weapons on the human body did little to relieve the anxiety of being on the receiving end.

Boomer didn't bother trying to allay Lanscom's fears. Now that he had the final go, his job was to concentrate on the mission at hand. The bus was carrying members of one of the factions of the newly formed Ukrainian parliament. A faction that was vehemently opposed to following the guidelines of the standing agreements on nuclear arms reduction between the United States and the Ukraine.

NATO inspection teams in the Ukraine to ensure treaty compliance had recently been forced to curtail their activities. The political situation was growing unstable. A NATO team had been attacked two days earlier by a mob, and the U.S. Congress was getting very vocal about sending 200 million dollars a year to the Ukraine to dismantle nuclear weapons when the job wasn't being done. The Ukrainian parliament, defying the Ukrainian president's signing of the START II Treaty, was making vague threats of nuclear blackmail as the country's economy slid into a morass. It was the politics of the late 1990's, and since military force was an extension of politics, Boomer was here to extend the wishes of the United States government.

Thirty-six hours ago, the issue reached crisis level. A Ukrainian Backfire bomber flying low toward Iraq had been intercepted over Turkish airspace by two American F-16s assigned to NATO. The Backfire had refused to land, and the F-16s had attempted to force it down. The result had stunned the world as the Backfire disintegrated in a nuclear fireball, taking with it the two American jets.

According to the intelligence analysts, the Backfire had been caught while trying to smuggle a nuclear weapon to Saddam Hussein's regime in exchange for desperately needed cash. When confronted with the possibility of capture, the crew of the Backfire had chosen suicide. The Ukrainians claimed the aircraft had wandered off course during a routine training mission and an on-board accident caused the explosion. It was a feeble excuse at best. No one seriously believed that the plane could be that far off course and the experts pointed out that nuclear weapons did not explode by accident.

The incident infuriated Congress. Claiming treachery and

deceit, it demanded that the START II treaty be scrapped. Boomer knew that in the biblical tradition of an eye for an eye, he was here to inflict hurt on those that had harmed the United States. In this case the radical politicians who had sent the Backfire on its fateful mission. Intelligence had placed them in a bus on this road. Boomer and his team were here to kill them.

Boomer wasn't exactly sure how his team's mission was going to affect things, but in a few minutes there would be fewer people opposed to NATO gaining positive control over the nuclear stockpile. Boomer, like most of his comrades in arms, drew no ethical lines when it came to nuclear weapons in the hands of extremists. Using the cold calculations of the professional military man, the potential body count of a rogue nuclear bomb weighed against the lives of the men approaching his kill zone left him with no qualms.

The lead car came around the bend and into sight, closely followed by a bus. Boomer twisted the focus knob on his goggles. The Ukrainian flag flapped from the radio antenna on the right rear of the car. It roared by, rapidly approaching the ambush area. Boomer looked at the bus and blinked. There was some sort of emblem pasted to the right side of the bus, next to the door. As the bus rumbled by below him, he tried to make it out; he could almost swear it was the globe/compass marking of NATO.

The car had entered the kill zone, and the bus was less than thirty meters away from the point of no return. Boomer knew he had less than two seconds to make a decision.

"Abort!" he hissed into his radio. There was no immediate reply. "Martin, abort! Answer me, goddamnit!"

A bright flash split the night sky, followed immediately by the roar of an explosion as a remotely detonated mine went off under the front tire of the lead car. The blast lifted the car twenty feet into the air and tossed the crumpled machine off the road. A line of fire seared from the area of Martin's team and slammed into the bus—the warhead of the RPG rocket detonating on impact. Designed to stop tanks and armored personnel carriers, the warhead tore through the thin metal skin and exploded inside, blasting apart flesh and machine with equal ruthlessness.

"Abort!" Boomer yelled helplessly.

Green tracers licked out from the hillside disappearing into the ravaged body of the bus, the crack of the PK machine gun filling the silence left by the explosions. Boomer could see men crawling out the windows of the bus, trying to claw their way to safety.

"Get the chopper here!" Boomer ordered Lanscom. He got to his feet and ran along the hillside toward Martin's position. He slipped and fell, grabbing onto a sapling to keep from rolling down the hill. As he got to his feet, he could hear the snap of AK-74s adding to the din of the PK machine gun.

Just as Boomer arrived at the kill team's position, the firing suddenly stopped. In the sudden absence of the sound of killing, the screams of the wounded echoed up the hillside.

The members of Martin's team were standing, peering down, weapons at the ready, the barrel of the machine gun glowing bright red. Boomer grabbed Martin on the shoulder, and the captain turned, startled, a glazed look in his eye.

"Why didn't you obey me?"

Martin blinked. "What?"

"I ordered you to abort, goddamnit!"

Martin shrugged and pointed downhill. "They were in the zone. There was nothing else we could do. It was too late."

"You didn't have to fire up the bus," Boomer retorted.

"What's the big deal?" Martin asked. "This was what—"

They both froze as an eerie voice floated up the hill, crying out in English: "*Oh God, help me!*"

"That's why!" Boomer yelled. "That was a *NATO* bus."

The members of the kill team stared at him. Boomer was looking down the hill, thinking furiously. Flames were flickering out of the engine of the bus. He could make out some movement among the bodies lying around the shattered vehicle. There appeared to be one or two unwounded

men down there, dragging the hurt to the shelter of the
drainage ditch on the far side. Lanscom and the other man
from his headquarters element came running up.

"Chopper's inbound, sir," Lanscom informed him.
"Two minutes out."

Boomer reached out and grabbed the handset for the Satcom radio. "Thunder Point, this is Mustang. Over."

"This is Thunder Point. Over."

Boomer's voice was harsh as he reported. "We've got a
fuck-up here. We hit the target, but it was a friendly. Looks
like a bus full of NATO inspectors. Over."

Colonel Decker didn't hesitate. "Get out of there ASAP.
Over."

"There's wounded down there. We need to help them.
Over."

"Negative, Mustang. Over."

"Let me talk to my six. Over," Boomer said, trying to
get a hold of his commanding officer.

"Your six is not available. Exfil immediately. You are
not to render any assistance. You are not to compromise
your presence. That's an order. Over."

Boomer held the handset, unable to reply. He felt the
gaze of the other members of his team upon him.

Colonel Decker's voice took on an edge of anxiety at
the lack of reply. "Mustang, do you hear me? Mustang?
Confirm that you will comply with your orders. Over."

"Let's get down there," Boomer ordered his men, dropping the handset.

"Thunder Point says to exfiltrate," Martin objected,
pointing at the radio.

"And I say let's get down there and help who we can.
We'll put the wounded on board the chopper and take them
back to Turkey."

Martin shook his head. "I'm sorry, sir, but we have to
obey orders."

Boomer stared at his executive officer. The sound of helicopter blades started to override the cries of the wounded.

Martin half lifted his AK-74, 17 a vaguely threatening
gesture in Boomer's direction.

"You're going to have to shoot me in the back if that's

what you're thinking,'' Boomer snapped. He turned and started downslope. Behind him, Martin lowered the weapon and grabbed the handset for the Satcom radio, rapidly speaking into it.

Boomer was less than twenty feet from the road, when the Hind-D changed its landing pattern, roared up the road, and the 12.7mm Gatling gun in the nose opened fire. Boomer threw himself to the ground as bullets tore through the carnage his team had wrought, effectively finishing the job. The survivors were caught in the open and thrown about like rag dolls as the heavy metal-jacketed bullets tore into them. The helicopter banked and flew back, doing another gun run, taking care of those who had hidden in the drainage ditch. The aircraft flared just beyond the wreckage of the bus and slowly settled down to land.

Boomer stood and stepped out into the road. He bent over the closest body. There was no doubt the man was dead, his chest was torn open and half his head gone. Boomer checked the pockets, then quickly ran to the other bodies. All dead and most unidentifiable. The rest of his team came running down the hill toward the beckoning doors of the helicopter. Reluctantly, Boomer turned and followed them, stepping up and through the door into the waiting womb of the cargo bay. The helicopter immediately lifted and headed south to safety.

Boomer had something in his hands, a small piece of plastic. Turning it toward the red glow of the cargo bay, he read the lettering. He briefly froze and a look of anguish coursed across his face. He stuffed it back into the pocket over his heart.

Boomer spent the rest of the return trip in silence, ignoring the other members of his team. The one time Lanscom nudged him, holding out the handset of the Satcom to answer an incoming message from Thunder Point, Boomer simply pointed at Captain Martin. Lanscom took the radio over to the executive officer, who spent a good portion of the trip speaking into the handset. Boomer unhooked his FM radio and stuffed the earpiece into his vest pocket.

The noise inside the helicopter, loud enough to drown

out any attempt at normal conversation, made the ride a curiously silent one. Each man was coming off the adrenaline rush of the action, and each was weighing the potential consequences.

At the airfield in northern Turkey, the helicopter landed and was immediately directed into a secure hangar where the doors swung shut as protection from prying eyes. The helicopter came to a halt. The sound of the engines decreased as the pilots began shutting the bird down. The side door opened and a soldier stuck his head in. "The Colonel's waiting for you."

As the other members of the team stood up to exit the bird, Boomer grabbed Captain Martin's arm and pulled him down into the seat next to him. "What the fuck happened back there, Pete?" he asked, finally able to be heard.

"What do you mean?" Martin asked, jerking his arm out of Boomer's grip.

"You told the pilots to strafe, didn't you?"

Martin couldn't meet his commanding officer's eyes. "Those were our orders."

"We killed our own," Boomer said. "You damn near killed me."

"You shouldn't have gone down there, Boomer," Martin said. The younger man shook his head. "It was messed up, but once the shit starts hitting the fan you got to play it out as it lays."

"That's what you call it?" Boomer asked incredulously. "Strafing wounded friendlies? Playing it out?"

Martin nervously shrugged.

Boomer poked him hard on the shoulder. "You ever pull a weapon on me again, I'll kill you."

Martin exited the aircraft without another word. Boomer angrily got to his feet and followed. In the hangar he walked to the brightly lit corner where the communications console was set up and the maps were tacked to plywood walls. Colonel Decker was there along with Colonel Forster, Boomer's immediate superior in Delta Force. Boomer's hand slid into the pocket of the greatcoat he was wearing and reappeared with two pieces of cloth. He threw them down onto the folding table in front of the two senior officers without a word. A small, blood-stained American flag with a Velcro backing along with a NATO blue beret lay there, frozen in the bright glow of the overhead lights.

Forster glanced at the patches, then at Boomer. "I heard. I'm sorry."

Boomer's eyes were locked on Colonel Decker's. He ignored the other members of the team as they gathered around, Captain Martin keeping a safe distance away.

"Do you have a problem, major?" Decker asked, breaking the uncomfortable silence.

Boomer stiffened. "No, sir, *you* have a problem. The target that you identified and confirmed for destruction was a busload of NATO officers from one of the inspection teams in-country. I took that shoulder patch and beret from one of the bodies. An American body."

"It was a mistake," Decker said. "We received some bad intelligence."

"Bad intelligence?" Boomer was stunned. "I counted at least six bodies outside that bus, and God knows how many were inside."

"It's done," Forster quietly said. "It was a mistake and it's done. Let it go, Boomer. There's nothing we can do right now."

Boomer twisted his head. "Let it go? Sir, my men just killed some of our own." His finger pointed at the patch, shaking with emotion. "How the fuck could Intelligence get that screwed up? You were tracking that damn bus since it left—."

"But we couldn't tell who was in it," Decker quickly interjected. "That was your job on the ground."

Boomer stepped back in surprise at the last comment. "My job? It was oh-dark-thirty in the morning there. Those vehicles were moving about forty miles an hour into my kill zone. You gave me final authorization for a go on the mission. I tried to abort," he said, throwing a hard look at Captain Martin, "but it was too late by the time I recognized the markings on the bus."

"Sounds like *you* made the mistake, major," Decker said.

Boomer took a step toward Decker, his eyes blazing.

"Listen," Forster said, holding both hands up and moving between the two men. "Let's not be getting into a pissing contest about whose fault things are. It's done. We've run seven different ops here into the Ukraine and this is the first one that went wrong. I don't like it. Nobody likes it, but our luck was bound to run out sooner or later. Let's be glad you all made it back all right, and we'll make damn sure something like this never happens again."

Decker picked up the flag and beret and stuffed them into his fatigue pants pocket, then turned an emotionless gaze on Boomer. "Your boss is right. We don't like it, but that's the way it goes sometimes. There are things going on that you aren't cleared to know. We were obviously fed false intelligence on this mission. It might even have been a deliberate setup. A lot of strange things have been going on since the interception of that Backfire. But it's done, and we need to make the best of it."

"The best of it?" Boomer asked. "How can you make the best of it?"

"That's not your concern, major."

"It damn well is my concern," Boomer replied angrily.

"Major!" Decker snapped. "That's enough." He turned to Forster. "I want this man relieved of duties immediately."

Forster bristled. "This is *my* command."

"It won't be much longer if you don't do what I say," Decker warned.

Forster glared at the other officer for several seconds before replying. "I'll take care of it. *You*," he added, still looking at Decker, "watch what you say to my people. This was *your* mission and you take responsibility for what happened."

Decker pointed at Boomer. "I want him out of this area of operations before close of business today." With that he turned and strode out of the hanger.

Forster waited until he was gone, then faced his subordinate. "I'm sorry, Boomer."

From the tone of his commander's voice, Boomer knew what the words meant. He was stunned. "You're going to let that asshole dictate what you do?"

"He works directly for the Joint Chiefs, Boomer," Forster explained. "I think the best thing to do is to get you out of here before someone goes headhunting to lay blame for this mission. It's for your own good. I'll cover your ass and take care of things here."

CHAPTER ☆ 2

The computer screen glowed in the darkened room. A woman sat in front of it, her glasses reflecting the electronic images. She was still except for the repetitive tapping of her right index finger on the scroll key. As her finger brought forth the words, she read:

18 DECEMBER 1945, EARLY MORNING
HEIDELBERG, GERMANY

"I'm dying, aren't I?"
The nurse put down the book she had been reading and stood—it was necessary in order for the patient to be able to see her. His head was immobile; a large plaster collar had been placed around the neck earlier in the day to replace the surgical hooks that had been implanted in his cheeks eight days ago to keep the head immobile and relieve pressure on the spine.
Colonel Hill, the hospital commander, had left standing orders that everyone was to stand in easy eyesight of the patient when addressing him. Given who the patient was, they were orders no one dared disobey.
The nurse leaned over and wiped the slight sheen of sweat off the old man's forehead without answering. The general bore her silence for almost ten seconds, the flinty eyes following her every movement.

27

"No one around here will tell me a damn thing," he rasped. *"They act like I'm an old lady who can't handle the truth. They even told me today that I'll be flying home on the thirteenth."* He finally caught her with his eyes; the only way he could keep attention nowadays other than with his voice. *"You can tell me, and I give you my word that I won't tell anyone."*

She met his gaze, her face blank, her voice flat. *"Yes. You're dying."*

A slight sigh was the only sign he'd heard. The eyes turned straight ahead, staring up at the ceiling. The nurse picked up her book and sat back down. For the rest of her four-hour shift the only sounds were the rustle of paper as she turned the pages and the general's steady breathing.

19 DECEMBER 1945, EARLY MORNING

"You're damn quiet," the general muttered.

The nurse briefly glanced up from her book, then resumed reading.

"Everybody else, all they do is talk, talk, talk, but they never say anything," he continued, speaking to the white-painted ceiling. The bed was in the middle of a sixteen-by-fourteen-foot space that had served as a utility room. It had been stripped bare for the general, the only private room in the hospital. There were two MPs outside the doors. They were necessary during the daytime to screen the visitors who streamed in. In the early hours of the morning, during the nurse's shift, she and the general were usually alone.

The old man coughed, his body shifting as much as his condition allowed. *"I appreciate you telling me the truth yesterday. A man ought to have the right to know the truth about himself. Especially when he's dying."*

The nurse slowly closed the book and stood, moving so that he could see her. She reached up and checked the collar. He caught the glint of gold on her left hand. *"You're married?"*

"Yes."

"You look damn young to be married. How old are you?"

"*Twenty.*"

"*How long have you been married?*"

"*Two years.*"

"*That's a long time during a war,*" the general muttered. "*Where's your husband? Is he in the service?*"

"*He was.*" Her voice was cold.

"*Where is he now? Mustered out?*"

"*He's dead.*"

The general's eyes narrowed. "*Dead? How?*"

"*The war.*"

"*Where?*"

"*Hammelburg.*"

The general averted his eyes, looking across the bed to the far wall for several minutes. The nurse stood still, silently staring down at him. Finally he looked back. "*Task Force Baum?*"

"*Task Force Baum,*" she confirmed.

The tip of the general's tongue appeared, flicking against his lips. His eyes lost their focus for several minutes, and silence reigned as each occupant of the room remained lost in their own thoughts. The general was the first to break the silence. "*That was a mistake.*"

"*I know.*"

His eyes flashed angrily. "*War is full of mistakes. I only made two.*"

"*One of them killed my husband and quite a few other good men.*"

He didn't seem to hear. "*Two in four years. But no one talks about what I did right. They only talk about what I did wrong and the things I said. They don't want soldiers any more, they want damn politicians. That's why they're pushing Ike. He's good at that horsecrap. They've got him all set to—*" He paused in midsentence as his mind reeled in, realizing his surroundings and the company.

The room returned to silence. The nurse sat back down, but she left the book lying on the floor, her gaze boring into the wasted body lying in the bed. After thirty minutes, the general spoke once, briefly, his voice so low it almost was inaudible. "*I'm sorry.*"

She picked the book back up.

20 DECEMBER 1945, EARLY MORNING

The question was purely professional. "How is he?"

The outgoing nurse shrugged. "Not good. He had a bad coughing spell slightly after ten. We gave him phenobarbital, but the coughing kept up. We followed that with codeine. He coughed up some blood twice and Dr. Spurling thinks it's an embolism. He's dyspnoic and suffering from cyanosis. Respiration is rapid and erratic."

She pointed at the bed. "We put him on oxygen and that's helped some. Dr. Spurling's on call. He was in here twenty minutes ago to take a look." She handed over the patient's chart. "He's sleeping now." With that, she was gone, leaving the room in silence.

The nurse checked her patient. His chest was rising and falling very slowly and with great difficulty. The eyes were closed. She was just about to sit down when the eyes flashed open and blinked. "They came today," he muttered under the oxygen mask.

The nurse frowned. The general had dozens of visitors each day. He had never before commented on any of them, not even his wife when she had flown in from the states with the famous neurosurgeon who had been able to do nothing to help the patient. She looked at the chart. His situation had most definitely taken a turn for the worse.

"Take it off," he said.

The nurse didn't argue. She reached forward and unfastened the oxygen mask, letting it lie next to his head, shutting off the valve on the tank.

He could speak more clearly now, although he had to pause between every few words to catch his breath. "They weren't satisfied . . . that I'm in here flat . . . on my ass dying. They were worried . . . that I still might cause . . . trouble." His breath came out in a long rattle. "I gave them their damn gold," he muttered. "You think they'd be . . . happy with that."

The nurse put the chart back and sat down.

The general hacked in what might have been an attempt at a chuckle. "They talked about . . . Task Force Baum too. Everyone blames me for . . . that because my son-in-law . . . was at that prisoner of war camp . . . but liberating that

camp wasn't . . . the real reason we sent . . . the Task Force
out.''

For the first time, the nurse looked interested. "Who
came today?" She stood so they could make eye contact.

The general took a few deep breaths. "Ike sent them.
Marshall's hatchet boy . . . Hooker, he was in charge. Flew
all the way in . . . from D.C. At least Beatrice kept . . . Smith
out. That simpering ass-kisser."

"Who's Hooker?"

His voice was a whisper. "The Line."

The nurse frowned. "The Line?"

The general closed his eyes. "I really am dying. I can
feel it. The doctors said . . . I was getting better, but—" He
paused, as if trying to collect his thoughts. "I said I was
sorry . . . about your husband. I am. But it wasn't . . . my
fault. Baum was sent out after . . . the damn gold . . . to get
it before the Russians did. I had to take the heat . . . and
make up that crap about the . . . prison camp when it all
went to shit. Hell, I could have given them the damn money
. . . they didn't need to try for the gold . . . we weren't even
sure where it was.''

"Gold?" The nurse asked.

"The Reich's reserves and . . . all the crap those Hun
bastards plundered. The Army found most of it . . . just two
months ago. Then we . . . The Line that is . . . had to give it
up . . . couldn't keep it quiet. But the other find . . . outside
Hammelburg . . . not much . . . about two million . . . that we
got and kept . . . or should I say they got it."

"Task Force Baum was sent out to find some hidden
gold?"

The general glanced at her, his eyes taking in her youth.
"The world's a hard place . . . the last four years have seen
to that. Dying on an expedition to . . . recover some lost gold
is just one of thousands of . . . reasons people have died over
the past years. No matter what the reason was . . . they were
still fighting Germans. And they did a hell of job of killing
. . . Krauts all the way in to Hammelburg. Shit, after all the
crap I've . . . been through, here I am dying of a damn . . .
broken neck from a car accident. But this . . . this stuff now
. . . this is going too far.''

"Why would this Line want gold?"

"They need money . . . for their plans."

The nurse was standing still, as if afraid any movement on her part might derail his train of thoughts. *"Tell me about The Line."*

21 DECEMBER 1945, EVENING

The nurse was coming out of the mess hall when she saw the crowd outside the west wing of the infirmary dissipating. She made her way through to the door and showed her ID to the MP on duty.

Inside, three other nurses were gathered around the duty desk, speaking in hushed tones. She ignored them and looked down at the duty officer's log. When she got halfway down the page, a single line entry caused a bitter smile to come to her lips:

GENERAL PATTON DIED AT 1745, 21 DECEMBER 1945, WITH SUDDEN STOPPING OF THE HEART.

"Did you hear?" the head nurse whispered to her.

In reply the nurse held up the medical report.

"No, I meant about the autopsy." The head nurse glanced around nervously. *"They're not doing one."*

"So?" The nurse was distracted, her mind elsewhere.

"So!" The head nurse leaned forward and spoke in a conspiratorial tone. *"That closes the investigation. No autopsy, no investigation."*

The nurse had been secluded during Patton's tenure at the hospital, doing nothing but work, sleep and eat. She had not bothered with the gossip that had flown about over the weeks.

The head nurse continued, feeling important with her information. *"I talked to a captain in Criminal Investigation. He told me that they were suspicious about the accident. That it might have been a deliberate attempt on the General's life. But now that there won't be an autopsy, there's no possibility of an investigation."*

"Who signed off on the release for the body without an autopsy?" the nurse asked, interested in who would want

to keep the accident from being investigated.
"Some colonel from Washington. A Colonel Hooker."

Major Benita Trace raised her head when the sharp buzz of the phone interrupted her, fingers paused above the keyboard as she prepared to continue her work. She stood, picking the portable up, and looked out at the ocean as she hit the on switch. "Hello?"

A voice in a heavy accent was on the other end. "Hey, sweetheart. Would ya like go to da Bronx zoo and see da boids and the toitles?"

A broad smile crossed Trace's face. "Boomer! Where the hell are you?"

"Well, that's a good question. Can't tell you exactly, since I'm not flying this dang plane, but somewhere about 35,000 feet over the Pacific, heading in your direction."

"You're coming here?"

"Yeah, my boss thought I needed some time off, so he wrangled me TDY orders to 4th TASOSC at Fort Shafter."

Trace frowned as she read undercurrents in Boomer's voice. "Is something wrong?"

"No, nothing's wrong. Listen, I'm on one of these credit card phones they got in the plane and I have no idea what this is costing me. I just wanted to make sure you were still in Hawaii. We should get together."

"Absolutely. When are you getting in? I can pick you up at the airport."

"My flight lands at 1030 but there'll be someone from the unit at the airport to pick me up and take me over to Fort Shafter to get inbriefed. How about this evening?"

"Great. When and where?"

"Well, I can tell you the when, how about 1900? The where is up to you. It's your island, not mine."

"All right, I'll make it as easy as possible. 1900 at the Hilton Hawaiian Village. You can't miss it. It's at the west end of Waikiki. If you can't find it, just ask. Meet me in the bar just off the main lobby."

"OK. 1900, Hilton Hawaiian Village. The bar off the lobby. Sounds good."

Trace was acutely aware of her racing heart. "Hey, Boomer?"

"Yeah?"

"I'm looking forward to seeing you."

His voice lapsed back into the exaggerated accent. "Me too, sweetie. See ya tonight."

The phone went dead and Trace slowly pressed the off button. She sat back down facing the computer screen, but her eyes were no longer taking in the words nor did she feel any inclination to write. Her brain swirled with mixed memories of the past.

She'd first met Boomer Watson at West Point in September of 1978. The incoming class of 1982, of which Trace was a proud member, had just finished their ten-day summer bivouac at Lake Frederick and marched back to the main post of West Point. With every mile the new cadets trudged from the lush mountains of the training area to the gray stone of the academic and barracks area, their anxiety level increased. They were leaving the brutal, two-month old cocoon of Beast Barracks for the unknown terror of the academic year. "Three-to-one," less than sympathetic upper class cadre members had chanted at the new cadets, referring to the academic year ratio where there would be three upper class cadets to every plebe as opposed to the survivable one-to-four ratio of Beast.

Trace was in First Company, and as such, was among the lead group to march past the Superintendent's house under the cold eyes of massed upperclassmen on either side of the road just returned from their own varied summer training. After passing in review in front of the Superintendent, the company commander halted his troops in front of Eisenhower Barracks. With his back to the Plain, he looked over his young charges and smiled. "The party's over! When I dismiss you, you are to pick up your duffle bags which are in Central Area and report to your academic year companies. You've all done well this summer. Keep up the good work in your academic year companies. Best of luck! First Company, dismissed!"

"First to fight, sir!" the plebes dutifully chanted, the last time they would yell the company motto.

Some party, Trace thought as she executed a right face and double-timed through the salley port to the left of Washington Hall into Central Area. Beast had been anything but fun. From her original squad of twelve new cadets, there were only eight left, the other four opting out of the excitement and returning to the civilian world. Trace herself had more than once seriously considered the lure of a civilian college where women—hell, human beings—were a bit more appreciated.

She joined the horde of green-clad first-year cadets scrambling like ants through the large pile of duffle bags, searching for the one with her name on it. Finding it, she was briefly flustered as to how to handle both the duffle bag and the rucksack on her back. She got a classmate to balance the duffle bag on top of the rucksack, bowing her head forward and almost pushing her to the ground. She slowly made her way out of Central Area, staggering toward the academic year company to which she had been assigned.

"What are you looking at, beanhead?" a voice exploded in her ear as she made her way up the ramp to New South Area.

"No excuse, sir!" Trace automatically snapped as she screeched to a halt, eyes locked straight ahead, or to be more accurate, given the weight on her back, straight downward. With only four approved answers—"yes, sir; no, sir; no excuse, sir; sir, may I make a statement"—her conversational options were somewhat limited. Out of the corner of her eye, she could make out the highly shined low quarters of an upperclassman edging up.

"Your damn right, no excuse, beanhead," the voice growled. An acne-faced man with the yellow shield on his collar denoting a second year cadet—a "yearling" in Academy slang—looked her up and down. "You're a mess, miss. You call those boots shined?"

"Ah, lighten up, Greg," a deep voice spoke from behind her left shoulder. "They just got back from Lake Frederick. How do you expect her boots to be shined?"

Trace kept her eyes straight to the front, as the cadet who had stopped her flushed red in the face and looked past her. "Mind your own business, Boomer." He turned back to her. "What company are you going to, miss?"

"I-1, sir."

"You mean India-One, don't you?" the upperclassman

corrected, using the proper military term.

"Yes, sir."

"Outstanding," he purred. "I'm in I-1, so we'll be seeing quite a bit of each other. You know what they call it I-1, don't you?"

Trace considered the potential traps that question entailed, weighed it against the vague constraints of the honor code, and finally answered: "Yes, sir."

"And what's that?"

Trace felt the sweat pouring down her back, adding to the wetness already there from the long hike back. "Inferno-One, sir."

"Damn right, miss"—he leaned forward and his hand pulled aside the strap of her rucksack and he read her nametag. "Miss Trace. Inferno-One. We're not like those party people over in 4th Regiment. The heat is on now and it's only going to get hotter. This is the 1st Regiment, and you'd better get your act together in a hurry. I will remember you. Next time I see you, those boots had better be spit-shined."

"Yes, sir."

The shoes turned and headed away down the ramp. Trace took another step and her knees buckled, the duffle bag sliding off her back, slamming into the ground, while she caught herself from smashing her face into the concrete ramp at the last second.

"Better leave that here, dump your ruck in your room, and come back for it," the deep voice suggested.

She quickly scrambled to her feet and locked up at attention. "I can handle it, sir."

The upperclassman named Boomer chuckled and wagged a finger at her: "Ah, now, now. Is that one of your four answers?"

Trace flushed, her head spinning from the heat and mental and physical exhaustion. "No, sir."

"I know they tried to brainwash all the common sense out of your head during Beast, but you're going to need to turn your brain back on now to survive. They can harass you all they want, but that isn't going to get you kicked out of here. Flunk a course or two, though, and you'll be out of here in a heartbeat. Got that?"

"Yes, sir."

Boomer moved in front of her, his dark eyes finally meeting hers. "One other thing, miss. The secret to survival as a plebe is to become invisible. And as a woman you aren't going to be able to do that. You might have in Beast, but in your academic company you're only going to have three or four other female classmates. You're going to be a shit-magnet. Understand?"

"Yes, sir." A bead of sweat was agonizingly making its way down her nose toward the tip, but Trace stayed locked in a rigid position of attention.

"You've already got someone's attention in your company and it'll only get worse. But the bottom line is, they can't do nothing to you. You may think they can, and it may sure seem like they are, but they really can't do anything to you unless you let it get to you. They can scream all they want, and waste your time up until 2000 every evening, but after that they have to let you study and that's what you have to concentrate on. In other words, decide real quick what's bullshit and what's real and don't let the bullshit get you down. Got that?"

"Yes, sir."

"There's a lot of people like Greg, but that doesn't mean you have to let them get to you, or that you have to become one. Right?"

"Yes, sir."

"All right." He chuckled and his deep voice attempted to get serious. "Now get out of my sight, beanhead. Move. Move. Move!"

Trace never forgot those words of advice in the following months. In retrospect she wondered if she would have made it if Boomer hadn't taken the time and effort to talk to her that day. At the time she had simply thought he was being nice. It was only after she'd been further indoctrinated into the Academy system did she realize that Boomer had been perilously close to being unprofessional by being nice to her. Nice was not a trait extolled in the Blue Book that ruled cadets' lives.

Leaning back in her chair, Trace stretched out shoulder muscles sore from her time at the keyboard. She had short dark hair, framing a thin, tanned face out of which two dark eyes blazed behind steel-rim glasses. Her fatigue shirt hung limply over the back of the chair and her camouflage pants were unbloused from the highly shined jungle boots. Trace was slender, one of the few women who looked good in the male-designed Army-issue battle dress uniform, which was actually to her disadvantage among her peers and the Officers' Wives Club and had proved to be disastrous when it came to a particular high-ranking male officer.

In 1992 the sudden opening of combat flight slots to female pilots had seemed to Trace as a particular stroke of luck. She'd just served in the Gulf War piloting a UH-60 Blackhawk air ambulance with the 82nd Airborne Division and had received a Bronze Star for valor when she'd flown a rescue mission for a team of Navy SEALs pinned down on the first day of the ground war.

Her excellent record and her skills as a pilot had garnered her a slot as one of the first three women to go through Apache flight training. Her husband, John, had not been thrilled with the idea. He was a classmate and they had married in the excitement and fear of graduation. He wanted the two of them to settle down with concurrent tours at graduate school and then back to the Military Academy as instructors. But Trace had loved flying too much and insisted on the opportunity that presented itself.

Trace had fallen in love with the powerful attack helicopter and graduated at the top of her class, despite subtle—and not-so-subtle—attempts on the part of both her male peers and instructors to sabotage her invasion of their aerial domain.

After graduating, she'd been assigned to the 2nd Infantry Division's Apache Battalion in South Korea in late 1992, while her husband was attending Johns Hopkins back in the States for graduate schooling. As the only woman in the unit, she'd faced a wall of hostility penetrated only by many of the men's attempts to get into her flight suit. They hated her, but they wanted to screw her, which in retrospect, Trace found to be an apt commentary on the state of women in the military.

Her new battalion commander, Lieutenant Colonel Warren, had been none too pleased to inbrief her. He didn't want her, but the Department of the Army had cut the orders and there wasn't anything he could do about it. His comments were succinct and to the point: make one mistake and she would be gone from his unit.

Two weeks after getting in-country, she'd joined the rest of the pilots at the base's officer club early one Friday evening for a "Hail and Farewell." It was an Army tradition to greet incoming members of the unit and to bid goodbye to those departing back to the States. Trace sat through the speeches and plaques for the farewells and waited for the hails. The new officers, Trace among them, were lined up to "Do The Lance."

The Lancers was the battalion's nickname, and the physical symbol of that nickname was an eight-foot bamboo lance. The long center of the haft had been hollowed out, the tip was now removed, and it was ceremoniously filled with beer. Each new officer was required to take the Lance and empty it in one continuous drink, never removing the end of the haft from their lips. Since it contained six beers, the first two officers, both second lieutenants, failed to the derision of the other officers of the battalion.

When it was Trace's turn, the volume level in the room in the officer's club reached new levels as they waited for her to fail. Trace, however, had learned the art of chugging from her plebe classmates in I-One on their lonely Saturday nights in Eisenhower Hall where the only thing they could do was drink as much beer as quickly as possible. Since the line for the draft beer was always long, they had quickly gotten into the habit of buying several pitchers each and getting swiftly drunk before having to return to their Academy cells at the stroke of midnight.

Trace took the lance from LTC Warren and proceeded to drink it dry to the consternation of the other pilots. When done, she turned it upside down and offered it as evidence to the disbelievers in the crowd. She thought the whole thing childish, but she knew if she wanted to fit in at all, this was one way she would have to try.

The rest of the evening proceeded with great quantities of beer being imbibed and ever taller tales of flying derring-do being told. Trace kept quiet and switched her drinking to coffee and soda. She knew better than to talk about her Bronze Star mission, or any of the other ones she'd flown in the Gulf. Coming from her it wouldn't command respect but animosity. She also knew better than to get further drunk around aviators, whose sexual reputation around the Army was built upon numerous O-Club excursions with women, married or not, in uniform or not, it didn't matter. Anything that was female and breathing was considered fair game. And here in this O-Club, Trace was the only female around other than the Korean waitresses.

By eleven, over half the officers had left to crawl off to the Korean bars outside the gates and link up with local women who were willing, for hard currency, to give in to the men's lust.

Trace decided it was time for her to get back to her BOQ room when she was stopped in the dark foyer of the club by LTC Warren.

"Where'd you learn to drink like that?" he demanded, his face bright red and his eyes blinking, trying to focus.

"Proper training, sir," Trace replied, trying to be diplomatic.

"So can you take it all down like that?" Warren slurred.

Trace had no doubt what he was referring to and tried to slip around him. She'd been in this situation before and knew that discretion was the better part of valor, especially with one's own battalion commander. She now accepted that it was going to be a very long year.

Warren reached out and grabbed her shoulder, which shocked Trace. "So do you swallow?" Warren was pressed up against her in the corner formed by a telephone booth and the wall.

"Sir, let go of me," Trace said, her stomach doing flip-flops.

Warren let go of her shoulder, but instead of backing off, he reached out with both hands and placed one directly over her left breast and began squeezing and, with the other, tried to unzip her flight suit from the top.

Trace stopped thinking and reacted. She swung an elbow, catching the colonel on the side of the head, knocking him against the phone booth. He let go of the breast and groped for her crotch. She grabbed both his shoulders, steadying her target, then exploded her knee upward with all her strength.

Warren gasped and immediately let go of her as he sunk to his knees now holding his own crotch. Trace turned and ran out the club, heading directly for her room where she locked the door and remained there all night, half afraid that someone would show up there pounding and demanding to be let in.

The next day she was shocked when Warren walked by her at morning PT formation, acting as if nothing had happened. After physical training, Trace approached the battalion executive officer, Major Ford, in his office and told him of the previous evening's incident. His immediate response was not gratifying as a worried look settled in on his face.

"Colonel Warren has a little drinking problem, Captain Trace." Ford offered a weak smile. "I'm sure he doesn't remember what happened."

"What are we going to do about what he did, sir?" Trace asked.

"*We* aren't going to do anything," Ford replied. "The colonel was drunk."

"That doesn't excuse what he did! He assaulted me," Trace said, trying to control her anger. "What happens if he does it again?"

"Just make sure you aren't around him when he's drinking and it won't happen again," Ford suggested sharply.

Trace gestured around. "This post is only slightly bigger than the airfield. Am I supposed to hide in my room when I'm not on duty because the colonel has a drinking problem and likes to grope women?"

"It's your word against his," Ford said.

"You just said he had a drinking problem," Trace protested.

"And if I had to testify, I would say he's the best battalion commander I've ever served under and I have no knowledge of a drinking problem." Ford leaned forward. "Listen, let it go. No one wants you here anyway. Make waves and they'll ship your ass out of here in a heartbeat."

Trace felt curiously calm. She was at one of those life points where you know there's a fork and once you choose your direction, there's no going back. She'd put up with the sexual harassment from her first day at West Point until

the present. She'd been exposed to some situations at West
Point that made Warren's drunken gropings seem insignificant, but she expected more from a forty-year-old battalion
commander, especially one she had to serve under for the
next year at an isolated base. In fact, one of the reasons—
in bitter retrospect the major reason—she'd married so
quickly after graduation was for the protection a wedding
band would give her among the wolves waiting in the ranks
of the real Army. But it was obvious that her wedding band
would be no protection here in Korea, especially with her
husband thousands of miles away.

"I want to lodge a formal complaint against Colonel
Warren," she said, her voice totally flat.

Ford looked like he had just swallowed a horse turd.
"What?"

"I am going to lodge a formal complaint against Colonel
Warren. I will file an assault charge with the military police
and a sexual harassment complaint through the chain of
command and with the division equal opportunity officer
at Camp Casey."

"You're crazy," Ford said.

Trace stood. "No, sir. I'm pissed." She turned and left
his office.

It had turned into a bloody mess that had gone all the
way to the 8th Army Commander in Japan. Trace had been
grounded during the investigation and that was used to
move her out of the Apache Battalion. The reasoning was
that a pilot should fly, not fight legal battles. So in the long
run, she'd lost as far as the Army was concerned. Warren
was allowed to finish his command if he attended the Army
drug and alcohol rehabilitation program. The sexual harassment charge disappeared under volumes of legal white-
washing. In Army thinking it was better Warren be an
alcoholic than a sexual harasser. Everyone remembered
Tailhook and no one wanted to be associated with either
the case or Trace.

She'd returned to the States four months early, never
having had a chance to fly the helicopter she'd been trained
for. She'd been shipped to Fort Meade and given a job in
public affairs. An assignment close to her husband, but one
which kept her away from helicopters. Aviation branch saw

her as a hot potato and a case of good riddance.

Of course, when she had returned from Korea, her home was one of those places where she'd hoped she could get some unconditional support. But she'd heard the tone in her husband's voice during their long distance conversations and she saw the look in his eyes when they met at the airport. There was no going back from such a look.

He'd stayed for six months until finally Trace had been forced to make him face the fact that he was only there out of some perverse sense of duty and pity. He was worried about his own career now, married to a woman who had gained an unfavorable reputation with the powers-that-be in the green machine. Ultimately, she knew that he had not agreed with her decision to press charges and that knowledge disgusted her. That he would rather her keep quiet about her being groped by another man, rather than possibly upset their career track, was beyond what she could take. Her husband moved out the next day, relieved to be able to put it totally on her shoulders and get on with punching his tickets up the rank structure. The divorce followed as soon as legally possible.

With her nothing job at Fort Meade and her husband gone, she'd been lost and confused. The injustice of what had happened to her in Korea and the stonewall of Army brass she'd run into had left her empty and alone.

That was when Boomer Watson had saved her life. She'd never told anyone that, not even Boomer. But she knew it was true. He'd made a special trip from Fort Bragg in between one of his constant deployments to visit her. And he'd kept in touch on the phone, calling whenever he got back from a deployment—sometimes in the middle of the night.

Then, two weeks after John had moved out, Boomer had appeared at Trace's office, wearing civilian clothes and sporting non-regulation hair with a beard. He was in for two weeks temporary duty. Something to do with an upcoming exercise. He never told her why he was at Fort Meade, but she suspected it had something to do with the National Security Agency which was also headquartered on post.

For two weeks they spent every minute off duty together.

On the third night, as he was getting ready to leave to go back to his BOQ room, she'd asked him to stay. He looked at her, grinned, and joined her on the couch. Two hours later, when he taken her in his arms, she'd pried herself loose and turned all the lights out, before taking her clothes off, going to the bed, and sliding under the covers, unseen.

The next morning she slipped out, getting into the shower while Boomer still slept. She was pleased when the curtain was pulled aside and he stepped in. He grabbed the soap and did the favors.

Later, over breakfast, she asked him how he felt about being with her. Boomer raised his eyebrows: "What about being with you?"

"Come on, don't mess with me. You know I'm a marked woman."

"Hey, I'm not messing with you. All I saw—and see— is a beautiful person and a beautiful woman—that I just made love to. The sex wasn't bad either. And you know me better than to think I give a shit about my so-called Army career. I'm just having fun down at Bragg. I don't care if they keep me a major the rest of my career. Sounds good to me."

He'd gone back to Bragg, and though they'd seen each other over the years, they'd never slept together again. It was as if they'd crossed a line for a reason, then put the line back in place and gone back to the strength of their friendship. Trace had read somewhere that if old lovers stayed in your life they were the truest friends and that was how she felt about Boomer. And now he was coming back into her life.

Trace shook herself out of her reverie and glanced at the clock. It was a quarter to nine. Time to be going. She shrugged on her BDU shirt, feeling the stiffness of the starched material. She saved what she'd written, shut the computer down, and the words faded from the screen as she left the house perched on the mountain side overlooking Barbers Point Naval Air Station.

She decided to take the fastest route to work, turning her Jeep Cherokee toward Makikilo Drive and H1. Even if her thoughts had not been on the pending arrival of Boomer Watson, there was no chance she could have spotted the two men dressed in black fatigues hidden 600 meters away on the heavily vegetated slope of Puu Makakilo.

The man with the rifle shifted the red illuminated laser aiming circle in the center of the scope reticle and tracked the Jeep as it moved toward the highway. The scope was mounted on a Remington Model 700, .308 caliber, single shot, bolt-action rifle on top of a tripod behind which the man sat crosslegged. A thin black cord led from the side of the large scope to a small black box on the ground. The box was a computer that combined the location of the rifle and distance and elevation to the target—determined by ground-positioning radar and the laser range and direction finder in the scope itself, along with weather data, particularly current wind direction and speed (calculated by a small anemometer which popped up on the top of the computer box), to automatically adjust the aiming circle in the scope. Except for the ability to keep the aiming point on target while pulling the trigger smoothly, the computer and scope made an expert marksman out of the most ordinary of shooters. The will to pull the trigger on a human target was, of course, assumed.

The man centered the small pointing circle on Trace's head and his right forefinger caressed the trigger. "Pow," he muttered. "One dead bitch." As Trace's Jeep entered H1, he pulled his eye away from the rubber cup on the scope. "Why are we just sitting here? Why don't we do it?"

"We wait for orders," the second man said, noting Trace's departure time and direction in a small notebook. "We aren't the only ones waiting for orders. There are other actions to be coordinated," he added vaguely. "We need to get everything and we need to know how she got the information."

He put the notebook away in his breast pocket and smoothly slid a double-edged commando knife out of a boot sheath. With a flip of his wrist, he threw the knife into the trunk of a tree ten meters away, the razor-sharp blade sinking four inches into the wood. "We have to go in and get the stuff first. Then grab her. Someone else says when."

CHAPTER ☆ 3

AIRSPACE. HAWAIIAN ISLANDS
29 NOVEMBER
9:30 A.M. LOCAL/ 1930 ZULU

The muted crackle of the plane's public address system woke Boomer from an uneasy slumber, and he cracked an eye. He peered out the window to take in the sights below as the pilot's voice described them: "On the left side of the aircraft, you have an excellent view of Pearl Harbor. The white structure just off the island in the center is the *USS Arizona* Memorial. We will be touching down shortly. Attendants, please prepare for landing."

The water below glistened. The bright green hills in the near distance were lush with vegetation. When Boomer craned his neck, he could see the urban sprawl of Honolulu to the east, poised between the mountains and the sea with the large silhouette of Diamond Head backdropped beyond the city. It seemed like more than twenty-four hours since the horror of events in the Ukraine and the hectic departure from Turkey.

The plane touched down. Boomer kept his seat, watching with detached interest as the aisles rapidly filled even as the plane taxied to the terminal. He was in no rush—he got paid whether he sat here or scrambled off the plane as quickly as possible. He waited until the crowd dissipated to slide into the aisle, the briefcase containing his orders in hand.

He smiled at the stewardess who was rotely bidding the departing passengers to have a nice stay in Hawaii. The stewardess's plastic smile became genuine for just the slightest moment and then he was gone, past her into the tunnel leading to the terminal.

Boomer rode the shuttle to the main terminal to claim his baggage. Beyond the meaning of the acronym, Boomer knew little about the the 4th TASOSC, his new unit. From vague memories from his days in the 10th Special Forces Group, he knew 4th TASOSC stood for 4th Theater Army Special Operations Support Command. Its mission was to plan and coordinate the support and sustainment of all Army Special Operations Forces operating in the Pacific region. To Boomer's experienced mind, that translated to a lot of paperwork and time on the telephone talking to support people. Clerk and jerk stuff, nothing very exciting.

Boomer hoped that the locale of Hawaii would make up for the boring work. He was still concerned with the events occurring at Delta Headquarters at Fort Bragg. He wasn't concerned about making general someday, but he did enjoy his job in Delta Force and didn't want to lose it. He didn't like being out of the loop, but Colonel Forster hadn't left him much choice. He knew his commander had picked Hawaii as the cooling-off place for Boomer because Forster knew the executive officer of the 4th TASOSC and was collecting an old debt. Forster felt it was far enough away from both Turkey and Fort Bragg for Boomer to ride out whatever storm Colonel Decker tried to raise, if any, over recent events. Forster had been of the opinion that the less said all around, the better. He hoped that was the way Decker would see it. "Take a couple of weeks in the sun, Boomer," Forster had said. "Enjoy yourself and get out of the rat race for a while. I'll cover for you."

Boomer located the correct baggage carousal and waited for his duffle bag and rucksack to appear. He spotted a young, female, Hispanic soldier wearing camouflage fatigues and jauntily sporting a red beret—indicating she was in an airborne unit—enter at the far side of the terminal. She was only about five feet, four inches tall, but she carried herself with a swagger, her slender form bopping about as she restlessly scanned the terminal.

The young sergeant looked uncertainly at the milling group of people. Boomer appreciated her predicament. It used to be easy to spot male military types by their haircut

when he first came on active duty in 1981. He remembered
when soldiers in his first unit, an infantry platoon at Fort
Riley, Kansas, wore wigs when they went into town off-
duty, anything to hide the distinctive short hair of the military. Nowadays though, short was in and the sergeant was
uncertain who to approach, her eyes flitting from man to
man. She in turn was getting a few appreciative glances
from some of the men.

Boomer let her wait until his OD green bags came up
the chute and he grabbed them. The sergeant took that as
a cue and ambled over.

"Major Watson?" she asked, taking in the longer-than-
regulation hair and civilian clothes.

"Yep," Boomer said, shouldering his ruck and getting
a closer look at her shining dark eyes.

To Boomer's surprise, the sergeant grabbed the duffle
bag, easily chucking the heavy bag over one shoulder.
"This way, sir. I got my car parked in the red zone. Colonel
Falk took us on a long run this morning, and I didn't get
done at the gym and everything until real late so I didn't
catch your plane coming in."

"No problem," Boomer said. "I wasn't going anywhere."

"The XO—that's Colonel Falk—got you a room at the
guest house," the sergeant added as she led the way out of
the building. "It's good till tomorrow, then you're probably
going to have to go out on the economy or maybe Tripler
might have something."

A fire-red Camaro was parked illegally and the sergeant
popped the trunk and deposited the duffle bag, filling the
trunk. "Put that in the back seat," she instructed.

Boomer complied and settled into the passenger seat. As
the woman started the engine, he leaned over and stuck his
hand out. "Major Boomer Watson."

The sergeant was briefly startled, then smiled, a smooth
row of white teeth showing up against her dark skin. "Shit,
sir, I'm sorry. Sergeant Vasquez. Everybody's jumping
through their ass in the tunnel and I guess my head's kind
of out of it."

"The tunnel?" Boomer inquired as Vasquez peeled

away from the curb and roared into traffic, ignoring the bleating of horns.

"Yes, sir. That's where we work. A system of tunnels built at the beginning of World War II. They cut right into one of the old lava flows. It's pretty neat. Actually there's three tunnels altogether that make up our place. They're all connected."

"What's everyone jumping about?"

Vasquez looked at Boomer as if he had just come from the Australian outback. "The President's visit. The whole Pearl Harbor gig. Security's going to be tighter than a frog's asshole. Especially now that the Iraqis are making a stink again, and all that crap with the Ukrainians. It's just a big mess. Hell, for all we know the sons-of-a-bitches have got a bomb now. There's speculation in the paper about what would happen if one went off here in Oahu while the President was here."

Boomer *had* forgotten much of that, not that the isolated launch base in Turkey had offered much in the way of current news. The President was due to arrive in Hawaii the following week to commemorate the fifty-fourth anniversary of the attack on Pearl Harbor. The word in the media was that he would use the occasion to make a speech concerning the MRA—Military Reform Act—that his party had just squeaked through Congress and which was awaiting debate in the Senate. Boomer had barely followed the heated coverage, although even a casual observer knew that the military as a whole was violently opposed to the act. He'd had more pressing problems on his mind the last six months, like staying alive and keeping his men alive.

Vasquez pointed to a massive building on the hillside far above the highway. "That's Tripler Army Hospital. Fort Shafter's just ahead." She jerked a thumb over his shoulder. "I guess you saw Pearl and Hickam Airfield on the way in."

"Yeah," Boomer acknowledged. "What do you do at the TASOSC?"

"I'm in Intelligence. I interpret imagery and do target folders. I did the folders on the radar sites that got hit by the Apache helicopters on the first day of the air war during Desert Storm," she added proudly. "The first shots of the war were fired using my stuff."

Boomer smiled to himself. He couldn't tell her that he'd been in Iraq on the ground long before those Apaches from the 1st Battalion of the 101st Airborne let loose their Hellfire missiles, officially beginning the war. One thing he had learned about the military: the need to feel like an important piece of the overall machine. Boomer recognized the reality that the military, by being the largest "corporation" in America, had so many pieces that almost everyone was a minor and relatively insignificant cog. And now that organization was facing major restructuring.

"How does everyone feel about the MRA?" Boomer asked.

Vasquez barked a short laugh. "Sir, you want to get in a fight, you mention those three letters around anyone in uniform. When it was the gays in the military thing a couple of years ago there were still a lot people who actually didn't give a shit. Live and let live they thought. But there's enough bullshit in the MRA that *everyone's* got something to be ragged off about, including the total drop of the gay unacceptability thing.

"You got the Marines about ready to bust a gut 'cause of the part that wants to integrate the Corps into the Army. Same with all the pilots being pissed about being made into one branch. You name the person and the act affects them somehow. We been downsizing and cutting back for years now, and now they hit us with this! Those fucking civilians in Washington don't understand."

Boomer settled back in the bucket seat and watched the countryside as Vasquez bitched on about the act, her language quite worthy of any infantry sergeant. He hadn't been too worried about the act himself, but now he wondered if he ought to be. Even with all the cuts coming in the Army he was pretty confident that Delta and Special Operations overall would not be cut. No matter what the world situation or level of "peace," Special Operations always had a real world job to do, as evidenced by his most recent missions in the Ukraine.

He had heard some rumbles that the Joint Chiefs of Staff were not keen on keeping Special Operations forces up to strength while having to cut their own prized Army divisions, aircraft carrier groups, and Air Force squadrons. Boomer had been exposed to the regular Army's distaste for Special Forces from the moment his infantry battalion commander had told him his Army career was over when Boomer filed a 4187 form requesting Special Forces training in 1983.

In those days Special Forces was truly a bastard stepchild. There was no Special Forces branch and any officer taking an assignment in the Green Berets threw his "career track" off the beaten path. In 1987, when Special Forces had finally been recognized as a separate branch by the Army, after great pressure from Congress, Boomer had been proud to pin on the crossed arrows that adorned the right collar of his battle dress uniform. In fact, nearly every major reform in favor of Special Operations Forces had required the passage of a law by Congress, which in turn had to be crammed down the throats of the reluctant conventional military leaders.

The other issue in the MRA that was causing a great amount of consternation was the proposal to basically eliminate the three service academies by converting them into one-year officer basic schools for all officers upon commissioning from ROTC or OCS programs. Boomer could well imagine the ulcers that was causing among most of his fellow graduates of West Point. He himself wasn't too sure it was a bad idea, considering the discrepancy in cost between a West Point graduate and an ROTC officer, and the small, if any, difference between the two once they were in the Army.

The Academy had been founded when there was no other way to produce quality regular Army officers. Today that wasn't the case. Of course, Boomer also had to admit that he would have had a most difficult time getting a college education if he had not been able to attend the Academy. In the years since graduation, though, Boomer realized more and more that he had paid for his four-year education in a currency more valuable than coin. He had paid with some of his heart and soul. He could see that most clearly when he looked at others his own age who had attended a "regular" college.

Vasquez took an exit off the highway and was waved

through the gate to Fort Shafter by an MP. A sign just inside warned all visitors that they were subject to search and that they had basically surrendered most of the basic rights guaranteed by the Constitution simply by crossing the invisible line separating the state of Hawaii from federal land.

A military post is a world unto itself and basically self-contained. Boomer had once been on temporary duty (TDY) at a remote base in Korea and had met people who had never been outside the gate into the Korean community other than passing through on a military transport bus. They lived for an entire year within the fence surrounding the compound. Military people were a curious combination of world-traveler—even the lowest ranking person usually having lived overseas—and xenophobic isolationist. It was not unusual for the highest-ranking general to have no idea what it meant to live in a community with people of different beliefs and occupations or have to deal with such civilian matters as having to pay health insurance.

Boomer took in Fort Shafter, correlating it to the map he had casually studied on the plane coming in. The major populated area of Oahu stretched from Diamond Head on the southeast corner of the Island, west along Waikiki and downtown Honolulu, to the International Airport and Hickam Field, Pearl Harbor, to finally Barbers Point Naval Air Station at the southwest corner of the Island. Fort Shafter was on the north side of Highway H1 which ran along all those points. The fort overlooked the airport and Pearl Harbor, with an excellent view of downtown Honolulu to the left. Shafter was one of dozens of military posts scattered about the Island and housed the Army's Western Command.

"I'll take you to the guest house, sir. You can throw on a uniform and then we can head to the tunnel," she added as she glanced at Boomer's hair.

They drove up to the motel-like guest house, and Boomer quickly stored his gear and changed into a set of starched BDUs. It felt funny every time he put on U.S. uniform after the civilian clothes and foreign uniforms he was used to in Delta. It was like changing part of his personality. He'd worn a uniform full-time from West Point in 1977 through joining Delta. He pulled a faded green beret from his bags and settled it on his head, checking himself in the mirror.

The beret was the original one he'd been issued on graduating the Special Forces Qualification Course in 1984. He'd been told several times in the course of his career to replace the worn hat with a new one, but he'd grown attached to this one. It had gone many places with him. The green cloth had that beaten, faded look that soldiers in Special Force secretly prized.

Vasquez's demeanor changed when she spotted Boomer walking out of the lobby. She noted the Special Forces Combat patch on the Major's right shoulder, and the Combat Infantry badge, Master Parachutist badge and scuba badge on his left chest. Beneath the Special Forces and Ranger tabs on Boomer's left shoulder, he wore the unit patch of the Special Operations Command (Airborne).

"You were in 5th Group during Desert Storm, sir?" she asked as they got back in the car.

"No. First of the 10th out of Tolz," he lied, automatically giving her the cover story that he'd been briefed on right after the Gulf War.

Boomer waited for the inevitable "What did you do?" but it didn't come, for which he was relieved. They were at the entrance to the tunnel in less than five minutes. Boomer looked at it with interest. A heavily vegetated lava ridge line was directly in front of them with a covered walkway leading up the side to a large vault door. Looking to his left he could see the ocean, with Honolulu off to the far left. To the right, the road ended in a housing area, behind which the mountains loomed, forming the interior of Oahu. It was a spectacular location, but it didn't appear that there were any windows in the office to enjoy the view.

"The XO will have to give you the door code, sir," Vasquez said as she punched into the numerical key pad on the side of the door. There was a loud beep and with great effort Vasquez slowly swung the door wide. "Air pressure makes it real hard to open in the mornings," she added as they stepped inside and the door swung shut on its own.

A tunnel painted pale green stretched ahead for more than a hundred feet. Vasquez led the way past wall lockers and turned right at the first set of double metal doors. A larger tunnel beckoned at a right angle to the first one. This tunnel was thirty feet across and the ceiling was curved, over twenty feet high at its peak. Desks were scattered about and the far end was walled off with glass, curtains hiding whatever was on the other side of the door in the center of the glass.

The home of the 4th TASOSC consisted of three main, parallel tunnels. Boomer was currently in the first. It housed the TASOSC's S-1 section (administrative and personnel), executive officer, and in the far end of the tunnel, separated from the others by the thick glass wall and curtains, the TASOSC commander. The middle tunnel held the TASOSC sergeant major, the communication's console, and at the far end, again walled off with glass, the TASOSC conference room. The third and most distant tunnel contained the Operations (S-3) and Intelligence (S-2) staffs. All the tunnels were connected by two side tunnels—one along the base, leading in from the vault door, and the other in the center, splitting each tunnel in half.

Vasquez led the way to a desk strewn with various papers and folders. "Sir, I got the major," she announced.

A lieutenant colonel peered up above the stacks of paper. He was small, with leathery skin stretched tight over his bones. A thin, gray crew cut gave him the indeterminate appearance of man somewhere between an old forty and a young sixty.

"George Falk," he announced sticking his hand out, "but you can call me 'sir,' " a genuine smile indicating that he did not take the remark too seriously.

Boomer smiled in return. "Boomer Watson, sir."

"Glad to have you, Boomer. Grab a seat and I'll get you tuned in to our operation."

"See you around, sir," Vasquez said, spinning on the heel of her spit-shined jump boots and heading off to a side tunnel.

"I see you've met our resident body-builder," Falk said.

"What?" Boomer asked.

"Vasquez—she competes in body building contests," Falk said.

Boomer twisted in his seat and watched the sergeant disappear with interest. That helped explain the way she handled his duffle bag. Boomer settled down into the beat-up gray chair and returned his attention to Lieutenant Colonel Falk. Boomer watched as he rustled through a stack of papers. "Damn, I had a copy of your orders here somewhere. Got them faxed in from Bragg this morning."

Boomer slipped a copy of his orders out of the file folder he was carrying. "Here you go, sir." They were fill-in-the-blank orders, assigning him to the 4th TASOSC until further notice. Typical orders for Delta Force personnel who were often sent to strange locations to do strange jobs without much notice.

"Thanks," Falk said, glancing at them. "You're going to be with us for a while?" he asked.

"I don't know, sir."

Falk pursed his lips. "Hmm. I got a call from Jim Forster on the secure line yesterday afternoon. He asked me to take care of you. Jim and I go back a long ways."

Boomer could tell Falk was fishing for information, but he figured he couldn't tell the man anything more than Forster had.

"You're going to have to get your hair cut," Falk added. "We're not that high speed and we get quite a bit of rank coming through the tunnel. A lot of people around here get their nose out of joint about important things like haircuts and shined boots and all that," Falk said, his own disdain for the regular Army clear.

"Yes, sir."

"Good. Well, glad you're here. We need the help. Forster told me to let you take it kind of easy, so I don't want to overload you. What's your area of expertise?" Falk looked at Boomer's uniform, making the size-up all Army people did upon meeting, noting badges the way a dog would sniff another upon first meeting.

"My primary is Eighteen," Boomer said. "My secondary is Thirty-nine—Operations."

Falk looked at Boomer with more interest. "Who were you with before going behind the fence?" he asked, using the euphemism among those in the know for people who went into Delta Force. The original Delta Compound at Bragg had been surrounded by a chain link fence with green strips of metal sown through it to provide some degree of protection from surveillance—thus the term that had developed for people going to work there. The new compound was bigger and had a correspondingly higher fence in a more remote area of the Fort Bragg reservation.

"I was originally branched Infantry then went SF in 'eighty-four. I was with 10th Group at Fort Devens, team leader and Battalion S-3 for a while; then the Advanced Course then I went to 1st of the 10th at Bad Tolz in Germany, where I had another team before heading back to Bragg."

"Good, good," Falk said.

The door at the far end of the tunnel opened and a major exited. A squeaky voice calling for Colonel Falk echoed over the major's shoulder.

"Excuse me," Falk said as he quickly walked away and entered the office, shutting the door behind.

Boomer recognized the other major as a man he had gone through the Special Forces Qualification Course with, Frank Wilkerson. He looked none-too-happy at the moment. "Frank, how's it going?"

Wilkerson looked at Boomer's long hair and glanced at his nametag. He tried in vain to crack a smile of greeting. "Boomer Watson, long time no-see."

The beret stuffed in Wilkerson's pants cargo pocket had a yellow tab sewn behind the gold major's leaf—another message that could be read by those in the fraternity. "Where are you assigned in 1st Group?" Boomer asked. "Fort Lewis or Okinawa?"

"Okie," Wilkerson said shortly. "Or perhaps it's better to say I was."

"What do you do?" Boomer asked.

Wilkerson's jaw tightened. "I *was* the commander of A Company, 1st Battalion."

"You just changed command?" Boomer asked innocently.

"No, I was just relieved two days ago."

Boomer had regretted his question as soon as he had asked it. Wilkerson's entire demeanor and tone had suggested bad news. Relief from command was an instant career-killer—about the worst thing that could happen to an officer short of death in combat, and there were many that probably would prefer the latter—at least it was honorable. Boomer was surprised: Wilkerson had been a squared-away and conscientious officer at the Q Course. To get relieved of command in peacetime usually required some gross violation of military regulations.

"I'm sorry to hear that."

Wilkerson jerked a thumb over his shoulder at the office he had just cleft. "It's bad enough I have to go back to Fort Lewis and get reamed out by the Group Commander when I get there, but this shithead has to have me come through here and stick his two cents in and he's not even in the chain of command."

"Who's that?" Boomer asked.

"The CO here—Colonel Coulder. He's a class-one prima donna. Thinks he's actually in charge of something instead of simply being a beans and bullets guy." Wilkerson slumped down in the chair Boomer had just vacated. "What the hell are you doing here anyway? I've never seen you here before and I come through here pretty often."

"I just got in today for some special work." Boomer replied vaguely, knowing that Wilkerson was trying to make sense of his non-regulation hair and the Special Operations patch on his shoulder.

"Beefing up for the President's visit?" Wilkerson asked, almost to himself. "Everyone's running scared after the incident in Turkey with the nuke." He looked up, his thoughts returning to his own situation. "Well, I guess I won't even be able to stay in the Reserves after this. My fucking career is over."

"What happened?" Boomer asked.

Wilkerson glanced around, making sure no one else was in earshot. "It was bullshit, man. Pure bullshit. I was set up."

"Set up?"

"I was assigned to take part in a command post exercise in Korea back in October. I got in-country, and they gave me my copies of the operations orders and playbook and all that other classified stuff. I had it in a briefcase. Well, I was on South Post Yongsan and I stopped at the Burger King there to get something to eat before heading down to

Taegu. I wasn't in the place more than two minutes, and someone popped out the lock on the trunk and took the briefcase. Turns out it was CID. It was all a set-up. They nailed my ass for a security violation.''

Boomer found it hard to generate sympathy. Being a courier for classified material meant never letting it out of your sight. ''It was probably some sort of counter-intelligence thing, Wilk. They do that stuff a lot in Korea. It's a hot zone.''

''I know it's a hot zone,'' Wilkerson hissed. ''And I know that I fucked up by leaving the shit in the car, but I'm telling you it was deliberately set up to get *me* relieved. I was deliberately sent on that CPX to get me out of the way in the first place.''

''Who would have done that?''

''I don't know, but there's some weird shit going on. I've had unusually high turnover in my company and the sergeant major and battalion commander have been stacking two of my teams—assigning people directly to ODAs while I was deployed. When I complained, they sent me on the mission to Korea.'' Wilkerson took another look around, then leaned forward. ''You know what my company is?''

Boomer frowned. ''What do you mean 'what it is?' It's a Special Forces company.''

''Yeah, but do you know what our primary mission is?''

Boomer shrugged, pretending to be uncertain about what his old comrade was talking about. ''I don't know. You guys out of Okie are targeted for Southeast Asia right?''

''B and C Companies are.'' Wilkerson's voice dropped to a whisper. ''A Company is the regional counter-terrorist reaction force. Just like Det A in Berlin was over in Europe. We work with Delta all the time. We're the first response guys for half the fucking world if any high-speed shit goes down. And somebody wanted my ass out of that command.''

Boomer had known exactly what A Company, 1st Battalion was. Part of the ''secret'' game, though, was to never let on that you knew anything. Boomer preferred to play at being stupid and to profess ignorance rather than try to do half-truths and explain what couldn't be talked about. He'd never worked with A-1/1, but he knew other's in his squadron of Delta had. A-1/1's job was to stabilize a threat situation in the Pacific until Delta could arrive on scene to deal with it. The five teams in the company were specially trained and equipped for the mission.

Wilkerson leaned forward. "You should see the guy that took over for me. They've got two or three promotable captains in the battalion that they could have given the company to. Hell, my senior team leader is on the promotion list. Or even moved someone in from Japan or Korea. But instead they bring some guy straight from Benning."

"Who's that?" Boomer asked, glancing over at the door Falk had disappeared through, hoping the XO would come back soon and get him out of this awkward conversation.

"Some fellow named Keyes. Major Geoffrey Keyes. I checked with some of my buddies at Bragg and they don't even think this guy is SF-qualified."

That caught Boomer's attention. Keyes was a classmate of his from West Point. Boomer remembered him well—Keyes had been ranked number one in Infantry Branch and number three overall in the class at graduation. At Ranger school Keyes had been in Boomer's platoon and had earned a reputation as a dick. Boomer had watched Keyes skate his way through, putting out effort whenever he was in charge of a patrol and being evaluated, but slacking off whenever he wasn't. Despite that, Keyes had been one of those gladhanders that walked on water and received maximum ratings. Someone who looked good but lacked substance. Boomer had not heard of Keyes going to the Special Forces Qualification Course. Last he had heard, Keyes was in the Ranger Battalion at Fort Benning, punching his regular Army career ticket in the elite infantry unit.

"Does he have an SF Tab?" Boomer asked, referring to the cloth tab awarded to graduates of the SF School.

"Yeah, he's got one. But hell, Boomer, you can buy one of those at clothing sales and sew it on. No one I know of ever saw him in a group. He's coming right from the 3rd Ranger Battalion at Benning. That doesn't make any sense."

Boomer commiserated with Wilkerson while he waited

for Colonel Falk to return, half his mind marveling at the tremendous capability of people to deny reality. First, Wilkerson *had* screwed up by leaving the classified material in his car unattended. Second, why would anyone want Wilkerson removed from command? Third, why would someone send a non-SF-qualified officer to take command of a Special Forces company? Sounded like Army politics to Boomer, but the bottom line was that Wilkerson had been wrong to leave the classified material in the trunk.

Boomer was relieved when Colonel Falk returned and Major Wilkerson wandered off to nurse his bitterness elsewhere.

Falk scratched his scant hair and peered at his desk, lost in thought for a few seconds. "So what have I told you so far?" he asked.

"You said I could call you sir, sir."

"That's it?" Falk sat down. "I got forty-five balls in the air right now and I'm dropping half of them so don't take it too seriously when I start ranting and raving. OK, Boomer, here's the deal. Everybody's jumping through their butt over the President's upcoming visit. JSOC, Joint Special Operations Command, got tagged to pick up some of the security out at Pearl since that's the military's turf. There's some other training operations going on, which you don't have a need to know about," he continued vaguely, "that's eating up all our time.

"So I need someone to take care of our normal message traffic and screen it for hand grenades with short fuses. Go through our incoming message traffic every morning when it comes in and see if there's anything that looks like it needs immediate attention and let me know. That shouldn't be too hard. To fill up the rest of your time, I also need our classified files purged."

"I've got a top secret Q clearance, sir," Boomer said, a bit surprised at the comment about training missions he wasn't cleared for.

"I know. That's why I'm having you look at the message traffic." Falk popped to his feet, and Boomer followed him into a side tunnel which opened onto a parallel tunnel, identical to the first one. Locked four-drawer filing cabinets lined one of the sides, while desks lined the other. A few officers and senior NCOs were at work there.

Falk pointed at the cabinets. "You can start at one end and work your way through. Don't worry if you don't make it through," he added with a smile. "Anything you do will be an improvement. No one's been through that stuff in years."

Falk looked up at the large clock on the wall. "The Old Man's got a briefing here in four minutes and I have to go down to USPACOM and take his place for the weekly staff meeting." He tapped Boomer on the shoulder. "Glad to have you."

Boomer watched Falk walk out of the tunnel, then turned to the file cabinets. He ran a hand through his long hair and smiled ruefully. Paperwork. Just as he'd expected.

CHAPTER ☆ 4

HONOLULU, OAHU, HAWAIIAN ISLANDS
29 NOVEMBER
7:00 P.M. LOCAL/ 0500 ZULU

Boomer had a hard time finding a place to park his rental car until he realized that with the temporary military parking pass he'd been issued at Fort Shafter, he could park it in one of the restricted lots on Fort DeRussy, right across the street from the Hilton Hawaiian Village.

In the less than ten hours he'd been in Hawaii, one thing that had already impressed Boomer was how strong a presence the military was on the island. From Pearl Harbor and Hickam Air Force Base in the south center, to Schofield Barracks taking up most of the interior, to Fort DeRussy and the military's Hale Koa Hotel staking claim to some of the most prime real estate in downtown Honolulu and along Waikiki Beach, there was no doubt that the U.S. military was the second largest industry in the islands after the tourism trade.

Boomer crossed from one industry to the other as he left the parking lot and neatly cut grass of Fort DeRussy and crossed the street where an auditorium with bright signs advertised Don Ho's Hawaiian Extravaganza at the Hilton Hawaiian Village. Directly ahead, he spotted the main lobby for the massive hotel complex. A piano bar beckoned off to one side and Boomer went in, scanning the tables. It was early and the bartender was watching a TV mounted at the end of the bar as he catered to the sparse crowd.

Trace was seated at the end of the bar and she waved him over, rising to greet him. She was dressed in slacks and a short sleeve blouse, a large shoulder bag was lying on a chair next to her. Boomer wrapped his arms around her and lifted her off her feet with an exuberant hug.

"Easy there," Trace laughed. "Nice outfit," she commented.

Boomer let her down and turned, modeling the garishly colored shorts and shirt he'd bought earlier at one of the downtown markets. "Pretty neat, huh?"

"It's definitely you." Trace pulled him down into a seat. "So tell me, what have you been up to?"

"You first," Boomer countered, not quite ready to get into his own story. "Last time we talked you were still at Fort Meade. I got a postcard with your new address and number here in Hawaii a month or so ago, but it didn't tell much. Where are you assigned now?"

Trace shook her head and her tone of voice indicated displeasure with her current assignment. "USPACOM at Camp Smith."

"Pacific Command?" Boomer repeated. "What do you do there?"

"Public relations," Trace said, as she signaled to the bartender. After ordering two beers, they turned back to each other.

"I didn't know the Army had a public relations specialty," Boomer replied. "And even if they did, that isn't what you trained for."

"They don't. Technically, I'm assigned as the assistant PACOM J-1—Personnel. But considering the Unified Commands don't control people in peacetime, there isn't too much for me to do other than sit around and dust off the war plans every once in a while. Thus my real job of public relations for the PACOM commander. Once they saw that I worked in the public affairs office at Fort Meade before CGSC, I was doomed."

"You couldn't get a flying job?" he asked.

"The people in D.C. figured that this was a good opportunity for me to gain experience working at a unified command. Learn what the other services are about and all that good stuff. That's the big push in the *real* Army now," Trace said. "No aviation battalion commander is screaming for me to be in their unit. This assignment's my latest exile."

"What do you do besides work?" Boomer asked.

"I write."

"Write?" Boomer repeated, surprised. His question had been more directed toward her personal life. This was an unexpected development.

"I'm working on a novel," Trace said. "Well, sort of a novel."

Boomer grabbed the two mugs the bartender brought and slid one in front of her. "Here's to old friendships."

They tapped glasses and were silent for a few minutes, each lost in their own thoughts and memories.

"So, what about you?" Trace asked, breaking the silence. "If you tell me what you do, will you have to kill me?"

"Pretty close," Boomer replied. "Kill you, cut off your head, and lock it in a safe."

"Sounds like I don't want to know."

"You don't," Boomer said.

"Something's wrong," Trace quietly said. "I could tell by the tone of your voice on the phone earlier today. And you don't look happy to be here in paradise or to see me."

"I *am* happy to see you," Boomer insisted. "I'm just beat. I was in the air all night and I didn't have much sleep before that."

"In the air coming from where?" Trace asked.

"So what's this book you're writing about?" Boomer attempted.

Trace smiled. "You're not very good at changing the subject. Don't they teach you guys a course on that at Bragg? The art of evasive conversation?" She didn't expect an answer. "I've only just started it. It's about West Point. Well, not exactly West Point. About a group of West Pointers who influence the country's policies in favor of the military."

"The infamous WPPA?" Boomer asked. When he had first come on active duty he'd never heard the term—West Point Protective Association—despite four years at the Academy. As far as Boomer could tell, the WPPA was an informal organization that existed wherever West Pointers scratched each other's back.

Trace picked her words carefully as she answered his question. "No, not exactly the WPPA. It's about a secret organization called The Line that's been in existence for over sixty years and really came into power after World War II."

Boomer was interested despite his own personal problems. "So how'd you think this up?"

"I didn't think it up," Trace said. She leaned forward. "Just before I left Fort Meade I was briefly assigned as Post Public Affairs Officer. While I was there we received a strange letter at the office. It was from this woman, Mrs. Howard, who was a nurse in the European Theater during World War II. In the letter she claimed to have been one of the nurses assigned to General Patton after his accident in 1945."

Trace paused in thought. "To make a long story short, she claims that just before his death, Patton told her about this organization called The Line that had been formed in the late twenties. And that it was getting ready to really expand its power at the end of the Second World War. So I took her story and I've been trying to make a novel out of it. Sort of 'what-iffing' it out, as if it were true."

"Why'd she send the PAO this letter?"

Trace shrugged. "She was sending letters to a whole bunch of people—the Pentagon, Fort Lee, everywhere. I just happened to be the only person who read it and bothered to talk to her. It *was* a pretty wacko letter but I thought it was kind of interesting. Plus, she was this nice old lady living in this home out in the country. No family, no friends. I guess I just felt sorry for her."

Boomer smiled, remembering Trace as the sort of person who took stray cats in even at West Point where it had gotten her in trouble. "Do you think Mrs. Howard's story was true?"

"I don't know," Trace said. "Her mind wasn't in the best shape. A lonely old lady reliving the past is not exactly an accurate source. But you know, ever since I started writing this, what she told me has really made me think twice. I think I've been getting slightly paranoid."

Boomer laughed. "We have a saying in Special Forces: 'Just because you're paranoid doesn't mean they aren't out to get you.'"

Trace didn't smile. "There's been so much strange stuff going on in this country in the last fifty years that it makes you wonder sometimes."

"Stuff like what?" Boomer asked picking up his mug.

Trace pulled a newspaper out of her shoulder bag. "Lots of things look different if you simply assume a different perspective. Take today's paper for example." She ran her hand over some of the headlines of the late edition of the Honolulu paper. "The MRA and the conflict between the Joint Chiefs and the President. Hell, the Army Chief of Staff came within a hair of uttering statements about the President at that AUSA convention on Tuesday that he could have been court-martialed for. Like that Air Force general last year who was forced to retire.

"Then there's everyone in the defense industry and the Pentagon screaming about the President cutting out funding for development of the Hard Glass anti-ballistic missile defense system. The nuclear blast over Turkey last week certainly made that move seem unwise.

"Or these NATO inspectors that were ambushed the other day and killed in the Ukraine. It's causing the President's foreign policy regarding the START II treaty with the former Warsaw Block to be questioned even further. Congress is passing a special resolution to freeze the disarmament funding for the Ukraine after this latest incident."

Boomer's hand halted in midair, a small bead of condensation dropping off the bottom of the mug and splashing unnoticed. "Let me see that."

He grabbed the paper and scanned the story.

AT LEAST THREE U.S.
SOLDIERS KILLED IN UKRAINE

President offers condolences.
Reaffirms disarmament funding.

MOSCOW (AP)

Three U.S. servicemen were among ten NATO nu- clear weapons inspectors killed in an ambush along a road outside the town of

Senzhary in the Ukraine. A representative of the Ukrainian government blames the attack on dissident forces trying to derail the START (Strategic Arms Treaty) II agreement worked out between the President's administration and the Ukraine. These same forces were also believed responsible for the attempted shipment of a nuclear weapon to Iraq two days ago that cost the lives of two U.S. pilots and the first non-test detonation of a nuclear weapon in over fifty years.

"The situation is somewhat confusing because we are working from reports relayed to us by Ukrainian authorities," an anonymous Pentagon spokesperson said. "We should have some of our own people at the site shortly. All we know is that a ten-man NATO team, which was comprised of three Americans, three Germans, two Dutch, and two Norwegians, was involved. The report we have received is that there were no survivors. Some Ukrainian military personnel were also killed in the attack."

The Administration's commitment to this mission comes amid increasing resistance from the Pentagon and calls from Congress for a pullout of American forces from the mission until the political situation in the Ukraine has been resolved. "I offer my deepest sympathy to the families and friends of the American soldiers who were killed in the Ukraine last night," the President said in a statement. "These brave Americans were engaged in a mission vital to continued world peace and security."

An anonymous source at the Pentagon reemphasized the position General Martin, Chairman of the Joint Chiefs of Staff, made public during testimony last week in front of Congress: "There's no way a handful of inspectors can ensure that these weapons are being accounted for and destroyed. We're talking about over 1,700 warheads. Piecemealing it like we are doing presently allows them to play a 'shell game,' switching warheads around. The only adequate response to this situation is a pullout of NATO forces until the political situation stabilizes in the Ukraine and increased emphasis on the Hard Glass ballistic missile defense system that the President has withheld funding for. The explosion over Turkey two days ago shows that without immediate, absolute positive control over those warheads, we cannot be sure where they will end up or how they will be used. We don't know for

certain that other nuclear weapons might already have been sold and be in the hands of unstable forces."

There are 32 other Americans among the peacekeepers . . .

Boomer was confused. "What connection do you see between this and your story?" he asked.

Trace shrugged. "The Backfire incident, these inspector deaths, both were the worst possible thing that could have happened. The Pentagon didn't want to send those people in, but the President overrode that at the urging of the State Department. Now there's a big whiplash effect, just like the Somalia peacekeeping operation a few years ago, and we all saw what happened there. And this is happening just prior to the President coming here and making his MRA speech. You could certainly make a case that these incidents are not good for the MRA."

"But what does that have to do with your novel?" Boomer asked, his mind still on the article.

Trace smiled. "Not much, really. I guess I'm just getting so used to writing fiction that I start playing 'what-if' with everything that goes on."

Boomer put the beer down on the table. "Do you think this Line is real?"

"I don't know. I'm making the story up," Trace said.

"But you didn't make up the original idea," Boomer noted.

"No, but like I said, this lady's mind wandered quite a bit when I talked to her two months ago. She was pretty bitter. Her husband had been killed in the war when he was in Patton's 3rd Army."

"But you must have checked her facts. Was she a nurse on the staff that worked on Patton after he had his accident?"

Trace nodded. "Yeah, that checked out."

"So, I'm asking you again, do you think it's possible that an outfit like this Line exists?"

Trace spoke slowly, as if considering her words carefully, picking up Boomer's serious mood. "I suppose it is possible. But I find it hard to believe that such an organization could be kept secret for so long."

"How much have you written?"

"I've done some research and outlining, but I've only worked on two chapters."

"And you've made it all up, based upon one interview with this woman?"

Trace nodded. "I'm writing it with the fictional premise: 'What if it were true?' I'm going back over the past fifty years and looking at various events that West Point graduates were involved in and making some speculations using what she gave me. There are a lot of areas I'd really like to research in depth. Lots of intriguing premises, if you accept my initial one and believe even half of what she told me, but I don't exactly have the time to do that. The stuff I did find scared me plenty."

Boomer pulled out his wallet, laying a twenty on the bar to cover the beers. "I'd like to go someplace quieter if that's all right with you."

Trace nodded. "We can go to my house."

"Would it be possible for me to see a copy of what you've written so far?" Boomer asked.

"I've got a printout at home on my desk. Why are you so interested in this?"

Boomer shrugged. "No particular reason. It's just kind of strange." He took her hand in his. "Enough pondering the world's problems. We've got a lot of catching up to do."

Trace leaned close, her shoulder touching his. "We certainly do. Why don't you follow me to my place?"

11:23 P.M. LOCAL

As if to release the pent-up stress of the past week, Boomer found himself wrapping his arms around Trace, pulling himself tight into her with a passion that surprised even himself. He could feel her moving with him. Then he felt her, a silky moist heat that felt so wonderful that he tried to stop her movements to savor the feeling a little longer. But the long slow spasms of pleasure shook him even as he held her in perfect stillness.

Later, they took their time. Boomer grinned at Trace's soft sigh as he barely kissed each of her closed eyelids, then did the same to her breasts. She nuzzled up next to him, gently urging him, her slender fingers fondling his chest. He took her hand, kissed her fingers and lost himself in her body. He enjoyed pleasing her and spent a long time bringing her to climax.

It was a perfect ending to a terrible week, Boomer thought, as Trace finally collapsed in his arms. He held her close, feeling her relax into sleep before allowing himself to drift into an uneasy slumber filled with visions of the hillside in southern Ukraine and the sounds of the screams of wounded men.

"They done yet?"

The man tapped the side of the night scope. "Yeah." He pulled back and turned off the power to the scope.

"One of the perks of the job," the first man said with a grin.

"Gonna be a shame to waste her," the second man said. "Who do you think the guy is?"

The first man lay down and pulled his poncho liner up around his neck. "Somebody she works with probably. He's not important."

"I hope they give us the word soon," the first man mused as he settled down for his shift whittling at a piece of wood with his knife.

30 November
5:30 A.M. LOCAL/ 1530 ZULU

In the soft glow of the desk light, the words on the laser-printed pages stood out clearly. Boomer sat cross-legged on the carpet and read them with interest.

11 JUNE 1930
U.S. MILITARY ACADEMY,
WEST POINT, NEW YORK

The smooth marble felt cool to Cadet Benjamin Hooker's hand. He gazed up the shaft of Battle Monument to the stars overhead, then up the Hudson River where the hulking presence of Storm King Mountain loomed to the left, a darker black presence against the night sky. It was a view that never failed to raise a strong feeling of attachment and sentiment in Hooker's heart.

Boomer shook his head. He'd seen that same view many times over his four years at the Academy and he couldn't quite say he'd had the same emotions. He continued reading, turning the pages as Trace's story unfolded. After finishing the last page of the second chapter, he put the draft of Trace's book down and glanced out the window at the dark ocean, then over at the bed where Trace was stirring. "What are you doing?" she asked sleepily, squinting against the small desk light he had on.

"Looking at your manuscript," Boomer replied. "I had trouble sleeping."

"Oh," she said, sitting up and leaning back against the headboard, her small breasts perfect in the morning light. She smiled. "I had a good time last night. You're an amazingly good lover for a guy like you."

"It takes one to know one," Boomer murmured in her ear.

She glanced at the glowing digits on the clock next to the bed. "You know what I mean by a guy like you, right?"

Boomer wrapped his arms around her and sigheed. "Yes, I do. I'm starting to wonder if I'm a guy like me." He'd caught her glance. "I know you have to go soon, but can I see you later? I need to be with you."

Trace nodded. "You can stay exactly where you are right now. It's been a while since a man needed me. Just stay in bed and rest." She smiled and added, "You'll need it later."

He cupped her breast and gently blew air across her nipple. "I'd love to, but I've got to make PT too and take a look at the message traffic. What time will you be in this evening?"

"I'm usually back by 1800," Trace said. She made her way to the shower. "Care to join me?"

Boomer stepped into the hot spray, his thoughts going back to a shower they'd shared so many years ago. He still hadn't told Trace what had sent him to Hawaii. He knew he wasn't authorized to do so.

"I read the first two chapters of your manuscript," Boomer said.

"What do you think?"

"Good writing," he said.

"I mean what do you think of the story?" Trace amplified.

"Interesting. I assume the first chapter about Patton was what that old woman told you."

"I made up the conversations, but basically, yes, that's what she recollected. It was strange to talk to someone who'd really been there taking care of Patton when he died."

"I don't understand the second chapter, though," Boomer said. "What does some cadet in 1930 have to do with Patton in 1945? I know you have Patton mentioning Hooker in your first chapter."

"Did you know that George Marshall was the deputy commander of the Infantry School at Benning from 1927 to 1932?" Trace asked in turn.

"Of course," Boomer replied. "How the hell would I know that?" he asked. "It was there in your manuscript. And you still didn't answer my question."

"I'm getting there. Did you also know that 160 members of the Infantry School during Marshall's tenure became general officers during World War II and that Marshall, as Chief of Staff, was the one man who made most of the personnel decisions in the war?"

"Besides plumbing the depth of my ignorance," Boomer said, "do you have a point to make?"

"My point is that a hell of a lot of power was concentrated in the hands of a few men during World War II, and most of those men were at Fort Benning during the years that Marshall was there before the war. At the start of World War II West Pointers made up only seven percent of the officer corps. By the end of the war they were less than one percent. Yet three of three Supreme Commanders, seven of nine Army Group Commanders, eleven of twenty Army Commanders and twenty of thirty-one Corps commanders at the end of the war were West Pointers.''

"The old boy network," Boomer said. "Happens all the time. Why do you think the Masons have a handshake?"

"Yeah, but *if* that old lady was correct, it's a little bit more than that," Trace replied.

"Your own manuscript notes that Marshall was a VMI grad, not West Point. Doesn't that blow your theory?"

"Not really. What better cover than to have someone like Marshall be the front man for The Line?"

"Now you're thinking like a Special Forces operator, not an aviator," Boomer said with a smile. "What about this Hooker character?" Boomer asked again. "Is he made up? Where do you get him from?"

"It's the name the nurse said Patton gave her," Trace said evasively. "If The Line existed, I think Hooker played a very special role in it. I'll show you what I mean later."

"Have you shown the manuscript to anyone?" Boomer asked.

"It's a long way from being done," Trace answered. "In fact those two chapters are the only ones written. I've got a lot of notes on what I'm thinking of writing. I sent off a synopsis and the first two chapters to a couple of publishers to see if they're interested. I'm not sure I'm ready to write four hundred or so pages without an idea first if the story is marketable. I *do* have to get to work," Trace added as Boomer's hands wandered.

"OK, OK," Boomer said, pulling his hands away. "It's just that I can't resist."

"Save it for this evening," Trace said, getting out and grabbing a towel.

"Is that a promise?" he asked as he followed.

"Written in stone." She dried off and then went out into the main room. Boomer watched her as she went over to a bookcase behind her desk. She pulled a thick, soft-covered book off the shelf. He recognized it immediately: the Register Of Graduates, published by the Military Academy Alumni Association. Trace tossed it at him. "Take a look at the class of 'thirty."

Boomer opened the book up. He easily found the class of 1930. Trace had tucked in the appropriate page a Xeroxed copy of what must have been Hooker's graduation picture from his year's *Howitzer*, the cadet yearbook. Even with the grainy Xerox quality, Boomer was caught by the dark eyes. He put the photo aside.

In the register each class up until 1978 was listed in class rank order; only with '78 did they get ordered alphabetically. Hooker's name was the second one listed in his class.

Benjamin Ross Hooker
B-ME 12 DEC 07: A-lge: FA: Rhodes Scholar 30-32: MA Oxford: OPD WDGS 41-45 (LM): BG 44: JA-MAG London 46-48: S & F USMA His 49-50: JA Secy Def 50-52 (DSM): Prof History USMA (Head of Dept 53-68) (DSM): Ret 69 BG: Secy Offc JCS 70-74: UP USSECCON 75-present: 1221 Whispering Brook Dr. Springfield VA45112.

Since Boomer was also listed later in the book, he could make some sense out of all the acronyms and abbreviations that listed a man's life's work in one paragraph:

Hooker was born in Maine on December 12, 1907. A-lge meant his appointment to West Point had come from the President as the son of a career military man. FA stood for field artillery, Hooker's branch of service. After Oxford, Hooker's next major assignment was in the office of the Operations Plans Division in the War Department—the people who had worked directly for Marshall and been the brains behind planning the entire U.S. war effort. Boomer was surprised to see that Hooker had spent the entire length of World War II in Washington. Most officers would have been fighting to get out and lead troops. That fact of Hooker's career at least fit with what Trace had written about him.

Hooker had been promoted to brigadier general in 1944 and then went to London to work in the Military Assistance Group there after the war. Boomer wouldn't be surprised if that organization didn't have a lot to do with implementing the Marshall Plan in Europe.

Then back to West Point as an instructor in the history

department from 1949 to 1950. Then to a Joint Assignment with the relatively newly established Secretary of Defense's office. Then back to West Point for a second time, this go-around as head of the History Department for fifteen years.

Hooker had retired in 1969, still at the rank of brigadier general, and had gone to work for the Joint Chiefs of Staff. Boomer assumed that was before legislation had been enacted requiring a certain amount of time before retired military could work in a civilian capacity for the Department of Defense.

"What's USSECCON?" Boomer asked Trace, who was lacing up her running shoes.

"I had to check. It's a private company called United States Security Consortium headquartered in Alexandria, Virginia," she said.

"What does the United States Security Consortium do?"

"I don't know. I got the name of the firm by calling around in the D.C. area, but that was it." Trace came over and pointed over his shoulder. "The interesting parts are the fifteen years he was head of the history department and the work he did for the Joint Chiefs. Hell, even what he did in the Ops division during the Second World War. This guy was in all the key places, but he always appeared to be a low-level player.

"During his time as head of history at West Point, he was gone over eighty percent of the time, doing special missions at the bequest of the Joint Chiefs of Staff. He was in Vietnam in 'sixty-one for almost eight months, going around the country, checking things out, and then going back to the Chiefs and reporting to them."

"Guess he didn't check them out too well," Boomer said, "or else we might not have gotten involved."

"Maybe he did check the situation out very accurately," Trace replied.

That startled Boomer. He considered the bio again. Head of one of the academic departments at West Point was a prestigious position. It held the rank of full colonel with automatic promotion to brigadier general upon retirement. "Hooker was promoted to brigadier general in 'forty-four," Boomer noted. "Did he take a drop in grade to go back to the Academy?"

"Yes," Trace said. "For all the high-speed jobs he did, this guy was never promoted beyond one star. Very strange for a Rhodes Scholar who was second in his class and did the job he did during World War II. From looking at his career track I got the impression he deliberately kept a low-profile image in his career."

Boomer put the register down and started putting on his PT uniform. "So, you still haven't answered my question. I would assume from what you wrote in your manuscript that this guy was a player in The Line."

"I don't think he would be just a player," Trace said, grabbing the keys to her jeep. "I think after a certain time period he was the number one guy in The Line—if it existed."

Boomer pulled on his grey PT shorts. "Can you use a real person like that in a work of fiction? Won't you get sued or something?"

"I'm just using his name in the draft. I'll change the name later on—make Hooker's character fictional. It just helps me in writing to use real names. Besides, when did you start worrying about the legalities of the publishing world?"

Boomer followed her to the door. The anxiety he felt the previous evening during the drive to her house was returning. Boomer was a man who survived by his instincts, but he was used to real situations that deserved fear. This was something different. He pulled her close and buried his face in the hollow of her throat. "It's not legalities that concern me, it's you. I just don't want you to get hurt or rejected."

Trace flashed a dazzling smile and kissed him on the tip of his nose. "The people who can hurt me already have. That's the only good thing about losing what's most important to you—you can stop worrying about losing it."

Boomer walked her to the Jeep. His words were lost in the engine noise. "I haven't lost it, Trace."

CHAPTER ☆ 5

**FORT SHAFTER, OAHU, HAWAIIAN
ISLANDS
30 NOVEMBER
6:45 A.M. LOCAL/ 1645 ZULU**

"Sergeant Major Skibicki," Falk said, raising his voice
so the man heard him, "take charge of the formation!"

Boomer looked at the senior NCO who walked to the
front of the gray-clad phalanx of soldiers. Skibicki was a
short man with a barrel chest and gray hair. His face had
the leathery look of a man who spent most of his waking
hours in the elements. Boomer noticed that one side of Skibicki's skull was slightly concave, and a nasty scar lay there
under his thinning hair. The name sounded vaguely familiar
to Boomer, and he tried to recall if he'd served with the
sergeant major sometime in the past.

Skibicki immediately began barking commands, moving
people about until they had enough room between each
soldier to do the exercises. Then they began: pushups, sit-
ups, crunches—a whole regimen of muscle-numbing work.
Boomer had thought he was in shape, but the older man
put them through exercises Boomer hadn't done since he'd
gone to scuba school several years ago. He noted Sergeant
Vasquez at the front of the PT formation. She was quite an
impressive figure in shorts and T-shirt as she pumped out
pushups, the muscles in her arms rippling from the exertion.

In twenty minutes, they were done. Skibicki reformed
the unit and returned it to Colonel Falk. The XO gave instructions for the various ability group runs and dismissed
the soldiers to finish the physical training on their own. He

waved for Boomer to come over as the groups dispersed.

"I'd like you to meet our sergeant major," Falk said, indicating Skibicki. "This is Major Boomer Watson. Major, Sergeant Major Skibicki."

"Sir," Skibicki extended a callused hand. Boomer met the hard grip and they stared at each other for a second before the sergeant major let go.

"Skibicki's the man you need if there's anything you want," Falk said. He pushed a button on his watch. "Well, I've got to get running." With that, the Colonel took off, his skinny legs carrying him rapidly away.

"Where are you in from, if you don't mind me asking?" Skibicki said.

"I'd prefer not to say," Boomer replied.

Skibicki nodded to himself, accepting the sentence as a fact rather than a rebuke. Boomer figured Skibicki could find out more about him with one phone call using the NCO old boy network than he himself could tell him.

Skibicki cocked his head like an old dog trying to remember a scent. "Was your father in the service?" he asked.

Boomer nodded. "Yes."

"Mike Watson? Special Forces?"

"Yes."

Skibicki nodded. "I thought so. I served with him in Vietnam. He was a good man. He saved my life."

Boomer stiffened. He'd never met anyone who'd known his dad in Vietnam. He'd read the official notification of death and pored over the Medal of Honor citation numerous times, but the pieces of paper gave him little information. "Were you with him when he was killed?"

Skibicki grimaced and tapped the left side of his head where Boomer had noticed the slight depression in the skull. "I got hit in the head during that mission. Damn near killed me. Now I got a steel plate. I was a young E-Five, full of piss and vinegar on my first tour with Special Forces. Your dad got me out of there still breathing."

Boomer leaned forward. "I'd like to talk with you about my dad. I never really knew him or what happened."

Skibicki nodded. "You were what—nine, ten?—when he died?"

"Ten."

"I remember him having pictures of his wife and son in the team house at the launch site. He was a good man." Skibicki idly rubbed the side of his head. "Are you sure you want to know what happened?"

"Of course I want to know," Boomer said.

The sergeant major looked at him hard. "You know the saying 'let sleeping dogs sleep?' or something like that."

"Yeah." •

"Maybe you don't want to know what happened to your dad."

Boomer returned the sergeant major's look, his body stiffening. "I want to know."

Skibicki nodded "OK. You're going to be here a while, right? We'll talk. Right now, we need to finish PT."

8:45 A.M. LOCAL/ 1845 ZULU

"Sir, there's an encrypted message for the commander in here," Boomer held out the one-inch binder that he'd picked up from the Fort Shafter Secure Communication/ Intelligence Facility (SCIF). The binder contained all the classified messages for the TASOSC received during the past twenty-four hours. "All the rest is routine traffic decoded by the SCIF and I've Xeroxed copies and put them in the appropriate boxes."

Lieutenant Colonel Falk looked up from the mound of paperwork that always covered his desk. He turned around and pulled open the drawer of a secure file cabinet behind him. Falk removed a small pad and tossed it to Boomer. "Break out the message and give me a hard copy to put in the CO's reading file." He noted Boomer's surprise. "I know that isn't the way it's supposed to be done, but Colonel Coulder's time is too important—or at least that's what he thinks—to be wasted on breaking out messages, and he delegated it to me, and I'm delegating it to you. Like you said yesterday, you do have a TS Q clearance. He's got a briefing at 0900 in the conference room and I don't have time right now."

"Yes, sir," Boomer said, taking the one-time pad with him to his desk in the next tunnel. Sergeant major Skibicki wasn't in from PT, and Boomer was anxious to talk to him.

Boomer sat down and matched up the page number on the pad to the indicator at the start of the message. A one-time pad consists of sheets of six-letter groups. Boomer took the unintelligible six-letter groups on the actual message, matched them with the randomly generated groups on the one-time pad and, using a trigraph which had standard three-letter combinations, he was able to decipher the message. Despite all the advances in technology, a one-time pad was still the most secure way to send a message because there were only two copies of the pads in existence— the sender had one and the receiver had one. Because the pad letters were randomly generated by a computer, there was no "code" involved that could eventually be broken down.

The only problem, thus Boomer's surprise, was that the owner of the one-time pad was supposed to be the one decoding the message. Having someone else do it was a breach of security. Boomer knew that on A teams, detachment commanders sometimes gave the team pads to their communications sergeants to make message sending and receiving easier because commo men had the three letter groups on the trigraph memorized, but he'd never agreed with that policy. He also wondered why the TASOSC commander was even using a one-time pad given the sophisticated transmitting and receiving machinery available at the Fort Shafter SCIF. An A Team used the pads because they only had a limited capability to carry encrypting machinery—thus the code itself had to be unbreakable. At fixed stations like Fort Shafter, the encryption usually was in the sending and receiving technology.

The letters flowed out under Boomer's pencil and the message slowly took form. He was surprised to see a Javis report appear—a format for a water drop zone report used by Special Forces.

TOCOMM	ANDERF	OURTHX	XTASOS	CFROMT
ASKFOR	CEREAP	ERJAVI	SMESSA	GECITE
ZEROON	ESIXFO	URTHRE	EAAAGU	MBOSHA
RKBBBF	OURTWO	ECHOJU	LIETSE	VENFOU
RFIVEE	IGHTEI	GHTZER	OCCCON	EEIGHT

SIXDEG	COASTG	UARDLI	GHTONE	POINTE
IGHTKI	LOMETE	RSDDDO	NEZERO	ZEROBY
SEVENT	WOZERO	AXISZE	ROZERO	SIXDEG
EEEONE	TWOZER	ODASHE	IGHTZE	ROFFFZ
EROZER	OSIXDE	GGGGEI	GHTZER	OTOONE
TWOZER	OMOUNT	AINSHH	HIRSTR	OBEMAR
KRPIII	INFILT	RATION	FOURTE	ENPERS
ONNELT	WOBUND	LEJJJD	TGTWOD	ECEMBE
RONETW	OZEROZ	EROZUL	UXXXXX	

Boomer took the deciphered six letter groups and made sense of them on another sheet of paper:

```
TO: COMMANDER FOURTH TASOSC
FROM: TASK FORCE REAPER
JAVIS
MESSAGE CITE ZERO ONE SIX FOUR THREE
AAA   GUMBO SHARK
BBB   FOUR TWO ECHO JULIET SEVEN FOUR FIVE EIGHT
      EIGHT ZERO
CCC   ONE EIGHT SIX DEG COAST GUARD LIGHT ONE POINT
      EIGHT KILOMETERS
DDD   ONE ZERO ZERO BY SEVEN TWO ZERO AXIS ZERO ZERO
      SIX DEG
EEE   ONE TWO ZERO DASH EIGHT ZERO
FFF   ZERO ZERO SIX DEG
GGG   EIGHT ZERO TO ONE TWO ZERO MOUNTAINS
HHH   IR STROBE MARK RP
III   INFILTRATION FOURTEEN PERSONNEL TWO BUNDLE
JJJ   DTG TWO DECEMBER ONE TWO ZERO ZERO ZULU
```

As Boomer finished, a shadow appeared over his desk. He looked up into the cold gray eyes of the full-bird colonel he'd glimpsed at a distance during PT. Boomer glanced down at the nametag on the man's starched fatigues and confirmed the identification: COULDER

"What are you doing, major?" The voice was the same high-pitched one he'd heard coming from Coulder's office the previous day.

Boomer snapped to his feet, holding out the piece of paper on which he had just written the formatted message. "Breaking out a message received this morning, sir."

Colonel Coulder snatched the message out of Boomer's hand and looked at it, then his eyes swiveled back up. "Who told you to decrypt a message addressed to me?"

"Colonel Falk, sir. He said to—"

"When my name is on a damn message, major, I want to see it immediately. Do you understand?"

"Yes, sir."

"Who the hell are you anyway?" Coulder demanded, slipping the message into a file folder under his left arm.

Boomer was very glad he had gotten his hair cut yesterday afternoon and shined his boots right after physical training. "Major Watson, sir. I'm here TDY."

Coulder searched his mind. "Are you the fellow Falk told me about yesterday?"

"I don't know, sir."

"From Bragg?"

"Yes, sir."

"Why are you here?" Coulder demanded.

"Area orientation, sir," Boomer answered.

Coulder stared at him for a few seconds, then held out his hand. At first Boomer thought he was offering to shake hands, but his next words corrected that assumption. "Give me the pad," Coulder ordered.

Boomer passed over the one-time pad. Coulder glanced at it, then turned and walked away, going into the glassed-off conference room at the end of the tunnel. Boomer sank into his chair. The original copy of the message he had transcribed with its six-letter groups was still on the pad of paper.

He now understood Wilkerson's anger and frustration yesterday. The last person he'd want to talk to after getting relieved of command was Coulder. Boomer hurriedly tore the top page off and stuffed it into his fatigue pocket, not wanting to risk another encounter with Colonel Coulder over the message.

Sergeant Major Skibicki had walked in while Coulder was addressing Boomer. The old NCO slowly sank down into his squeaking desk chair after the colonel departed and kicked his feet up on the scarred desktop. "Finally met the boss, I see."

"Is he always so friendly?" Boomer asked.

"You caught him on one of his good days," Skibicki said. "Normally he would have locked your heels."

"I'm getting a little too old for that kind of crap," Boomer said.

"I *am* too old for that crap," the sergeant major said. "He tried to do it to me once, right after he came here and took over. Right in front of the troops at an inspection formation. Talk about unprofessional. I told him he could shove that shit up his ass. We haven't had too many discussions since then."

"What did he do?" Boomer asked.

"He tried to get me relieved, but SOCOM told him he could shove that. I was the only Special Forces sergeant major on the island and they were damned if they were going to PCS another one here just because he couldn't get along with me." Skibicki grinned. "Besides, the sergeant major at SOCOM, Billy Lucius, owes me one, and I want to retire here. Don't need to be getting shipped back to the states and turn right around."

"How many years do you have in sergeant major?"

"Twenty-nine." Skibicki gestured around the tunnel. "I came on active duty in 'sixty-four; then had a two-year break in service after coming back from my third tour in 'Nam in 72. Back on active duty in '74, so I seen it all.

"This assignment is my last hurrah. Baby-sitting a bunch of headquarters pukes and making sure the police call outside the tunnel is done properly. I've got more time in uniform than any other person on this entire island. I've got more time in grade than Sergeant Major Finley up at the 25th Infantry Division at Schofield. Yet here I am."

"How did you—" Boomer halted as Sergeant Vasquez walked in and handed a folder to Skibicki.

"Here's the duty roster, sergeant major." She gave Boomer a smile as she exited the tunnel.

The gesture hadn't been lost on Skibicki. "Damn Army sure has changed. You saw her at PT?"

"Yeah. Made me feel out of shape," Boomer said.

"Well, be careful of her," Skibicki warned. "We get a

lot of people through here TDY, and Vasquez likes playing with 'em. Don't matter if it's officer or enlisted as long as it has a hard dick. Get your head between her thighs and she'll crush it like a melon.''

''I'll keep that in—'' Boomer froze, his eyes locked on a figure that had just walked out of the middle side tunnel and was heading for the glassed-in conference room. Boomer slid his seat back until he was hidden from view by the bank of classified filing cabinets.

''What's the matter?'' Skibicki asked, his eyes following Boomer's. ''You know that guy?''

''Yeah, I know him,'' Boomer answered. The door to the conference swung shut and through the glass, Boomer could see the backs of the people attending the meeting, all facing Colonel Coulder who stood at a podium, a map of the island of Oahu pinned to the easel to his left rear. Sergeant Vasquez walked in, handed a folder to Coulder and left the conference room. She gave Skibicki and Boomer another smile as she exited the tunnel.

Boomer, still hiding himself from direct view of the people in the room, watched as Coulder started talking, wishing he could read lips. ''What are they talking about in there?'' Boomer asked.

The sergeant major shrugged. ''Don't know. I'm the senior enlisted man in the tunnel and no one tells me shit.''

''Who are they?''

Skibicki looked and checked off people with a glance. ''As you know, the full bull at the podium is our exalted leader, Colonel Coulder. The guy with the thinning blond hair works in J-3, Operations, up at USPACOM. I don't recognize the major or the other colonel who''—Skibicki threw a questioning glance at Boomer—''you apparently know, but I don't.''

''That colonel is from the JCS. He's the Special Operations liaison. His name is Decker,'' Boomer said.

Coulder was slapping his pointer on the blue marking ocean, off to the west of the island. Suddenly Coulder stopped and looked straight through the glass at the sergeant major. He snapped something and the major stood up and drew the curtains on the far side of the glass, blocking off the view.

"Assholes," Skibicki said angrily. "That's fucking insulting. I've served in this man's Army since Christ was a corporal, and they're hiding things from me like they don't trust me." He rubbed his grizzled chin. "Special Ops liaison from the JCS, eh? There's some weird shit going on around here lately."

Boomer relaxed slightly now that he couldn't be spotted, but he was anxious to be out of the tunnel before the meeting broke up and Decker came out. He was absolutely the last person Boomer had expected to run into here.

Boomer turned his attention to more personal matters. "Hey, sergeant major, is there some place on post where we can go get a cup of coffee and a donut?" Boomer asked, wanting to get the story about his father out of the old man as much as he wanted to avoid Decker.

"Yeah." Skibicki stood and grabbed his green beret, squashing it down on his iron-gray hair. "Let's go talk. It stinks in here."

The snack bar Skibicki took Boomer to was an old World War II structure. One of thousands of "temporary" buildings, constructed during the war at dozens of Army posts and then used for the next fifty years by the military, another curious example of the spending practices of the defense establishment. Billions could be spent on a new airplane, but purchasing a new boot or better living quarters for the actual soldier was usually very low on the priority list. Boomer figured it was more a question of contractor and politician than soldier needs.

Inside the building, Boomer grabbed a couple of cups of coffee and a plateful of donuts and joined Skibicki who was joshing with the little old woman who worked the register.

"Boomer, meet Maggie Skibicki, my mom," the sergeant major said. "Mom, this young fellow is Boomer Watson. I served with his dad."

"Well, you are getting old, aren't you, Ski? I don't want to think what that says about me," she joked. "Pleased to meet you, Boomer," Maggie said as she took his money. Her face was wrinkled with the years, but her eyes were a piercing blue that had lost nothing over time. They gazed at Boomer, and he felt that look cut into him.

"Nice to meet you," Boomer replied.

Skibicki led the way to a corner table where he sat down, his back square in the corner, facing the empty room. "Mom's been here at Shafter for over twenty years. She used to work up at Schofield Barracks.

"My dad was retired Navy. Mom's what they call a Pearl Harbor survivor. She was living out by Pearl back in 'forty-one. Dad was on board the *Enterprise*, so it's one of those strange twists of fate that she was here for the attack on Pearl Harbor and he wasn't. They used to joke about that all the time. He spent thirty years in the Navy. He died about four years back. Mom's past mandatory retirement age, but she's got a special exception from the post commander to work. She likes to get out and be around people. You ever need to know anything about this island, you ask her."

Boomer glanced across the room at the old woman with slightly different eyes. All he knew of the attack on Pearl Harbor were newsclips and boring lectures at West Point.

"You need to go out there to Pearl," Skibicki continued. "It's very interesting. Ask Maggie about it if you get the chance."

"You said you served with my dad?" Boomer prompted.

Skibicki nodded. He reached into the breast pocket of his fatigues and pulled out a piece of cardboard and carefully unfolded it, revealing a faded picture inside. "You ever heard of Projects B-50 or B-57?"

Boomer nodded. "We used their after-action reports when I was in 10th Group to help write our team SOPs. B-50 and B-57 were the cross border operations 5th Group ran during the war to gather intelligence."

Skibicki laid a photograph on the table top. A very young-looking Skibicki wearing tiger-stripe fatigues and sporting a CAR-15 stood next to another American, also wearing the distinctive fatigues and holding a short-barreled grenade launcher in one hand and an AK-47 in the other. Four indigenous soldiers, dressed in fatigues and carrying AK-47s stood in front of the taller Americans. Boomer instantly recognized the second American as his father.

"There weren't that many of us in SF at any one time, although this was in 'sixty-nine when they were taking any

Tom, Dick, and Harry and giving them a beret and shooting them across the borders because we were taking such high casualties,'' the sergeant major explained. ''I was in the 173rd Airborne during my first tour, and when I went back for my second, they were hurting for bodies so they were taking even non-SF people into the recon teams. Any idiot that was dumb enough to volunteer and had combat experience was accepted. So that's how I became Special Forces-qualified in 'sixty-eight.''

He tapped the photo. ''This was recon team Kansas. Each team was named after a state. This picture was taken a week before we went on our last mission.''

Skibicki took a sip of coffee, then continued. ''Let me give you some background so you understand what happened. 'Sixty-eight and 'sixty-nine were bad-ass years in the war. It was after Tet, and, despite what those pissant reporters said, we were kicking ass. The fucking NVA had run for the hills and was licking its wounds across the borders in Laos and Cambodia. The only time they showed up to fight was when they were sure they could hit us by surprise. So in order not be surprised, in October of 'sixty-eight, the Blackbeard Collection Plan was instigated by some Intelligence dink in Saigon. The idea was to coordinate all surveillance and reconnaissance assets running operations near or over the borders.

''Project Gamma, of which project B-57 was a part, was the Special Forces' contribution to the Blackbeard effort. And even though we only supplied six percent of the total flow of information to MACV, our stuff turned out to be over half the good intel. That was 'cause we went in on the ground and put our beady little eyeballs right on the shit. We didn't fly over at thirty thousand feet and guesstimate or drop in sensors that fucking deer could set off and the Air Force would waste a couple of hundred thousand dollars worth of bombs on making venison. When we said something was there, it was there right in front of us.

''Anyway, we would work off of humint—human intelligence—about possible enemy locations. We'd get some info, then go in and verify. Well, in early 'sixty-nine our sources started drying up. And the info we were getting was tainted. We lost several teams. They just went out, and it was like they disappeared into a black hole. We later found out what was happening: there was a double-agent at Nha Trang turning the teams.'' Skibicki waved his hand. ''I'll get back to that.''

''In May of 'sixty-nine we got information about an NVA regiment staging right across the border from an A Camp at Tong Le Chon so we were ordered to go in and check it out. Your dad was the team commander, I was the man with the radio, and we had four 'little people'—Montagnard natives—along for security.''

Skibicki's eyes were unfocused as he remembered. ''It was supposed to be a quick in and out, just to check to see if the bad guys were preparing to attack. It wasn't straightforward though. They moved us out of the normal launch site to another place. It was somewhere I'd never seen before and it sure wasn't SF run. We got a briefing from some CIA dude assigned to CCN—Combat Control North—and they gave us a spook straphanger. Your dad didn't like that one bit, but that's the bitch of being in the green machine; our's is but to do and die, right?''

Skibicki didn't wait for an answer. ''So we went in on one slick. We had two Cobras flying cover—two Cobras painted black. Air America at work. You wouldn't believe the amount of stuff the CIA had working over there. Just the little I saw at that camp hinted at an operation beyond anything that's ever been written or talked about.

''Everything went to shit from the word go. We didn't go in where we were supposed to. I had no idea where the fuck we were but it certainly wasn't across the border from Tong Le Chon. Your dad was arguing with the spook. Right there on the fucking landing zone they're having a God-damn argument. Talk about giving you the shits. Your dad wanted us out. The spook overruled him. Your dad had me come up on the guard net and call for extraction. CCN denied it and told us to continue mission. Except now we didn't know what the fuck the mission was, other than go with this spook and watch his ass. And that guy was none too happy about us coming up on the radio trying to get out of there.''

Skibicki shook his head. ''If I'd have known then what I know now, I would have greased the spook right then and there and called in a 'prairie fire'—that was our code word for emergency extraction. We had our own air assets and we could have gotten out, although there would have been hell to pay later. But we still had that good Army training: follow orders, even if you don't know where the fuck they're coming from. I'll tell you one thing I learned from that: if you ever get in the position where you got to kill someone to keep the shit from hitting the fan, kill 'em, drive on, and don't say a fucking word about it. That's what we should have done.

"But I hadn't learned that yet. So, there we were over the border, moving west and north along this ridgeline to some mysterious fucking rendezvous when we got hit. We had one of the little people at point and he got his shit blown away." Skibicki looked Boomer in the eyes. "You ever been on the receiving end in an ambush?"

Boomer shook his head, remembering the screams of the wounded near the bus.

"But you been shot at right?"

"Yeah, I've been shot at."

"Well," Skibicki continued, "you know it isn't like in the movies. It was confusing as crap. Your dad was screaming for us to break contact and move downridge. Not the preferred direction, but we didn't have much choice since they already had the high ground. Of course the spook didn't know our immediate actions drills, but he knew enough to get out of the way and run. We broke contact, leaving behind two of our little people dead and the rest of us all hit somewhere. I had shrapnel wounds all along my left side from a grenade, but fear can be a mighty motivator. We beat feet, leapfrogging. Two men laying down a base of fire, two running, then alternating. The spook helped some, he had a Swedish K and he emptied a magazine now and then over our heads.

"To make a long story short, we ran until we hit the first piece of open ground we could find. The spook got on the radio and called in for extraction from his people. Then we got hit on the edge of the PZ. Those son-of-a-bitches, whoever the fuck they were, wanted us bad. The spook got hit right at the start—caught a round through the chest. We lost the last two Montagnards and your dad took a round through his thigh. I was bandaging up the spook, trying to seal off his sucking chest wound, when I opened up the small ruck he was carrying, looking for anything I could use to block off the air coming out of the hole in his lung.

"There was gold in there. Four fucking bars of gold." Skibicki laughed bitterly. "Of course that shit wasn't very useful at the moment. That's when I got hit again." He tapped the side of his head. "Lucky I got a thick skull."

Skibicki fell silent and Boomer waited for a few seconds. "Then what happened?" he finally asked.

"The black Cobra gunships came in. Your dad directed their fire using the spook's radio. Jesus, he was great, Boomer." Skibicki shook his head wonderingly at that day so long ago. "A true fucking professional. I was half out of it. I couldn't see a damn thing; my eyes were full of blood, and I had a hell of a headache," he said. "I just kept firing in the general direction of the bad guys which wasn't hard to do since we were surrounded.

"Your dad carried me out to the slick that came in. He threw me on board and he went back to get the spook. That was a big mistake. He was carrying the spook back when they got cut down. The bad guys must have brought up a heavy machine gun by that time and they opened up from the treeline. We got the bodies on board and the pilots got us the hell out of there in a hurry. The bird took a lot of hits on the way out but it got back in one piece." Skibicki looked at Boomer. "Your dad and the spook were KIA."

"But that's not what his citation read," Boomer said. He knew a bit about classified operations and he was confused. "How did my dad get a Medal of Honor for a cross-border mission? I thought all that stuff got buried deep. Hell, there's guys who got wounded on some of those cross-border missions who still can't get VA treatment since their wounds aren't recorded anywhere because they weren't legally supposed to be where they were when they got hit. The citation said he was killed defending an A Camp in South Vietnam, not across the border."

Skibicki gave a wicked grin. "I did that. Me and the Special Operations Commander in-country, Colonel Rison. I was in the hospital recovering when Rison came to ask me what had happened. When I told him, he wrote up the award just as you saw it. The CIA backed the story. It was a trade-off. I kept silent about what really happened and your dad got the CMH. It was the least we could do for him.''

"What *did* happen?" Boomer asked. "What was that guy carrying gold for?"

"You know what CIA stands for, don't you?" Skibicki didn't bother to wait for an answer. "Cocaine in America. Those guys were running a whole 'nother show over there. Still probably are.''

"It was a drug operation?" Boomer asked, not as shocked as he probably should have been; his years in Delta had shown him a thing or two about the real world.

Skibicki shrugged. "I don't know that for sure, but what the hell else would that guy be carrying gold bars into the jungle for? He might have been paying some mercenary groups that were in the CIA's employ. At least that was what the spooks briefed me afterwards, but I think that's a bullshit cover story. If we were going in to pay off mercenaries, why didn't we just land at the mercenaries' camp. If we were paying them, they should have been friendly, right?''

Skibicki shook his head. "No, I heard enough and seen enough over there to know. It was a drug op. Gold for drugs, which they could turn a big profit on back here in the states. How the hell do you think they can fund all their bullshit? And those people who were after us wanted us a hell of a lot more than the VC and NVA usually did. They wanted us real bad to absorb the casualties they took.''

"But what about the Army?" Boomer asked. "Didn't the Special Ops commander—this Colonel Rison—do anything about his people getting caught up in that?"

"Listen, Boomer. I don't know what the hell you've been doing, but let me tell you a few things I've learned in my time. One is that you don't fuck with the CIA. And the other is that the CIA and the top ranks of the Army are wired in tight. It's us guys wearing the green beanies who are on the outside. Everyone always thinks the CIA is some world unto its own, but you just need to look at its history to see that it was formed right out of the Army at the end of the Second World War. And its aims and the Army's have never been very far apart. Hell, Boomer, whenever you give someone a whole lot of power, then cloak it in secrecy in the name of national security, you got the ingredients for some bad shit to happen.

"Hell, that whole fucking war was just like a big game for some of them people. Think about it. What the fuck were we doing? We didn't fight it to win, and we didn't fight it to lose. We just sort of dicked around until the damn civilians had enough of it and made us come home."

Boomer had heard it all before from other veterans. He was surprised, though, when Skibicki leaned forward and grabbed his arm.

"You went to West Point, didn't you? I heard you took the Presidential from your dad's medal."

"Yeah," Boomer said, extracting his arm from the other man's fierce grip.

"That's pretty ironic," Skibicki growled, "considering how it was West Pointers that got your dad killed."

"What do you mean? You said it was the CIA."

"Colonel Rison was a West Pointer. He told me about some of the shit that was going on. Hell, they tried to court-martial him about six months after your dad got killed."

"What happened to him?" Boomer asked.

Skibicki shook his head. "He ran into the establishment and they broke him. And he was one of them too, a West Pointer, but they busted his ass. We damn near had the closest thing to a revolt that the U.S. Army ever saw when they arrested Rison at group headquarters in Nha Trang. A camps all over the country were locking and loading and ready to fight it out with the regular Army. Hell, all us guys in SOG were ready to fly into Saigon and waste those regular motherfuckers at MACV headquarters."

"Rison was arrested?" Boomer asked. "For what?"

"Remember that double agent I mentioned earlier?" Skibicki paused and seemed to consider what he was saying and then changed his mind. "You don't want to get into all that." Skibicki waved a hand. "Forget what I said all right? I've heard so much bullshit in twenty-nine years in the service that I can't remember what's real and what's not. Forget it."

Despite Boomer's attempts at rekindling the subject, Skibicki refused to talk and Boomer reluctantly went with him back to the tunnel. He spent the rest of the morning going through the classified files, destroying out of date folders and inventorying what was left. His mind was only half on his job, and just before lunch he cornered Skibicki, who was in the very rear of the tunnel, pulling maintenance on scuba equipment.

"Sergeant major, do you know someone at Bragg in the schoolhouse who can check records?"

"What kind of records?" Skibicki asked, carefully leaning a scuba tank against a wall locker.

"Q Course graduates. Or, more specifically, eighteen qualified officers."

Skibicki nodded. "Sure." He glanced at the large dive watch on his wrist. "Only problem is that it's 1200 here. That makes it 1700 on a Thursday afternoon on the east coast. They'll all be at the Green Beret club at Bragg sucking down brews."

"Can you do it first thing tomorrow?"

"Who do you want me to check on?"

"A major named Keyes."

"The new CO for Alpha, 1st of the 1st?"

Boomer nodded.

Skibicki's heavily tanned arms rippled as he hoisted the air tank and settled it in place in the wall locker. "That battalion in Okinawa has been fucked up for twenty years, sir. Never could quite figure out what was going on out there. They had that big shitstorm eight years ago about running demo into Thailand and selling it on the black market. Hell, *60 Minutes* did a special on it. Then they had that plot to kill one of the company sergeant majors."

Boomer had heard about some of that. It had been a bad blemish on the name of Special Forces in the media. Every so often there was an article about some Green Beret doing something stupid, and it tainted the entire Special Operations community. One of the most aggravating things for Boomer was when he walked into a bookstore and saw the book *Fatal Vision* with the green beret with the old 5th Group flash and the medical corps insignia on the cover. The subject of the book, McDonald, had not even been Special Forces-qualified, yet he had always been referred to as the "Green Beret Doctor."

There was no doubt that some Special Forces people went over the edge occasionally. When an organization attracted highly qualified people as SF did, it invariably attracted its own share of highly qualified wackos. When Boomer had gone through selection for Delta Force, he had to go through severe physical and mental challenges that had knocked out over ninety-five percent of his classmates. Then the survivors had undergone a rigorous psychological screening to find out if they could handle the stress of the job and were mentally stable.

In retrospect, Boomer found the psych screening amusing, although at the time it had been very serious—several otherwise highly qualified individuals who had passed all other tests had been washed out on the word of the psych panel. Boomer had to wonder what kind of stable personality they were looking for: one that was capable of performing brutal tasks, yet not enough of a sociopath to ignore orders.

All those thoughts brought Boomer's mind back to the matter of 1st Battalion, 1st Special Forces Group. "I heard the battalion commander out there got relieved over that black market stuff."

Skibicki took out talcum powder and began sprinkling it on the rubber cuffs of a dry suit. "Nope. He finished his tour and got his little command box checked off. They said he wasn't responsible. That he didn't know what was going on in his own unit."

"You heard anything about strange personnel procedures out there?" Boomer asked.

Skibicki put the talcum powder down. "We don't use this scuba gear too much here, but we're authorized four dive slots. I pull one, Colonel Falk has one, and we got two open." He looked at the patch on Boomer's chest. "You definitely want to get some diving in while you're here. We got some great water. I'll sign you out a complete set."

"I'd like that," Boomer said.

Skibicki leaned back against the walllocker and folded his massive arms. He spoke slowly. "Yeah, there's some weird shit going on in 1st Battalion. I'll check on that name for you.''

The scuba gear reminded Boomer of the message in his pocket. "One other thing, sergeant major. Do you know of a jump scheduled for early morning on the second?"

"Saturday morning? No."

"Ever heard of a Task Force Reaper?"

"No."

"Ever heard of a water DZ named Gumbo?"

"Yeah. That's off the northeast corner of the island. We use it once in a while for water jumps."

Boomer pulled the message out of his pocket and silently handed it over. Skibicki scanned it. "If someone's jumping Gumbo Saturday morning, I sure as shit should have heard about it because there ain't too many people that can be drop zone safety officer for a water jump on this island other than me. I should have been tasked for bodies to pull drop zone safety. According to safety regs you have to have one boat per jumper. It's a damn nightmare. I don't know why the colonel hasn't told me about this."

"Maybe they aren't having any safety boats," Boomer said. "Maybe the colonel doesn't want you to know about these people coming in. He got kind of pissed when he saw that I had broken the message out."

Skibicki's eyes widened slightly. "If they ain't using safety boats, then they're violating about twenty fucking regulations. And that means they're planning on drowning their chutes and not recovering them. You know how much a chute costs? Sounds to me like someone's planning a real-world operation."

"Any idea where these people are from?" Boomer asked.

"Not a clue, and I don't think I'll be going to ask the colonel either. He don't want me to know, I don't fucking know." Skibicki answered, handing back the message.

Boomer pocketed the piece of paper and hesitated. He had one last question, triggered by Skibicki's comments. "Sergeant major, have you ever heard of an organization called The Line?"

Skibicki paused ever so briefly, then answered almost inaudibly, his eyes locked on the scuba locker. "No."

"You sure?" Boomer pressed, picking up the hesitation. "The reason I'm asking is cause you said my dad's death was caused by West Pointers and I've heard that there was this group of West—"

"I said no," Skibicki snapped, glaring at Boomer. He turned and looked away for a few seconds, regaining his composure. He reached into his pocket and pulled out a business card and handed it to Boomer. A green beret with a knife across it was embossed on it. Along the top it said PARATROOPER, RANGER, SPECIAL FORCES, WORLD TRAVELER, SINGER, SALESMAN, BULLSHIT ARTIST. Skibicki's home and work address and phone numbers were listed in the center. At the bottom the rest of Skibicki's qualifications were listed: REVOLUTIONS STARTED; ORGIES ORGANIZED; ASSASSINATIONS PLOTTED; BARS EMPTIED; ALLIGATORS CASTRATED; TIGERS TAMED; VIRGINS CONVERTED; OTHERS SATISFIED.

"I only did that shit in my younger days," Skibicki said, noting Boomer reading it. "You need anything, you give me a call, OK? I don't know why you're here, but it sounds like you might be needing some help."

Boomer took the card. "Thanks, sergeant major, but I'm just here TDY for a couple of weeks to take it easy."

"Uh-huh," Skibicki, said, turning back to the equipment. "Well, be careful taking it easy."

CHAPTER ☆ 6

MAKAKILO, OAHU, HAWAIIAN ISLANDS
30 NOVEMBER
1:30 P.M. LOCAL/ 2330 ZULU

It was payday, a significant event for the military. Although most soldiers now had direct deposit twice a month, the last duty day of the month was still formerly known as payday. It was usually designated as a half day of work with the morning being given over to such vital military acts as a Class A (dress) uniform inspection.

Trace had forgotten that it was payday when she'd told Boomer what time she'd be home. Camp Smith, where she worked, was a small post run by the Marines nestled in the foothills of Halawa Heights. It was the headquarters of the U.S. Pacific Command (USPACOM) and also housed Headquarters Fleet Marine Force Pacific.

USPACOM was the Unified Command for military forces in the Pacific. When Trace had arrived in Hawaii and been assigned to USPACOM she'd been astounded at the clutter of commands and headquarters all camped on the island of Oahu. The command and control system for the armed forces of the United States was anything but simple, and Trace had spent several days simply studying the flow charts of organizations to get oriented to her new environment.

In the U.S. military there are six unified commands which cut across service boundaries: USEUCOM (European Command); USPACOM (Pacific Command); USLANTCOM (Atlantic Command) which is mainly a Navy show; USSOUTHCOM (Southern Command) which is primarily in Army hands, covering Central and South America; USCENTCOM (Central Command) which received fame and fortune under General Schwarzkopf during the Gulf War and ignominy for the embarrassments in Somalia; and USREDCOM (Readiness Command) in charge of forces in the continental United States.

While those commands sound very cut and dried and split the world up quite neatly in various areas, the actual practice of those commands was somewhat ludicrous as Trace had learned at USPACOM. During peace, the Unified Commanders controlled no troops (other than the staff—such as Trace—assigned to their headquarters). The separate services controlled their own forces during peacetime and jealously guarded that right.

Thus in Hawaii, the USPACOM commander could order a car to take him down to Pearl Harbor, but until the Joint Chiefs decided to give him operational control (OPCON) in time of crisis, he could only stare at the ships in the harbor and the jets at nearby Hickam Field which were, respectively, under the control of the admiral who commands the Pacific Fleet and the Air Force general who had the title of Commander of Pacific Air Forces. The Army troops at Schofield Barracks would salute the USPACOM Commander, but they answered to a three-star Army general at Fort Shafter who held the title of WESTCOM (Western Command) Commander.

The various services on Hawaii—indeed throughout the US military establishment—only worked together at the very lowest or the very highest of levels. At the lowest level, Trace could get on the phone and call a buddy of hers at Kaneohe Marine Corps Air Station and get some flight time in a Huey helicopter to keep her flight status current. At the highest level, joint exercises were scheduled—such as the annual Team Spirit in Korea—where the services grudgingly agreed to work together and the Air Force would actually allow Army troops inside their cargo planes and Navy pilots might acknowledge the presence of Air Force planes in the same sky. But in the middle levels it was as easy to coordinate a Navy ship into an Army exercise as it was to get Congress to agree on a new gun-control bill.

Trace knew it was this intractable system-wide separation that the President was trying to address in the MRA. Because not only did the gulf between the services threaten their operational capabilities, it was devastating when it came to the world of weapons and equipment procurement. Only under the greatest of stress—usually the threat of loss of funds—would the Air Force and Navy agree on, say, a jet fighter to be jointly developed and purchased. And in the process they usually ignored the bastard stepchild of military procurement, the Marine Corps, which was one of the major reasons the MRA Commission had recommended the Marines be integrated into the Army.

Trace had entered the military listening to horror stories of interservice incompatibility, such as the Navy SEAL teams in Grenada that were attacked by Navy planes because their radios didn't work on the same frequencies. It was that same lack of communication in a different form that was sending her home at 1:30 in the afternoon rather than her usual 6:00 P.M. The senior Army officer on the USPACOM staff had announced the previous week that his troops would work the full day, but that directive had run counter to the USPACOM Chief of Staff's (a Navy officer) instruction that all service people were to be given the afternoon off. The brief squabble had been resolved in traditional military fashion: since the Chief of Staff was a one-star admiral and the senior Army man was a full colonel, the troops went home after lunch.

Such weighty matters seemed to fill up the time for the USPACOM staff at Camp Smith, Trace thought as she swung her AMC Jeep onto H-1 and headed west, happy to be missing the rush-hour traffic out of Honolulu. She was glad for the time off. It would give her some time to clean the house up before Boomer got there. She knew that Boomer would be working a full day. The only troops in the Army that ignored such things as payday were Special Operations troops.

Trace continued west past Waipahu and turned off on Kunia Road, then made an immediate left on Cane Haul Road, a small gravel road that ran through the sugarcane fields. She was renting her house from a Marine Lieutenant Colonel who was currently at sea for eight months. It was a good deal, and Trace enjoyed being away from the monotony of Army housing.

The colonel had bought the land years ago when Makakilo City was first being developed. It was a choice location, well up on the slope leading to Puu Makakilo, the hilltop from which the area received its name. It was a one-story house, the edge of which was on stilts, hanging over the hillside, looking toward the ocean. In dry weather Trace liked going the ''back way'' as she called it, taking Cane Haul Road up between Puu Kapuai and Puu Makakilo. This brought her to the house from down the shoulder of the mountain, rather than up the tar road the other less adventurous residents used.

She stopped in the driveway and disengaged the four-wheel drive before getting out. She slipped her key in the lock and stepped into the main foyer which opened onto the large living room facing the ocean.

Trace was shocked to see a man dressed in black standing over her computer, his figure frozen in mutual surprise at her unexpected entrance. A second man was on the balcony, looking *down* toward the main road, which explained why she had come upon them unannounced. They both wore black balaclavas over their faces and had small backpacks slung over their shoulders. The room was trashed. The couch had been slashed apart, drawers emptied, picture frames shattered.

The first man swung up a large-bore pistol and pointed it directly at Trace. ''Don't move and you won't get hurt,'' he hissed.

''How'd she get here?'' the second man asked, coming into the room from the porch.

''That's what I was going to ask you,'' the first said. ''Cover her.'' The second man produced a pistol as large as the first's.

Trace froze but her eyes were searching the room, looking for anything she could use as a weapon. She could see a bat she used for softball, but it was too far to be practical. The man shoved her computer display over. It thudded onto the carpet, the glass screen somehow staying intact. He expertly flipped open a butterfly knife with one hand and slashed the razor-sharp blade through the cords at the back of her hard drive base unit, which he tucked under one arm.

"Got it all?" the second man asked.

The first man nodded. He walked over and cut the cord for the living room phone. The two men looked at Trace, then glanced at each other, as if trying to come to a consensus.

They took too long. A shadow loomed behind Trace in the doorway and a familiar voice called out in a Bronx accent. "Hey, sweetheart, what ya' doing?"

Trace dove to the right as one of the men fired, the round splintering the doorjamb, the gun hardly making any noise at all. "Watch out, Boomer!" she screamed as she scrambled behind the dubious cover of the couch.

Boomer didn't have to think to think. Thousands of hours in the killing room in the Delta Force compound had automated his response. He had his 9mm pistol in his hand in a flash. Boomer fired as he dove across the doorway to the cover of the other side, letting loose two quick shots into the room, caught between trying not to get shot himself and concern for Trace's position.

The cost had escalated beyond what the two men were willing to pay. They'd assumed after forty-eight hours of surveillance that Trace would follow the same pattern she had for the past two days both in terms of time of return and direction of return. They bolted for the balcony. Together, they leapt over and disappeared. Boomer carefully slid into the room, his Browning High Power at the ready.

"You OK?" he asked.

"Yeah," Trace answered.

Boomer kept moving. He flattened himself just inside the balcony door, then "pied" his way around the corner, muzzle of the pistol leading, taking the corner in sections. He spotted the two men scrambling up the slope. As he took aim, they disappeared into the jungle. Following was not the wisest option; for all Boomer knew they were inside the treeline waiting in ambush.

"What did they get?" Boomer asked, walking back into the room and examining the full extent of the damage as he put a fresh magazine into his pistol.

"I don't know," Trace replied. "The only thing I saw them take was my computer hard drive."

Boomer sat down at Trace's desk and looked at the cut wires. "Why didn't they take the whole computer?"

"They probably would have if I hadn't caught them in the act."

Boomer shook his head. "It doesn't make sense. How much could they get for the hard drive?"

Trace was searching through her desk. "My checkbook's still here and some cash." She continued searching. "The manuscript is gone."

"The manuscript?" Boomer repeated. "Your book about The Line?"

"Yes."

"It was on your hard drive, too, wasn't it?"

"Yes."

"What about back-up disks?"

"My disks were in this drawer." She lifted up an upside down drawer, then searched wreckage on the floor. "They got them." She looked at the bookcase behind the desk. "They took all my notes too."

"You must have caught them just as they were ready to leave. The hard drive was the last thing they needed." Boomer walked out to the railing and glanced up. The slope was very steep—not the easiest way to get to the house.

Trace followed him out there. "I'm going to get the bedroom phone and call the cops."

After Trace left, Boomer sat down in a wicker chair and gazed out at the ocean several miles away as he collected his thoughts. When she came back in, she sat down across from him. "They'll be here soon."

"Why would someone want to take the manuscript?" Boomer asked.

"You think this was all about two chapters of a manuscript?" Trace asked.

"When it's obvious, accept the obvious," Boomer said. "That's what they took, that's what they came here for. And it looks like they were getting ready to waste you when I stumbled in here."

Trace remembered looking down the barrel of the pistol and the cold eyes of the man holding it and shivered. "Why were you back so early?" she asked.

He reached out and took her hand, feeling the trembling

in it. "They had sexual harassment awareness training scheduled for the afternoon, and since I'm an expert on sexual harassment, and I'm not really assigned to the unit anyway, I thought I'd take the afternoon off and greet you when you got home."

"Who do you think they are?" Trace asked, sitting down on his lap and leaning against him. He ran his hand through her short hair.

"I don't know."

"Why did they want the manuscript? What good is it going to do them, whoever they are?"

"I don't know," Boomer said. "You tell me."

"Well, maybe someone thought it would be a best-seller," Trace joked nervously, "and they wanted it."

"Do you have a list of the publishers you sent your book proposal to?" Boomer asked.

"I don't need a list," Trace said. "There were only two. Lister Press in Las Vegas and Air Force Institute Press in Boulder. They're both small publishers known for doing military non-fiction and an occasional work of fiction. I figured that would be my best shot."

"What do you know about those publishers?"

"Will you tell me what you're getting to?" Trace asked.

"Someone came here and stole your manuscript and all records of your manuscript. Who knew of the manuscript's existence besides those two publishing houses?"

Trace paused in thought. "That's it. Besides you, I haven't told anyone else about it."

"Anyone at work?"

"No."

"All right," Boomer said. "So therefore someone from one of those two places sent those people here or, more likely, they forwarded your submission to someone who sent those people here."

Trace's eyes widened as she finally understood. "You're saying The Line exists and they did this?"

Boomer shrugged. "Actually, no, I don't think The Line exists, but I do think someone wanted your manuscript."

They heard a car pull up in the drive. They walked to the door and reached it just as two men in khaki pants and colorful shirts arrived on the other side.

"Inspector Konane," a large, dark-skinned man announced, holding out an ID card and badge. "My partner," he nodded at the other man, "Inspector Perry."

Perry was short and compact, several shades lighter than his partner. He hung in the background as Konane entered and looked around. "Tell me what happened." He flipped open a notebook and wrote as Trace relayed the story. When she was done, he looked at Boomer.

"Let me see your gun."

Boomer pulled out his Browning High Power and handed it over.

"Do you have a license to carry?"

Boomer reached into his wallet and removed the special federal license all Delta Force operatives had to carry a weapon anywhere in the United States and on airlines.

Konane seemed disappointed that Boomer did have a license. Boomer noted that the policeman wrote down his name and license number in his notepad.

Konane pulled out a card and handed it to Trace. "When you make a list of everything that was stolen, fax it to the number on this card. If you think of anything else, call me."

"That's it?" Trace asked as the two cops turned toward the door. "Aren't you going to check for prints or something?"

"Ma'am," Konane said, "this was a robbery. We get a dozen of these a day. Once you get us a list of the property we'll put it into the computer and keep an eye out. Since you say the men were wearing masks you can't give us a description more than their height and approximate size. We really don't have much to work with."

"This wasn't just a simple robbery," Boomer said.

"Oh no?" Konane waited

"We were shot at," Boomer said. "That's attempted murder."

Konane nodded. "True, but we still don't have anything more to go on at the moment. Like I said, we'll see if anything stolen turns up. Once you get us a list of what was stolen, of course."

"What about the slugs in the wall?" Boomer demanded. "Aren't you interested in those?"

Konane sighed. "This isn't like a cop show on TV. OK?"

Boomer shook his head, but he didn't say anything. Konane had Trace sign the report and they were gone.

Boomer felt the pocket of his shirt. "Give me the phone. There's someone I want to call." Boomer pulled out the card Skibicki had given him and dialed the number.

"Skibicki," the voice on the other end growled.

"Sergeant major, this is Boomer Watson."

"What's up, sir?"

"Can you get out to Makakilo City right away? I need to talk to you."

"Reference?" The sergeant major succinctly asked.

"My friend just got robbed here and both of us got shot at."

"You call the cops?"

"Yeah, but they weren't much help," Boomer said.

"What's the address?"

Boomer got it from Trace and relayed it.

"I'll be there in a half hour." The phone went dead. During the wait, Boomer and Trace cleaned up the house as much as possible, although there was little they could do about the bullet holes in the wall.

Skibicki arrived and Trace and Boomer told him what had just happened as he checked out the place.

"You didn't get a good look at them?" he asked Boomer.

"No. I heard Trace yell and didn't know what the setup was inside so I just tried to clear the room out by returning fire. They ran up the hill there and I spotted them just before they hit the tree line."

Skibicki took out a pocket knife and dug into one of the bullet holes in the wall, extracting the spent round. "Nine millimeter. Had to be subsonic since you say the weapons were silenced, and this round didn't penetrate very far into the wall. Your ordinary crook doesn't carry silenced weapons."

He walked out to the patio and looked around. "If you're right about professionals here to steal the manuscript, they most likely had the house under surveillance. And if I was going to surveil, I'd do it from there," he added, pointing

up to the lush vegetation adorning Puu Makakilo. ''That's
where they ran, right?''

''Let's take a look,'' Boomer suggested. They went out
the back door and began scrambling up the hill.

Skibicki led the way, snaking through the vegetation, following the trail the two men had made in their scramble to
escape. They came to the small clearing where the two had
obviously spent some time, judging by the cigarette butts
littering the ground. It was a perfect place to watch the
house.

Boomer and Skibicki quartered the ground, searching.
Finally Boomer halted and pointed. ''They had either a
scope or rifle set up here on a tripod. Maybe a camera.
They were watching you for a while, Trace. Normal bur-
glars don't sit for a couple of days before they rob a
house,'' he added.

Skibicki walked over to a tree and noted the numerous
scars torn into the wood. He turned and checked out a faint
line scratched in the dirt with what looked the toe of a boot.
''Not bad,'' he muttered noting the placing of the impacts
and the distance of the line from the tree.

''Do you think they'll come back?'' Trace asked as the
went back down the hill.

''I don't know,'' Boomer said. ''If all they wanted was
the manuscript and your notes, then they won't be back.''

''That doesn't make much sense,'' Skibicki said.

''What doesn't?'' Trace asked.

''They may have gotten the manuscript and all her stuff,
but she still has everything in her head, right?''

Trace nodded.

''Then they'll be back,'' Skibicki concluded.

Boomer had to concur with that reasoning. ''It's probably not safe to stay here,'' he said.

''If you're right,'' Skibicki said, ''I've got a place where
you'll be safe.''

PACIFIC PALISADES, OAHU
30 November
4:30 P.M. LOCAL/ 0230 ZULU

The place Skibicki chose for Boomer and Trace was his mother's house, high along the slopes of the Waiwa Forest Reserve, six kilometers due north of the East Loch of Pearl Harbor.

Maggie welcomed them and after a brief huddle with Skibicki settled Trace down in her spare bedroom. The four of them met in her living room, brightly lit by the sun in a descending hover over the mountains to the west.

"This is ridiculous," Trace said. "I mean, I just got shot at for Christ's sake and the police act like it's no big deal."

"The crime rate is so high nowadays," Maggie said. "I remember when you could leave your house unlocked all the time. I used to never lock my car, no matter where on the island I went. Now I have to carry a can of mace on my key chain."

"I don't think the cops are going to do much about this," Boomer said. He looked at Skibicki. "What do you say we do a little work on our own?"

Skibicki nodded. "What do you have in mind?"

MAKAKILO, OAHU, HAWAIIAN ISLANDS
30 November
7:30 P.M. LOCAL/ 0530 ZULU

Although night was settling over the mountainside, the two men had no trouble maneuvering. Their night vision goggles took what light there was and computer-enhanced it to provide a greenish version of daylight inside the lenses.

One of the men set the tripod for the Remington 700 down, then carefully screwed the rifle onto the tripod. He flipped the on switch for the rifle's night scope and gave it a few seconds to warm up, before trading his goggles for the view through the scope. He scanned the house, then the immediate area.

"Anything?" the other asked.

"House is dark, no cars parked outside."

The second man sat down, leaning his back against the

small pack he was carrying. "The woman comes back, you do her, first clear shot you get. Take out her trigger-happy boyfriend too and anybody else."

The first man smiled and settled in comfortably behind the scope.

CHAPTER ☆ 7

Boomer watched as Skibicki unlocked the footlocker that was bolted to the back of his jeep. The drawer on top held tiger-stripe fatigues, their fabric worn with time. He lifted the tray to get to the contents beneath. He grabbed a Calico M-950-A machine pistol and checked its functioning. It had a built-in sound-suppressor that gave it a short, stubby barrel. The body consisted of a pistol grip and an open bolt assembly facing up.

Skibicki reached in a black bag and pulled out a cylindrical magazine—the most unique feature of the Calico. The magazine, two and a quarter inches in diameter and a little over seven inches long settled into place on top of the weapon, overhanging the rear slightly. Totally unlike any other magazine Skibicki had ever used, the fluted cartridge carrier in the center of the magazine held seven 9mm bullets and the helix around the cartridge carrier held forty-three more rounds, giving the moulded plastic contraption a fifty-round capacity and outgunning any other pistols and automatic weapons around.

Skibicki slipped a shoulder harness over his head, hooking the pistol to the right side and sliding a spare magazine into the open pouch on the left. He took a small cloth brass-catcher and slipped it over the bottom ejector, ensuring that his brass would stay with him if he had to shoot.

He removed a second Calico and handed it to Boomer. "Fifty rounds in the magazine. It operates closed-bolt, re-

111

tarded blowback, like the H&K MP-5 you use in Delta.''

Boomer slid the magazine on top of the housing and chambered a round. He checked the heft of the weapon, sighting down the raised sights across the small parking lot where they were leaving Skibicki's jeep.

"You can fire one-handed," Skibicki said. "Real smooth operation. It goes up and slightly right at first, then settles down on target. You can fire all fifty rounds in one burst if you want." He handed over two additional magazines and a shoulder holster. "You got a laser sight on top. Switch is here," he added, tapping the side of the gun. He handed over a set of PVS-7 night vision goggles and slipped on his own set. "Ready to go for a walk?"

They'd driven back trails through the jungle north of Puu Makakilo until they were about a thousand meters away from a hill on the northeast side. The side opposite Trace's house. They left the jeep behind and started through the vegetation, allowing the bulk of the hill to shield them from the site they'd found the previous day. After carefully checking both directions, they scampered across Palehua Road, the same road Trace had used when she'd unexpectedly come upon the men.

As they got closer to the summit, Skibicki slowed down. Boomer matched the veteran's pace. They went around the side of the hilltop. When Skibicki went prone, Boomer dropped to his belly also, and they remained frozen for fifteen minutes. Boomer caught a faint whiff of cigarette smoke borne by the landward breeze and his finger curled out and flipped off the safety on the Calico. He tapped Skibicki and then touched his nose. Skibicki nodded.

They began moving down the hillside at an excrutiatingly slow pace, often pausing for five to ten minutes, using the rustle of the wind to cover their movement. They didn't have to exchange a word, the two men moving as a unit. An untrained person would have thought their progress unbelievably slow, but Boomer appreciated the older man's stealth.

After two hours, they finally reached a point on the edge of the small clearing, slightly to right of the tree that had been marked by the knife throwing.

Boomer scanned the clearing, taking in the two men and

the sniper rifle set on tripod. One man was watching the house through the scope on the top of the rifle. The other was lying down, his back against a rucksack. Several cigarette butts were in the dirt next to him.

Boomer and the sergeant major watched them for a half hour waiting to see if there was any change to the routine. Finally, Skibicki glanced at Boomer, who nodded. He edged sideways until he was about fifteen feet away from Skibicki. When the sergeant major stood, Boomer did also, the pistol held steady in his right hand, muzzle centered on the man at the rifle.

"Just hold it right where you are," Skibicki said.

Boomer was surprised when the one on the right rolled left, reaching for a pistol in his shoulder holster. Skibicki fired a sustained burst, the first round hitting the sniper rifle, ricocheting off, then he walked the line of bullets into the man, hitting him four times in the chest as the weapon the man had been reaching for cleared its holster. It fell to the dirt next to dead fingers.

If the second man had reacted promptly, his partner's death might not have been in vain, but he froze, caught between reaching for his own pistol and surprise.

"Hands up," Boomer said.

The man bent forward to stand up, and his right hand brushed his pant leg. Boomer's training kicked in and he fired, his bullets stitching a bloody trail up the man's stomach and chest. The man's arms flew wide as the bullets knocked him backwards. The Calico handled smoothly, the unique balance of weight caused by the non-traditional magazine allowing it to be fired accurately with one hand.

Boomer walked over to the body and checked the hand. A knife was clutched in the dead fingers.

"Good job," Skibicki said.

"Damn," Boomer replied, his fingers gripping the handle of the Calico tightly. "Why didn't they surrender? We had them cold."

"It was us or them," Skibicki replied. He pointed at the sniper rifle. "They weren't sitting here waiting to have a discussion with Major Trace. I'd say they were going to finish the job by putting a bullet in her head to completely erase all the information."

"But why?" Boomer asked. He gestured around the clearing. "I don't understand why that manuscript is so damn important."

Skibicki was searching the bodies, pulling out their wallets. "Oh, fuck," he muttered. "It just got worse." He tossed one of the wallets over.

Boomer rubbed his forehead to forestall a growing headache when he saw that the man carried an ID card from the DIA: Defense Intelligence Agency. "Oh shit," Boomer said. "We're fucked."

"It was us or them," Skibicki repeated. He looked up. "You sure those guys yesterday didn't try to identify themselves to Major Trace?"

"She would have said something if they had. They didn't act like they were there on legal business from what I saw."

"They didn't act that way here either. They should have talked to us."

"Maybe not," Boomer said. "Hell, if I had two guys draw down on me in the dark, I'd probably go for my gun too. Goddamn," he kicked the trunk of a tree. "What's going on?"

Skibicki drew a couple of black balaclavas out of the men's backpack. "They also have silenced weapons. I'd bet a month's pay that the ballistics on those guns matches the slugs in the wall down there."

"That still doesn't justify our shooting them," Boomer said.

"They fucking didn't freeze when I told them to," Skibicki growled.

Boomer was shaking his head. "We didn't identify ourselves." He laughed, but there was no humor to it. "Shit, what could we identify ourselves as? 'We're two guys with semi-automatic pistols running around in the fucking dark. Put your hands up'."

"They robbed Trace's house," Skibicki said. "They shot at you both."

"Yeah, I know that." Boomer walked over and put the ID back in the vest pocket of one of the bodies. There was a key in there. He pulled it out and looked at it in the dim light. Room 456, the Outrigger Reef Hotel. He put the key back in the pocket. The man's dead eyes were staring at the sky, reminding Boomer of the ambush several days ago in the Ukraine. No matter where he went, death seemed to be following. But here on a hillside in Hawaii was the last place he'd expected it.

Boomer slowly stood. "Well, I guess I'll call our friends in the police department."

Skibicki nodded. "You go down to the house. I'll go back and bring the jeep around by the main road and join you there."

"All right." Boomer made his way carefully downslope until he got to Trace's house. He went inside and pulled out the card he'd been given earlier in the day. He dialed the number and the phone was picked up on the second ring.

"Oahu PD."

"I'd like to speak to Inspector Konane," Boomer said. He didn't expect the man to be on duty at this time, but the phone clicked and Konane identified himself. Boomer quickly related what had happened and Konane said he was on his way and for Boomer to just hold where he was until they arrived.

Twenty minutes later a pair of headlights cut through the dark, but it was Skibicki's jeep. Boomer told him that the cops were on the way and Skibicki joined him in the drive, pulling out a cigarette and lighting it.

Konane and Perry arrived five minutes after Skibicki.

The inspector didn't waste any time. "Where's the bodies?"

"This way," Boomer said, grabbing a flashlight.

Boomer led, with Skibicki right behind and the two cops bringing up the rear. He crested the hill, stepped into the clearing and froze. It was empty. No bodies. No weapons. No backpack. Nothing. The dirt was scuffed where the bodies had been. That was it.

"Well?" Konane said, walking around Boomer. "Is this the place?"

"Yes." Boomer looked at Skibicki, who raised his hands helplessly.

"And?" Konane pressed.

"They were here," Boomer insisted. "Two men. They were armed. They had a sniper rifle trained on the house."

"You Delta Force guys like playing games don't you?" Konane said. "This some sort of exercise?"

"No." Boomer turned to Skibicki. "You tell them."

"Everything he told you is true," Skibicki said. "There were two men up here and when they tried shooting at us, we killed them."

"And the two bodies just got up and walked away?" Konane didn't wait for an answer. "Listen, it's the middle of the night and we've been on duty for twenty hours. I have half a mind to call your commanding officer and jerk a knot in his ass and yours. *This* isn't a military reservation here and you can't be playing your games."

"But—" Boomer began, but Skibicki grabbed his arm. "Let 'em go," Skibicki hissed.

The walk back to the house was in silence. Konane and Perry gave a few more dire warnings about false crime reporting and departed. As soon as the car pulled out of the drive, Boomer turned to Skibicki. "What happened to the bodies?"

Skibicki shook his head. "I don't know. I went straight down to the jeep. I didn't hear or see anybody. Maybe they had a back-up team nearby that moved in and sterilized the site."

Boomer walked into the house and dropped into a chair. "What's going on?"

Skibicki sat across from him on the couch. He pointed at the portable phone they'd used to call the police. "You need to get your friend out here. She's the one they want, so she's the key."

Skibicki gave him Maggie's number and he called. She put Trace on and Boomer told her to come without telling her what had happened.

Boomer and Skibicki waited, each lost in his own thoughts. By the time Trace arrived, Boomer had mulled over a few things. First, he told her what had happened. At the news of the killings, Trace's reaction matched Boomer's: "Why? What is going on?"

"It has to be the manuscript," Boomer said.

"What's so important about the manuscript?" Trace asked. "That shit happened fifty years ago."

"This Hooker fellow is still alive," Boomer noted.

Skibicki sat upright. "What was that? What did you just say?"

"I said General Hooker is still alive. He's a character in Trace's manuscript."

"A real person?"

Boomer nodded. He explained the two chapters: Hooker graduating and being inducted into The Line and Patton's death as described by the nurse.

"I'll be a son of a bitch!" Skibicki exclaimed when Boomer was done. "I saw Hooker in Vietnam. He was a hatchet man for somebody high up in the Pentagon. He was one of the straight-leg pukes that tried to do away with Special Forces after the incident in Nha Trang."

"Apparently Hooker's been behind a lot of things," Trace said.

"So you're saying maybe Hooker is behind this?" Boomer asked.

Skibicki shrugged. "I don't know, but from what you just told me, I think he'd be a little upset about his name in this manuscript. You're intimating that he was involved in Patton's death. Just think: what if he was? He certainly wouldn't want that to come out, even though it is fifty years later. Who knows what other dirt he's hiding?"

"I guess it's possible," Trace said. "The nurse's story was just so outrageous that it never occurred to me it could be real and someone who was involved would come after me."

"That might also explain why the DIA was watching you," Skibicki added. "Hooker probably still pulls a lot of weight in the Pentagon. He could get the DIA to do his dirty work."

"What do we do now?" Trace asked. The sun was just beginning to rise in the east.

"You all get to work," Boomer said. "Sergeant major, can you cover for me this morning?"

"You have an idea?" Skibicki asked.

"Yeah, I have an idea."

"Remember your last one," Skibicki warned.

HONOLULU
1 December
8:00 A.M. LOCAL/ 1800 ZULU

The Outrigger Waikiki was easy to find, standing just to the east of Fort DeRussy Beach Park and Museum. Boomer parked at the museum and strolled down the beach past the hotel. It was a bit early for tourists, so the beach was almost deserted.

Boomer was tired, but adrenaline was providing the energy now. He'd killed before on missions overseas, but never in the States and never under such confusing circumstances.

He wondered why the two men were staying at the Outrigger. The Hale Koa, a military-run hotel on the Fort DeRussy reservation was just a couple of hundred meters down the beach. And then there were all sorts of BOQs at various posts all over the island where the two men could have stayed if they had been on official orders. So perhaps they were at the Outrigger because this mission wasn't official?

He walked into the lobby of the hotel as if he belonged, stepped into the elevator and pushed the button for the fourth floor. He was wearing shorts and the loose-fitting shirt he'd worn to meet Trace. He'd traded the Calico back to Skibicki for his Browning High Power and it rode comfortably on his left shoulder.

The doors opened on the fourth floor and Boomer stepped out. He checked the small sign. 456 was to the right, several doors. He strode up to a maid and flashed his federal ID. "I need to have Room 456 opened."

The woman did not react the way Boomer expected. "I just opened it for you people. What did you do, lock yourself out?"

"You just—" Boomer turned, and the door to the room opened. A man pushing a luggage rack piled high with scuba tanks came into the hallway. He looked up at Boomer and their eyes locked, the cleaning lady looking from one to the other.

If there was one thing Boomer had learned early in his military career—not just learned but ingrained into his psyche at Ranger School—was when in doubt, attack.

He charged forward, feinted with his right leg and snapped a left leg kick into the bottom of the man's jaw. There was an audible click as teeth smashed together. Boomer grabbed his shirt and pulled the unconscious body into the room. He stuck his head back out. "It's OK," he called out to the maid. She stared at him for a second, then shrugged and walked away, muttering to herself.

There was no one else in the room. The luggage rack was still in the hallway, but Boomer did a quick search of the man first. Another DIA ID card and badge, which Boomer appropriated. A gun in a shoulder holster. Something was folded on the inside pocket of his suit jacket. Boomer pulled it out. A topographic map of Oahu.

He heard the elevator open. Boomer stood and checked the hallway. Two men were approaching and when they saw him they broke into a run. Boomer slammed the door shut and threw the bolt. Thuds rained down on the door as Boomer spotted his only option. He ran out onto the small balcony. There was a small concrete extension surrounded by a chest-high railing. Boomer climbed onto the railing, steadying himself with his hands on the bottom of the balcony above. Carefully he slipped his hands over the edge of the concrete lip. He avoided looking at the ground forty feet below. As the door splintered open, Boomer swung a leg up, then the other. Standing up, he hopped over the railing and got out of sight.

He heard feet clatter onto the balcony below. "Where'd he go?" a man's voice asked.

"Either up or down," another voice replied.

"He's going to have to go down to get out. Let's move."

Boomer hoped the room was empty. He opened the sliding door and went through the room into the hallway. The elevator was in the center, the fire stairs to the right. No choice really. There was no way Boomer would want to fight his way out of the close confines of a small box.

He took the stairs two at a time until he hit the second floor, then he slowed down, his sneakers making no noise as he carefully took the next corner. Boomer drew his Browning. He made the last turn, muzzle leading and the first thing he saw was another muzzle pointing at him.

"Freeze!" the DIA agent yelled.

Boomer didn't stop moving, taking the last couple of stairs, weapon pointed directly between the man's eyes. The agent backed up to the outside door.

"I said freeze, asshole!"

Boomer continued until the muzzle of his gun pushed up against the man's forehead, pressing the back of his skull against the steel door. The agent's gun was correspondingly against Boomer's face, but the man's hand was shaking and his eyes were wide open trying to focus on the metal tube pressing into his skin. This was not at all something he expected or had been trained on. With his free hand, Boomer effortlessly snatched the man's gun and tossed it away.

"Good night," Boomer said, rapping the cold steel of the barrel against the agent's head. He slid to the floor unconscious. Boomer leaned over and checked the man's hands, then he pushed the outside door open and squinted in the bright sunlight.

CHAPTER ☆ 8

FORT SHAFTER
1 DECEMBER
9:10 A.M. LOCAL/ZULU

"Major Keyes isn't Q course-qualified," Skibicki said to Boomer as the letter entered the tunnel.

Boomer replied by tossing the ID card and map onto the sergeant major's desk.

"What's this?" Skibicki asked.

Boomer quickly related going to the motel and his encounters there.

When he was done, Skibicki picked up the card. "Let me see if I can find out what's going on."

"How?" Boomer asked.

Skibicki took an old spiral notebook out of a drawer. "NCO network." He flipped through until he found what he was looking for. He grabbed the phone and began dialing.

While he was doing that, Boomer unfolded the map and studied it. There were pencil marks in the upper left corner, on the blue next to the land. Boomer remembered something, but before he had a chance to take the thought further, Skibicki slammed the phone.

"He ain't DIA."

"What?"

Skibicki flipped the card to him. "Your buddy there, John Regan, if that's his real name. He isn't DIA."

"But he had this on him," Boomer said, looking over the ID.

Skibicki gave Boomer a look normally reserved for idiot

privates. "Yeah, and the two guys we blew away had these too and they were doing some breaking and entering earlier in the day. These cards are their cover so they can go about their business. I talked to a sergeant major buddy of mine over at DIA headquarters and he checked their open *and* classified records. This guy isn't listed in either."

"Then who the fuck is Major John Regan?"

"It'll take a while for me to check around," Skibicki said. "We also have to consider the possibility that this guy might not be military at all. I think we've stepped in some deep and dark shit here."

Boomer tapped the map sheet. "Remember that water jump I told you about?"

"Yes?"

Boomer pointed at the pencil marks off the northwest coast of Oahu. "Is that Gumbo Shark DZ?"

"Yes."

"And those guys had scuba gear," Boomer said.

Skibicki put those two pieces of information together. "DZ coverage."

"That's the way I figure it," Boomer said. "Which means there's a hell of a lot more going on here than someone simply wanting Trace's manuscript." Boomer sat on the edge of Skibicki's desk. "Let's go back. You said Keyes isn't Special Forces-qualified?"

"Right. His orders for command of A Company, 1st Battalion, were cut in DC—right at Department of the Army personnel—not at Special Ops Headquarters at Bragg. That explains how they can slot someone who isn't qualified into that slot."

"How the hell can they do that?" Boomer asked.

"Well, it's like this. Someone with a lot of rank orders someone in personnel to sit down at a typewriter and type the fucking orders, then put them in an envelope and mail them. Whoever gets them salutes and says 'yes, sir, yes, sir, three bags full,' because the signature on the bottom has a few stars behind it." Skibicki's voice dripped sarcasm. "This is the only job in the world where you wake up in the morning and they tell you, 'Well, hey, bud, we want you to go and get your ass shot off,' and the only option in your bag of retorts is to salute and say 'yes, fuck-ing-A, sir.' "

Skibicki leaned forward. "You still don't get it, do you, Boomer? When the system says it will happen, then it *will* happen. They could have cut orders assigning an orangutan to be commander out there at Alpha company and the fuck-ing battalion commander would have handed the guidon to a monkey."

"I get it," Boomer snapped back. "I've played the game."

But Skibicki wasn't done. "Those guys we killed could be Company. Sooner or later they're going to backtrack to us, if they haven't already. Our names are on that damn police report."

"But what's the CIA doing operating inside the States?" Boomer asked.

"I just said they *might* be CIA," Skibicki said. "There's so many damn private armies running around sanctioned by the government it could be anybody. Hell, you guys in Delta are just the tip of the iceberg."

Boomer leaned toward Skibicki and spoke in a low, mea-sured tone. "Do you think there's a connection between these guys here on the island and 1st of the 1st."

"If those are Keyes' guys making the jump," Skibicki answered.

Boomer pulled out the copy of the JAVIS report from his breast pocket. "What about the plane for this water jump? If we can find out about that, then maybe we can get an idea what's going on. We need to know if it's com-ing from Okinawa."

Skibicki started turning pages in his spiral notebook. "That will take a little while."

"I'll give Trace a call and fill her in on what's going on," Boomer said. He went to the desk across from Ski-bicki and dialed Trace's work number. When she came on the line, he related what had happened at the hotel and their discoveries so far. As Skibicki hung up, Boomer told her to come to the tunnel.

"The plane isn't from the island," Skibicki said. "And it ain't from the mainland. At least it's not listed in the Military Airlift Command master files."

Boomer looked at the message and considered the contents in a different light. "Why fourteen men and two bundles for a water jump? Why not two full teams? That would be twenty-four people."

"Can't fit twenty-four on a Combat Talon with bundles. Especially if the bundles are rubber boats. Normal load for a rubber boat drop from a Talon is two boats and fourteen personnel," Skibicki replied, referring to the modified MC-130 transport plane that the Air Force used for special missions.

"That makes sense," Boomer said. "Then it's probably a Talon doing the drop. They'll be able to come in low to the coast of the island and not get picked up on radar. Hell, I talked to one of those Talon jockeys last year, and he said they flew right up on the aircraft carrier *America* at wave-top level and never came up on the radar screens."

"Plus they're pushing bundles," Skibicki said. "That means ramp jump from a 130. It's a bitch to get a bundle out of anything larger than a 130."

"What about SOW?" Boomer asked, referring to the Air Force's Special Operation Wing that had all the MC-130 Combat Talons under its command. "They're not under MAC control. Anything on their location?"

"I checked that too. My buddy at Eglin Air Force Base in Florida says that two of their Combat Talons are deployed and he isn't saying where, but I got the impression they were over in Europe supporting NATO missions. They moved the squadron of Talons that used to be stationed in the Philippines to Japan. It's too early for me to be checking there."

Skibicki tapped the phone. "The problem is every time I call someone on this thing, the chances increase that someone's going to get counter-curious about my questions. Besides, I don't think these people are going to be dumb enough to have the flight plan for this operation listed anywhere," Skibicki concluded. "Not if they're using fake DIA ID cards for cover"

"Come here," Boomer said. He led the sergeant major into the empty conference room and closed the door behind them. He pointed at the large map of the Pacific posted on the wall. "I agree that the flight plan for the aircraft flying this mission will probably be classified and we won't be able to get a look at it. But how far is it from Okinawa to the drop zone here?''

"About 4,000 miles," Skibicki said, having flown across the Pacific numerous times in his career.

"Mission range on a Talon without refueling is 2,800 nautical miles, which is a little over 3,000 miles," Boomer said, figuring the numbers on a notepad. "Which means—"

"Which means if the plane is coming from Okie they're going to have to in-flight refuel," Skibicki said, catching Boomer's logic. "Which means we can check on KC-10 tanker missions scheduled for the night of the jump. I'll get on it as soon as they wake up. Most of the tankers in the Pacific fly out of Guam.''

"All right, let's play with this a little," Boomer said. "Let's assume it's fourteen guys from 1st Group under Keyes command jumping in tomorrow night with rubber boats. What's the plan?''

"It's got to involve water," Skibicki said. "They could just as easily do a rough terrain jump into the center of the island.''

"I disagree," Boomer said. "A water jump is the most secure way to go. They can drown the chutes, get accountability for everyone, and come ashore together. They try a rough terrain drop on the island they could lose someone or somebody could break a leg.''

"We're on an island," Skibicki said, circling his finger around his head. "That means we're surrounded by water. Odds are, they're going to come from the water to do whatever they have planned.''

Boomer looked at the calendar. "They're jumping at 1200 Zulu on the second. What's that local time?''

"0200 local time on the second—Saturday morning," Skibicki calculated.

"Who's jumping?" Trace asked from the door of the conference room. "Sergeant Vasquez told me you were back here.''

Boomer quickly brought her up to speed, then went back to the problem.

"So what are they coming here for?" Boomer asked. "And what do you think this means?" He reached into his pocket, pulled a ring out, and looked at it.

"What do you have there?" Skibicki asked.

"I took this off the man I knocked out at the hotel." Boomer turned it around. "Class of 'eighty-four."

"West Pointer," Skibicki said, taking the ring and looking at it.

"Whose is it?" Trace asked.

Boomer took the ring back and looked on the inside. "Peter Killington."

Trace shook her head. "Don't know him."

"Let me run his name," Skibicki said. "Find out where he's assigned."

They waited as Skibicki made several phone calls. When he was done, his face indicated that the news wasn't good. "There is no Peter Killington listed on active duty or in the reserves."

"Another person who doesn't exist," Boomer said.

Skibicki held up a hand. "Just because he's not listed doesn't mean he isn't in the service. I remember when I was in 7th Group our battalion XO didn't get picked up for lieutenant colonel. When he sent a letter to the board asking why, they sent the letter back saying he had not been considered because they never saw his file. He didn't exist.

"Turns out, his previous assignment was with the ISA— Intelligence Service Agency," Skibicki clarified for Trace. "A high-speed unit that did a lot of covert work. People in that unit are buried deep and their records pulled."

"So you're saying these people could be military but working under deep cover," Trace said.

Boomer nodded. "You won't find my name listed anywhere at the Department of the Army. But that still brings us back to the question: who are these guys working for?" A thought struck him. "Decker!" Seeing the looks on their faces, he explained. "Colonel Decker—he was here in the tunnel the other day. He's the one who—" Boomer paused as he realized what he was about to say. Then all the pieces came together, and Boomer staggered back. He grabbed a chair to steady himself and sat down.

"Are you OK?" Trace put a hand on his shoulder and leaned over.

"Oh my God," Boomer muttered. "Oh my God."

CHAPTER ☆ 9

"Sit down and let me explain from the beginning," Boomer said, forestalling Skibicki's and Trace's questions. He began with the mission into the Ukraine, sketching out the events and the people involved. Trace was shocked to learn that the inspectors had been killed by Boomer's team, but Skibicki seemed none too surprised.

"You think it was deliberate?" he asked Boomer.

"Yes. Especially after seeing the fall-out in the press over the deaths. I think we were sent there to kill exactly who we killed and I think Decker knew it from the start."

Then he described seeing Decker in the tunnel, the strange happenings in A Company, 1st Battalion, 1st Special Forces Group, with Wilkerson being set up and relieved and Keyes taking over. He added the mysterious jump scheduled for the night of the second with the men in the hotel room who happened to have a load of scuba gear.

"Combine all that with the military's unhappiness over the MRA and the existence of The Line—"

"Possible existence," Trace cut in.

"This doesn't look like just possible," Boomer said, pointing at the ring he'd taken off the man at the hotel. "Nothing here has just been a coincidence.

"Anyway," he conceded, "add in the 'possible' existence of this Line organization, and I think we have a bad situation here."

Trace shook her head. "I don't understand what 1st of

127

the 1st has to do with this. So you've got a new CO for A Company 1st of the 1st. One who's politics are sort of right wing.''

"But he's not SF-qualified," Boomer noted.

Trace continued on. "And he's taking over because the last commander said he got set up to be relieved and his company is getting new people in that he doesn't have authority to slot where he wants. Did they set up his making the mistake that got him relieved?''

"They're stacking a couple of teams there," Boomer insisted, giving his explanation for events on Okinawa.

"Uh-huh," Trace said. "And you have these fourteen people and two bundles jumping into a water DZ on the night of the second off the coast.''

"Most likely those same teams from 1st of the 1st," Boomer said.

"But how can you connect them to The Line. If The Line exists?''

"I don't have a direct connection," Boomer ceded. "But I think someone, somewhere, is pulling some strings and most of the principal players are West Pointers.''

"So are we," Trace interrupted.

"Yeah, but we aren't Rhodes Scholars," Boomer said sarcastically. "If they only pick a couple of people every few years, I'm not too surprised they didn't pick us to be part of their little organization.''

"Speak for yourself," Trace said, trying to smile. "I ranked in the top twenty of my class.''

"Shit, Trace," Boomer said. "Get real. You could have been number one and they wouldn't give you the time of day. The Line probably had a shit fit when Congress passed that law allowing woman into the Academy. The damn superintendant at the time threatened to resign.''

"Let's get back to facts," Trace said. "We have no proof that The Line exists. All I had were the muddled memories of an old lady. And what does that have to do with my manuscript? The men in the hotel were connected to the men you killed behind the house. You're only connecting them to this jump because of their scuba gear—''

"The map," Boomer said tapping it, "locks them together.''

"OK, they're connected," Trace said. "If this is all fact, what are they here to do?"

Boomer rubbed his eyes, his voice cracking with fatigue. "When is the President arriving?"

Trace slumped back, the disbelief apparent on her fine features.

Skibicki silently went to a table in the corner of the room and pulled out a sheet of papers with a classified stamp on the cover. "This is the OPLAN for security. He arrives on Ohau the morning of the sixth. He's attending a fundraising dinner at the Royal Hawaiian on the night of the sixth, then the ceremony at Pearl on the morning of the seventh. He's scheduled to commemorate the anniversary with a minute of silence at 7:54 A.M., the time when the attack started. His speech is set for 8:00 A.M."

"So we have six days."

"Hold on one second," Trace said. "How do you come up with a plot against the President? I think you're stretching here, Boomer."

"Hey, you're the one who's writing the book," Boomer replied. "You're the one that told me about The Line."

"But I was talking about fiction. A novel, Boomer, you know like Stephen King and John Grisham."

"You based it on facts as told to you," Boomer said. "You just automatically assumed she was senile. What if she's floating with all her oars and told you the biggest secret of the century? God, Trace, it's as if she told you the mob shot JFK and you called Joe Bonanno and said, 'Hey, wanna hear a good story?' "

"Calm down, both of you," Skibicki said. He was looking at the map. "The water jump. It makes sense now. The President's speaking at Pearl Harbor; that has quite a bit of water in it, last I checked. If I was going to plan an operation, knowing the security that the President always has, I don't think I'd come at him on land."

"You think it's an assassination?" Boomer had not taken it to that drastic conclusion. "I don't think they'd go that far. More likely they have something planned to politically hurt him."

"I don't even know that *anything's* planned," Skibicki countered. "We're just speculating here. We got some

strange shit going on and we're checking it out." He looked
at the map. "The President's exact itinerary is classified,
but there's one place and one time everyone knows exactly
where he's going to be: the *Arizona* Memorial at 7:54 A.M.
on the seventh of December. If I was doing a target folder,
I'd start with that fact. And the Memorial is in the center
of Pearl Harbor, which just happens to contain a lot of
water," he added, looking at Boomer.

Skibicki sat down in the seat marked commander and
swung his boots up on the conference table. "Let me ask
Vasquez to do some checking."

"Vasquez?" Boomer repeated.

"She's smart and she's hooked into the intelligence ap-
paratus on this island like you wouldn't believe. She can
go up to PACOM or over to Pearl and check on damn near
anything. Hell, she's got a direct computer line into the
NSA back on the mainland."

"What will you tell her to look for?" Boomer asked.

"Anything out of the ordinary," Skibicki said. "In fact,
I'll set it up like I would if *I* was going to do a mission.
Have her check to see if anyone else has done any checking
on information about the President's visit or about security,
or the setup at Pearl. Anything."

"Sounds good," Boomer said. He turned to Trace. "Try
to remember. Is there a way to learn more about The Line?
If it's real it had to have had a history. More than just
involving Patton. Sixty years is a long time for a secret
organization."

"You've made up your mind this thing exists and you,"
she said, pointing at Skibicki, "think they're going going
to kill the President. Do I have this right?" She waited and
their silence was her answer. "Hell, then I have the entire
history of The Line. It's my outline. The stuff I made up
last month that now turns into fact."

Boomer grabbed her hands. "Listen, Trace. You don't
want to believe it, but those guys at your house had a sniper
rifle loaded with a bullet that had your name on it. Maybe
that's why. Maybe taking the nurse's story and whatiffing
through history like you did is exactly what happened. Can
you talk to this woman again? Is she still still alive?"

Trace was pale, her hands trembling in Boomer's grip.

She nodded with resignation. "She lives on the mainland. I'll have to go, won't I?"

Boomer nodded, but his brain was racing over the events of the last few days. He turned to Skibicki. "You told me that you saw Hooker in Vietnam."

Skibicki was looking at the map. "Yeah?"

"If The Line exists, Hooker's one of them. You said he was involved in what happened at Nha Trang with your commander."

Skibicki nodded. "Yeah, he was."

"Does Colonel Rison know anything about The Line?" Boomer asked.

"Who's Colonel Rison?" Trace asked.

"The Special Operations Commander in Vietnam in 1968," Skibicki replied.

"Why would he know about The Line?" Trace asked.

"It's a long story," Boomer said.

Skibicki flipped open his spiral notebook one more time. "Let's find out. Last I knew Rison retired to New York. Up in the Adirondacks." He checked his watch. "It's just after two in the afternoon there." He turned on the conference room speakerphone, punched in the number, and waited.

After two rings, the other end was lifted and a strong, but very guarded voice came out of the box. "Hello?"

"Colonel Rison?"

"Yes? Who is this?"

"This is Sergeant Major Skibicki calling from Fort Shafter in Hawaii."

"Earl Skibicki?" The voice warmed considerably. "How are you doing, you young fool?"

"I'm not so young any more, sir."

"Hell, none of us are, son, none of us are. What can I do for you?"

"I've got some people here that want to talk to you. You remember Mike Watson, RT Kansas?"

"Hell, yes, I remember him."

"Well, I'm with his son, Boomer Watson. He's a major now, assigned out of Bragg."

"I guess from the echo I'm on a speaker," Rison said.

"Yes, sir," Skibicki answered.

"Well, Major Boomer Watson, your dad was one hell of a soldier. Who else do you have there?"

"I'm Major Benita Trace, sir. I'm a friend of Boomer's."

"What can I do for you?" Rison asked.

Skibicki gestured at Boomer, who took the cue. "Sir, this is Boomer Watson. I appreciate what you said about my dad. The sergeant major told me about his last mission. We have a problem and Sergeant Major Skibicki says you might have some information that could help us out." That earned a glare from Skibicki, but Boomer didn't have time to play games.

The voice hesitated. "What do you need to know?"

Boomer took the plunge cold. "Sir, have you ever heard of an organization called The Line? It's a group of—"

"Wait a second," Rison's voice snapped. "Skibicki, you still there?"

"Yes, sir." The sergeant major sat up straight in his chair.

"Verify for me the name of the mascot at the B-50 base camp in early 'sixty-eight."

Skibicki nodded. "We had a mangy old dog there named Crazy, sir."

"And who did what with the dog every Friday night he was in camp?" Rison demanded.

Skibicki glanced at Maggie and Trace. "Uh, well, sir, Howie Mendenez used to get plastered, then take the dog in the club and—"

"All right, that's enough." Rison interceded. "You're Skibicki, but I won't talk about this over the phone."

Boomer leaned forward. "Sir, this is important. We need to—"

"No, young man, you listen to me. You want to know about that organization, you come here and talk to me."

Boomer looked at Trace. She shrugged. He turned back to the phone. "Sir, that's no possible right now. We—"

"It mustn't be that important to you, then," Rison replied sharply.

"It's very important to us," Boomer protested. "But we're in Hawaii and we need to know now. There are things going on that are vital to national security."

There was a loud snort of derision. "I've heard that bullshit before. I don't who the hell you or the young woman are. I know who Skibicki is, but they've turned others on me before. I won't talk over the phone." He paused. "You want to see me, you come to me."

"Wait one minute, sir." Boomer hit the hold button on the phone, then turned to Trace and Skibicki. "What do you think?"

"I think if you want to know what the colonel knows, one of the two of you ought to go talk to him," Skibicki said. He pointed at Trace. "I think she ought to go. We're going to have to guard her if she stays here. This way we can get her to the mainland and out of sight for the time being, while we figure out what is going on."

"We don't have much time," Trace added.

"Can you go?" Boomer asked.

Trace nodded. "I can get leave this evening. If he's in New York, I can see Mrs. Howard. Maybe she does know more."

Boomer took it one step further. "Will you go?"

"This is so crazy," Trace said. "I know everything you say fits a pattern but—"

"People have died, Trace," Boomer said. "That we know for sure." He pointed at the phone. "Rison acts like he's heard of The Line."

"Rison does know something about The Line," Trace agreed. "And I guess I'm the one who started all this with my manuscript. I want to know what he knows."

Boomer reached over and turned the phone on. "Major Trace will come to talk to you, sir. She can meet you in New York."

"I won't be here," Rison said. "Meet me Saturday in Philadelphia."

"Philadelphia?" Boomer asked.

"Yes. The Army-Navy game. I'll be seated in section GG. Row Twenty-three. Seat One." There was a click, then a loud dial tone buzzed through the room.

Boomer turned off the phone. "Rah-rah-rah-boom. On brave old Army team," he began to chant in a derisive voice.

"I've heard it before," Trace snapped. "What are you

two going to be doing while I'm seeing Rison?'' she demanded.

"We," Boomer said, "are going to try and find out several things. We need to know the departure airfield for the plane. That will give us a good idea who's dropping in. So while you're in Philly enjoying the game, we'll be greeting our incoming guests.''

Trace pulled out her wallet, removing her credit card. "Let me call the airlines and see what they have leaving this evening for the mainland." She paused. "I can't believe I'm doing this."

Boomer stood up. "Believe." He pointed at the phone. "Rison knows about The Line and I think The Line is here on this island. We've got six days to uncover what they have planned."

CHAPTER ☆ 10

"Think I ought to take this?" Trace asked, holding up a black sweatshirt with a large number twelve silkscreened onto it. The Army mule, hooves kicking, was on each shoulder. "This is from my firstie year, December 'eighty-two. We all took off our dress gray in the fourth quarter to cheer." She laughed at the memory. "We got our butts kicked."

"That was the game out in California wasn't it?" Boomer asked.

"No, it was in Philly. We lost twenty-four to seven that year."

Boomer vividly remembered the four years of Army football he'd watched. Every cadet did, because, like it or not, you were a fan once you were a cadet. The Academy took the money for season tickets out of every cadet's pay. A plebe who didn't go to a home game wouldn't have lasted the first semester hazing.

Of course everyone went. What else was there to do on Saturday afternoon at West Point? The one concession the Academy made for home football games during Boomer's time was shortening Saturday morning classes. But that wasn't so the cadets could get ready for the game. It was so they could get back to the barracks and change into full dress uniform for the parade for the American public prior to every game.

The culmination of every season was the Army-Navy

135

game. The team could lose all ten prior games, but all that went out the window when the classic interservice show-down rolled around. Boomer had never particularly enjoyed having to stand during every game, another great West Point tradition. He especially remembered standing in the fourth quarter during a 55-0 drubbing by Baylor his plebe year. Not his idea of fun.

"You have everything?" he asked, as Trace stuffed the sweatshirt into her overnight bag. Trace had spent the afternoon getting her leave approved and Boomer had stayed with her the entire time. Skibicki was back in the tunnel trying to unearth new information.

"I guess so."

"Let's roll," he said grabbing the keys for her truck.

Boomer watched the rear-view mirror the entire way to Honolulu International Airport, but he didn't spot anything. He parked in the short-term garage. Boomer showed his special federal ID to the guard at the security gate and he was allowed to pass with the Browning High Power hidden in its shoulder holster. They arrived at Trace's departure gate with a half hour to spare. Boomer choose seats for them where they could watch the center of the terminal.

"Am I off on a wild goose chase?" Trace asked, leaning back in her seat and regarding Boomer with skeptical eyes. "And yes, I know people have died. But the more I think about it, the crazier this all sounds. You're talking about the military taking action against the government. We've never had anything like what you suspect in the history of this country. I know the MRA isn't very popular, but hell, there's always been unpopular stuff going on."

"When I arrived in 10th Group for my first Special Forces assignment, my company commander was a fellow named Major Stubbs," Boomer said. "When I went for my inprocessing briefing with him, he gave me a couple of books to read. He told me that being in Special Operations meant that I had to think differently and I also had to understand the history of covert operations."

"This have anything to do with what I asked?" Trace asked, fingering her ticket and watching the waiting area.

"Bear with me a minute," Boomer said. "I was thinking about this because of that chapter in your manuscript, the one about Patton and the Second World War. One of the books I had to read was about covert operations in Europe during that war. The title of the book, *Bodyguard of Lies*, came from a quote by Winston Churchill. He said: 'In wartime, Truth is so precious that she should always be attended by a bodyguard of lies.'

"I've heard it said that truth is the first casualty of war," Trace said.

"Maybe it's just misplaced," Boomer replied. "Anyway, anyone who's studied World War II has heard about the city of Coventry and how Churchill had advance warning of the bombing raid there but didn't inform the populace of Coventry because doing so would tip off the Germans that the Brits had broken the German secret cipher with Ultra. That's one case where the bodyguard was the truth being withheld. But in this book, the author spent a lot of time talking about the Resistance in France and the Allies' SOE, Special Operations Executive, the American contribution of which was called the OSS, Office of Strategic Services, from which both Special Forces and the CIA draw its lineage.

"The SOE sent agents into occupied France to work with the Resistance, particularly wireless operators to relay information back and forth. Of course the Germans weren't too keen on that and ran counter-operations and managed to scarf up quite a few of these wireless operators along with their radios and ciphers. The Germans then set up a false network. Communicating back to Britain as if the agent was free and doing his or her job.

"After the war there were a lot of accusations that the SOE parachuted agents into Resistance nets that they knew had been compromised. Particularly female agents."

"Why women?" Trace asked.

"The feeling at the time was that the Germans would not believe that an English gentleman would sacrifice a woman in such a manner. Deliberately giving her false information in training, then handing her right over to the Germans to eventually give up that false information as truth under torture prior to being executed."

"Jesus," Trace whispered. "Is that true? Did that happen?"

"The author of the book said there was no proof,"
Boomer said. He snorted. "Of course there was no proof.
Who would have been stupid enough to document such a
thing? Everyone wants proof, when all they really need to
do is look at what really happened, instead of what they
hoped happened.

"What I took from the book was that those radio operators had three security checks. The first was a cipher to
encrypt the message. If they were captured before they
could destroy their cipher, then that could be compromised
and used by the Germans without the receivers in Britain
knowing. The second was a security check—a code word
each agent had memorized that was supposed to be in every
message. If the code word wasn't there, the SOE people in
England knew the message was being sent under duress."

Boomer looked at Trace. "There were numerous messages sent that lacked these code words, yet the SOE han-
dlers still sent agents into those nets. The excuse they used
after the war was that they thought the radio operator had
forgotten to include the safety code word. Can you believe
that?" He didn't wait for an answer. "I'm sitting in an attic
in occupied France transmitting valuable information to England and I'd forget to use the security code word that
would verify my message as legitimate? Not likely."

Boomer shook his head. "The third one though, is the
most damning. Every radio operator who sends Morse
code, which is the mode they used then and we still train
on in Special Forces, has what we call a 'fist.' That's each
individual's way of tapping the key. If you listen to someone long enough, their fist is like their personal signature
and it can't be duplicated. Quite a few of those messages
that came back setting up drop zones for new agents not
only lacked the proper security codeword, but the radio
people at SOE headquarters could tell that the fist was not
that of the radio operator they'd worked with in training."

Boomer's voice hardened. "No matter how much they
deny it, they *knew* at SOE headquarters that some of their
nets had been compromised and they still sent people into
them.

"After reading all that," he continued, "there was one
damn thing I was sure of, and it was the reason Major

Stubbs had me read that book: I learned never to trust the 'official' story. I think there's a good chance The Line exists, and I think we've got to give that chance our best shot. If we're wrong, no harm no foul, but if we're right . . .'' He left it at that.

He reached into his pocket. "There's something I didn't tell you last night when I told you about what happened in the Ukraine." He laid a plastic military ID card in Trace's lap. It was smeared with dried blood. "I took that from one of the bodies at the ambush site. I didn't show it to Decker."

Trace looked at it, reading the name through the red film. JOHN K. STUBBS. She raised her eyes to meet Boomer's.

"I had known he was working some kind of NATO deal. Most of the officers who work those sensitive assignments are Special Forces because of their background and training," he said. "The man who taught me not to believe what I'm told died because I believed the bullshit they were feeding me over there in Turkey. I can't let this rest, not after that and what happened at your house."

The waiting area was beginning to empty as Trace's flight began boarding. Boomer put the ID card back in his pocket and stood. Trace threw her overnight bag over her shoulder. "I understand," she said. She turned for the gate.

"Take care of yourself and be careful," Boomer said walking with her, both stopping just short of the gate.

Trace stepped forward and wrapped her arms around him. "You take care of yourself. Let's hope this turns out to be for nothing."

"That would be nice," Boomer conceded, returning her hug.

Trace hesitated. "The other night. That was like it was down in Texas, wasn't it?"

Boomer hesitated, then answered slowly. "I'm not sure what it was, but I don't think it was like Texas."

Trace smiled knowingly. "Yeah, I didn't think so." She leaned forward and held him tight. "Please don't say anything, Boomer. Just hold me hard and know I need you." She let go just as suddenly and rapidly walked to the gate and disappeared.

Boomer stood there feeling the emptiness she had left. "Please be safe, Benita," he whispered.

On the far side of the boarding area, Sergeant Major Skibicki watched the embrace, the Calico hidden in his shoulder holster. He waited until Trace had entered the tunnel before approaching Boomer.

"Sergeant major," Boomer said, surprised to see him. "What's up?"

"I thought I'd come by to make sure Major Trace got off all right," Skibicki replied, walking out of the boarding area with Boomer. "Vasquez wants us to meet her at the NCO Club at Shafter."

"The NCO Club?" Boomer asked.

"I don't trust the tunnel now," Skibicki replied.

"Does she have anything?" Boomer asked.

"I guess she'll tell us that," Skibicki said.

FORT SHAFTER, HAWAIIAN ISLANDS
1 December 1995
7:00 P.M. LOCAL/ 0500 ZULU

The NCO Club at Fort Shafter was a round building with a central bar on the top level that had a beautiful view of the ocean. On a Friday evening it was packed with soldiers enjoying the end of another work week. Skibicki led Boomer through the throng until they spotted Vasquez at a table near the large windows. Two young soldiers were seated with her, vainly trying to get her attention.

"Get lost," Skibicki growled placing a hand on the back of one of the men's chair.

"Hey, screw off—" the soldier's words froze in his mouth as he took in the grizzled old sergeant major and the officer standing behind him. "Sorry, sergeant major, I was just trying to talk to the lady," he tried explaining.

"The lady is a sergeant," Skibicki said. "And she's *my* sergeant, and I need to talk to her, so hit the road." The two scattered and Skibicki and Boomer took their place.

"I didn't need the help," Vasquez said. "They were amusing."

"No time for amusing," Skibicki replied shortly. "What have you got?"

Vasquez shifted her dark eyes to Boomer, then back to Skibicki. "I checked on the KC-10 situation for tonight like you asked me."

The young sergeant pulled out a notepad full of scribblings. "Most tanker missions in this area of operation are flown by the Pacific Tanker Force of the 65th Strategic Squadron, which is located at Andersen Air Force Base on Guam. That falls under the command of the Pacific Air Forces headquartered right here in sunny Oahu at Hickham. I've got a friend at PACAF who owed me," she said with a smile that made Boomer wonder about the debt.

"He checked and he found a KC-10 tanker departing Andersen at 0430 zulu on the first. It's scheduled to do a mission at 0830 zulu, at coordinates 178 degrees, twelve minutes east longitude, and twenty-three degrees, fifteen minutes north latitude."

"Which is where?" Skibicki asked.

She had an 8.5-by-11 Xeroxed map of the Pacific in her notebook and she unfolded it and placed it next to the paper. She drew a small circle on it. "Right here. Five hundred and fifty miles southeast of Midway." She consulted her notes again. "The KC-10 is to remain on station to do another mission at the same spot at 1530 zulu. It's scheduled to return to Andersen at 1930 zulu."

"A second mission?" Skibicki said. "Two aircraft?"

Vasquez shook her head. "No. Same aircraft. Once going in and once coming out. I checked, using what you gave me, that it might be a Combat Talon that's getting the gas. A 0830 Z refuel at this spot," she tapped the mark, "given the Talon's mission speed at altitude of 260 knots, puts the Talon here at Oahu at 1200 Z. Given that they come in low level the last fifty miles or so to get under radar."

Boomer nodded. Exactly the time for the drop on the message.

"You weren't able to find out anything about where the four Talons of the 1st SOS are?" Boomer asked, referring to the 1st Special Operations Squadron which was stationed at Kadena in Japan.

''No, sir. That stuff is tightly classified and my buddy doesn't owe me time in Leavenworth.'' Vasquez continued with what she had. ''My figuring, though, has the same thing for the return of the mission aircraft. The second top off at 1530 Z gets the Talon on its way back to Kadena or wherever. I think it's coming out of Japan or Okie because the refuel makes sense at that point. It's just about 3,000 miles from those islands, which is the safe operational range of the Talon. Then they got a thousand miles in to here, a thousand back, another top off, and the 3,000 miles back to home base.''

''Son of a bitch,'' Boomer muttered looking at the map, impressed with Vasquez's interpolations.

''She's good, ain't she?'' Skibicki said proudly.

Boomer looked at his watch. ''That means they're in the air now. Hell, they'll be refueling in three hours.'' He looked around at all the people in uniform drinking beers and laughing together. He was only three days removed from lying in ambush above a road in the Ukraine. He felt the hard plastic edge of Stubbs' ID card pressing into flesh through his thigh pocket. ''We're going to have to check out the jump. Get an idea of what they're up to.''

''Already thought of that,'' Skibicki said. ''I drew some gear out of the tunnel for us to use. We'll get to that in a little bit.'' He turned back to Vasquez. ''You find out anything else?''

Vasquez pocketed her papers and map. ''Not really.''

''Not really?'' Skibicki repeated. ''What the fuck does that mean?''

Vasquez shrugged, used to the sergeant major's gruff manner. ''You told me to check for anything weird going on around the island, sergeant major. There's some weird shit going on with SOSUS and the imaging people over at Pearl.'' She paused. ''If I knew what was going on with you two, I might know what's important and what's not,'' she added.

''SOSUS?'' Boomer asked. ''What's that?''

Vasquez enjoyed showing off. ''The sound surveillance system the Navy uses to track submarines. The first SOSUS systems were put together in the fifties and the sixties and laid along the Atlantic Coast. Then they put in Colossus, which is along the Pacific Coast. Then the Navy boys got real smart. They moved it out to the Russians to catch their subs as they put to sea. The Navy put systems off the two major Russian sub ports at Polyarnyy and Petropavlovsk.''

"What's that got to do with Hawaii?" Skibicki asked impatiently. "Those are over near Europe."

"Slow down, sergeant major, I was getting to that." Vasquez leaned forward. "The Navy's been adding to SOSUS all along. We got a line not far off the coast of the islands. It's some pretty wild shit. The system consists of groups of hydrophones inside large tanks—and I mean large. My buddy over at Naval Intel says each tank is as big as the oil storage tanks at Pearl. These things are sunk down to the bottom. They're all connected by cable and the cable is buried. That's to prevent the Russians from trailing cable cutters off their ships or subs and severing the lines." Vasquez shook her head. "Man, there's real shit going on out there under the waves all the time. It's a whole 'nother world.

"Anyway," she quickly said, noting Skibicki's growing impatience, "what the Navy did not too long ago was really smart. The various systems could pick up subs, but they weren't too exact in pinpointing location. Some whiz brain figured that since the hydrophones are real sensitive that if all the systems could be coordinated, they could get accurate fixes using triangulation from various SOSUS systems."

She pointed down at the map. "Say the one off Hawaii picks up a sub. All they got is one direction and the sub is somewhere along the line. But if the one off the West Coast can pick up the same sub, then you got two directions. Draw a second line and bingo.

"They hooked all the SOSUS systems together using FLTS—that's Fleet Satellite Communication System. The Navy's got five satellites up there in fixed orbits. Well, my buddy is hooked into FLTS and when I discreetly inquired if there was any weird shit going on, he told me they picked up a bogey sub this morning on SOSUS; only it wasn't a bogey, it was a friendly."

"You've lost me," Boomer said, his head still spinning from all her acronyms.

"Well, here's the point," Vasquez said. "Most Navy subs patrol at the discretion of their own skippers within a large designated area, particularly the boomers, the nuke-firers. That way no one can find them and no one can give up the secret of where they are since the only ones who know where they are are on board. But the Navy realized after hooking the SOSUS system together that they had to be able to tell friendly subs from unfriendly. I mean, since our own Navy doesn't know exactly where half its own subs are, and certainly doesn't know where the Russkie subs plan to be, then when SOSUS pinpoints a sub, there has to be a way to know whether it's friendly or enemy."

Vasquez smiled. "After all the friendly-fire hoopla after the Gulf War, the Navy figured it would be bad to sink one of their own subs if we ever fought the big one. So every U.S. and NATO sub has an ID code painted in special laser reflective paint on the upper deck."

"What good does painting a code on the deck do?" snorted Skibicki. "They stay submerged all the time."

Vasquez waved a finger under his nose. "Modern technology, sergeant major. The Navy can read the codes by pinpointing a sub's location using the SOSUS, then using one of the FLTS satellites firing off a laser downlink. They use a high-intensity blue-green laser. It penetrates the ocean to submarine depth and gets reflected by the paint and the satellite picks it up and reads it. It's not useful in finding subs without the SOSUS because the ocean's a damn big place and a sub is pretty small.

"So now every friendly sub has this code. The satellite beams down where SOSUS says there's a sub and they get no reflection, then they know they have a bad-guy sub.

"Well, the computer dinks at Pearl had them an underwater vehicle on their SOSUS about 400 miles off the coast, southwest. When they checked with FLTS and flashed the laser on it for an ID they got a hit and a friendly prefix, indicating it was one of ours, but the identifier code wasn't in their book."

"Meaning?" Boomer asked.

"Meaning that there's a friendly sub off the coast, but it's not one of the subs the Navy, or any of our allies, say they got." Vasquez shrugged. "So, I'd call that kind of strange. My buddy says when he talked to his watch commander about it, he was told in no uncertain terms to forget about it.''

Boomer glanced at Skibicki. "What do you think?"

Skibicki looked like he had a bad headache. "I think we can't do diddly squat about a sub 400 miles off-coast and I don't have the slightest clue what it might have to do with all that's going on. But we can go eyeball a parachute drop a mile off." He tapped Vasquez on the shoulder. "Good job on the KC-10 stuff."

CHAPTER ☆ 11

Trace felt like she was the only one in the terminal other than the people cleaning the floor. She'd landed two hours ago and she had two and a half hours to go before continuing on the last leg of her journey. The runways outside the large windows were lit and there was activity as an occasional plane made its entrance or departure, from what she could see, mostly UPS and Federal Express cargo planes, but it was only a tenth of the traffic daylight would bring.

Trace had slept on the flight in from Honolulu and she felt marginally refreshed. The departure from the island had been unusual. She felt that she and Boomer were entering new territory. He'd always seemed to be there in her life at important, turbulent junctures, but then he was gone when the sailing was smooth. She didn't think it was deliberate, but she wondered how it would be if they could spend time together when circumstances were a bit more normal.

She remembered the second time she'd run into him at West Point. It was two months after their first meeting on the ramp leading to New South Barracks. The first weeks of the academic year had passed in a tension-filled blur. As one of five female plebes assigned to I-1, Trace and her gender comrades had indeed been shit magnets as Boomer had predicted. She'd drawn duty as head mail carrier during

Reorganization Week, the first week of the academic year.
It was the harshest job a plebe could be assigned.

Contrary to the federal law not allowing a third party to
control mail, an interesting attitude for a school funded with
federal dollars, cadet mail was delivered by the plebes of
each company. The Cadet in Charge of Quarters (CQ) went
to the cadet mail room and picked up the mail for all the
cadets in the company. Bringing it back, he dumped it in
the orderly room and waited for the head mail carrier to
come back from class at 11:30 A.M.

That first week Trace quickly learned one of West
Point's unwritten axioms: cooperate and graduate. She'd
walked into the barracks, squaring corners and walking
along the inside wall as required, to be handed the heavy
bag of mail accumulated from a summer of misroutes and
girlfriends already missing their boys.

She'd staggered to her room with the precious cargo and
dumped it open on her bed. She'd been given a listing of
all room assignments by the company first sergeant when
he'd briefed her. She began sorting, trying to get it organized as her two roommates scuttled about the company area,
grabbing their classmates and corralling them into the room
to help deliver. It all had to be dispensed prior to lunch
formation and the clock began ticking almost immediately
as the plebe minute caller outside her room sounded off:
"Sir, there are ten minutes until lunch formation. The uniform is as for class. For lunch we are having hot dogs,
french fries, iced tea, and Martha Washington sheet cake.
Ten minutes, sir!"

Trace tried to ignore the echoing screams of upperclassmen hazing the minute callers for real or imagined mistakes
as she thrust mail into her frightened classmates' hands and
told them which room to deliver it to. The fact that they
weren't supposed to be "gazing about" as they moved out
at 120 steps per minute in the hallway made looking for
room numbers a perilous proposition. God help the plebe
who entered the wrong room or got caught looking around
to make sure it was the right room.

Trace wasn't quite sure how she survived that first week.
Those fifteen minutes each day before lunch twisted her gut
and kept her awake at night with worry. She spent her eve-

nings reporting around to upperclassmen rooms to explain every single screw-up in delivery. She also learned a lot about her classmates as she noted who was willing to put their neck on the line to help her in her duties and those who covered their own ass and made it out to formation ahead of the ten-minute bell in order to try and beat the "plebe chasers," second-year cadets assigned to harass plebes not making it into formation on time.

It was a "damned if you do, damned if you don't" scenario. And it was designed to be that way, Trace later realized once she was on the other side as an upperclassman. Plebes learned to be amazingly efficient. By the end of the academic year, they could get the mail out in less than two minutes. Also, those classmates who were dicks, heading out to formation trying to escape the hassle of getting hazed delivering mail, were hazed for not helping their classmates out.

Cooperate and graduate was the rule, forged in the flames of verbal and mental abuse. It was such a strong rule, that in many cases the honor code stood a distant second as the occasional cheating scandals that rocked the Academy showed. It was the one thing the Academy didn't display to the outside world whenever a newspaper came around and wanted to know why so many cadets would get implicated in a scandal. And despite the scandals, the loyalty classmates showed each other had the potential to be a valuable trait, or it could be abused.

Trace had survived that first week and the following ones, but there was no doubt that as a woman she was at a disadvantage. The secret to survival as a plebe was to become invisible, an impossibility for five women among thirty-four plebes in the company. And to make it worse, the senior class—called firsties—of 1979, was the last class to graduate West Point all-male and they had a particular hatred for the female gender. There were two women in I-1 from the class of '80, the first year group of women, but they hung low, having already endured an inhuman amount of abuse, simply biding their time for graduation. They didn't offer any special solace to their younger comrades, feeling that acceptance among peers was more important than acceptance by gender.

It was during a situation involving a firstie and one of the females from the class of '80, that she ran into Boomer for a second time. It was a Tuesday evening in October and they were attending a lecture in the auditorium at Eisenhower Hall by the Army Chief of Staff, a former superintendant of the Academy.

Seated by company, Trace found herself in the uncomfortable position of being between the company first sergeant, Cadet Frankel, a man with a reputation as a "flame," and her platoon sergeant, Cadet Jean Woods.

"Neck back, beanhead!" was Frankel's first words to her as they settled into the seats in Eisenhower auditorium. "I want you back a fist distance away from the rear of the chair."

The order wasn't correct, since there was no requirement for plebes to sit braced at the lecture, but such reasoning was academic due to the reality of Frankel's position as first sergeant. Trace figured an hour of sitting braced beat a week of hazing so she pressed her chin back, until she could feel the skin fold in on itself. She was disappointed that Woods didn't say anything, but she also understood Woods' position. Trace scooted forward in her seat the required distance, the same posture she had to adopt in the mess hall for every meal.

Frankel leaned over. "Do you know what my class's motto is, smack?"

"Yes, sir."

"Well?" Frankel waited.

"Top of the line, 'seventy-nine, sir." Trace said, sensing Woods' uncomfortable shifting to her right.

"Yeah, that's the official one," Frankel said, "but do you know what every member of my class is putting on the inside of our rings?"

"No, sir."

He pulled off his ring and waved it in front of her nose. "LCWB," Frankel said. "Know what that stands for?"

Woods turned the other way, and Trace gave the only answer she was allowed. "No, sir."

"Officially it stands for Loyalty, Courage, Wisdom, and Bravery," Frankel said. "But in reality it stands for Last Class With Balls."

"Hey, Frankel, that's enough," Woods protested.

"I don't want any shit from you, you—" Frankel's retort was interrupted by a familiar, deep voice cutting in behind her, as the next company took its seats.

"Hey, smackhead, chill out."

Trace didn't move, aware of the attention of Frankel, and also aware that Boomer was just a yearling, well below Frankel in the chain of command.

"I said relax, chill out, sit back, take it easy," Boomer said with a laugh, leaning forward from his place behind her.

"Who the hell do you think you are?" Frankel snapped, twisting in his seat. "This is *my* company, yearling, so butt out."

Boomer laughed. "Hey, hero, you want the Army Chief of Staff to see a plebe sitting here in the fourth row braced? How come none of the other beanheads in your company are braced? You wanna be stupid, be my guest."

"Watch it, Watson," Frankel growled.

"Hey, Frankel, I know you're an asshole, you know you're an asshole, but do you have to show the whole world that you're an asshole?" Boomer replied.

"That's it, Watson! I'm writing you up for insubordination!" Frankel cried out, reaching into his pocket and producing a pen and paper.

"Fine," Boomer replied hotly. "And write yourself up for hazing at the Chief of Staff's address while you're at it."

Trace was surprised when Woods interceded again. "He's right, Frankel. She shouldn't be braced here."

Frankel's face turned several shades of red as he tried to control his temper. "All right, Trace. At ease." He turned to Boomer. "But I'm going to have your ass, Watson."

Trace later found out from talking to Boomer that Frankel had been Boomer's second detail Beast Squad Leader and Boomer detested him. The incident in Eisenhower Hall had cost Boomer four hours walking the area for insubordination, but Boomer said it was worth it.

Trace also remembered the content of the Chief of Staff's speech. The speech had been about the Academy's role and if Trace had not been so concerned about surviving the hell flying on around her, she might have paid more attention at the time. The most interesting thing about the speech was that it clearly laid out where the Academy was heading, yet the cadets were so young and simply wanted to survive that they really didn't give a damn what they were being changed into.

Trace had looked the speech up a few weeks ago as part of her research for her manuscript. A transcript had been printed in the *Assembly,* the publication of the West Point Association of Graduates (AOG). Reading it had chilled her.

With over 4,000 cadets in attendance, the Army Chief of Staff had talked about the Academy from a perspective the cadets had only begun to glimpse.

"West Point has been in existence for 176 years. In that time we have graduated over 36,000 men. From the war of 1812 through the recent conflict in Southeast Asia, we have provided the moral spirit for our country's Army. Never has this spirit been more important than in today's society.

"Just down the river in New York City—less than fifty miles from here—you can see a vision of the depths our society has sunk to. Drugs are rampant on the street. Crime is at an all-time high.

"Even further down the East Coast, in our nation's capital in Washington, our leaders are caught in a malaise of inaction. But is that so surprising? One can not act unless one has the moral base to act from. That is what you are being exposed to in your four-year journey through the Academy. It is a journey that, upon graduation, will lead you through the wilderness of modern society with the moral tenets of discipline, loyalty, and honor to carry you when times seem bleak.

"It is our duty to give back to our country that which West Point teaches us. In a world that sorely lacks those moral tenets, it is our responsibility to stand up to the rest of the country as a guiding light, a way out of the troubled forest of moral decay.

"Duty, honor, country," the Chief of Staff intoned the Academy motto, evoking in all the cadets present the speech by Douglas MacArthur in front of the Corps in 1962 that every cadet had to memorize as plebes. "Never has our country needed our sense of duty and honor more.

"In the upcoming years, as you spread out around the world to serve in the active Army, I call upon each of you to remember your duty to your country. I call upon you to pursue a more active role in our society—even beyond that demanded by your role as officers. That is no longer sufficient, as the recent debacle in Southeast Asia clearly shows. Men who walked the long gray line before you served honorably there, but they were let down by a lack of moral fiber in our very society. We cannot keep our heads in the sand and simply look outward for our enemies. We must also search within the borders of our country and fight them in the way the Academy has taught you: with perseverance and courage in what you have been taught here!"

Trace remembered that the Corps had given the Chief of Staff a standing ovation, more for not taking up the full hour allocated, allowing them to get back to the barracks earlier for study or rack time, than for the content. But if one considered the existence of The Line, Trace began to understand how such speeches were allowed at an institution funded by the very society it so often lambasted. She had done some research and learned that the Chief of Staff's comments were by no means isolated. West Point existed in a timeless vacuum that only occasionally noted the changes of the outside world, and then only to contemplate what effect West Point could have on the outside world, rather than the more natural opposite.

As the airport slowly came alive, Trace wondered what experience, if any, Colonel Rison had had with The Line, and what a man who had been relieved of his command in a combat zone would have to say about West Point and The Line. She had a feeling it would be very different from the Chief of Staff's speech.

CHAPTER ☆ 12

KEAWAULA, OAHU, HAWAIIAN ISLANDS
1 DECEMBER
11:45 P.M. LOCAL/ 0945 ZULU, 2 DEC

Boomer slid the magazine on top of the housing and chambered a round. He and Skibicki were at the end of the paved road that wound its way up the west coast of Oahu. A sign indicated that the rest of the way was off limits to vehicles. And, as if to reinforce the message on the sign, the road turned into a potholed dirt trail.

"Switch for the laser sight is here," Skibicki added, tapping the side of the gun. He handed Boomer his night vision goggles. "Ready to go for a walk?"

"How far is it?" Boomer asked, shouldering the weapon and stepping out with Skibicki onto the dirt road.

"About three and a half klicks. We should make it in plenty of time." Skibicki pointed landward, toward the steep slopes that towered up. "See those lights up there?"

"Yeah."

"That's the Kaena Point satellite tracking station. All that land on the high ground is military reservation." He pointed down. "Maps show this road going around the point and continuing on the north side, but as you can see, you can't drive it. It's washed out at some points. Hardly anyone ever comes up here other than some fishermen during the daytime. Coast Guard's got a lighthouse on the point itself but it's unmanned."

Boomer remembered that detail from the DZ message. "Sounds like they picked the one place off-shore of Oahu where you could do a water drop and not have civilians on the beach," he continued.

"Roger that," Skibicki said.

Boomer felt the warm night breeze, and reflected how different the coastal breeze was than the bitter arctic air he'd felt in the Ukraine. He wasn't quite sure what to expect this evening. His hope was that they would at least confirm that it was a jump and maybe find where the jumpers came ashore and camped out. It was still five days before Pearl Harbor Day, and Boomer hoped that Trace would come up with something concrete so that the information he discovered tonight could be given to the proper authorities whoever they were.

AIRSPACE 200 MILES WEST OAHU
2 December
1:00 A.M. LOCAL/ 1100 ZULU

The interior of the Combat Talon was illuminated by red light so that everyone inside could maintain their night vision. The airframe was a modified C-130 Hercules transport, an aircraft that had served as the workhorse of the Air Force for four decades and was still going strong. The interior was large enough to hold five cars end to end, but the front half of the Talon cargo bay was blocked off by thick, black curtains, separating the flight crew from the jumpers in the back.

The Air Force men in the forward portion of the cargo body were button-pushers and screen-watchers. It was their job to defeat electronic threats to the aircraft, allowing it to perform its stated mission of penetrating deep inside enemy airspace without being detected. This mission was considered a milk run by both the screen-watchers and the pilots up front. There were no mountain valleys to be negotiated at low level, where they could look up and see trees and the slopes above them; no electronic threat from enemy anti-aircraft systems to be thwarted; no special navigating problems as—unlike electronic silent missions—they were linked into the Navy's FLTSatcom network and their computers could locate their position on the move to within five meters every one one-thousandth of a second. The in-flight refueling had been the most exciting event and it had gone off without a hitch.

As loadmaster, Master Technical Sergeant Johnson was the man who worked both sides of the curtain. He was a member of the aircrew, but his job was to ensure that whatever cargo or personnel was loaded into the rear half of the Talon got to its departure point intact. For him, this was no milk run. He had fourteen personnel packed into the cargo bay along with two Zodiac rubber boats and other gear. The men's parachutes and rucksacks were strapped down on the back ramp and they had mostly slept for the ten hours they'd been in the air.

"We've got a TOT of sixty minutes," the pilot's voice sounded in the portable headset Johnson wore.

"Roger that, sir. I'll wake up our sleeping beauties." Johnson walked over and tapped the man who had identified himself as the leader of these men when they'd onloaded.

The men wore no insignia or rank or organization patch—just black wet suits—and they had not identified themselves or their organization when they'd boarded the aircraft in Okinawa. Johnson didn't find that surprising. The Talon often flew missions for hard-eyed men with no indication of who they were or what their mission was. Johnson's job was to get them out of the plane intact at the right place and time, not to ask questions. In fact, he knew if he asked questions, he'd be looking for a new job as soon as they landed, if he was not locked in the brig.

"One hour out," Johnson yelled over the roar of the engines.

The man cracked an eye and nodded, immediately nudging the man next to him, passing the signal down. Johnson was always impressed that men who were about to jump out of a perfectly good airplane could sleep so easily.

Johnson went to the back ramp and began unfastening the cargo straps holding down the parachutes. The men in the wet suits paired off into buddy teams and began rigging their parachutes. The dimly lit interior didn't affect the men's efficiency. Johnson had seen in-flight rigs on routes through rough terrain where the constant jerking of the aircraft had thrown the men around like rag dolls, and the floor of the plane had been coated with slippery vomit from airsickness. He was glad for the smooth and level flight two hundred feet above the wavetops.

It took the men twenty minutes to put their chutes on, hook their rucksacks up underneath their reserve chutes in front, rig their weapons, and stuff their swim fins underneath the waistband of their parachutes and secure them with a safety line. Then they sat back down and started their wait. Johnson could feel the change in atmosphere inside the aircraft. The adrenaline was beginning to flow.

KAENA POINT
2 December
1:30 A.M. LOCAL/ 1130 ZULU

"Should be due north of us," Skibicki said. "Track will be from left to right."

Boomer twisted the focus on his night vision goggles and surveyed the ocean. The cresting waves were glittering green lines with sparks flying off as the spray pounded the rocks. The ocean beyond was a greenish-black slate out to the horizon where stars glittered brightly in the computer enhanced image.

He and Skibicki were hidden in the sand dunes of Kaena Point on its north side. The small Coast Guard lighthouse was to their right rear and unmanned as Skibicki had said. Five hundred meters inland, the ground swooped up precipitously to Puu Pueo, the beginning of the mountain chain that was the backbone of the west side of Oahu.

"Do you think they'll come ashore here?" Boomer asked.

"I wouldn't," Skibicki replied. He pointed with the muzzle of his Calico. "The shore here is rocky, and as you can see the waves aren't very gentle. They'd get pounded pretty bad trying to swim in here. If those two bundles they're jumping are boats, I think they'll go one of two ways: east and try to beach somewhere opposite Dillingham Air Force Base, which is an old abandoned airfield on the inland side of the Farrington Highway that runs along the coast there. The only problem with going that way is that the mountains are very steep and if they are trying to go inland, they got one hell of a climb.

''The other possibility is that they go south,'' Skibicki continued, pointing to their left, and then to their rear, where the coast came in. ''Lots of beach they can land on. Also, that's the best way to eventually get to Pearl. Hug the west coast all the way around, then along the south, and into the harbor. They could take a couple of nights to make the move and do it without getting spotted if they're very careful. Going around clockwise to the east they'd eventually have to round Diamond Head and pass Wai-kiki—not exactly the most secure way.''

''The message said the RP for the jumpers would be marked by IR strobe,'' Boomer noted. ''I don't see anything out there.''

''Normally the strobe would actually be at the RP,'' Skibicki said. ''However, in this case, they might track the aircraft from land and flash an IR strobe when the aircraft is at the RP. I got the impression that the IR was just a safe signal that the jump could proceed. Hell, those damn Talons got such good navigating equipment that they'll release those jumpers within ten feet of the planned RP.'' Skibicki pointed at the mountains. ''If I was running this drop, I'd be up there somewhere, almost on level with the aircraft.''

Boomer glanced down at the glowing face of his watch. ''We'll find out in twenty minutes.''

Four hundred meters to their right rear, on the other side of the lighthouse, two figures carrying rifles moved silently through the darkness, the snout of their night vision goggles centered on the lighthouse, beyond which Boomer and Ski-bicki lay.

FINAL CHECKPOINT
2 December
1:40 A.M. LOCAL/ 1140 ZULU

''Charlie Papa Fourteen at my mark,'' the navigator said. ''Five, four, three, two, one. Mark.'' He checked the numbers on his screen. ''We're two seconds ahead of schedule,'' he announced.

''Roger,'' the pilot said. ''What about electronics?''

His answer came from the countermeasures officer in the front half of the cargo bay. "I'm getting atmosphere bounces off the radar from the International Airport but we could go up another six hundred feet and they wouldn't have a clue we were here. No sign of ships or other aircraft."

"All right," the pilot said. "Johnson, we're twenty minutes out."

In the rear of the plane Master Technical Sergeant Johnson relayed the time until drop to the jumpmaster, who turned to the other men seated on the web seats and extended both hands, fingers spread wide. "Twenty minutes!" he screamed, repeating the gesture twice to give them the visual count.

The jumpmaster then turned to the two rubber Zodiacs and checked the cargo chutes rigged on each, hooking their static lines to the steel cable—one of which ran the entire length of the cargo bay on each side, ending far in the tail well. At loading, Johnson and his assistant loadmaster had placed the Zodiacs in position, one on each side, nose facing the rear. Each boat rested on a metal pallet, and the attaching points for the cargo chutes were on each corner of the pallet.

The boat was attached to the pallet with cargo webbing, all centered on one quick release inside each boat so that once in the water, the pallet would release and sink, leaving the boat floating on the surface. The forty horsepower engine for each boat was tied down inside. The pallets were held to the inside of the aircraft with one length of cargo webbing attached to the back of each pallet, tied to an O-ring on the floor of the aircraft.

"Ten minutes," the pilot's voice announced in Johnson's headphones. He gave the information to the jumpmaster who again relayed it to the jumpers.

"Break the chem lights," the jumpmaster instructed Johnson. He obliged by cracking the two chem light sticks taped to each Zodiac—one on the prow, one on the stern.

"Six minutes." This time the routine changed. The jumpmaster stood and hooked his own static line hook to the right cable, just behind the hook for the right boat. He then turned to the men. "Six minutes!" he called out extending five fingers on one hand and one on the other.

"Outboard personnel stand up!" he yelled, pointed to both sides of the aircraft, then gesturing up with his palms. Six men on his side of the aircraft and seven on the other stood, holding onto the side of the aircraft for support.

"Hook up!"

Each man unhooked his static line snaphook from where the jumpmaster had placed it on the carrying handle of the reserve parachute over his belly and attached it to the steel cable, open end facing out. The jumper then slid a slender metal safety through a small hole in the hook, insuring that the snaphook could not reopen.

The jumpmaster curled his fingers, thumb to forefinger, and moved them back and forth. "Check static lines!"

Each jumper rechecked his hookup to the cable, then traced the yellow web of the static line as far as he could until it disappeared over his shoulder, making sure that it was clear and free. He then checked the man's in front from where it appeared over his shoulder to where it disappeared into the pack closing tie of the parachute itself. The last man on each stick turned to face the front of the aircraft and had the next-to-last man check his. An improperly routed static line could cause the jumper great difficulties after exiting the aircraft and lead to him being hung up and battered against the aircraft.

Johnson felt his weight thrust slightly forward—he knew that was the aircraft slowing down from almost 300 miles an hour, to jump speed of 125 knots, and that the plane was three minutes out from the drop zone. Johnson took the strap for the monkey harness he wore and hooked it into a O-bolt on the side of the floor of the aircraft just short of the hinge where the ramp began. He played out enough slack so that he could make his way the end of the ramp and then cinched it tight so he couldn't fall out once the ramp opened.

"Check equipment!" The jumpmaster waved his arms, palms toward his chest. Each man started from his head and worked down, making one last check on their gear, a few semi-squatting as much as the gear would allow to make sure that one of their legs straps was not routed over a testicle.

The noise level on the inside increased abruptly as the ramp began to open. A thin horizontal crack appeared, rapidly growing wider as the top portion of the ramp disappeared into the cavity that housed the large tail of the aircraft and the lower ramp began leveling out.

"Sound off for equipment check!"

The last man in each stick slapped the man in front on the rear, yelling "OK," and the message was passed up until the front man in each stick looked the jumpmaster in the eye and reported "All OK, jumpmaster!"

The jumpmaster immediately turned toward the open ramp and gingerly made his way around the side of the right Zodiac. He held onto the hydraulic arm that had lowered the ramp and stuck his head out into the slipstream, peering ahead to try and make out the island of Oahu which should be approaching on the side of the aircraft. Satisfied, he came back in and took his place at the front of his stick.

"One minute," the pilot radioed to Johnson. "You got the secure signal?" he asked the co-pilot, who was wearing night vision goggles. The co-pilot leaned forward and peered down to the right, where Kaena Point protruded into the ocean. He spotted a flash of light from the IR strobe in the sand dunes near the lighthouse. "Roger. We're good to go." The pilot relayed the information to the loadmaster.

Johnson grabbed the jumpmaster's shoulder and gave him both the time warning and strobe information, then wedged himself in between the bundle and the skin of the aircraft.

"One minute!" the jumpmaster gave his last time warning. The eyes of all the jumpers were wide now, the adrenaline flowing freely. The red light high up above the ramp glowed brightly.

Johnson felt his knees buckle and knew that meant they were thirty seconds out and the pilot was bringing them up from 200 feet above the waves to jump altitude at 500 feet.

"Stand by!" the jumpmaster called out, edging forward until he was as close as he could be to the Zodiac. Johnson drew his knife from its sheath, making sure that his assistant loadmaster on the other side of the plane had his out and was watching him. He then focused on the red light.

"Go!" the pilot yelled in the headset at the same moment the light turned green. The razor-sharp edge on John-son's knife went cleanly through the webbing holding the Zodiac's pallet. The pallet slid off, the chute deploying almost immediately and the chem lights disappearing into the darkness below. The jumpmaster was right behind it, waddling off the edge of the ramp and disappearing from sight, the only reminder of his presence the deployment bag fluttering the air behind the aircraft, still held by the static line. The other six jumpers in the right stick followed, less than half a second between each man.

As the last man in the right stick cleared the ramp, John-son chopped his arm down, indicating for the other load-master to cut his boat free. The other stick was gone in less than four seconds. Johnson stood and walked to the edge of the ramp, feeling the tug of the safety harness pulling him back. A row of chutes were deployed behind the path of the Talon, the first jumpers already in the water. Johnson turned back and activated the static line retrieval system. A large bolt on each of the static line cables slowly pulled the deployment bags back in. Once they were clear of the ramp, Johnson informed the pilot, and they closed the ramp and dropped back down to 200 feet, pulling a hard left turn at the same time to head for home.

KAENA POINT, OAHU, HAWAIIAN ISLANDS
2 December
2:00 A.M. LOCAL/ 1200 ZULU

"I counted fourteen jumpers and two Zodiacs on pal-lets," Boomer said, the sound of the MC-130 Talon fading into the noise of the surf. The darkened aircraft turned left and disappeared, but not before Skibicki and Boomer had had a chance to positively identify it—there was no mis-taking the "whiskers" on the nose for the Fulton aerial recovery system unique to that aircraft.

"Same here," Boomer edged up on the sand dune until he was kneeling on top in order to be able to see out into the ocean. He caught sight of one of the Zodiacs as it rode a wave then it disappeared again. The chem lights made it easy to pinpoint the boats. Each chem light, almost invisible to the naked eye at this distance, showed up like a spotlight in the night vision goggles. Boomer knew the men out there weren't happy about having to use the lights, but it was a better alternative to splashing around in the water and not being able to find the boats. As the waves moved he could make out figures moving over the sides of the boats—the jumpers climbing on board. Boomer knew the routine well; he'd done it himself numerous times.

The first man in would check for gas—at night by smell—to make sure the fuel bladder hadn't ruptured. As soon as the second man was aboard, they would free the engine from its place on the floorboards and mount it with the engine's clamps on the rear center of the transom. They would also secure it with a retention cable that was anchored on one side of the boat, so they wouldn't lose the engine in case the boat capsized. It was secured to only one side so they would be able to right the boat from the water.

"Hear it?" Skibicki asked.

"Yeah." Boomer caught the cough of the engine starting. The sound of its running was lost in the surf and distance. He knew the two boats were holding in place, waiting to collect all their swimmers. Then they would be off, but which way?

Skibicki twisted around and glanced inland. "I didn't see any IR strobe," he noted. "Maybe there wasn't one, or maybe there was another message."

"Could have been down in the dunes," Boomer noted. "They could see it from the cockpit."

"I didn't see any coverage either," Boomer said.

"They could be out there blacked out," Skibicki said.

The lights on one of the boats suddenly went out. All were aboard. Boomer focused his attention on that spot, maintaining its location through his goggles, catching sight of the low-lying silhouette as it crested each swell. He was unaware of the wavering red dot of light that had suddenly appeared in the center of his back. The dot shifted, moving over to Skibicki, at first also centering on the back, then slowly moving up toward his head.

"I think they're turning east," Boomer said, turning to Skibicki. He threw himself forward and grabbed the sergeant major, the two of them toppling down the beach side of the sand dune as a shot rang out.

Boomer flipped off the safety on the Calico. "He's got laser sights. Somewhere up near the lighthouse. Must be security for the jump and our IR strobe man." He was calculating rapidly, assessing the situation. "We need to break left."

"No," Skibicki said. "We got to get back to my jeep. We got to go right." He jerked a thumb over his shoulder. "The rocks are slippery, but if we get down in them, we can circle around."

Boomer accepted that this was Skibicki's terrain and that the older man had more combat experience. Skibicki moved out, crouching low, keeping the sand dune between them and the lighthouse.

Boomer was glad he was wearing running shoes as they started moving across algae-covered rock. His sneakers were soon soaked, but he maintained a degree of traction. He kept the Calico ready for use in his right hand, using his left hand to steady himself. He felt exposed, knowing that someone with a night vision scope and laser sight was out there in the dark, waiting and watching and that the bullet would hit before he even heard the crack of the rifle.

The roar of the waves crashing onto the rocks thundered in his ears. Boomer kept his neck craned inland, watching the nearest dunes. He crabbed sideways behind Skibicki as they made their way around the tip of the point and started moving down the southwestern shore.

As Boomer hopped from one large rock to another, he slipped, falling into a large tidal pool. He kept his face up, desperate to keep the goggles from getting soaked and shorting out. He stood up in waist-deep water, and gained his footing, only to be knocked over as the next wave rushed in, and then sucked back out, dragging him with it. He slammed the edge of the telescoping stock of the Calico between two rocks and grabbed hold with both hands to keep from being pulled out into the ocean.

Skibicki clambered up onto a tall rock to Boomer's right and held out his left hand, holding on precariously with his right, his weapon hanging free on its sling. "Come on!"

Boomer reached, but there was a two foot gap between their extended fingers. He was inundated up to his neck as the next wave roared in. With a hiss, the water poured out, pulling him down to his knees. In the pause before the next wave came in, he unhooked the Calico and slapped the barrel into Skibicki's hand. With the sergeant major giving a hard tug, Boomer got to his feet and climbed up onto the rock, escaping the wall of water that cascaded in.

Boomer was soaked to the skin but the goggles still functioned. Skibicki moved inland about ten meters to avoid a repetition of the experience. They continued for twenty minutes, then Skibicki halted. "The road's right ahead."

Boomer remembered that when they had come up the road, it had cut close in to the west shore, leaving no space for them to maneuver between the ocean and the steep cliffs.

They sat still for ten minutes, searching the darkness with their goggles, waiting for any sign that the unseen sniper was aware of this chokepoint. The thunder of the surf continued unabated and there was no movement in the dunes to the left, where the sniper would have a clear field of fire up the road.

"I'll go first," Skibicki said. "Cover me until I get about twenty-five meters down the road. Then I'll return the favor."

Boomer scooted up to the edge of the road on his stomach, then snuggled the butt of the Calico into his shoulder. The red dot from his laser sight showed clearly in his goggles, allowing him to easily aim it. He picked the center of mass of the largest dune. "Go."

Skibicki leapt to his feet and sprinted onto the dirt road, immediately turning right. Boomer caught the flash of the rifle firing, a hair before the sound of the rounds going off reached him. He fired on automatic, directly at the muzzle flash of the sniper. The Calico worked just as Skibicki had promised, the muzzle staying smooth and level, the empty brass flowing out of the bottom ejection port.

Boomer was rewarded with the muzzle flash of the sniper's weapon abruptly going up, then silence.

"Skibicki!" he yelled.

"I'm all right," the sergeant major called back from his prone position on the far side of the road, where he was nudged up against the cliff face. "Son of a bitch missed me."

"Think there's more than one?" Boomer asked, sweeping the muzzle of his weapon along the dune. "I got the one that shot at you."

"I don't want to wait around and find out," Skibicki replied. "I'll cover you. Move!"

Boomer didn't need to be told twice. He got to his feet and ran, feeling the skin on his back contract and his shoulder hunch in anticipation of a bullet slamming into him. He was almost abreast of Skibicki when he heard the sound of firing to his rear. He dove right, rolling off the edge of the road and slamming into the wet rocks, feeling the jagged edge of one leave its painful imprint on his right side.

Skibicki returned fire with a long stutter of rounds from his silenced weapon. "You OK?"

Boomer wedged himself between two rocks and sucked in a painful breath. He felt along his side and winced as his fingers touched. "I think I busted a rib."

"If you're breathing you're OK," Skibicki returned. "I hit the second one. Let's book."

"I'll cover," Boomer said as he edged up and peered over the edge of the road.

Skibicki didn't bother answering. He got to his feet and ran down the road, disappearing where it bent inland, the cliffs covering him. "Set!" he yelled.

Boomer jumped to his feet, ignoring the stab of pain that jabbed into his side. He joined the sergeant major and leaned over, trying to draw rapid shallow breaths. "Fuck, that hurts."

"Pain is weakness leaving the body," Skibicki said, peering carefully around the rock face to see if they were being followed. "Let's make like a duck and get the flock out of here."

They started out at a steady jog and Boomer stoically bore the pain. They reached Skibicki's jeep and stowed the weapons under the seats. Boomer leaned back in the passenger seat, bending slightly to the right. Skibicki started the car up and they headed down the highway.

As overhead lamps flashed by, Boomer tenderly opened his shirt. The skin was broken and blood was slowly oozing from a jagged tear in his chest. He felt through the blood and torn skin. "It's cracked," he announced.

"First aid kit's in the back," Skibicki said, checking his rear-view mirror. "Stop the bleeding, and I'll put a wrap on it once we get a chance to slow down."

"What about the cops?" Boomer asked.

Skibicki snorted. "Fuck the cops. We're in deep shit here and I don't think we're on the side with the bigger firepower. If this Line exists, you can bet your ass they're wired in deep at all levels of bureaucracy. We call the cops and tell them we just shot some people out at Kaena Point, and all we're doing is turning on a searchlight and pointing it at ourselves and we've already done that twice. Three times and they'll lock us up."

"Where are you going?" Boomer asked, tearing off a piece of tape to put some gauze over his wound.

"Maggie's," Skibicki replied. "I'll drop you off there. You'll be safe. I've got some checking to do on other things."

"Like what?" Boomer asked.

"Listen," Skibicki said. "Whoever these guys are who just parachuted in, they had security here on the beach and that security damn near wasted our ass. The shit's starting to hit the fan, and I'm going to go around on shit watch. Seeing where it hits. I know people all over this island and I want to find out what they know. Particularly about the President's visit." Skibicki taped his watch. "It's two December. We only got five days to get to the bottom of this."

CHAPTER ☆ 13

As Trace sped north, Secret Service agent Mike Stewart drove across Memorial Bridge to Fort Myer, the military caretaker post for the nation's capital. Bordering Arlington National Cemetery and home to the 3rd Infantry—the Old Guard—Fort Myer also was home for the chairman of the Joint Chiefs of Staff, within short commuting distance of the Pentagon.

Stewart was thirty-three, relatively new to the Secret Service, having joined five years ago after a six-year stint in the Army. He was tall, slightly over six foot and solidly built, projecting the type of physical image the Secret Service wanted surrounding the President. His crew cut was sprinkled with premature gray. Although he enjoyed his job, the constant stress wore through at times.

Stewart rolled into Fort Myer, past the stately brick buildings housing the 3rd Infantry, and pulled up to the small chapel that had served as way station for most of the bodies destined for interment at Arlington. Today, the body in the casket at the front of the chapel was that of Lieutenant General Wayne Faulkner, the fiery commander of the Army's III Corps, who had been best known to the public during operation Desert Storm for leading the 5th Armored Division faster and farther through enemy territory than any armored commander in history.

More newsworthy though, was an event after Desert Storm, and in the second month of the fledgling presidency.

Faulkner had joined the President on a fact-finding mission to Poland and in a snafu typical of the early months of the administration, he'd been rudely bumped off the helicopter flying to a meeting with former Warsaw Pact political and military leaders.

The bump had been bad enough—with CNN broadcasting a fuming General Faulkner in his ribbon-bedecked uniform standing at the airfield, trying to commandeer a ride on a subsequent flight—but the President's press secretary had thrown gasoline onto the fire by getting caught on a mike she thought was dead saying, "We don't need those damn toy soldiers screwing things up any more."

The remark had cost the young woman her job, but it had cost the President more, Stewart knew. The President's already-strained relationship with the military fell to an all-time low, and he'd spent the last two years striving to patch up an unfixable break.

As Stewart drew to a halt outside the chapel, he reflected that the President's presence at Faulkner's funeral later today was a gesture that they all probably could have done without. The unexpected death of the well-liked General had caught everyone by surprise, and with the MRA still a burning issue, the presence of the unpopular President at the funeral was going to leave a bitter taste in everyone's mouth.

The only bright spot was the location. As advance security man for the visit, Stewart liked the fact that everything was going to occur in the closed environment of the military post. The military might not like the present President, but Stewart knew he could count on 100 percent support for security and that all the wackos would be on the outside of the fence surrounding the base, not on the inside.

"How's it going, Mike?" A man wearing a long black raincoat and an Army dress hat greeted him as he stepped out into the chill air. Silver eagles glinted on the man's shoulder, and a subdued MP arm band was on his right shoulder.

"Pretty good, sir." There was no need for Stewart to call Colonel Hines 'sir' but Stewart had spent six years in the Army and old habits were hard to break. He also had learned to grease the skids of politeness every place he went. Other agents doing advance security came into places like gangbusters, making demands and treating the local security folks like minions. Stewart didn't like that approach, especially at places like Fort Myer and with people like Colonel Hines who he had to deal with often. People usually reacted well to a little respect.

Hines's report was the usual for the area. "We're secure. I sent a detail through the cemetery, and it's clean. I've got men posted at all gates, and the route to the gravesite is blocked for 400 meters on either side."

Stewart glanced at his watch. "The President will be coming in by chopper in thirty minutes. I'll give you departure notice." He looked at Hines, sensing the colonel was bothered by something. "Anything wrong?"

Hines shrugged. "Just the general's widow. She's not too happy about the President coming here. In fact, I would say she's kind of pissed."

"Any press on post?" Stewart asked.

"No. I did what you asked and closed it down. One of the Arlington Ladies is with Mrs. Faulkner, and I hope she'll be calm by the time the President gets here."

"Arlington Ladies?" Stewart asked as he checked the frequency on the radio he wore on his belt and slipped the earpiece into his left ear.

"They're volunteers who go to every funeral at the cemetery. They're a great help. Most of them have someone in their family buried here so they can really talk to those who've lost loved ones."

"Has this Arlington Lady been cleared?" Stewart asked, regretting the question as soon as he asked it.

Hines's face clouded with anger. "Mrs. Patterson—the lady assigned to this funeral—has a husband and a son buried here, KIA Korea and Vietnam. I think that's clearance enough."

"Sorry," Stewart said. "That was a stupid question." A voice crackled in his ear. "Chopper's lifting off. They'll be here about ten minutes early, so we need to get this going at nine-fifty."

Hines frowned but uttered no word of protest. "I'll inform Mrs. Faulkner."

Stewart walked across the street to the parade field where the 3rd Infantry practiced their intricate drill and ceremonies. When Stewart had been in the 1st Cavalry Division at Fort Hood, the 3rd Infantry had been regarded as a showboat unit, not worth much in terms of real infantry. He watched carefully as two soldiers set out beanbag lights to mark the landing zone for the President's helicopter.

Beside the fact that this was a military post, Stewart felt comfortable security-wise because this trip was unannounced. The President had only decided the previous evening to attend the funeral and the only ones informed of the decision had been the Secret Service, Colonel Hines at Fort Myer and General Faulkner's aide, who'd informed the family. One of the primary rules of security was that the chances of a random attack on the President were much lower than a planned one. If a visit wasn't announced, the threat indicators were usually very low.

Stewart heard the Marine Corps CH-53 helicopter long before he saw it. "Gull, this is Julius, are we clear?"

Stewart spoke, knowing the acoustic mike built into the plug in his ear would pick up his words and transmit them. "Julius, this is Gull. You are clear to land."

The aircraft came straight in, landing with a slight flair of blades. The staircase on the side was folded out and the lead men for the President's security detail stepped out. The President followed along with several of his key people. Stewart knew more about the Administration than most reporters who covered the White House beat because he was on the inside and more importantly, because Secret Service agents were treated like part of the furniture, with much being said in front of them that would not be said in front of anyone else.

The man right behind the President was someone who Stewart always paid careful attention to, because the President paid careful attention to him. The person the President relied on for political expertise in the vicious and unfamiliar political waters of Washington was the man walking at his right side, inside the inner circle of Secret Service protection. James Jordan was the senior senator from Vermont and the man who had helped guide the President through the minefield of the campaign trail and his first three and a half years in office.

Jordan was every inch the distinguished senator, from his full head of white hair, to his erect carriage and bearing. The sound of his New England accent preaching a new brand of middle class liberalism had become very familiar to all Americans, and there were many who wondered why Jordan had not sought the nomination himself, not knowing that the senior senator was more than content to sit on the less stressful side of the desk in the Oval Office. Jordan had a reputation in Washington for a brilliant mind. Stewart knew he'd saved the President's political bacon more than once with his observations and suggested plans of action.

The party went into the chapel. Stewart waited outside and he was joined by his immediate superior, Special Agent John Rameriz, radio code name Julius, shift commander of the President's personal detail.

Rameriz had a large manila envelope under his arm. He extended it to Stewart as the chapel doors closed and the service began inside.

"Oh Christ," Stewart said. "Where to now? Not Iceland again."

Rameriz smiled. "Ah, Mike, I'm giving you a good deal."

"Yeah, right," Stewart said as he took the envelope. "There's no such thing as a good deal on this detail."

"How does sun, bikinis, and a room on Waikiki sound?" Rameriz asked.

"I may have to take my last statement back," Stewart said as he looked at the orders inside.

"You leave this evening. You do the initial run through with the locals and then I'll join you on the fifth. The threat assessment is in there along with all the names we need the locals to run for us. We've got four Class A's," he said, referring to people who made it to the top of the Secret Service list of persons who had threatened the President in some manner, "who we need picked up."

"No problem," Stewart said, checking the rest of the papers.

Rameriz smiled. "I told you this was a good deal. I've already faxed those names to Hancock who's in place there with the VP's second detail. All you have to do is double-check. Hancock has also initiated security briefings with the locals so you only have to check on that too.

"We got you a room at the Royal Hawaiian. That's where the Boss will be staying and attending a dinner the night of the sixth. We've never done that hotel before so we need you to do an assessment. That's the reason you're going so much earlier. That should leave you plenty of time to catch some time on the beach. Any questions?"

"No, sir."

"Good, then you might as well go and get packed. I'll close out here."

Stewart walked past the Army detail decked out in dress blues standing next to the caisson and horses, ready to take General Faulkner to his final resting place in Arlington.

A figure in an Army-issue raincoat stepped out of the chapel and walked up to Stewart. He recognized the face as the man drew close. Stewart stiffened, almost locking his arms to his side at attention. "Good morning, sir."

"Good morning," General Maxwell replied.

"Terrible loss, sir," Stewart said, uncertain as to why Maxwell had approached him.

Retired General Roy Maxwell was the man that the President's party was touting as his successor. Maxwell had guided the successful intervention into—and the even more successful departure out of—Bosnia as NATO Commander. It had proved to be a bright spot on an otherwise dismal international record for the Administration. Maxwell had retired shortly afterward.

Stewart had been present at the first meeting between Maxwell and the President. He could tell the President had been bothered that the man his party saw as an apt successor was being foisted upon him as an adviser. After several meetings (Stewart noticed) the President came to value the general's keen mind, and he was forced to admit that if someone else was to pick up the reins, it would be the retired general. Maxwell appealed to a broad base of Americans because of his military background, and the party—although in the manner of American politics it was never publicly discussed—appreciated that he was an African-American.

Maxwell was whipcord lean and despite the civilian

clothes he wore under the raincoat, his military life was stamped on his bearing. A product of South Central LA, Maxwell had worked his way to an ROTC scholarship at a local university and followed that with a highly successful thirty-year career in the military. He had surprised many when he retired as he had been the odds-on favorite to become the next chairman of the Joint Chiefs of Staff, but his presence as political journeyman at the President's side went a long way toward explaining that decision.

When Maxwell spoke, his voice was a deep, reassuring bass. Maxwell glanced over at the chapel. "Faulkner was a good soldier. He did his job and he did it well." The general glanced at the envelope in Stewart's hand. "I've been informed that you are departing immediately for Hawaii to prepare security for the President."

"Yes, sir," Stewart replied.

"Uh-huh." Maxwell pulled a pipe out of his pocket. "Going to be a pretty contentious trip."

Stewart remained quiet. If Maxwell wanted to smoke a pipe and talk, that was fine with him. "What do you think of the MRA?" Maxwell asked.

"I don't know, sir."

"You were active duty before you joined the Secret Service, right?"

"Yes, sir."

"Then you must have an opinion," Maxwell said.

"Sir, that's not my job."

Maxwell chuckled. "I have a most difficult time trying to tell the President that the military is not the monolithic, single-minded organism most seem to believe."

"It seems to be unified in its stand against the MRA," Stewart noted. "At least that's the media take," he amended.

Maxwell shook his head. "Every person in uniform can find some part of the MRA he doesn't agree with. The act covers a lot of ground."

"What do you disagree with, sir?" Stewart asked, trying to keep the conversation away from his own opinions. It was part of the Secret Service unofficial code that one always kept one's opinions to oneself.

Maxwell puffed, then let out a smoke ring. "The melding

of the Marine Corps into the Army. That was never even
remotely proposed by any committee affiliated with the military: They got that part from that independent review
panel, all civilian backgrounds by the way. I know that it
would be more cost-effective to integrate the two services,
but there is a factor that is worth a hell of a lot more than
any dollar amount and that is the pride and spirit of the
Corps.''

Stewart felt uncomfortable. He didn't believe that General Maxwell was just making idle conversation, but he
couldn't imagine his purpose.

''What *I* think isn't important either,'' Maxwell continued. ''Now, what the Joint Chiefs thinks is. Nobody likes
to lose their job. The MRA totally restructures the JCS and
cuts a lot of the fat. Also, they don't want to lose the academies.''

Stewart was surprised at that succinct assessment and
glanced at the general. ''Out of all that, you're saying
they're worried about the academies as their number two
priority, sir?''

Maxwell looked at him. ''The chairman and three of the
four service chiefs are graduates.''

''But even so,'' Stewart said, ''that's relatively minor in
the overall scheme of the MRA.''

''Not to them it isn't,'' Maxwell said. ''I said earlier that
the military is not monolithic, but the graduates of the academies are another story. They've exerted influence in the
military well beyond what should reasonably be expected.
You're asking the Joint Chiefs to kill their own offspring.''
Maxwell took off his steel-rimmed glasses and rubbed his
forehead. ''You're a graduate of the Academy, aren't
you?''

''Yes, sir.''

''You don't seem too concerned. You just said that doing
away with the academies was a minor point.''

Stewart shifted his feet uncomfortably. ''I was a turn-
back, sir.''

Maxwell put his glasses back on. ''A what?''

''I had to go through my plebe year twice. It took me
five years to graduate.''

''No love lost then for West Point, eh?''

"Not really, sir."

"Then you won't mind my saying that I believe the academies, as they are, may have outlived their usefulness. They either need extensive revision, which the JCS and the academies themselves have vigorously resisted for decades, or they need to be abolished." Maxwell abruptly changed the subject. "You know the President is making a major policy speech about the MRA at Pearl Harbor?"

"Yes, sir."

"He scraped the MRA through Congress," Maxwell said. "Of course, with what just happened in the Ukraine and Turkey, he's catching quite a bit of flack." Maxwell sighed. "There are some shortsighted people around. We're pumping millions into the Ukraine, but the Pentagon's solution is to pour billions into Hard Glass, a system most objective researchers say won't work. Even the contractors admit they can't guarantee a hundred percent protection. We can't guarantee a hundred percent solution in the Ukraine either, but it should prove cheaper doing it the political way. And it does have a higher probability of success.

"Of course, we've got to consider the jobs that are affected by Hard Glass. Those billions aren't going into a vacuum, they're going into our economy. Those millions into the Ukraine are going into a black hole as far as the people in Congress are concerned. Ukrainians don't vote and they don't contribute to PACs."

Stewart had been in Washington long enough to have heard it all before. Every clear-cut issue dissolved into a morass of special interests, many of which had little direct bearing on the issue itself. Sometimes Stewart wondered how the republic had worked so well for so long.

"I'll be going to Hawaii with the President," Maxwell said.

"Yes, sir."

Maxwell's back was ramrod straight and his eyes were now on the rows and rows of white grave markers. "I served in Vietnam. I fought the war my country ordered me to fight to the best of my ability and tried to bring home in one piece the men who served under me. Those men who died at Pearl Harbor fifty-four years ago did what they were ordered to do. I have always followed legal orders. I ordered men on missions in Bosnia where they died; those orders came from the President. That's the way it works." Maxwell tapped out his pipe on the palm of his hand. "Do me a favor," he said.

"Yes, sir," Stewart automatically responded.

"Be careful and be very thorough with your Pearl Harbor check."

Stewart blinked. "Sir?"

Maxwell tapped the side of his closely cropped head. "Humor an old soldier's intuition. I've got a bad feeling about this whole trip and I'd appreciate it if you'd be extra careful in preparing for the President's trip, particularly with regard to the military installations he'll be visiting."

Stewart nodded, "Yes, sir, I'll do that."

Maxwell laid a hand on his shoulder. "Thank you." With that, he turned and walked into the chapel, leaving a confused Stewart alone on the chilly hillside among the graves.

PACIFIC PALISADES, OAHU
2 December
5:00 A.M. LOCAL/ 1500 ZULU

Boomer drowsily awoke from an uneasy dream and turned over. He froze as the pain from his ribs shocked him totally awake. He gingerly swung his legs out and touched the floor before sitting up on the couch. He glanced out the window into the darkness and was surprised to see Maggie's figure silhouetted against the night sky. She was wrapped in an old housecoat and smoking a cigarette, looking out at something.

Boomer carefully slipped on a shirt and slid open the glass door. Maggie turned and smiled. "Having trouble sleeping?"

"A little."

"How's your side?"

"Hurts like hell, but I've cracked ribs before. It just takes time to heal. As long as I don't laugh too hard, I'll be all right."

"Not much to laugh about right now is there?" Maggie asked.

"No, there isn't."

"Sit down, relax," Maggie said, pointing at one of the wicker chairs on the porch. A thermos was on the table along with a couple of mugs. "Help yourself to some coffee." She settled into the seat, drawing her coat in tight around her frail shoulders. "Ski's told me what's going on. It's a pretty sad thing."

Sad wasn't exactly the word Boomer would have used to describe the events of the past week. He remained silent and looked over the low lying ground sloping into the ocean. The *Arizona* Memorial was a bright block of white, lit by searchlights in the middle of Pearl Harbor. The International Airport was just coming to life as red-eye flights landed every ten minutes.

"Ski told me your father was killed in Vietnam," Maggie said. "My oldest son, Peter, died there too. Ski probably didn't tell you that."

"No, he didn't. I'm sorry," Boomer said.

"It's strange. A generation either way, and we both lost someone in the same war. You know, my generation looks at that war differently than yours. For us it was this long, slow slide that didn't make any sense. We grew up in the Depression and then went through the dark years of World War II. It was especially dark here in Hawaii where every day you could look out at the harbor and see how bad things were.

"Then things turned around. Coral Sea. Midway. Guadalcanal. On through the islands. The war in Europe ended. Then the bomb. No one questioned the bomb back then. We were so tired of death and war. We just wanted it over. And after what the Japanese did here, we weren't exactly in the mood to be very sympathetic.

"After the war we all thought everything would be so bright and the world would be a better place. And it was. At least it appeared to be. The fifties were wonderful, but there was a cloud over everything. The Cold War. The war in Korea. No one quite understood that war. The Red Scare!" Maggie laughed. "It all seems so stupid now, but it was so real then."

She lit another cigarette, then pointed with the glowing end at the harbor. "But the question I've been asking myself: 'Was it real?' "

Boomer took a sip of hot coffee. "Was what real?"

Maggie didn't answer him directly. "I get up every morning at four-thirty and sit out here for an hour. I've been doing that for fifty-five years." Maggie sighed. "You know, some people claim Roosevelt knew we were going to get attacked on December seventh and he let it happen. Did you ever hear that?"

Boomer nodded. "I've heard it, but I never really got into it."

"Oh, there's been volumes written about it," Maggie said. "*I've* gotten into it," she added. "I've read all the books and even done some studying on my own. It bothers Ski that I seem so obsessed by it all, so we don't talk about it any more.

"I was here when the bombs started falling. Ever since that morning I've never been asleep at dawn here in Hawaii." She paused. "I wasn't where I was supposed to be that morning."

She glanced over at Boomer, who was still, his head cocked attentively. "Ski told you my husband, George, was on the *Enterprise* and they were out at sea on the seventh. We lived down there in Pearl City in a nice little house we'd bought about six months earlier. But I wasn't in my house, in my bed, on the morning of the seventh. I was over at the bachelor officers quarters at Pearl in someone else's bed that morning."

Maggie paused again and Boomer didn't know what to say. Maggie glanced at the darkened house, then back at Boomer. "I've never told Ski about all this. I wanted to years ago, but George told me it was better to let sleeping dogs lie. And then Peter, Ski's brother, was killed in Vietnam and it seemed better to let it lie. But all that's been happening the last couple of days, it just seems some of it is coming alive inside me again."

Boomer didn't quite understand what she was saying, but he knew enough about people to keep quiet and let her say what she felt she had to.

Her voice was wistful as she continued. "The man I was

with was a lieutenant on the fleet staff—Jimmie. What a wild man. You wouldn't know it to look at me now, but I cut quite a figure back then.

"Jimmie worked in Navy Intelligence. He certainly shouldn't have been in bed with me on the morning of the seventh," she added with a low chuckle. Her voice turned sad. "None of those boys should have been asleep that morning. Jimmie was the man who picked up the telegraphs when they came in and brought them to Admiral Kimmel's G-2, so he was able to get a lot of information."

She poured a cup of coffee, then wearily leaned back against the wicker. "We all knew war was coming. It was inevitable. Europe was in flames. France had fallen. England was surrounded. The Japs were expanding everywhere.

"We knew it was coming, but we didn't think it was coming here. We thought the Japs would have to be crazy to attack here. All you had to do was look down in the harbor to know that. Those ships were so beautiful and proud.

"Jimmie and I talked about it a lot. He was stationed shoreside and George was always at sea so that made things convenient. Bull Halsey was in charge of the *Enterprise* task force and he ran his ships hard. *He* didn't want to get caught here in the harbor at least.

"Jimmie said that the Philippines would get attacked for sure. Wake. Singapore. Malaya. Hong Kong. But not Pearl he said. At least not until a month before the attack. Then he started saying things that worried me." She paused and took a drag on her cigarette.

"Did you ever hear of Magic?" Maggie asked, the question catching Boomer off-guard.

"The Pacific version of Ultra?" he asked.

Maggie nodded. "It was the codeword for the machine they used to break the Japanese code." She stopped as if reconsidering what she was saying. "Listen, this Line organization that Ski says you think exists, didn't Trace say it started before World War II?"

"Yes. She says it started in the late twenties."

"With Marshall and other top people in the Army?" Maggie pressed.

"Yes."

She nodded. "Marshall was chief of the Army at the time of Pearl Harbor. He was on the Ultra list that got to look at Magic intercepts. Did you know that President Roosevelt was taken off the Ultra list for a while just prior to the attack here?"

Maggie leaned forward, not waiting for an answer. "Jimmie saw all the Magic intercepts. The ones they forwarded here to Admiral Kimmel and General Short, the Navy and Army commanders on the island. He was only a messenger but he was in a position to see a lot.

"But more important than the ones they forwarded are the ones they didn't forward. Many historians have looked at the record and deduced that Army and Navy headquarters in Washington had sufficient information to indicate that an attack on Pearl Harbor was imminent. That's why some believe the President was the one who decided to withhold the information in order to drag us into war.

"But no one has even considered the fact that maybe it all stopped at Marshall's desk. That maybe the President didn't know beforehand either. It was the military's responsibility to know and they did know. And they allowed it to happen.

"And why?" Maggie asked, her voice rising. "Because although we all felt war was inevitable, most people didn't want it. Isolationism was at an all-time high. We didn't want war and nothing short of what happened out there"—she pointed out to the harbor—"could have galvanized the country into war fever. We went from a depression and isolationism in three short years to become the most powerful military force on the face of the planet!"

Her words chilled Boomer. Since hearing about The Line he had only obliquely considered what such an organization would have done. To think that military men would have allowed the attack on Pearl Harbor to occur when they had foreknowledge was abhorrent to him and his training. But Boomer also remembered his words at the airport to Trace about the bombing of Coventry. "Surely they wouldn't have allowed such a devastating defeat," he objected.

"I don't know," Maggie replied. "On one hand, I don't think they thought it would be the disaster it was. Jimmie told me that the Navy was sure that the harbor was too shallow for torpedoes to be used and since dive bombing was still very inaccurate they felt the fleet was relatively safe in the harbor. But on the other hand, my husband told me that when Task Force 8, the *Enterprise* task force, sailed out of Pearl *before* the seventh, Admiral Halsey put them on full war footing. Any ships they spotted were to be sunk, any aircraft shot down.

"So why the two different attitudes? Here at Pearl we were asleep. On board the carriers, the heart of the fleet and the true objective of the Japanese attack, they were on full alert, ready to fight.

"And Marshall did send an alert message to General Short and Admiral Kimmel on the morning of the seventh. A message that arrived in time only to become a historical document after the fact, rather than a warning. A cover-your-ass telegram that was used to relieve Kimmel and Short from their commands in the aftermath." The chair creaked as Maggie shifted position.

"You know, not only was there ample evidence pointing to foreknowledge of the attack in Washington, but they did things here that almost aided in the attack.

"The night of the sixth, the radio station here, KGMB, stayed on all night, broadcasting. It usually went off the air for the early morning hours, but that night the Army paid for it to stay on. Their reason was to help guide in some B-17s flying in from the mainland, but those radio waves also helped guide the attacking Japanese force to the island.

"And did you know that the tunnel you're working in now was where the radar element up at Kahuku Point called to warn of the incoming attack flights? And that some Army officer there ignored the warning? But what if he didn't just blow it off out of ignorance?"

Maggie shook her head. "I'm sorry. It's so confusing and there are so many strange things that happened that day that I guess I see a conspirator behind everything. I do know what happened to me that morning though.

"I was in the BOQ at Pearl when the first bombs fell. Seven-fifty-four A.M. on Sunday." She looked up at Boomer with tears in her eyes. "I'd left my daughter in the care of our Filipino housekeeper. When we heard the first explosions, we thought it was a drill. Jimmie ran to the window and saw what was happening, and he ran out the door half-dressed, going to his post at headquarters. I looked out. It was unbelievable. There was smoke and fire everywhere. The Japanese were flying just like a practice drill in perfect formation and the ships were sitting ducks.

"When the *Arizona* got hit, the concussion blew out the windows in the room and jarred me out of my shock. I was cut and bleeding, but it got me moving. I threw on my clothes and ran out. I remembered when I got out, that I'd left my car at the house. Jimmie had driven me and he'd taken his car to headquarters. I started running through the streets."

Maggie shook her head slowly. "My housekeeper took my daughter and tried to drive away to the hills. I guess she thought the island was getting invaded. I didn't find the car until the next day. I spent twenty-four hours wandering the streets, looking, until a neighbor took me in his car to look for them. We found my car inland. A Japanese pilot must have strafed it. Maybe he thought it was servicemen heading for Schofield Barracks. Maybe just to get rid of ammunition before heading back to his carrier.

"They were both dead. It was my fault. I should have been with them. I had to tell George when he got back." She took a deep breath. "God bless his heart. He stayed with me."

She looked up at Boomer with tears flowing freely down her cheeks. "It was my fault, but my daughter wasn't the only one who died that day. They were still hearing the desperate taps from sailors trapped in some of those ships for weeks, until they finally died. And if this Line exists and it knew about the attack beforehand and allowed it to happen, then there's no place in hell hot enough for those bastards!"

CHAPTER ☆ 14

The satellite dish in Maggie's backyard shifted position slightly, then settled in place. Inside the house, Boomer sat on the couch and watched the pre-game show for the Army-Navy game.

The front door opened and Skibicki walked in, looking like he had not had a moment of sleep.

"What's up, sergeant major?"

Skibicki gratefully accepted the mug of coffee Maggie handed him. "Thanks. Nothing. Everything's quiet." He looked at the screen. "Let's hope Trace made it there."

"What's the plan for today?" Boomer asked.

"I talked to Vasquez. She's doing some more snooping." He threw a newspaper down on the table. "I noticed an interesting article in the back pages. We've been concentrating so hard in one area, we've lost track of some other aspects of this whole situation."

Boomer tore his eyes from the screen. "What do you mean?"

Skibicki sat at the table and Boomer joined him. "If there is a plot to get to the President, then what?"

"I don't think the plot is directly against the President," Boomer said.

"Just play along with me, then," Skibicki bargained.

"All right," Boomer said, "what if there is a plot to attack the President? What are you talking about?"

"I mean, what would their plan be after they got rid of

185

the President?'' Skibicki said. ''They're not going to do this in a vacuum. If the President disappears or is killed, what happens?'' He didn't wait for an answer. ''The Vice President takes over. And guess where the Vice President is going to be this weekend?'' He tapped the newspaper. ''Vacationing on the North Shore of this island at the Turtle Bay Resort playing golf.''

''No shit?'' Boomer grabbed the paper. ''Hell, he's arriving this morning.'' He looked up at Skibicki. ''Maybe those guys jumping in this morning weren't going after the President. Maybe they had responsibility for a secondary target right where they came in.''

Skibicki nodded. ''That's why I got Vasquez checking the Intel nets. We may have had tunnel vision about this jump, thinking it was the main event, but it just might be the sideshow.''

The sound of the football announcers filled the silence in the room.

''That sub,'' Boomer said, breaking the quiet, ''the one Vasquez said her friend had on the SOSUS but wasn't listed in the Navy books. That might be part of this.''

''Already thought of that,'' Skibicki said. ''I'm having her do a complete check of the sea around the island. Not just what SOSUS has, but imagery from the Intelsat. I'd love to have her do a Keyhole look at the island itself to see if we could find where those jumpers and their boats went to earth, but doing that would raise red flags all the way to the Pentagon. Plus, I don't know if any of the Keyholes pass over here.''

''A Keyhole look,'' Boomer said, referring to the latest spy satellite that could read the information off a cigarette pack, ''wouldn't be much good here. They probably sunk the Zodiacs anyway,'' Boomer said. ''If they're using F-470s, they can waterproof the engines, sink the boats, and then recover them when they need them using CO_2 canisters on board.''

Skibicki nodded. ''Yeah, and the guys on land would be deep under cover.''

''You two can sit here and speculate all day,'' Maggie said, her attention on the TV screen, ''but if your cute young friend doesn't get some solid information about The

Line from this colonel of Ski's, you might as well be whistling in the dark.''

The doorbell rang and Skibicki opened it. Vasquez walked in. She had a briefcase that she carried directly to the table and opened. The others gathered round.

''Got some strange stuff going on at sea,'' she began. ''That unidentified SOSUS contact I told you about is closing in on the island. About two hundred kilometers due east now. Now there's a second submarine contact.''

''Another unknown friendly?'' Skibicki asked.

''Negative, sergeant major. This one is listed. The USS *Sam Houston*. I looked it up,'' she added. ''It's a missile carrier.''

''No, it isn't,'' Boomer interrupted, catching Vasquez by surprise. ''The *Sam Houston* is an Ethan Allen Class sub. They used to carry Polaris missiles, but those are out of date now. The *Sam Houston* was taken out of service in the early eighties and reconfigured for Special Operations. They removed the missile control system and most of the empty missile tubes. Some of the missile tubes were converted to act as air locks for swimmer exit. It's also fitted to accept two DDS assemblies.''

Seeing Vasquez's blank stare, Boomer explained. ''DDS stands for dry dock shelter. It's something the Navy's developed to be mounted on the deck of submarines to carry SDVs—swimmer delivery vehicles. You can go directly from the inside of the sub into the DDS, and load up the SDV while maintaining an airtight environment.

''You can also use the DDS to lock out a large number of swimmers from the sub, all at the same time.''

''Lock out?'' Vasquez repeated.

''Exit the submarine while it's still submerged,'' Skibicki explained. ''So this sub is one of the ones the Navy has modified for Special Operations?'' he asked.

Boomer nodded. ''After they retired the USS *Greyback*, the first Special Operations submarine, they converted the *Sam Houston* and the *John Marshall*, both Ethan Allen Class. They've also modified about eight of their Sturgeon Class to mount the DDS. I've done some work on the *John Marshall*,'' he added to explain his knowledge.

Skibicki considered the information and tallied it with

what he knew from joint exercises on the island. "Navy Special Warfare Group One at Pearl has got two DDSs and four SDVs in a secure holding area, or at least they have space for them. They might be out there mounted on the *Sam Houston* right now."

The sergeant major slapped his palm on the table. "It makes sense. The Army guys get the land target, the VP, up on the north shore. The Navy boys get the target in Pearl. They could get right up to the *Arizona* Memorial in an SDV. Hell, they can mount goddamn torpedoes on the Mark IX SDV. They can sneak into the harbor, stand off, and fire a torpedo and blow the shit out of everyone standing on the memorial."

"But I thought we were worried only about the Army?" Maggie threw in. "I thought The Line was from West Point."

"Shit, I bet they got a chapter at Annapolis," Skibicki growled. "They probably got one at the Air Force Academy too."

Boomer felt uncomfortable with all this talk of plots and assassination. It just didn't jive with what he believed and had seen in his time in service. But he also remembered pulling the trigger and killing those two men the other night and that didn't jive either. If he took away the blinder that told him the military would never do such a thing, then anything was possible.

Vasquez pulled out some satellite photos. "The sub ain't all, sergeant major. Take a look at that."

"What the blazes is that?" Skibicki said.

A massive ship floated in the middle of an empty sea. What appeared to be a huge oil-drilling derrick took up the entire center of the ship, towering over it. An Army helicopter sat on a landing pad on the stern. A broad wake behind it indicated the ship was moving.

Vasquez smiled. "I had to go to the library and do some research to find out. It's not listed in the current ship's logs down at Pearl. It's the *Glomar Explorer*."

"And what's the *Glomar Explorer*?" Boomer asked.

"You ain't gonna believe this," Vasquez said. "It was built in 1973 by Howard Hughes for the CIA."

"Say again?" Skibicki exclaimed. "To do what?"

"To recover a Russian sub that sank northwest of here."

"Start from the beginning," Boomer said, unsure of where, or even if, this new piece fit in the puzzle.

Vasquez consulted the notes she'd scribbled. "The *Glomar Explorer* was built by Hughes to mine minerals off the ocean floor. Or at least that's the cover story he told the press and even the people building it. It was constructed at York, Pennsylvania, and is over 200 meters long. They spent about 400 million of the tax payers' dollars on the thing without the taxpayers knowing about it. To get it to the Pacific, they had to sail it around South America because it wouldn't fit through the Panama Canal.

"Anyway, it was actually built to be part of a secret CIA mission called Project Jennifer. While the ship was built on the East Coast, they built a companion craft called the HMB-1, Hughes Marine Barge, in California. It's about a hundred meters long and built like an underwater aircraft hangar."

"Underwater?" Boomer asked.

"The barge is submergible. It's got a giant claw, remote TV camera, and lights. It can dock with the *Glomar* in the well of the ship underneath the derrick. They went after the sub in 1973, and I couldn't find out whether they got it or not. One report says they got part of it. Another says they didn't. Whichever, the whole thing had to be scrapped after the press got a hold of the story."

"Why did they spend 400 million dollars trying to get a Soviet sub?" Skibicki asked. "You could build your own sub for that much back then."

"They wanted the cipher codes that sank with the submarine."

"What for?" Skibicki asked. "The Russians would have changed their codes once they realized they lost the sub."

"Apparently, the CIA wanted to decode back traffic that they'd recorded over the years but been unable to break. Get information on how the Soviet missile fleet operated."

"What a crock," Skibicki muttered. "Fucking CIA."

"So what's it doing now?" Boomer wanted to know. "Is it still working for the CIA?"

"I don't know," Vasquez replied. "I don't know if the barge is underneath the *Glomar*," she said, pointing at the imagery. ''The wake looks funny, but I'd have to consult a Navy expert at wake interpretation and since there's only one guy who does that at Pearl and it's a Saturday and I'm doing this unauthorized—''

''I get the message,'' Skibicki said. ''The important thing is, what is the *Glomar Explorer* up to now?''

''It's been docked out at Sausalito, California for over a decade. I read one account where the government, after the Cold War ended in 'eighty-nine, even tried to sell or lease it to the Russians to help recover their other lost subs. There was one newspaper report saying that it was bought by some civilian corporation and refurbished a year and a half ago.''

''Who bought it?'' Boomer asked.

''I couldn't find the name of the company.''

Boomer looked at the picture one more time. ''Again, the question is, what's it doing?''

''I don't know, but it looks to me from the imagery like it's heading for a rendezvous with that unidentified sub,'' Vasquez said.

''Not the *Sam Houston?*'' Skibicki asked.

''No, the bogey,'' Vasquez replied.

''Possible explanation?'' Skibicki snapped.

Vasquez paused, then gave her thoughts. ''This unknown friendly sub, obviously it's highly classified, even more so than the Special Operations sub. I'd say this *Glomar Explorer* would make an excellent at-sea tender for a sub that never wanted to enter a harbor or even surface at sea where it could be seen. If the *Glomar Explorer* is carrying the HMB-1 barge, they could berth this sub with the barge underneath and carry out maintenance and resupply totally out of view of satellites or aircraft.''

''The question is, what's so classified?'' Boomer asked. ''Some sort of cutting-edge technology stealth submarine? I heard the Navy was using some sort of floating barge out of San Diego to cover up their testing of a stealth surface ship.''

''This sub isn't so stealthful,'' Vasquez pointed out. ''SOSUS picked it up. And this barge is underwater, not floating.''

''Then what is it?'' Boomer repeated.

"I'll try to find out," Vasquez volunteered, "but it isn't going to be easy."

Boomer turned to Skibicki. "What now?"

"Maggie can monitor the phone in case Trace calls," Skibicki said. "Let's take a ride up to the North Shore and poke our noses around where the Vice President is. Maybe we can trip over something. If not, then we can go by the tunnel this evening and see what we can dig up. They have a copy of the President's classified itinerary in the vault. We can also see if we can get some more information on these vessels ourselves."

INTERNATIONAL AIRPORT, OAHU, HAWAII
2 December
7:10 A.M. LOCAL/ 1710 ZULU

Special Agent Stewart had chased the sun from the east and lost only a little ground with a delay in Dallas-Fort Worth. He was met at Arrivals by Mike Newman, a member of the Second Team, the security detail for the Vice President.

Newman hustled him out of the airport and into one of the Service's vans, which had been flown to Hawaii aboard an Air Force C-5 transport. As he pulled out of the parking lot, Newman pointed at a file folder tucked into Stewart's side panel. "Got all your information there. We've already screened the threat list. Honolulu PD will pick up the four A's today and give you a call to confirm. They'll detain them for the duration of the Boss's trip.

"I'm taking you to the Royal Hawaiian. You've got one of the rooms on the fourteenth floor. The entire floor is reserved for the President. We're staying up on the North Shore at the Turtle Bay Hilton. The VP is taking in the golf course.

"The name of the Hawaii PD point of contact is in there," he continued. "He's a good guy. So is the local FBI rep. It's been pretty quiet."

"What about the military?" Stewart asked. "I've got to do the prelim for the President's speech at Pearl and I need to get a hold of whoever is in charge of security there."

He was uneasy about General Maxwell's request and had pondered it during the flight. He wasn't sure whether Maxwell was concerned about a physical threat to the President, which was the Secret Service's area of responsibility, or a political threat in terms of an embarrassing incident, which was the purview of the President's advisers. There was no doubt that there was bad blood between the military and the President, but Stewart had no idea what could come of it.

Newman pointed across Stewart's chest and out the window. "That's it right there," he said. Stewart looked out. He could see gray ships riding at anchor and a white building just off an island. "That's the memorial. The whole installation is a secure area. I'll give you the name of the Navy guy in charge." Newman laughed. "Hell, we're on a damn island. Security's been a piece of cake so far. Enjoy yourself."

Stewart leaned back in the seat and tried to do just that, but Maxwell's words stayed in his head. He cursed to himself. So much for having a good time. Stewart knew he wouldn't be able to relax until this whole trip was over.

PHILADELPHIA, PENNSYLVANIA
2 December
12:30 P.M. LOCAL/ 1730 ZULU

Trace didn't think about needing a ticket to get into the stadium until she'd parked the rental car twelve blocks away and walked to Veterans Stadium. The game was sold out and the ticket booth locked and closed. It was a nice day for early December in Philadelphia. The weather was in the low forties and the sun was shining brightly.

Between the stadium and the Spectrum, she could see the Corps of Cadets lining up, 4,000 strong. To their left, the Brigade of Midshipmen was already beginning its march-on, entering the stadium.

Trace mingled in the civilian crowd near the stadium, searching for someone hawking tickets. She ended up paying fifty dollars in cash for an upper-level seat, a rather deep investment for a game between two non-nationally ranked teams. But, as Trace well knew, the Army-Navy game was much more than a simple football game. It was an event.

When Trace had entered West Point in July of 1978, the game in early December had been the first time she'd been allowed off-campus in the six months since entering Beast Barracks. At that time, the Academy had bussed all the plebes down to the game Saturday morning and back on the "vomit comet" that evening. In the few hours the plebes had between the end of the game and the mandatory bus formation to return, most tried to imbibe as much alcohol as possible at tailgate parties and local hotels, leading to a grim scene on the four-hour ride back up to New York.

From talking to more recent graduates, Trace had heard that the Academy had modernized slightly, allowing all cadets—even plebes!—the weekend off as long as they showed up for the march-on and game and weren't on disciplinary restriction.

The new freedoms being allowed cadets were bitterly protested by old grads of which Trace assumed she now was one. She didn't follow the old grad "make it as hard for them as it was for me" theory. After graduation, she had seen several of her classmates, unused to responsibility, since almost every of aspect of their lives as cadets had been dictated, fail miserably when given the authority and responsibility of being platoon leaders in the Army. Trace had often wondered where and how the Academy thought the magical maturation from being a cadet to being an officer occurred. In her time they certainly had never treated her and her classmates as responsible, thinking adults prior to sending them forth into the Army.

Trace made her way into the stadium and began heading for the section Colonel Rison had indicated. The midshipmen had finished their march-on, done a few traditional cheers, and were now beginning to file off into their place in the stands. Trace noted that many of the naval academy students were drunk, unable to march in step.

Trace remembered carrying a bottle of Jack Daniels on the inside pocket of her dress gray overcoat to the game in 1981 and mixing the liquor with Coke in a can during the fourth quarter and sharing it with her roommate in the stands. The alcohol fuel helped explain the enthusiastic cheers of the Corps of Cadets in that game as time ran out and their side was being pounded by the Navy 33-6. Alcohol was one of the ways cadets dealt with living in a high-stress environment. And from intimate experience Trace knew that the stress was very real. In her first six months at the Academy, she had not had a period. Finally gathering her courage, she had gone on sick call to get checked. The doctor at the hospital had told her that such a thing was not uncommon among female cadets and advised her not to worry.

"The Corps of Cadets!" the speakers in the stadium blared as the announcer welcomed the Corps. "Duty, honor, country. The long gray line. From the United States Military Academy on the Hudson River at West Point. Distinguished cadets include Ulysses S. Grant. Robert E. Lee. Douglas MacArthur. George S. Patton. Dwight D. Eisenhower."

Trace wondered why they never mentioned Custer or Edgar Allen Poe who had managed a little time at the Academy. One of the pieces of knowledge she'd been required to memorize as a plebe was the answer to the question "Who commanded the major battles of the Civil War?" The answer, according to the Bugle Notes issued to every cadet was: "There were sixty important battles of the war. In fifty-five of them, graduates commanded on both sides; in the remaining five, a graduate commanded one of the opposing sides." Boomer had once half-jokingly told her that that helped explain why that war lasted so long.

Trace paused on the second level of the stadium and watched as the thirty-six companies that compromised the Corps of Cadets marched onto the field in large gray blocks. The announcer called out the brigade commander and his home town, then each regimental commander, every battalion commander, and every company commander as the designated unit took its place.

The midshipmen were still filing into the seats as the cadets began their rote cheers, something the entire Corps had spent three late afternoons the previous week practicing. One thing Trace had always found a bit amazing about West Point was the way enthusiasm was dictated. "Spontaneous pep rallies" prior to games were planned, which sort of defeated the entire purpose of the event. The last meal that the football team ate in the mess hall before a game was called "Joe College" night, where, in the mighty leniency of the powers-that-be, cadets could wear a civilian shirt with their uniform pants to the dinner meal. In some convoluted thinking, that small taste of normalcy was supposed to increase morale rather than increase awareness of the differences of Academy life from mainstream America. It was a tribute to the desperation of the Corps, that it *did* increase morale.

Trace listened as the 4,000 members of the Corps dutifully shouted out a less-than-spontaneous cheer written decades earlier, led by gold-and-gray clad rabble rousers:

> *"Away, away, away we go,*
> *"What care we for any foe?*
> *"Up and down the field we go,*
> *"Just to beat the Navy.*
> *"A-R-M-Y! T-E-A-M!"*

Trace looked down and caught the guidon for Company I-1, her home for her first two years at the Academy. She'd survived the inferno, and after two years, during the scramble, where all third year cadets were reassigned to new companies, she'd been assigned to the last company in the Corps—I-4. She'd found life in 4th Regiment to be a bit more laid back, the only major problem being that as the last company to pass in review during a cadet parade, cadets from A-1 were already back in their barracks, showered, changed, and up in the parking lots two miles away departing on leave while I-4 was still saluting the flag while passing in review.

She continued to make her way around the stadium. The seat that Rison had indicated was right beside where the Corps of Cadets was to be seated, and when the cadets finished their cheers, they flowed into the stands, making her going slow. She halted, hand over heart, when the national anthem was played. As soon as it was over, she was caught in the reverse tide as cadets poured back onto the field to form a welcoming cordon for the team to come onto the field. Most of the cordon was made up of plebes

who felt obligated to be out there, while savvy upperclassmen took the best seats in the stands during their absence.

Across the stadium, the welcoming cordon for the Navy
team was more subdued, reflecting a less intense attitude
by the seamen. Trace slipped her way through the crowd
of cadets and halted short of her destination, scanning the
crowd. She was standing in the aisle, next to row AA, so
she counted up six more rows. A man with silver hair glint-
ing out from underneath a black watch cap and wearing
long tan coat sat there, a blanket over his lap. His face had
the complexion of worn leather, and his eyes were clear
and blue. Those eyes were glancing about the stadium and
they came to rest briefly on Trace, meeting her gaze, then
moving on.

Trace edged her way into the cadet section, wanting to
wait a bit and let all the seats be filled before approaching
Rison. A cadet glanced at her civilian clothing, gave her
credit for her twelfth man sweatshirt, but still confronted
her. "Excuse me, ma'am, but this seating is for military
only."

Trace pulled out her ID card.

The first class cadet backed off. "Sorry, ma'am."

The Corps exploded in cheers as the Army team appeared, running between the two walls of cadets that extended the length of the field. Trace glanced over her
shoulder. Rison was watching the field. She edged herself
into the crowd, determined to wait for the game to start
before approaching him.

The Corps cheered again as Army's wishbone offense
punched the ball into the end zone, giving their team a 7-0
lead. The cannon went off and the Corps broke into "On
Brave Old Army Team."

Trace took the opportunity to slide through the crowd
and reach the aisle. She started up toward the man she
assumed was Rison when a hand gripped her arm. She spun
around.

"Easy, miss," the man who held her arm said. A solid
block of human being, over six and a half feet tall, her
accoster smiled, the bright flash of teeth easily visible
against his coal black skin. His head was completely hair-
less and his skull was an ebony bullet. "You the one who

wants to talk to the colonel? Major Trace?''

"Yes," Trace said, feeling the steel grip of his fingers relax not the slightest.

"You got some ID?" the man asked.

"In my wallet," she replied.

The man nodded down toward the field. "Let's get closer to the action."

"Hold it," Trace said, pulling back futiley. "I came to talk to Colonel Rison."

"He'll be talking to you, miss. But down there. And after I see some ID."

Bowing to the implacable, Trace allowed her guide to lead her down toward the field level. He flashed some sort of ID at the MP standing guard to the field, and then they were down there, standing on the Astroturf behind the far end of the Army bench and in front of the wave of gray that was the Corps.

"OK, let's see the ID," the man said, finally releasing her arm.

Trace pulled out her wallet and showed him her military ID. She was surprised when he pulled a small notepad out and checked her ID card number against a list. He looked over her shoulder and nodded. Trace turned and the man who'd been in the seat walked up, his blanket carefully folded and hanging over his left arm.

"Major Trace," he said, extending his right hand. "I'm Bob Rison."

"Sir," Trace said, not sure what to say.

"This is Harry," Rison added. Harry bowed slightly, but his eyes were looking beyond, scanning the crowd and the other people near around. "You'll have to excuse his manners, but he happens to be rather protective of our mutual welfare."

A beach ball floated by, was picked up by one of the Army rabble rousers and thrown back up into the stands. "So, what is it you wish to know?" Rison asked.

"What do you know about an organization called The Line?" Trace asked.

Rison gave a sad smile. "Young lady, that is like asking what do you know about American history for the past fifty years."

"The Line exists?" Trace said, leaning toward Colonel Rison.

He gazed out at the field, where the Navy team was making a counter-drive down the field. "Let me start from the beginning. My beginning. I graduated class of 'forty-nine. Went to Benning for Infantry Basic, then to Japan. I was with the 1st Battalion, 21st Infantry Regiment, Task Force Smith, first on the peninsula in South Korea when Truman committed U.S. ground forces in 1951.

"We got our asses kicked. We were understrength, undergunned, and no one gave a shit about us. We had nothing that could stop their Russian made T-34 tanks. Our bazookas just bounced off the front armor.

"I remember one afternoon after we'd counterattacked all day, retaking a hill we'd lost the previous night. I found one of my classmates on the hill. He must have surrendered, but we didn't yet know what that meant. The Koreans, and later the Chinese, they didn't think like us about things like surrendering.

"My classmate was naked; wrapped in barbed wire, arms to his side; they'd doused him in gasoline and set him on fire. Burned him alive. I had to cut his finger off to get his ring. I was amazed someone hadn't stolen it, but they must have missed it in the dark. The ring was the only way I was able to identify the body. After I got wounded the first time, I came back to the States and gave his widow the ring."

Rison held out his left hand. The fingers were bare. "I stopped wearing my ring then."

For the first time Trace noticed that he was holding something under the blanket. He caught her gaze. "Silenced .45." He smiled the same weary smile. "Just because I'm paranoid doesn't mean they aren't out to get me."

The words echoed in her ears and she heard Boomer say them. It was something all Special Forces men seemed to have in common. Trace started as an explosion roared off to her left, bumping into Rison. He steadied her with his free hand. Smoke drifted across the field from the Navy cannon. The score was tied and the cheers from the brigade across the field were deafening.

"Who do you think is after you?" Trace asked, remembering the men in her living room.

"The Line knows about me, and it knows that I know about it. We have maintained a very uneasy truce over the years."

"How have you managed that?" Trace asked.

"My knowledge of The Line won't die if I die. In fact, the way I set things up, my knowledge becomes public knowledge, and The Line doesn't want that. A lot of people in many places would be hurt if information about The Line became public. However," he added, "it appears that you and your friends in Hawaii might have upset that delicate balance."

Rison turned his gaze back to the field. "I served twenty-one years. I was like you. Or like I think you might be," Rison amended, noting the ring on her finger. "I believed. I still do actually. In this country, that is. But I no longer believe in West Point or the Army."

He huddled close, his words a steady drumming on her ears, overlaid with the noise of the crowd. "I never even heard of the Line until I was in Vietnam. I arrived in country for my second tour in late 'sixty-seven. I was placed in command of the Special Operations branch of MACV-SOG. That's Military Assistance Group Vietnam, Studies and Observation Group. Basically every man wearing a green beanie in-country answered to me. And that's why The Line approached me.

"They never liked Special Forces. In fact, they hated us. Still do, I suppose. SF was Kennedy's baby, but until Vietnam got going hot and heavy, we weren't something the regular Army folks had to worry about. As commander of SF in Vietnam I had about 2,000 Americans under my command. But Special Forces' primary mission was to be a force multiplier. When you counted the indigs—indigenous troops that we basically trained and controlled—it was a whole different matter entirely and that's why The Line came to me."

He paused as the crowd cheered the Army fullback who broke through the Navy line and rambled for thirty yards before being dragged down from behind.

"There was a wide variety of people working under our

structure. We had the CIDG—Civilian Irregular Defense Group—about 45,000 strong but pretty much worthless in a stand-up fight; our mobile strike forces, about 10,000 strong, and some of those were ass-kicking troops, mainly the Montagnards in the hills; and various other units we ran. I was in command of the third largest friendly force in South Vietnam behind the ARVN and the regular U.S. Army. And in 'sixty-seven and 'sixty-eight The Line needed our cooperation.''

Rison seemed to return to the present, and he looked at Trace's attentive face. ''You don't need to hear all that. Suffice it to say I was approached. They sent one of my classmates. He was a one-star. Assistant division commander of the Americal Division. I listened to his plans. He gave me all the details, but left it to me to figure out what the details added up to. Boy, that son of a bitch laid it on sweet and heavy and threw so much bullshit in to the air, I almost didn't see the big picture.''

Rison's voice turned angry. ''They were keeping the war going. That was it. That was their only goal. They didn't really want to win. They certainly didn't want to lose. The war was just too damn good to let go of. For the officers it was a career ticket punch, but this asshole justified it by saying that it kept our forces in 'fighting trim.' Jesus those were the exact words he used: 'fighting trim.' I wonder when the last time *he* went out to the field was. That war *destroyed* our Army. It destroyed it long before we pulled out in 'seventy-three.

''And, of course, there was all the money to be made manufacturing the gadgets to fight the damn thing. That they justified too. I found out Korea was the same. That's why I told you about finding my classmate. You can't test weapons systems adequately without a war, after all. And if a lot of those weapon systems, such as helicopters, happen to get destroyed and we have to pump more money into the companies making them, well, so much the better.

''And do you know how many West Pointers there are working in the defense industry? How many ring-knockers are sitting in boardrooms of companies that supply the tools we use to fight? And of course they justify it with reasons other than profits: got to keep those companies in business to keep our defense industry strong. We must 'maintain the structural integrity of our military-industrial capability.' That's what one of my classmates told me.

"That hillside in Korea was the beginning of the end for me, but it took me twenty years to find out. Vietnam was . . ." Rison paused and collected himself. "Skibicki can tell you what happened in Vietnam." He looked her in the eye. "Why do you want to know about The Line?"

"We think there might be something planned in Hawaii during the President's visit next week," Trace answered. "Maybe some attempt to discredit the Administration."

Rison snorted. "I wouldn't put it past the sons of bitches to kill the President." He ignored Trace's shock. "They think they're fucking God. Makes sense with all that's going on, the MRA and the cutbacks. I'm surprised they waited this long. You need proof right?"

Trace was glad that Rison was getting to the heart of the matter. His talk of Korea and Vietnam had frightened her. The thought that she was up against an organization that had controlled history shook her to the core and was far beyond the depth of the worst fears she had conjured up flying here. "Yes, sir."

The crowd was going crazy. Army had the ball, first and goal at the three. The wishbone was lining up, pointed toward the end zone.

Rison gave a broad grin, the first time Trace had seen the troubled look slip from his face. He handed her a sealed envelope. "You're going to have to go back to West Point. It's all there. What they were always afraid I would reveal."

His grin turned to a surprised look as the Army cannon boomed, celebrating the successful sweep into the end zone. A red splotch appeared on his chest and he sagged into Trace's arm. "Go!" he hissed.

Harry was there, lifting the colonel out of her arms, his eyes flashing around the crowd. "You'd better run, missy. *They're here.*"

Trace turned helplessly, staring at the crowd that stretched up above here. Where was the gunman? She turned back. Harry had his arm around Rison, practically lifting him off his feet and was heading for one of the tunnels off the field. She spotted three men in long dark military coats making their way toward the two. She spun in the other direction. Two similarly dressed men were coming toward her along the Army sideline. There was no way out.

Trace sprinted forward and grabbed one of the female rabble rousers. "Old grad rocket," she yelled at the young girl, showing her her ring and pointing at her twelfth man sweatshirt. The rabble rouser caught the idea and relayed it to the other cheerleaders. "Old grad rocket!" they bellowed out through their megaphone.

Trace glanced over her shoulder as she stepped in among the rabble rousers. The two men were halted by her sudden noticeability. Trace put her arms at her side and faced the Corps which was had just finished cheering the second Army touchdown of the day.

The head rabble rouser let out a long whistle through his sound system as Trace slowly brought her arms up over her head. She reached the top, then dropped them. The Corps roared out "BOOM!" She continued on, leading the cheer as best as she could remember, following the lead of the rabble rouser next to her.

> "Ahh. USMA, Rah! Rah!
> "USMA, Rah! Rah!
> "USMA, Rah! Rah!
> "Hoo-Rah! Hoo-Rah!
> "AR-MAY! Rah!
> "Team! Team! Team!"

The Corps exploded in applause as the cheer finished, but Trace was at a loss. There was only so long she could hide in plain sight.

"Pass her up!" somebody yelled and Trace knew the way out. She ran forward to the four foot wall at the base of the stands, above which the Corps stood. Two large cadets leaned over and grabbed her, pulling her up. They lifted her overhead and Trace was passed overhead, floating above the Corps, supported by their arms.

She didn't even feel the hands that groped her. Her mind was numb, stunned by what had just happened. She rode above the field of gray dressed cadets to the top of their section. She staggered as she was put down on the ground. She spun about. Which way to go? The two men were trying to follow but they were hopelessly caught in the mass of celebrating cadets thirty rows below.

A walkway beckoned, leading outside. Trace instinctively headed for it. The roar of the crowd was muted as she went through the tunnel. Trace ran along the outside ramp that circumscribed the stadium, occasionally bumping into the wall, looking over her shoulder. She was operating on automatic, fleeing, not sure where to go or what to do. She just had to get away. Rison was shot and what he had told her about The Line was overwhelming.

"Just go," she whispered to herself. "Just go."

Exiting the stadium proved to be much simpler than entering—no ticket required. The game was still in progress and despite the Army lead, Trace knew the crowd would stay until the end, then disperse to tailgate and hotel parties all over Philadelphia.

She slipped out the same gate she'd entered the stadium, looking over her shoulder constantly for the men in raincoats. She paused on the sidewalk outside the stadium. Where had she parked? It took an effort for her to remember. Tenth Street. She looked back at the stadium. No sirens. No police. No ambulances. What was going on?

She felt her pocket as she moved quickly down Tenth Street, toward downtown Philadelphia. The envelope Rison had given her was still there. No time for that now. She turned right onto Oregon Avenue and spotted the rental car where she had left it. As she started the car, she again wondered why she wasn't hearing sirens heading to the stadium.

Trace started the car and turned right onto Fifth Street. Checking the rear-view mirror she saw no one in pursuit. "Just keep going," she whispered to herself, her hands gripping the steering wheel with a death grip.

A sign beckoned for I-95. It penetrated Trace's shock. North. Mrs. Howard was north along I-95. West Point was also north but that was thinking too far ahead.

The white line on the side of the interstate was her focus. As each mile passed and she slipped out of the city limits of Philadelphia, her emotions slowed down and doubt crept in. Should she have run? What had happened to Rison? Was he dead? Did Harry get him out? Who were the men in the raincoats? Were they The Line?

Crossing the Delaware River into New Jersey, Trace had to stop at the rest area. She parked at the far end, away from the other cars. Leaning her head forward on the steering wheel, she collected herself.

After an hour, she was able to pull the map out of her bag and check it. Mrs. Howard was in a nursing home in Princeton, about ten miles north. Trace checked her watch. It should still be visiting hours. With a steadier hand she started the car engine.

CHAPTER ☆ 15

PRINCETON, NEW JERSEY
2 DECEMBER
5:12 P.M. LOCAL/ 2212 ZULU

"Visiting hours end at five," the nurse said, barely glancing up from her novel.

"I just flew in from Hawaii," Trace said. "Could I see Mrs. Howard for a minute."

The nurse looked at her clipboard, looked at Trace, then stood. "Let me get Mrs. Johnson, my supervisor."

Trace fidgeted at the counter. She knew she should call Boomer and check in. Why had Rison said she would have to go to West Point? What was there? Trace knew she should have looked in the envelope he'd given her by now, but she just wasn't ready.

A distinguished looking black woman appeared at Trace's elbow. "Excuse me, I'm Mrs. Johnson, the shift supervisor. I understand you're looking for someone?"

"Yes, Mrs. Howard," Trace said, exasperated at the inefficiency, piled on top of what had happened today.

"Are you a relative?"

"No, I'm an old friend. I met her a couple of months ago and I was in the area, and I thought I'd stop by."

"Ah, that explains it," Mrs. Johnson said. She reached out and lightly laid her hand on Trace's arm. "I'm sorry to tell you that Mrs. Howard passed away last week."

"Passed away?" Trace dully repeated.

Mrs. Johnson glanced at the nurse and gently drew Trace away from the counter. "It was quite tragic. We think the fire must have started when Mrs. Howard fell asleep smoking in bed. We warn our patients about that, but there are some things you just can't control.''

Trace didn't remember Mrs. Howard smoking. As a matter of fact, she remembered Mrs. Howard having an oxygen tank next to her bed and using it often throughout their conversation. Not exactly something congruous with someone who would smoke in bed. ''This happened when?'' she asked.

''Late Wednesday night,'' Mrs. Johnson said. ''The body was shipped to New York. A distant cousin, I believe.'' She pulled out a notepad. ''May I have your name please?''

Wednesday night. The men had broken into her house on Thursday morning, Hawaii time. That equaled early Wednesday evening East Coast time. Mrs. Howard's name and address had been in the notes that had been stolen from her desk.

Trace remembered what Boomer had said about coincidences. She turned and walked away from Mrs. Johnson, straight out the door, and got into the car and drove. If The Line was willing to kill an old lady in her sleep, this was not a place to be giving her name.

She didn't notice Mrs. Johnson standing at the doors, writing down the license number of her car as she pulled out of the parking lot. The woman then walked back to her office and retrieved a file folder from a locked cabinet. She checked a card clipped to the front of the folder and dialed the number.

When the phone was picked up on the other end, she spoke quickly, excited to be taking part in something she had seen only on television. ''Agent Fields?'' Getting an affirmative response, she rushed on. ''Someone stopped in to see Mrs. Howard and I'm calling you like you asked me to. She wouldn't leave her name, but I did get her license number.''

Mrs. Johnson relayed the number and then answered questions posed to her by the man on the other end, describing Trace and the car as best she could. She was a bit disappointed when the man hung up on her with only a curt thanks. She'd expected more from the nice young man from the National Security Agency who had taken Mrs. Howard's body and briefed her that this involved the country's security and to call him if anyone showed up inquiring about Mrs. Howard.

Twenty miles away, Trace stopped at the first motel she could find, numbly signing the guest registration and taking the key. She carried her bags into the room and locked the door, making sure the deadbolt and chain were on. She stripped off her clothes, leaving them in a pile on the floor, then her sweatshirt on top. She turned the shower on, the water steaming hot, and stepped in.

As the drops pounded on her skin she remembered the old lady, lying in her bed with a comforter tucked up around her frail chin, telling her story of war fifty years ago and the death of a young husband whose picture was in a frame next to the bed. And now she was dead. The tears came and Trace pounded the wall in her mixture of grief and anger.

Trace pulled Rison's letter out of the pocket of the shirt she had worn under the sweatshirt. She was tucked up in the bed, the blankets pulled tight around her, the only light coming from the lamp on the nightstand. She could hear the rumble of traffic from the interstate. She'd tried calling Boomer twenty minutes earlier, but there'd been no answer at Maggie's house.

Trace slit open the top of the envelope and removed several pieces of paper. The cover letter was handwritten, the letters firmly formed.

I first became aware of the existence of a secret organization inside the Army in 1969 when I was in command of U.S. Special Operations forces in the Republic of Vietnam. I was approached by a classmate of mine—Brigadier General Matthew Broderine. The first two meetings I had with him at my headquarters in Nha Trang left me confused. I was uncertain why the assistant division command of the Americal Division wanted to talk to me and he did not make the purpose of his visits clear to me until our third meeting on April 12, 1969. In retrospect, I assume the first two meetings were to feel me out, although I would also have to say he did a very poor job of doing that based on the results of our third meeting.

*I am attaching on the next page a verbatim tran-
script of that meeting. I normally taped all personal
and telephonic conversations in my office after
having had several unpleasant experiences with the
CIA. The original tape of the conversation and all copies were stolen—but that comes later.*

Trace turned the page to a slightly yellowed document.

RISON: Good afternoon, Bill. What can I do for you today?

BRODERINE: Afternoon, Bob. Glad you could make time
to see me.

RISON: You said something last time about my camps in
your division's area of operations. Is there—

BRODERINE: Oh, everything's fine. Just fine. Actually, I
was talking with the general in Saigon the other day
and we were discussing you.

RISON: Discussing me?

BRODERINE: Actually, we were discussing the Montagnard issue.

RISON: What issue?

BRODERINE: Oh, come on now, Bob. Don't play cute
with me. We both know the ARVN would just as soon
go into the hills and kill Montagnards as they would
NVA. In fact they'd probably prefer killing your—
what do you call them? "Little people"? We also have
information that the Montagnards are stockpiling
weapons and ammunition for what they think is the
war after the war—their war for independence after the
threat from the north is defeated. Some of the people
in Saigon are very nervous about that and they've ex-
pressed their concern to the general.

RISON: And you're expressing it to me.

BRODERINE: The general did want me to feel you out on
it.

RISON: On what exactly?

BRODERINE: He wants to know if you think there's a
chance of the Montagnards going their own way.

RISON: They're fighting under the South Vietnamese flag.

BRODERINE: There's no need to get defensive, Bob. It's just that some people think you've got a wild card here, and we want to make sure we know how it's going to play.

RISON: This isn't a game we're involved in here. It's war. For now the Montagnards and the South Vietnamese have the same enemy. I think that's good enough. The "Yards" can outfight any ARVN outfit any day of the week, and those people in Saigon need to remember that. They also need to remember that if the Montagnards stop fighting, the VC will have control of the highlands in less than a month and this country will be history.

BRODERINE: We're aware of the strategic scenario. But there are larger issues involved here. Issues that are not of concern to either the government in Saigon or the Montagnards.

RISON: What issues?

BRODERINE: This war—don't you see what it is? We kicked their ass in Tet. They shot their wad. Hell, it's going to take those sons of bitches two or three years to get back up to strength in the north. They tipped their hand too soon and we handed them their ass in a sling.

RISON: I agree. If Washington would let us go, we could make a clean sweep of it.

BRODERINE: Washington! Hell, those pansy asses in D.C. couldn't fight their way out of paper sack. And this is just the sideshow any way. The real war is over in Europe.

RISON: We're not at war in Europe.

BRODERINE: We've been at war for twenty-four years over there.

RISON: What are you talking about?

BRODERINE: That's not important right now. What is important is that the general wants to know what his options are. He thinks we can downgrade our U.S. strength here and maintain the status quo. He wants to know if he can count on the Montagnards to remain a stable force.

RISON: Downgrade? We need to finish this thing. If we put every swinging dick we have in-country into the bush, we could have this thing done with by the end of the year. You yourself just said we've hurt them bad. We need to finish them while they're down.

BRODERINE: That's not the plan. Can the general count on your people?

RISON: Whose plan are we talking about? Since when does the general make foreign policy? He's not the National Command Authority.

BRODERINE: Listen, Bob, wake up. We've got two or three years of breathing space now. We can keep rotating people in and give them combat experience. Keep things going on the procurement side. After that, who knows? We can always keep the North under our thumb with the bombing. But the general feels it is essential that we maintain things as is. Those are his instructions.

RISON: From who? That isn't what Washington is putting out.

BRODERINE: Damn it, Bob. Forget Washington. They're out of the loop on this. This is *us*. You're one of us. You understand.

RISON: Don't wave that fucking ring in my face, Bill. That ring says we serve and follow orders. We don't dictate policy.

BRODERINE: We do when there's shooting involved. And we do when it involves being ready to defend our country. We can't allow that to remain in the hands of the civilians. They've screwed it up repeatedly and it's our blood that is spilled every time. This is the first war we've gotten into in this century where we've had the time to prepare. And the bigger war is just waiting over there in Europe and we need this one to remain prepared for it.

RISON: Who the hell is this "we" you're talking about?

BRODERINE: The Long Gray Line, Bob. It's been around a hell of a lot longer than you have and it will be here long after you're gone.

RISON: Is that a threat?

BRODERINE: Take it any way you want, colonel. The bottom line is, your people do what we tell you to do, or we'll gut you and your organization.

RISON: Are you done, general?

BRODERINE: I'm done.

END OF TRANSCRIPT

Trace rubbed her forehead. She turned the page and Rison's writing continued.

They didn't fool around. They did gut me and my organization, but all that's history and you can find that story elsewhere. If you're reading this, I am most likely dead and you are just finding out about the existence of The Line. And the thing you need is proof. I don't have the tapes of that conversation, and even if I did, it would be claimed a forgery. But I do have proof. To find it, you're going to have to go to West Point. Go to Custer's grave. Exactly one foot to the left on line with the front edge of the base of his gravestone—between his and his wife's grave—and one foot down, you'll find proof. Godspeed.

Trace folded the pages and slid them back in the envelope. At least she knew where she needed to go next. She picked the phone up and dialed Maggie's number again.

CHAPTER ☆ 16

PACIFIC PALISADES, HAWAII
2 DECEMBER
4:48 P.M. LOCAL/ 148 ZULU

Boomer and Skibicki trooped into Maggie's house covered in mud. They'd spent the last several hours scouring the north coast, searching vainly for any sign of where the previous night's jumpers might have gone to earth. They'd finally called it quits after getting Skibicki's jeep stuck on one of the countless back trails. They were both exhausted.

Maggie met them with a laundry bag to take their dirty clothes. "Your friend Trace called an hour ago," she informed them.

"Is she all right?" Boomer asked, pausing in the middle of unlacing his boots.

"She says she's fine, but she thinks Colonel Rison is dead."

"Dead?" Skibicki repeated, focusing all his attention on Maggie.

Maggie gestured for them to forget about the mud and follow her into the kitchen. "She didn't talk to me long. She said that she talked to Rison at the game and he was shot while they were talking. She escaped. Before he got shot, Rison gave her an envelope with some information in it that says the Line exists. She's on her way to West Point to get Rison's proof."

"West Point?" Boomer said. "That's going into the lion's den. What kind of proof is she going for?"

"She didn't say," Maggie replied.

213

''Did she leave a number where I could call her?'' Boomer asked.

''She said she didn't think it was a good idea to give her location over the phone,'' Maggie replied. She threw a newspaper down on the table. ''I just picked a copy of the evening paper. You might want to look at it.''

Boomer picked it up and scanned the front page. His eyes immediately focused on a story on the bottom left.

TWO BODIES FOUND
AT KAENA POINT

A local fisherman discovered the bodies of two men at Kaena Point early this morning. Both men had been shot but police were unwilling to release any more information. The identity of the men has not been released.

Boomer checked the rest of the article, but it yielded little information. ''The police have found the bodies from last night,'' Boomer said, laying the paper down.

''Any ID?'' Skibicki asked, pouring himself a cup of coffee.

''Not according to the paper, but we don't know what the police have. What about the weapons we used?''

''I deep-sixed those,'' Skibicki said. ''That's one of the things I took care of while I was gone.''

Boomer was relieved that those pieces of evidence were gone.

Maggie wasn't done. ''Trace also said for you to get the story about what happened to Colonel Rison in Vietnam from Ski.''

Boomer turned to the sergeant major. ''What does that mean?''

Skibicki wearily sank down into a chair. ''Rison was the best damn commander I ever served under. What it means is that Rison probably didn't have the time to tell her about what happened to him when he ran afoul of The Line.''

''And you know?'' Boomer demanded.

''Yes, I know.''

Boomer was agitated. ''Why didn't you tell me everything you knew?''

"Because I didn't have proof and I didn't really know what was going on," Skibicki snapped. "Rison had the proof and the real knowledge. And now Trace is going after it. I also didn't make all the connections with what happened back then with what's going on now. It's been a long time."

Boomer sat across from him. "Tell me what you do know."

Maggie bustled over with mugs of coffee and sat on the other corner of the table as Skibicki gathered his thoughts.

"When you first came to me about The Line, I tried to blow you off. I didn't know why you were asking me, and quite honestly, I thought you might be from them. They want that proof back too. They want it bad—bad enough to kill for. It was only when I realized who your dad was that I knew you probably weren't from The Line, but even then I had to play it safe."

Skibicki looked off, out at the ocean. "I ran into The Line when Rison did—way back in Vietnam. Of course I didn't know it was called The Line or anything about it. That all came later. It was after the mission where your dad died. We were running operations constantly so there wasn't any time to stand around and contemplate things. I got a new team. This time I was the team leader, we were so short of personnel.

"I also got a new assignment. Command and Control North, MACV-SOG. We were also under B-57, Project Gamma, but we weren't going west. We were going north, right into the little shitheads' backyard and snooping around. We were also crossing into Laos to get earlier readings on stuff moving south through there and into Cambodia on what everyone called the Ho Chi Minh Trail, but it wasn't just one trail—it was a whole complex of trails and roads and supply depots and staging areas.

"You got to understand something else that was going at the same time, something that was affecting Special Forces throughout the theater. A lot of our A Teams in 5th Group proper were working with the Montagnards—had been for years. And that was a big burr under the skin of the South Vietnamese government. In 1964, the Montagnards in the Ban Me Thout region had actually rebelled

against the government, and it was only with the greatest
of diplomacy that the Special Forces advisors in the area
were able to keep the peace.

"The teams working with the Yards were always caught
between a rock and a hard place. The Yards were damn
good fighters, but they hated the South Vietnamese as much
as they hated the North and if you remember rightly, our
government's policy was to support the South, not the
Montagnards."

Skibicki shook his head. "I'm not sure about the exact
political maneuvering. All I know is what Colonel Rison
told me afterwards and what I saw myself. Rison said that
he was approached by someone sent by the MACV Commanding General in Saigon and told to back off on supporting the Montagnards. They wanted us to disarm over
fifty percent of our indigenous forces. Rison refused to do
that, so the regular Army assholes started doing whatever
they could to screw with our operations. Since they also
had the help of the CIA, you could tell that someone really
high up was rocking the boat.

"In the middle of this bullshit we were trying to fight a
war. And it was starting to go badly in B-57. We still had
to deal with our counterparts in the LLDB—the South Vietnamese army—and sometimes it was hard to tell who was
more of a threat, the LLDB or the VC. Our counterintel
guy was picking up information that our fucking LLDB
counterparts were selling ammunition and weapons to the
North Vietnamese. So much for democracy and the free
enterprise system.

"We tried tightening down the screws on security at
CCN headquarters but we were still losing people on missions and it was obvious there was a leak. But it wasn't
like we could just call time-out and put all our energy into
finding out where the leak was. Our counterintel guys went
to work on it and we kept getting on board the choppers
and going out not knowing if our mission was compromised from the word go. You want to talk about having a
shit feeling in your gut, you try that someday, flying into
the badlands not knowing whether your whole OPLAN has
been compromised and the bad guys were waiting for you
to get off the bird.

"Then my team, RT Texas, went on a mission in, well, let's simply call it a classified area, although I can tell you now that it was north of the DMZ. We came across what had been an enemy base camp. It was empty. We searched the place, sometimes you'd be amazed what you can find left behind, and hit paydirt: we found some film negatives that had been discarded in a pile of trash that had been half burnt. We brought those back with us."

Skibicki laughed, a low growl that held no mirth. "We had the double-dealing motherfucker on film: one of our LLDB agents, Ta Chon, meeting with North Vietnamese in uniform. We brought the son of a bitch in and wired him up to the polygraph and he flunked it. Shit, he was sweating bullets and we knew that he knew we knew."

Skibicki paused and Boomer and Maggie both impatiently waited for him to continue. The sergeant major took a deep breath, then picked up the story.

"I was ready to pop Chon right then and there. Hell, I'd lost friends on those teams he'd compromised. Rison was down in Saigon at some damn meeting, so he was out of the net. The FOB executive officer, Lieutenant Colonel Killebrew, wasn't authorized to make such a command decision, so he went to the CIA for instructions. In reality, he wanted to turn Chon over to them and he knew that would take care of that. We'd done it before. The spooks liked fresh meat. Plus there was always the possibility the Company could triple Chon and turn him back against his own people and we could scarf up the rest of his buddies.

"But what Killebrew didn't know was that the CIA was wired in with The Line and they were waiting for something like this. I didn't know it either when I went to the CIA safe house outside Nha Trang with Chon. The asshole I talked to wouldn't take Chon. He suggested to me that we 'eliminate' Chon ourselves since we had such strong evidence. Hell, he didn't suggest it, he practically ordered me to do it."

Skibicki stretched out his massive arms and glanced at the other two occupants of the room. The only sound was the wind blowing off the porch moving a chime back and forth.

"We took Chon back to the FOB. Then me and another

guy, we shot Chon up with morphine, took him out into the bay, cut a vein so that the sharks would find him, and I popped him twice in the head with my High Standard .22. We weighed the body down with chains, and dumped him overboard.'' Skibicki said it all flatly, like he was describing a trip to the laundromat.

"It was all said and done by the time Rison got back to the FOB from a MACV command and staff meeting in Saigon. I went in with Killebrew and briefed Rison on what had happened. I think he knew right away that something stunk about the way the CIA spook had reacted, but fuck, the body was already a body. Couldn't resurrect the son of a bitch. We made up a cover story to explain Chon disappearing. We said we sent him on a cross-border op and we never heard from him again. And that wasn't that far out because, like I said, we were losing lots of people over the fence.

"The shit hit the fan the next day. Somebody, and to this day I swear it was the CIA, even though they produced some low ranking, non-SF Intel dink to go public, blew the whistle.

"That's all the general in Saigon needed. He called Rison up and asked him what happened. Rison gave him the cover story. The general blew a gasket, since he already had heard the true story and had Rison arrested. In the middle of a war, our own people arrested a full bull colonel in the U.S. Army!

"They also picked up Killebrew, me, and the other fellow who helped me, a guy named Harry Franks. We were charged with murder.'' Skibicki shook his head, still incredulous after all these years. "Here we were, in the middle of the most fucked-up war you've ever seen, and we're getting charged with *murder* for wasting a double agent. It was enough to make you cry.

"Well, even the general couldn't keep a lid on it. The press got a hold of the story and it hit the headlines all over back in the states. There was a big public outcry over Americans getting jailed, even if we did kill someone. Hell, John Wayne had made a movie about the Green Berets; people liked us. And by then most everyone was sick of the war and it looked like we were just being set up, which we were, except no one in the public knew the real reason.

"So it didn't work out quite like the general wanted. He didn't get to see Colonel Rison and the rest of us go to jail, but he did at least get the colonel out of the way. Rison's career was over. Never mind the murder, there was still the fact that he had lied to the general when he gave him the cover story. After all," Skibicki's voice dripped sarcasm, "we were only supposed to kill people, not lie about it.

"The real thing that got us off, though, was what had started it in the first place—the CIA. They wouldn't allow their people to testify, so that sort of stalled the whole thing out. After all, my defense was that I'd been told to waste the little motherfucker by the spook. There was no way the Company was going to put one of their own on the stand under oath.

"The general didn't waste any time in trying to get Special Forces in-country under his control, though. Rison was still in the brig down in Saigon when the general appointed some leg colonel from his staff to take over the FOB. The son of a bitch tried to put on a green beret and not only was he not SF-qualified, he wasn't even jump-qualified. The FOB sergeant major, old Terry Hollihan, a good man, had a fucking fit. He told the sorry SOB to take the goddamn jump wings and beret off.

"The colonel then tried to get around SF by going down to the LLDB jump school and getting airborne-qualified by doing a few chopper blasts. It was a real shame when he broke his leg on the third jump." Skibicki grinned a wicked smile. "Of course that might have had something to do with Hollihan's jumpmaster inspecting the colonel's gear just prior to the jump. I guess the man was lucky he was alive. I'd have cut his damn static line."

Skibicki's face turned serious. "But all that's a roundabout way to get you to what you really want to know. We got off. They dropped the charges. But Rison knew that he had to do something or The Line would kill Special Forces.

"So he came to me and Harry and Lieutenant Colonel Killibrew and we talked about it. We needed something on them. Something to act as a countermeasure. There wasn't much the officers could do. Rison had to go back to the States. His career was over. Killibrew was reassigned in-country. But before he left, Rison pulled a few strings and Harry and I disappeared into the Studies and Observation Group under deep cover with one last mission assigned to us by our former commander: get something on The Line.

"We went after the only lead we had, the assistant division commander of the Americal who had come to Rison in the beginning of the whole mess. We went down to the Americal AO and followed that officer everywhere. Hell, that unit was so screwed up, we could have wasted the man and the rest of the Division staff and it would have taken them a couple of days to realize it. We just put on regular fatigues, sewed an Americal patch on the shoulder and meandered around the big shitpile they called Division headquarters. They had so many ash and trash men there, it was amazing they could put a squad in the field. Everyone just figured we belonged and no one questioned us.

"It took us five weeks before we got what we were looking for. Some VIP from the States flew in to Saigon and then came up to the Americal. He went straight to the ADC—didn't even talk to the Division Commander, who spent most of his time drilling holes into the sky in his command and control helicopter, getting his rocks off listening on the radio to people dying five thousand feet below.

"We knew this VIP was something special. He wore unmarked fatigues and he was old. And he wore a big-ass ring on his left hand. Ain't no mistaking one of those Hudson High rings. So I left Harry with the ADC and followed this guy back to Saigon. He was staying at the MACV compound in VIP quarters. I did some checking and found out his name: retired Brigadier General Benjamin Hooker on special assignment from the Joint Chiefs of Staff. I told you about meeting him in 'Nam," Skibicki added defensively as Boomer glared at him. "Officially, he was retired and working for the Joint Chiefs. But in reality he was checking up on The Line's little war."

Boomer stood up and walked over to the window, then came back, his mind churning. "What happened?"

"I waited until Hooker was at a meeting at the MACV compound and I broke into his room. I was looking for anything. I still didn't even really know about The Line or who Hooker was. I hit paydirt. Right there in his locked briefcase.''

"What did you get?'' Boomer asked, unconsciously leaning forward.

"His diary. Starting from 1926, the year he entered the Academy through 1969.''

Boomer whistled.

"What did it say?'' Maggie asked.

Skibicki held up a hand. "Whoa, slow down. I only glanced at it to make sure it was something we could use. I didn't have much time. I got out of the BOQ and went over to a friend of mine who worked in an office there at one of the MACV buildings. I made a copy of the diary page by page, but I didn't read it. I checked a few pages here and there and what I saw scared the shit out of me. You won't believe some of the stuff this guy was involved in.

"Anyway, that same day I packed the original in a secure pouch and gave it to a SF guy I trusted who was rotating back to the States with orders to hand deliver it to Rison. I sent the copy by FOB courier to Killebrew. Then I went back to the American headquarters, gathered Harry in, and we went back to CCN to our job fighting the real enemy.''

Skibicki fell silent.

Boomer waited a little bit, then felt compelled to ask questions. "Is that what Trace is after? The original diary?''

"I don't know,'' Skibicki said. "If Rison sent her for proof, I imagine that's what he would send her after. It's what he must have been using all these years to keep The Line off his back and from tearing Special Forces apart.''

"But why is it at West Point?'' Boomer asked.

"The purloined letter theory,'' Maggie suggested. "You know, hide it in the last place people would look for it. Right at the place it all started.''

"What did Rison do with the diary back in 1969?'' Boomer wanted to know. "Why didn't he expose The Line?''

"Expose The Line?'' Skibicki repeated incredulously. "We were trying to save our ass and Special Forces' existence. The best Rison hoped for was a truce. A Mexican standoff.''

"What about Killibrew? What did he do with his copy?''

"Killibrew didn't do shit with his copy,'' Skibicki said, and for a moment Boomer mistook the bitterness in Ski's voice as being directed at his former executive officer. "Lieutenant Colonel Killibrew is officially listed as missing in action. Two days after I got the copy of the diary to him, he disappeared while on a flight from Nha Trang to the FOB. I find it rather curious that the plane he was on was a contract one flown by a merc in the employ of the Company. The merc pilot was supposedly lost in the crash also, but I wasn't very surprised when I just happened to spot him two years later in Bangkok while I was on R & R.''

"Did the mercenary tell you what happened to Killibrew?'' Boomer asked.

"Before he died, he did.'' Skibicki looked Boomer in the eyes. "They killed Killibrew, and that's one of the reasons we 'didn't do' anything. Rison took care of the original and took care of dealing with The Line. They backed off and we backed off and that's the way it's been for twenty-six years until you showed up here in Hawaii and Trace started writing her book. And now the Colonel's dead too.''

FORT SHAFTER, HAWAII
2 December
6:50 P.M. LOCAL/ 450 ZULU

Skibicki parked the jeep on Radar Hill Road, one street removed from the tunnel. In between the two streets a lava ridge separated Boomer and him from their destination.

"We'll leave it here. I want to see if anyone's in the tunnel first and going up a dead-end street isn't my idea of going in smart,'' Skibicki said. "The fake DIA guys have to have our names by now from the cops so I wouldn't be too surprised to see company waiting for us.''

Boomer didn't say anything. His mind was occupied with thoughts of Trace and what had happened to her today. He was less than thrilled about her going to West Point tomorrow, but there wasn't anything he could do about it and that was what rankled him the most. He had thought he'd be getting her out of harm's way by sending her back to the States.

They went up the ridge, getting down on their bellies as they came up to the crest. Peering over the top, they could see that the parking lot in front of the TASOSC tunnel was empty. Skibicki scanned the surrounding terrain in the fading light. "Looks clear. Let's go."

They stood and made their way down to the vault door. Skibicki picked up the phone that was on the concrete wall to the left of the door.

"What are you doing?" Boomer asked.

"On the weekend and at the end of each duty day the tunnel alarm is activated by the last person to leave. I have to call the Provost Marshall's office to have them turn the alarm off."

Skibicki dialed the number and talked to the duty sergeant. Then he punched in the code on the numeric keypad and pulled the door open. The was a rush of air as the pressure equalized and they stepped in, letting the door lock behind them.

Skibicki led the way to his desk where he pulled out a large keyring. "Keys to everything in here," he said. "So the enlisted people can clean everyone's office," he added.

They went to the end of the first tunnel and he opened Colonel Coulder's office. Boomer watched as Skibicki began spinning the dials on the secure filing cabinet behind the commander's desk.

"You have his combination?"

"Vasquez is security manager for the tunnel. She has all the combinations," Skibicki said as the tumblers clicked and he opened the top drawer. "So, naturally, that means I have all the combinations." He quickly began scanning the folders inside. "Since Coulder was in on the brief with Decker, I have to assume he's in on whatever's going on. He's a ring-knocker, too."

Boomer searched the colonel's desk while Skibicki worked the files. He looked up when Skibicki slapped a folder down on the desk. "The rest of the President's schedule. What wasn't in the OPORDER in the conference room."

"And?" Boomer asked.

"The night of sixth. After the President attends the fund-raiser downtown. A national command and control exercise is scheduled."

Skibicki considered the information he had just read to Boomer. "We've been focusing on the ceremony in Pearl Harbor, but that sounds like a good time for The Line to make its move. They'll have the President on their turf. Most likely on Looking Glass," he added, referring to the modified 747, E-4B command and control aircraft. "I heard one of them was flying in, but I assumed that was simply because the Joint Chiefs were coming."

"Maybe," Boomer said. "But I've got to tell you, despite everything that's happened the past several days, I find it hard to believe that there is a plot against the President."

Skibicki threw down the folder. "*You're* the one who said your mission you were on in the Ukraine was a set-up."

"Yeah, but there's a big difference between that and a plot directly against the President. In the history of our country there has never been—"

"Fuck!" Skibicki exclaimed. "Listen, Boomer, get your head out of your ass. First off, we've *had* the military go against the government numerous times before. Remember MacArthur during the Korean War? Some of the generals during the Civil War?

"You may have been behind the fence at Bragg for the past couple of years," Skibicki continued, "but I've been out here in the real Army. People are not happy. They haven't been happy for years. In fact, they're downright pissed. Our benefits are getting eaten up by fat cats sitting in Washington. They'll cut *our* benefits but not their own.

"We don't have a contract guaranteeing any of the things we enlisted for. If Congress wants to change retirement benefits for the Army, they simply pass a law. As they did a couple of years ago by changing the base pay computation for retirement pay. Not a big deal by itself, but when you start adding in all the piddly shit over the past ten years, it comes to a lot. There's been a betrayal of trust. We put it on the line for this country, expecting that the benefits we enlisted under would be there when we retired and they're not."

Skibicki was on a roll. Boomer had never seem him so agitated. "The President's flying out here to make a speech at Pearl Harbor, over the graves of men who died because their peacetime military had been cut to the bone after World War I. It's not so different today.

"Add it up, Boomer. The cutbacks. Hard Glass getting sliced. The Backfire incident. The bullshit missions that have killed soldiers and kept thousands away from their families for months on end: Bosnia, Somalia, Haiti. Pile on top of all that the MRA and you have a pile of C-4 just waiting for a fuse to be dropped in and ignited.

"The thing you've got to accept, Boomer, is that people are scared," Skibicki said. "They will never admit it, but they are. They're threatened—from the Joint Chiefs down to the lowest snuffy. Scared people don't act according to logic. And sometimes they act in ways that are destructive all around. That's what I think we're seeing here."

"You seem to have thought about this a lot," Boomer said.

"I haven't exactly been overwhelmed with work here the past year or so," Skibicki said.

Both their heads snapped up as they felt the air pressure change. Boomer had his Browning High Power out.

"It's probably Vasquez," Skibicki said, but he had a gun in his own hand also. They waited until a figure turned the corner at the end of tunnel one. They both relaxed as they reconized the newcomer.

Vasquez was wearing biker shorts and a sleeveless shirt, both of which accented the sleek lines of her sculpted muscles, but her tousled hair and drawn face looked like she had had a rough night. She had a can of soda in her hand and popped the top as she entered Coulder's office. She looked around, then settled into the colonel's chair.

"What do you have?" Skibicki said without preamble, ignoring her breach of etiquette.

"This one is gonna cost you big time, sergeant major," Vasquez said. "I want off the duty roster for the next two months."

Skibicki waved that aside. "What have you got?"

Vasquez looked at Boomer. "First off, sir, you was right. That Ethan Allen Class sub—the *Sam Houston*. It isn't a current missile carrier. It works for Navy Special Ops."

"The question is," Boomer said, "is what is it doing now?"

"It's heading for the unidentified sub and the *Glomar Explorer*," Vasquez said, laying out her Xeroxed maps. "The other sub moved in and has been lying still for the past twelve hours, here, about 150 miles southwest of Oahu. The *Glomar* is steaming toward it and should rendezvous in about six hours. The *Sam Houston* is closing in on both of them very slowly and at its current rate of speed should be in the immediate vicinity the afternoon of December sixth."

"What about the other sub?" Skibicki asked. "Anything on what it is?"

Vasquez took a deep breath. "Sergeant major, what I'm about to tell you is classified Top Secret, Q Clearance. Don't ask me how I got the information. Just trust me that I got it and it's true. If anyone finds out that I know, never mind that I told you, we're both going away for a long time."

Skibicki nodded and looked at Boomer who also nodded.

"The bogey sub is called the SHARCC. That's S-H-A-R-C-C," she added, spelling out the acronym. "It stand for Submerged Headquarters and Reserve Command and Control. It's the Navy's version of Looking Glass, the post-attack airborne command and control system for use in case all our fixed facilities get nuked."

Boomer looked at Skibicki who returned the eye contact.

"We got Looking Glass coming in also for a command and control exercise." Boomer said. "Why both?"

Skibicki rubbed his chin. "I never heard that we had an underwater system like that, but if you think about it, it makes sense. The airborne platforms were designed in case of nuclear war. That way the national command could take to the air and become less of a target. The only problem is that Looking Glass can only stay airborne for so long. Even with in-flight refueling, they eventually have to land somewhere. But this sub could probably stay out at sea for six months or more."

Vasquez nodded. "It's a nuclear-powered boat, using the same keel as the Ohio Class missile subs, but set up totally different on the inside for command and control. My source tells me there are two of them, one in the Atlantic and this one in the Pacific. My source also tells me that since they were launched two years ago, they have never gone back into port."

"What?" Skibicki said. "How can they do that?"

Vasquez tapped the imagery she'd brought the previous day. "The *Glomar*. It shuttles between the Pacific and the Atlantic. The SHARCC can dock with the underwater barge, then be brought up into the hold of the *Glomar* for repairs and maintenance. The crews are rotated then too. Since the SHARCC never surfaces, it can never get spotted."

"So maybe this C&C exercise on the sixth will be on board the SHARCC involving both the Joint Chiefs of Staff and the President," Boomer said.

There was a long pause before Skibicki spoke. "Now it all makes sense," he said. "It's not going to be Pearl on the morning of the seventh. They're going to take down the SHARCC from the *Sam Houston* on the sixth while our friends from Okinawa take out the Vice President up at Turtle Bay.

"If that SHARCC is set up just like Looking Glass then once they have it, they can cut in and take over all command and control for the military and even use the emergency overrides to cut into all civilian satellite traffic. Since practically all television feeds through satellites nowadays, they can effectively control the media."

"It's perfect," Boomer said. "No one will even know."

"We need to report this," Vasquez said.

"To who?" Skibicki asked.

"Someone," Vasquez said. "We can't just let this happen."

"We don't know for sure that it is going to happen," Skibicki said.

"But we know *something* is going to happen," Vasquez exclaimed.

"The problem is that we have no proof," Boomer said.

"What about the men who attacked you at Kaena

Point?'' Vasquez asked. ''It was in the paper. The police have the bodies.''

''If we brought that up to anyone,'' Boomer said, ''it would only cause Skibicki and me to be thrown in jail.'' He looked at the phone on the colonel's desk. ''No, what we need is solid proof that The Line exists, and Major Trace should be calling anytime.''

''How about if I go to the police?'' Vasquez offered. ''I wasn't involved in the shooting the other night and I can tell them all that has happened and what you all are afraid is going to happen.''

''We still have no proof,'' Boomer replied.

''But at least the President could be warned,'' she argued. ''He doesn't have to go out to the SHARCC for the exercise and maybe the Vice President could leave Turtle Bay early or something. We wait for proof, we might be waiting a long time,'' she added.

''Trace will come up with something,'' Boomer said.

''We still have two days,'' Skibicki reminded them.

Boomer thought about it. ''Even if the information about the *Sam Houston* and the SHARCC is correct, *and* there is a plan to take down the SHARCC if these guys have planned this correctly, and there's no reason to believe they haven't, then I'm sure they have one, if not several, backup plans.''

Skibicki agreed. ''If the night of the sixth doesn't work, they still can come into Pearl Harbor on the morning of the seventh off the *Sam Houston* using the SDVs. Those guys are trained on that kind of infiltration and they'll be infiltrating their own back yard.'' He made a decision. ''We don't hear anything from Major Trace by tomorrow morning, we're going to have to take action regardless.''

''So what do we do in the meantime?'' Boomer wondered aloud. ''We're—'' He paused as the air pressure changed again.

They all turned and looked. As the first person turned the corner, Boomer drew his gun again. It was Decker and he wasn't alone.

''Take them!'' Decker yelled as he dove behind a desk.

Boomer fired once then hit the deck as the pair of men who had followed Decker opened fire with submachine guns. The glass that had separated Colonel Coulder's office from the rest of the tunnel exploded inward.

Boomer stuck his hand up over the three-feet-high wall and fired blindly. He heard the roar of Skibicki's gun a few feet to the other side and glanced over. The sergeant major was hunched behind the wall also, firing blindly to keep them from getting closer.

"You OK, Vasquez?" Skibicki yelled out.

"Yeah, but I wish I was smaller," her voice came from under the colonel's desk.

Chips splattered off the wall as the intruders fired again.

"They aren't asking us to surrender," Boomer hissed to Skibicki.

"I noticed," Skibicki replied.

"What now?" Boomer asked as he fired another couple of rounds.

"We know the tunnels. They don't," Skibicki said.

"So?"

"Remember the locker where I was inventorying the scuba gear?"

"Yeah?"

"We go there." Skibicki raised his voice. "Vasquez, on three we head for the scuba locker."

"Roger that, sergeant major."

"Uh," Boomer said, "what about the bad guys?"

"One," Skibicki yelled. "Two." He rolled over, put his back to the low wall and fired at the antiquated fuse box in the corner of Coulder's office. With an explosion of sparks the tunnel went dark. "Three."

Boomer stood and vaulted the wall, keeping low. He didn't fire, nor did Skibicki.

The men with Decker fired blindly, bullets scattering all over the room. Their muzzles made bright flashes and Boomer took the opportunity to fire right at one of the stuttering lights. A startled yell of pain rewarded his effort and the firing stopped on both sides.

To the best of Boomer's recollection the side tunnel was only about ten feet to his right. He duck-walked, bumping into a desk, recoiling, pushing right, breathing hard. He hit the wall, then felt it give way to open space. Someone brushed by him, moving quicker. He was in the side tunnel.

He stood up and moved quicker. He could hear light footsteps in front of him and followed.

"Damn!" Boomer hissed as he ran into a wall with his forehead leading.

"This way," he heard Vasquez whisper. Boomer headed in the direction of the voice and a pair of hands grabbed him and pulled him into the scuba locker. They could hear Decker's voice echoing through the tunnel they had left.

"You won't get out! We have the front door covered."

Boomer heard a screech of metal, then Skibicki's voice explaining what was going on. "There's an air duct back here. It'll be a tight fit. I know it comes out on the back side of the lava flow. I went up there one day and checked."

"You ever been in the duct?" Boomer asked, tucking his High Power back in the holster, then feeling his forehead. His hand came away wet with blood.

"No," Skibicki grunted and there was the sound of something metal hitting the floor.

"So how do you know it's a tight fit?"

"I'm hoping it's a tight fit rather than no fit," Skibicki said. "I'm going in. Follow me."

Boomer helped Vasquez up after the sergeant major. Then he climbed up himself. He was in a four-foot-diameter ridged steel tube that angled up at almost sixty degrees. Boomer began climbing, bracing his boots against the ridges. After what he estimated to be about twenty feet he bumped into Vasquez's sneakers.

"What's the matter?" he asked.

"It's getting tighter," Vasquez's voice was strained.

Boomer soon found out what she meant. The tube halved in size and jigged to the left before resuming its climb. Boomer got stuck halfway into the jig. His hips were stuck. He felt cloth and skin tear as he popped free.

Boomer blinked. Although Vasquez filled almost the entire width of the pipe, he could see a faint light seeping through around her. The light suddenly grew much brighter as Skibicki punched off the cap on the air duct.

Boomer made the last few feet. Vasquez's hands came down, grabbed his collar and pulled him out faster than he could move his feet. Boomer looked around. They were on the far side of the lava ridge from the tunnel just as Skibicki had promised.

"Let's get to my jeep," Skibicki said. "This way."

CHAPTER ☆ 17

The sun had raced around and come up again, bathing
the east coast of the United States with light. Trace had
spent an uneasy night in the motel. She'd wanted to call
Hawaii again, but there was nothing more to say and it was
the middle of the night there. She'd relayed the important
information in her phone call to Maggie. Maybe she could
talk to Boomer later today.

Through the leafless branches of the trees lining the highway, Trace could see New York City off to her right. She'd
entered the Palisades Parkway at its start point, near the
George Washington Bridge and that had brought back
memories of Boomer. She remembered his telling her that
he'd grown up in the shadow of that bridge on the other
side of the river.

As she drove, the route paralleled the river. The Hudson
flowed in its glacial bed past her toward the Atlantic and
on the Jersey side, high cliffs—named the Palisades by
Henry Hudson when he'd first sailed up the river—looked
down upon the dark water.

Trace felt a familiar feeling ignite in the pit of her stomach, overshadowing even the present crisis she in. She
was returning to the Point. Like Pavlov's dog hearing the
bell, her body responded to four years of psychological and
emotional strain and terror. Every West Pointer going up
the Hudson felt it, no matter what the occasion for their

233

return. Trace often imagined that even an old graduate being assigned to take over the Academy as superintendent felt it. There was no getting over the memories of Beast Barracks and four years inside the gray walls of the Academy.

It didn't matter how far along on the Army chain of evolution a graduate was. The Point kept him or her in its grip. Even first-class cadets nearing graduation would aimlessly wander the barracks halls on Sunday nights in their tattered gray bathrobes or sweats, feeling the oppression of another week looming. In the Academy's perverse way there was even an official ditty for the mood listed in the issued Bugle Notes (the cadet bible) called the Sunday night poop:

Six bells and all is well.
Another weekend shot to hell.
Another week in my little gray cell.
Another week in which to excel.
Oh, hell.

The last two words were uttered with all the anguish and exasperation only a cadet could muster.

As she crossed the state line from New Jersey to New York, the Palisades Parkway veered away from the river and moved inland, crossing under the New York State Thruway. The terrain grew more hilly, and Trace passed the turnoffs for New City and Harriman State Park. The closer she got, the greater her anxiety.

Looping around the bulk of Bear Mountain, the parkway came to an end at a traffic circle. The first right led to Bear Mountain State Park. The second to Bear Mountain Bridge and Anthony's Nose on the far side of the river. The last exit, before looping back on oneself, was Route 9W. The sign pointed the way to Fort Montgomery, Highland Falls, and, ultimately, West Point.

Trace took the turn, going by the Revolutionary War sites of Fort Clinton and Fort Montgomery. For a young country like the United States, West Point was about as old and venerable a site as could be found to place a military academy. It was geography that fixed the name, and it was geography that dictated the early military significance of the site.

She passed through the small town of Fort Montgomery and took the turnoff on 218 into Highland Falls, the town that lay just outside the main gate to the Academy.

Since Trace's day, the Academy had expanded south, gobbling up what used to be Ladycliff College on the river side of the town and turning it into an extension of itself, housing the museum and a brand-new visitors' center. Trace had not been back to West Point since graduation and she turned into the visitor center to get acquainted with any further changes that might have occurred since her day. Besides, she was still somewhat at a loss about how to proceed. She didn't exactly envision herself digging up Custer's grave on a bright, wintery Sunday morning. That might attract a bit of unwanted attention. She had never been in the cemetery during her time as a cadet and she had no idea how many people visited it or how accessible Custer's grave was.

Despite the early hours, busloads of tourists were there at the center, eager to see how their tax dollars were being spent. Their official tour guides were the wives of officers assigned to West Point—a keen public relations move. The women could talk about their "husband's cadets," in a motherly tone, giving the impression of the Academy being one big happy family. That there were numerous off-limits signs posted all over the Academy saying "Authorized Personnel Only," wasn't noticed by most of the tourists. The signs blocked off all the barracks and academic areas from the public. A less naive person might wonder what it was the Academy didn't want the public to see. After all, there was no classified training going on at the Academy and it was fully funded by the taxpayer.

Trace walked past a group waiting to board their bus and entered the center. A large gift shop to the right sold practically every article of clothing ever made with the valuable addition of a West Point emblem stenciled on it, along with assorted coffee mugs, glasses, pennants, bumper stickers, and posters. In the other direction, an area housed several displays telling about "life" at the Academy.

Trace veered left and stopped in front of a display, star-

ing across the velvet ropes at a "typical cadet's room."
She was reminded of the different rooms she had inhabited
in New South Barracks. Memories came back to her in
waves, each one leaving a trail of emotion as the thought
receded: the cold, winter nights that never seemed to end
until they turned into bitter, gray mornings where plebe
roommates would talk to each other only to pass essential
survival information like who the officer of the day was,
while they prepared their room for the daily AMI—morning inspection; the sunny spring days with the trees high
up on the cliff behind the barracks just beginning to show
green and having the feeling in her chest that she just
wanted to explode and be somewhere else and be doing
anything else, not sitting here in her room studying Napo-
leon's campaigns, afraid to walk out the door for fear of
being stopped and hazed.

Trace had heard that there were some plebes who were
so afraid of leaving their room to go to the latrine that they
urinated in the sinks in their rooms. She was glad she had
never been that desperate, although she and her roommate
had ended up eating toothpaste, they'd been so starved in
the third week of Beast Barracks. Toothpaste was authorized, but they couldn't buy food at the small cadet store.

They'd been broken, some swiftly, some more slowly,
depending on the strength of character each individual
brought on R Day. By the end of the first day each new
cadet had received a hair cut, been put in uniform, and
marched in formation to Trophy Point where they'd sworn
their oath of allegiance to the United States. By that time,
half of them would have marched in step into the Hudson
if told to do so, they were so disoriented. And instead of
backing off, the pressure had increased through the years
at the Academy until what resulted was a "graduate," able
to recite MacArthur's duty-honor-country speech and the
number and weight of the links in the Great Chain.

But they were not only supposed to be able to recite
facts, Trace knew. They were supposed live Duty-Honor-
Country. And she had tried as best she could for thirteen
years in the Army. But something had gone wrong, badly
wrong.

Trace curled her fingers around the rope blocking off the

room and tried to remember who she was before she arrived at the Academy. Because she now realized she no longer was who she had been when she'd graduated. And since her four years at the Academy had taken her previous life from her, she felt totally empty and drained.

Tears flowed for the second time in twenty-four hours, but these were not tears of anger, but tears of profound loss for the idealistic seventeen-year-old girl who had walked into a meatgrinder in 1978 and seventeen years later finally realized she had gained nothing and lost everything.

From the visitor center it was only 200 yards to the main gate of the Academy grounds proper. As Trace drove to the gate, she wasn't surprised when the military police-woman on duty waved her through despite the fact she had no Department of Defense decal on the windshield of the rental allowing access to the post. Because it was such a tourist attraction, West Point was an "open" post, meaning that anyone could enter.

Behind Trace, the MP's head swiveled and noted the license tag. The MP dashed inside the small building that stood in the middle of the gate and picked up the phone. She dialed the duty NCO at the Provost Marshall's office.

On the other side of post, the duty NCO put down the phone and looked in the instruction binder he was issued when coming on duty. A new piece of paper had been paper-clipped to the front of it. The description of Trace's car and its license tag number was there, with orders to be on the lookout and to report it if spotted to the phone number listed. The NCO noted that since the phone number had only five digits, it had to be on-post. He dialed and it was picked up on the first ring.

"Major Quincy."

"Sir, this is Sergeant Taylor at the Provost Marshall's office. We've spotted that red Beretta coming through Thayer Gate."

"How long ago?"

"Not more than a minute. Do you want me to alert my patrols?"

"Negative," the major said. "Just order your people on

patrol to look for it. If it's spotted, your people are not to approach but simply to keep the car under observation and report to you. You will immediately give me a call. Is that clear, sergeant?''

''Yes, sir.''

''I say again, you are only to report back to me. Your people are not to approach the vehicle or alarm the driver in any way.''

''Yes, sir.''

The phone went dead. Sergeant Taylor was curious and also somewhat irritated with the officer's attitude. He pulled out the reverse directory phone listing for West Point and looked up the number he had just called, wondering what office he had talked to. The five digits were listed under the office of the superintendent.

Taylor's irritation disappeared. Whatever was going on was at the highest levels possible at the Academy, and one thing Taylor had learned after three years of duty at the Academy: there was the law, then there was the superintendant's law, and the second one had overruled the first one on more than one occasion in Taylor's experience. He remembered the time an MP had caught a pair of male cadets, naked and in a rather awkward carnal position up at Redoubt Number 4. The two cadets had been gone from the Academy the very next day and the MP shipped off to Korea with orders to keep his mouth shut. The story never made the blotter report or the news and that was the way West Point wanted it.

In the same manner suicides among the Corps of Cadets were totally blanketed with secrecy along with drunken accidents by senior cadets in their shiny new cars. Avoiding negative publicity was more important than anything else, even the law. Taylor wondered what the driver of the Beretta had done to draw the attention of the superintendant's office.

In fact, he wondered so hard about it that it reminded him of something else that the Provost Office sergeant major had told him and he picked up the phone and made another call.

*   *   *

Trace was surprised by the number of cars going onto the post this early on a Sunday morning in front of her. She was part of a line of a dozen or so vehicles. Trace accelerated through onto Thayer Road, passing the Thayer Hotel on the right and Buffalo Soldier Field to her left. At the end of Buffalo Soldier Field, she came to a stop sign. The road to the right went down to the river, 200 feet below. Straight ahead was the cadet area, and to the left, the road wound its way up to Michie Stadium and Lusk Reservoir and the various housing areas.

A small temporary sign indicated going to the left for the Scout Jamboree at Target Hill Field, and the other cars all turned in the direction, which helped explain the unusual amount of traffic. Trace went straight, deciding to go around the Plain before heading toward the cemetery. A low stone wall and concrete walk was on her right. As a pair of cadets jogged by, Trace thought of the hundreds of times she had made the run out to Thayer Gate and back from the barracks, a round trip of about two miles.

Officers' quarters crowded the hill to her left and then she came to a fork in the road. Straight ahead, the road dipped down, running between Mahan Hall and Thayer Hall. To the left, the road passed between the cadet barracks and the academic buildings. Trace turned left and very slowly drove by. Sunday morning was when the Academy was at its least active, and there was little sign of life as she passed New South Barracks, her home for her first two years. Not for the first time she wondered what sadistic mind had decided to cover every building with gray stone. Certainly not the most inspiring building material and with the current overcast sky, one that was sure to dampen even the most buoyant heart.

Bartlett Hall, home to the hard sciences taught at the Academy, was on the right while old Pershing Barracks, still standing from the days of MacArthur, was to her left. It was there that Trace got her first real surprise on the grounds. The road, which used to continue straight ahead and go around the Plain, was gone. The Plain had been expanded since her time, and where the road had been there was now only smoothly cut grass. Her only option was to turn to the right and go by the library. Trace stopped the

car, glancing in her rear-view mirror to make sure no one
was behind her. She stared out at the green surface of the
parade field, remembering sweating out there in the fierce
summer sun, learning to march. About the only good memory she had of the Plain was her final parade just prior to
graduation when she finally could believe that she would
be out of the Academy after four long years.

Trace continued on, her mind and heart overwhelmed
with memories. She had a job to do, but she found it difficult to not pluck at the scar tissue that surrounded her
core. Whether positive or negative, the Academy was a part
of her life. What she had learned after years of active duty
and more recently, the revelations about The Line, still
couldn't totally eradicate the four years spent at her ''Rock-
bound Highland Home.''

Trace was surprised to hear the distant chatter of helicopter blades and she twisted her head to watch an aging
Huey helicopter fly by, then dip down over the horizon in
the direction of the river on the north side of the Academy.
The road curved around, following the contour of the Plain,
overlooking the Hudson River below. Trophy Point and
Battle Monument went by on the right and Trace was reminded of the chapter in her manuscript that had started
this whole mess.

Old houses that were quarters for the permanent faculty
at West Point, the heads of each department, lined the road
to her left. She wondered which one Colonel Hooker had
lived in during his long tenure as head of the history department. The entrance to the cemetery, directly across the
street from the fire department, appeared on her right. The
old cadet chapel had been transplanted here in 1910, stone
by stone, after the present chapel had been built, and stood
just inside the gate.

Trace went past the entrance to the cemetery and continued to the post exchange parking lot. The cemetery was
now off to her right, shielded from the parking lot by a line
of eight-foot-high trees. Trace parked and sat still for a few
minutes, collecting her thoughts. The PX wasn't open yet.
That was obvious from the fact there were no other cars in
the lot. The post gas station was directly ahead and it too
wasn't open.

Trace remembered Boomer's statement about being paranoid, but she felt there was no reason why she couldn't at least go into the cemetery and find out exactly where Custer was buried. Despite her time at the Academy, she had never entered the cemetery; she'd never had reason to.

Trace left the car and walked through a gap in the trees at the edge of the parking lot. Among the grave markers in front of her, one immediately stood out: a massive concrete pyramid, at least twenty feet high. She followed the gravel road around, checking out the stones as she went. Many of the markers were relatively new, within the last several decades, so she knew she had to get to the older section of the graveyard.

Passing the pyramid, which on the other side showed itself to be a mausoleum, she came upon another elaborate marker, this one consisting of several columns holding up a roof with an eagle on top. She recognized the name: Major General Daniel Butterfield, born October 31, 1831, died July 17, 1901. Butterfield, a graduate, was the man who had written the traditional military bugle call Taps among many other accomplishments in his life.

Trace knew she was getting closer to Custer as the markers got older. A large tree hung over an obelisk at the edge of the next row of graves. A small placard was nailed high up on the tree and Trace walked up and read it: "FAGUS, SYLVATICA, PENDULA, A WEEPING BEECH," it said, identifying the tree. Trace walked around the tree and looked to see over whose grave it wept. The bronze plaque on the base of the obelisk told all:

GEORGE A. CUSTER

LT. COL 7TH CAVALRY

BVT. MAJ. GENL. U.S. ARMY

BORN

DECEMBER 15TH 1839 HARRISON CO. OHIO

KILLED

WITH HIS ENTIRE COMMAND

IN THE

BATTLE

OF

LITTLE BIG HORN
JUNE 23RD 1873

Trace pulled out the letter and looked. It said the diary
was to the left of the base of the monument, between Custer's and his wife's grave. But there was no grave to the
left, just the weeping tree.

Trace went around the obelisk, to the other side. A
bronze buffalo head stuck out of the side facing the tree.
On the far side, a soldier on a horse was emblazoned, along
with the family name of Custer at the base. To the left, a
long, stone grave marker read:

ELIZABETH BACON
WIFE OF GEORGE A. CUSTER, MAJOR GENERAL U.S.A.
APRIL 8, 1842; APRIL 4, 1933.

The top edge of Mrs. Custer's marker was on line with
the front edge of her husband's. The diary lay in between.

The cemetery was on a level with the Plain, a hundred
feet above the Hudson River. A hundred and fifty feet from
Custer's grave, there was a low stone wall, then the heavily
wooded ground on the other side precipitously descended
down to Target Hill Field at river-level where Trace had
spent many an afternoon playing soccer in intramurals. She
could hear the descending whine of a helicopter engine
coming from that direction; it must be the Huey that had
flown by while she was driving around the Plain shutting
down. The sewage treatment plant for the Academy was
also down there, and the smell of the plant was well known
to cadets because every time they had to take their two-
mile physical fitness test run, the course went out past the
treatment plant and then back.

Trace looked about in the immediate vicinity of the
grave. The cemetery was empty, and this spot wasn't visible from either the PX parking lot or the building that
housed the caretaker of the cemetery. To the left of the
Custers, Trace was interested to see the name Robert An-
derson, the commander of Fort Sumter when it was fired
upon at the beginning of the Civil War. She wondered who
else that had been such an integral part of the country's

history was buried here, but now was not the time. The PX would be opening shortly, and she needed to go in there and get the equipment to uncover the diary.

The doors to the PX were unlocked at exactly at eleven, and Trace was the third person in. She went to the back of the store where the four seasons section was and quickly found what she was looking for—a small hand spade that she could easily fit into the pocket of her coat. In hardware she picked up a measuring tape and took her purchases to the front. She was required to show her ID card before paying, then she made her way out into the parking lot.

The weather was still cold and gray with a low overcast sky. Trace could hear distant cheers coming from the vicinity of the track and field stadium down at river-level below the cemetery, next to Target Hill Field. She passed her car and slipped between the trees into the cemetery. She walked directly to Custer's grave.

There was still no one about, so Trace kneeled in the hard earth and pulled out the tape measure. Two feet to the left, on line with the front of the gravestone. She dug the point of the spade into the earth and began digging. She was grateful the ground wasn't frozen or else it would have required dynamite to make any sort of penetration. Trace felt very exposed as she continued to dig and kept glancing about, keeping an eye out.

In the PX parking lot an MP car pulled up to Trace's rental car, noted the license tag, then drove away to park near the main PX itself. The MP in the car picked up his radio mike and called it in to Sergeant Taylor. Within four minutes a van pulled up, and a major—identified as Quincy by his nametag—and a young captain stepped out. The MP pointed out the car to them.

Quincy glanced around, then pointed at the PX. "She must be inside." He jabbed a finger at the MP. "You stay here and watch the car." He grabbed the other officer. "Let's go, Captain Isaac." The two entered the PX and began a systematic search of the store.

The spade hit something solid about ten inches down. Trace continued to excavate, adding to the small pile of dirt

next to the hole. She brushed away with her fingers and
exposed a red plastic surface. She carefully dug around,
until she reached the edges—about ten inches long by eight
wide. She pressed the point of the spade in along the sides,
breaking the box free from the dirt. After four minutes, it
came loose and she held in her hands a plastic box, the
seams wrapped in duct tape. It was heavy, as if whatever
it contained was solid and filled most of the space inside.

"She's not in here," Captain Isaac said. They were
standing at the checkout counters, having been through the
entire store twice.

Major Quincy looked out into parking lot, noting the
location of the car, and thinking furiously. "Could she be
at the gas station?"

Isaac shrugged. "Let's check it out."

The two officers double-timed across the parking lot and
after a brief look inside, insured that the object of their
search wasn't there. "Where the hell is she?" Quincy muttered.

Isaac pointed. "The cemetery?" he guessed.

"What would she be doing in there?" Quincy asked,
moving before Isaac had a chance to answer. The two
headed for the break in the trees.

Trace shoved the dirt back into the hole, but the absence
of the box left a depression there that would be noticeable
to the first person passing by. She pulled her key chain out
and flipped open the small knife attached to it and began
cutting open the duct tape to see what was inside.

"There she is!" a voice cried out.

Trace looked up and she didn't have to consider the situation very long. Two officers, their long black raincoats
flapping in the wind, were racing toward her. She tucked
the box under her arm and ran in the opposite direction,
straight for the wall enclosing the cemetery. She made it
there with a fifty-meter lead on her pursuers. She looked
down the rock-and-tree-strewn slope on the other side, unable to see the bottom. She knew it had to come out around
Target Hill field, and she also knew that that was putting
herself in a dead-end situation, but a glance over her shoul-

der convinced her that it was better than the one she was currently in. The two officers had drawn .45 caliber pistols from the pockets of their raincoat and the lead one—a major from the oak leaves on his collar—halted briefly and fired, the round cracking by. Trace threw herself over the wall and began scrambling downhill.

Quincy and Isaac made it to the wall in time to see Trace disappear into the woods below. "Follow her!" Quincy ordered. "I'll get the van and meet you there." He turned and ran back to the PX parking lot.

Trace cursed as she slipped on the steep slope. She dropped the box as she desperately grabbed with both hands for a low tree branch to arrest her fall. The box continued downslope on its own. Trace followed it at a slightly slower pace and reclaimed it when it lodged next to a small boulder. She could hear the yells from what must have been the scout jamboree at the stadium off to her far right. She glanced over her shoulder and couldn't see any pursuit, but she assumed there had to be. She didn't know how they had found her. Maybe the damn checkout women in the PX were scanning IDs for all she knew. At this point it didn't really matter.

Trace tried to come up with a plan as she continued down. She knew that there was only one way out once she got to the bottom. Target Hill Field was a level area surrounded on two sides by the mountains and on the third by the Hudson. She would have to go to the right, past the sewage treatment plant. She also knew that whoever was after her also knew that and they could cut her off. She increased her pace, ignoring safety for speed.

She broke out of the trees just to the left of the sewage treatment plant and skidded to a halt, trying to catch her breath as she looked around. The Huey helicopter she had seen was parked in the middle of the nearest soccer field.

She heard a distant yell above and behind her. No time and no other options. She ran forward to the helicopter. It was open; the crew must have been over at the scout jamboree. A sign giving the aircraft's specifications was leaning up against the open left cargo door; obviously the aircraft was a static display for the scouts to look at later in the day.

Trace swung open the left pilot's door and settled into the seat. There wasn't time to do it by the book, the way she'd been trained at Fort Rucker over ten years ago. She flicked the generator switch to start and opened the fuel flow. She grabbed the throttle and rolled it to the start position while pulling the start trigger. She was rewarded with the turbine engine slowly whining to life. She breathed a short prayer of thanks that the battery had been up to power as she watched the N-1 gauge—the indicator of the engine's RPMs—slowly rise. The engine was still warm from its recent shutdown, so the startup was much faster than starting a cold engine.

Out of the corner of her eye she spotted one of the officers emerge from the woods and look about. The N-1 gauge hit fifteen percent, and the blades overhead began to slowly turn. The officer stared at the helicopter in surprise and then began running forward. Trace increased torque on the throttle, turning on the inverter switch, going to full power. She knew she was risking overheating the engine, but the options seemed limited as the officer pointed his pistol at her from forty feet away and fired a shot. The bullet ricocheted off the Plexiglas to Trace's right, cracking it.

She pulled in the collective with her right hand, keeping the engine at full throttle. With a shudder the helicopter slowly lifted. The officer fired again, missing wildly. Trace kicked the pedals, putting the bulk of the helicopter between her and the man. She wasn't surprised to see a van skid through the chain link fence surrounding the field and come bouncing straight toward her. She pulled further up on the collective and the gap between the skids and the ground grew. With only twenty feet of altitude, she pushed the cyclic over with her left hand and headed along the ground, away from the van.

"Come on, baby, come on, give me some power," she pleaded as the old Huey strained under the punishment. She leveled off, still only twenty feet above the ground, with the bulk of Storm King Mountain less than 400 meters away. Trace pulled back on the cyclic, slowing her forward progress, and put everything into the cyclic, gaining altitude as quickly as possible.

She cleared the foothills of Storm King with barely five feet between the skids and the highest tree tops and was off to the west, disappearing from the sight of the two officers below.

"What do we do, sir?" Captain Isaac asked, holding his empty .45 in his hand.

"The bitch has got to land somewhere," Quincy said, "and when she does, she's ours. Let's go alert all the local airfields and the State Police."

Trace's options were rapidly dwindling. The thickly overcast sky was pressing down on her, forcing her to stay below 1,500 feet altitude. With the mountainous terrain that surrounded West Point, there were only a couple of directions she could fly. Out the right window, the tree covered slopes of Crows Nest and Storm King Mountains loomed, stopping her from going north. To her rear, the low valley of the Hudson beckoned, but Trace instinctively didn't want to go the easy way—that's where they would look first. South, Bear Mountain blocked the way.

In her haste to simply get away from Target Hill Field, she'd headed west and passed over Washington Gate less than a minute ago—the rear entrance to the Academy from Route 293. For the present she was following the road, fifty feet above the black ribbon. She tried to remember as best she could the surrounding terrain. Following the road was the safest route for the moment. She knew the New York State Thruway was about a dozen miles to the west and she estimated she might be able to follow that to the north and land at Stewart Airfield, a former military airbase, that had been turned over to civilian authority several years previously. Trace figured she had a good chance of landing there and getting away in another rental before the alert went out.

At the West Point MP station, Sergeant Taylor received a call from the superintendent's office less than two minutes after getting the radio call from two of his MPs about shots fired near the cemetery and Target Hill Field. He wasn't surprised when the superintendent's aide told him to ignore all reports and that nothing had happened.

Taylor instructed his MPs to stay away from whatever was going on and to forget about it. Then he picked up the phone and called the same number he had called earlier after realizing he was dealing with the supe's office.

He started speaking as soon as the other end was picked up. "Harry, it's Sergeant Taylor. Something's happening."

Long Pond flashed by on the left, then the flashing yellow light indicating the turnoff for Camp Buckner. Trace banked right, overflying the long barracks that made up the summer training encampment. Popolopen Lake appeared and Trace flittered across the surface, continuing on a southwesterly direction. She knew the Bull Hill firetower was somewhere off to her right, but the cloud cover was so low, the tops of the hills were completely covered.

Doubt began to creep into Trace's mind. Did 293 intersect the Thruway or did it loop back to Route 6 and Bear Mountain? She had driven out this way numerous times as a cadet but that was over a dozen years ago. Of one thing she was certain: the Thruway was to the west, and it was her best and only shot through the mountains and to Stewart Airfield. She remembered seeing the four-lane highway from her plebe field training at Lake Frederick which she knew was very close, somewhere off to the right. With her hands full of cyclic and collective, there was no way she could check to see if there were any charts in the helmet bag next to the seat. A helicopter needs two hands to fly; let go of the controls even for the briefest of seconds and the aircraft will immediately attempt to invert and destroy itself.

A gap appeared in the solid line of green to Trace's right as the terrain descended below the clouds, an opening heading due west. Trace made her decision and turned, heading directly into the opening. A pond appeared: Lake Frederick? Trace wondered. She was caught between the gray clouds less than a hundred feet above and the black water thirty feet under her skids. The far side of the pond was a solid wall of trees. She was forced to turn left again, southwest, following the pond's surface.

The pond gave way to swamp and Trace slowed to an airspeed of less than thirty knots. She was looking out to the right when something appeared in the corner of her eyes. As she spun her head about she screamed a curse and pulled in on the collective as she slammed the cyclic over. High-tension wires were directly ahead, looming down out of the clouds and attached to a tower to her far left.

For a brief second Trace thought she'd make it as they flashed beneath the cockpit. The toe of the right skid didn't clear. It hooked on the topmost wire. The helicopter tilted and the blades flashed through the steel wires, destroying the wires and themselves in a split second. The helicopter went from an aerodynamic object to a rock.

Trace's hands were still struggling with the dead controls when the cockpit slammed into the rock wall face, then tumbled to the ground below, coming to a rest in a pile of broken tree limbs, crumpled metal, and shattered Plexiglas.

CHAPTER ☆ 18

From the hillside Boomer could clearly see the *Arizona* Memorial and the entire harbor spread out below him. He was above the Pacific Palisades in the jungle that clung to the side of the mountains. Skibicki had driven them there in the dark, going up an old trail until it gave out in a small clearing, hidden by the overhanging trees.

Boomer glanced over. Vasquez was in the back seat, sleeping. Skibicki had strung a hammock between two trees and was quietly snoring.

Boomer looked along the southern coast of Oahu in the quiet splendor of the rising sun. He wondered if any place could be further from the cold gray walls of West Point in December than Hawaii? Boomer couldn't imagine the Academy on the slopes of Diamond Head. Such martial learnings seemed so far removed from the tropical paradise around him. But he only had to look down at the harbor and the constantly lit white building above the rusting hulk of the *Arizona* to know that war had come here too.

Boomer twisted the focus on the binoculars. There was a launch heading out to the Memorial. He scanned it. Everyone on board was Navy except for one man in a suit. As he checked the man out, a sound to the side drew his attention.

It was Skibicki stirring. The sergeant major swung his feet to the ground, still supported by the hammock. "How's the head?"

251

Boomer reached up and felt the bandage the sergeant major had applied in the dark. "I've got a little bit of a headache, but other than that, it's all right."

Skibicki glanced down at the harbor. "What's up?"

"Not much," Boomer replied. "What's the plan now?"

Skibicki stood up. "We wait. I'm willing to bet that there will be no sign of what happened last night in the tunnel, but I'm sure that there will be someone posted there, waiting for us to come back. There's not much we can do right now.

"We wait," Skibicki repeated. "Let's hope Trace comes up with something today."

"And if she doesn't?" Boomer had to ask.

"Then we will have to do something."

Eight kilometers to the south, Mike Stewart tried hard to look suitably impressed as he was briefed.

"At precisely zero-seven-fifty-four the *Antietam*, an Aegis cruiser, will pass in review right *there*," the Navy captain said, pointing across the harbor, the crisp starched line of his dress whites accentuating the movement.

Stewart wished he didn't have to wear this damn suit everywhere. He could feel a trickle of sweat down his back despite the off-shore breeze and the sun not being much over the horizon yet. Stewart was standing on the edge of the *Arizona* Memorial, gazing out across the harbor at the sleek gray ships riding at anchor. He wondered how the Navy officer managed to look so cool and collected.

"At zero-seven-fifty-four plus twenty seconds, a flight of F-16 Fighting Falcons will fly in from the north," the captain said, pointing toward the lush green hills bathed in the bright sunlight, "in a missing-man formation, and head out sea. At zero-seven-fifty-four plus forty seconds, the bugler will begin playing Taps, at which time the President's party—"

"I have the time schedule of the ceremony," Stewart interrupted as gently as possible. "Getting back to security. What about sea and air control? The media will certainly have helicopters and chartered boats, and you also will have private boats coming—" Stewart stopped at the captain's bark of a laugh.

"There will be *no* problem with either unauthorized aircraft or vessels." The captain swept his arm around the harbor. "Everything you see here is Navy. No ship can get into this harbor without us clearing it at the mouth. We will have Marine Corps helicopter gunships on station to keep away any unauthorized aircraft."

Stewart was more than satisfied with all that he had seen and been briefed on so far—yet General Maxwell's words echoed in his ears: ". . . *particularly with regard to the military installations he'll be visiting.*"

But Pearl was as safe as you could get, Stewart reasoned, as he followed the captain to the launch that was waiting to take them ashore. As he made the short hop into the boat, Stewart glanced down and through the green water the rusting round hole that had once been the mount for one of the *Arizona's* main guns was clearly visible. He felt a momentary chill. There were hundreds of bodies still entombed in the wreckage there. That thought immediately led him to the realization that those men had also thought themselves safe that Sunday morning so many years ago, nestled in the bosom of the Pacific Fleet.

The words came to the forefront of his mind as clearly as if General Maxwell was there speaking them: What if the very security offered here was the threat itself? "Bullshit," Stewart muttered out loud.

"Excuse me?" the naval officer asked, perplexed.

"Nothing," Stewart said. He reeled in his wild train of reasoning. Damn General Maxwell, he thought; until this trip was over, Stewart knew his mind would have no rest, but he had no idea what he was supposed to be looking for.

Boomer put the binoculars down. Skibicki and Vasquez were heading down into town to get some fast food, while Boomer remained behind. No sense in all three of them being in the same place in public.

Boomer knew the man in civilian clothes on the memorial and he knew where he worked. He registered that fact and filed it for future use. He didn't like Skibicki's plan of waiting but he didn't have any better ideas at the moment. But if they didn't hear from Trace by tomorrow

morning, Boomer now had an idea what he was going to
do.

ALEXANDRIA, VIRGINIA
3 December 1995
6:30 P.M. LOCAL/ 2330 ZULU

The old man in the high-backed chair twisted the ring
on his finger as he listened to the report over the secure
phone. His aide shifted uncomfortably on the other side of
the desk when the phone call ended.

''Your men did poorly,'' Hooker said.

''Yes, sir,'' the aide acknowledged.

''The superintendent is very upset.''

To that the aide had nothing to say.

''And worse,'' Hooker continued, ''this woman—this
Major Trace—she's still unaccounted for. The helicopter
has not been reported anywhere.''

''I have my men still looking, sir.''

''I will have to take care of this personally,'' Hooker
said.

''Sir, I don't think—''

Hooker cut off the protest. ''We have reached a critical
juncture and I can't leave this to amateurs any more.''

''Yes, sir.''

''Do you know what she dug up at West Point?''

''No, sir.''

Hooker leaned back in his leather seat. ''I believe I
know,'' he murmured. His voice became sharper. ''Delay
my flight to Oahu for a day. I want to get a resolution on
this problem. File a flight plan for New York.''

''Yes, sir.''

CHAPTER ☆ 19

**WEST POINT MILITARY RESERVATION,
NEW YORK
3 DECEMBER
7:00 P.M. LOCAL/ 2400 ZULU**

Pain from the left leg was the first thing Trace felt. It was a dull, deep throbbing midway up her thigh. She said a brief prayer of thanks for the feeling because it let her know she was still alive. She blinked, clearing her eyes. It was dark out, and there was no sound, not even the usual noises of the forest. The interior of the cockpit was deathly quiet, and she could barely make out the shapes of objects inside and nothing outside.

Trace forced herself to keep still as she did an internal inventory of her body, gently flexing various muscles, working top to bottom. She almost fainted from the explosion of agony when she got to her left leg and attempted to flex her quadracep. Broken at the very least. She looked down, but it was too dark to tell. She knew something was across the top of the legs, as she could feel a straight pressure across both.

Other than the leg, though, she felt reasonably OK, considering the state the helicopter was in. A few bruises and bumps, but nothing major. She reached out with her right hand and flicked on the overhead cabin light. At least there was still some juice in the battery.

In the dim glow of the overhead she tried to see what her situation was. Still in the pilot's seat on the right side, Trace's body hung in the harness. But it wasn't just the harness that held her in place. The control panel had buckled and the metal edge above where the various gauges had once been was now pressed down against her legs. A red seepage on both legs showed where the metal had cut into flesh.

The helicopter lay against the side of the mountain, a pile of torn and shattered metal and Plexiglas. The main rotor had twisted on impact and sliced through the rear half of the bird, separating the tail boom from the main cabin. Trace knew if it had come down in the opposite direction it would have bisected the cabin up front and her body in the process. The steel support cable that had hooked under the right skid had snapped and now lay coiled underneath the aircraft, pointing back toward the still-standing power lines.

The left windshield had shattered upon impact with a boulder on the ground, spraying the inside of the cockpit with shards of clear plastic, flecks of which had cut Trace's hands and face. The gaping hole also allowed in the chill night air and the hint of moisture. Trace again tried moving and a low moan escaped her lips—no way she was using her left leg. She grabbed the edge of the control panel with both hands and pressed. It ignored her attempt. She tried again. Nothing.

She checked her legs as best as she could. The bleeding appeared to have stopped, for which she was thankful; the specter of bleeding to death was all too real under these circumstances.

Trace then reached up and switched the radio frequency to the emergency band. She pushed the send trigger on the collective but there was no rewarding hiss of broken static indicating she was transmitting. She tried again. Silence. Trace switched frequencies. Still nothing. After five minutes, she finally gave up. The impact must have broken the radio. At the very least she knew the condition of the helicopter meant the antenna had been sliced when the tail boom was cut off.

She cast her mind about, searching for a way out of her situation, but the options were not just limited, they were nonexistent. She would have to wait and hope.

"What now, recondo?" Trace asked herself out loud. These very hills on the military reservation were where she had earned her "Recondo" badge her second summer at West Point. Billed as a mini-Ranger school, the eight-day-long Recondo training was designed to introduce "year-lings" to the basics of patrolling but, more fundamentally, was designed to introduce cadets to the military practice of being forced to perform difficult mental and physical tasks while under the influence of stress, and sleep and food deprivation. "Good training" Boomer would call it, and Trace knew he was right. Combat was one of the highest stressors a human could go through and it was almost always under the worst possible conditions.

Despite her predicament, Trace had to grimly smile as a freezing rain began to fall outside. It seemed things were getting even worse.

Trace leaned back in the pilot's seat, as comfortable as she could be with immobile legs. She forced her mind away from her pain and discomfort and traveled back. She remembered Camp Buckner and the time her patrol of twenty-six cadets had charged a small hill defended by a squad of 82nd Airborne soldiers. They'd run screaming at the top of their lungs up the grass-covered slope to be met by a barrage of smoke and CS grenades. Hacking and coughing from the tear gas, they'd turned and run back downhill as swiftly as they had advanced. All except one classmate, Trace's bunkmate, Linda Greenberg, who'd simply frozen, standing still among the stinging gas.

Since the powers-that-be had not thought to issue the cadets gas masks—and the 82nd was not supposed to be using the gas—the cadets could only stand at the bottom of the hill and watch as Linda gagged and vomited all over herself, until finally the gas dissipated. At which point, not to Trace's surprise—she'd already seen enough in her first year at West Point—her male classmates had gathered around Linda and ridiculed her for embarrassing them in front of the enlisted men of the 82nd squad who were laughing from on top the hill at the spectacle of the female cadet covered in puke. They were especially thrilled when it was discovered that Linda had also lost control of her bladder under the effects of the tear gas.

Trace had taken Linda away from the jeers of their class-mates and cleaned her up as best as she could in a nearby stream, giving her the extra set of fatigues from her rucksack to wear. A week later, just after the formal graduation from Recondo training where the cloth patches denoting successful completion of the training were given out by the cadre from the 10th Special Forces Group, the cadets of Trace's company had held their own ceremony where they gave out their own awards. Linda was issued a pair of rubber panties and a vomit bag. Trace was given a Recondo patch made of moleskin—the medic's tool to treat blisters—a reflection on the six runs she'd missed with foot problems during the summer training.

It was sexist and it was brutal and most certainly "politically insensitive" in modern jargon, but as Trace sat there pinned in the pilot's seat, she also knew it was reality. The Academy had not been designed to prepare cadets to enter the normal world. It had been designed to prepare them to lead in combat and that in itself was the most brutal of all man's endeavors, despite such trappings as glory and honor. That cadets could be so nasty to those who failed to live up to their own standards was not surprising.

A moan escaped Trace's lips. Her leg was throbbing again, even stronger than before. She closed her eyes and gritted her teeth. Trace suddenly remembered the plastic case. She twisted her head and looked between the seats where she had jammed it on takeoff. It was still there.

That was all that mattered right now. Trace reached for the case, but the pain that jolted out of her right leg was enough to blanket her mind in darkness.

4 December
7:45 A.M. LOCAL/ 1245 ZULU

Trace hacked and coughed her way awake. Her chest felt terrible and she had a pounding headache. She blearily opened her eyes and quickly closed them. In the pale gray daylight, her current predicament was all too real. She could see the rock wall just in front of the cockpit and the tangle of metal.

She opened her eyes again and looked down at her legs. There was a dull throbbing pain coming from her left leg and although it was much less than it had been last night she knew if she didn't get help soon, that the situation was going to be very serious. She tried the radio again, on that faint optimism people in grim situations have that something might have changed for the better. It hadn't.

She glanced around, inventorying everything within reach. The survival vest with its knife. The plastic box. The crushed instrument panel. The overhead controls.

Very carefully, Trace reached down with her left hand and picked up the box. She drew the knife from the survival vest hooked to the right wall behind her and slit the layers of duct tape around the seam. It took her a while and she was glad to have something to keep her mind off her situation although it took an inordinate amount of attention for her to do this simple task. With the tape gone, she found that a small clasp kept the two sides closed. She unfastened it and opened the box.

Inside, an object wrapped in black plastic awaited her gaze. She drew out the object and slowly began peeling away the inside layers of protection. Whoever had hidden this had certainly wanted to make sure that it was protected from moisture. With her fingernails, Trace tore open the last thin sheaf of plastic and touched leather. She completely uncovered the object, and a leather-bound diary rested in her hands. On the cover, embossed in gold, were the initials: BRH.

With grimy fingers, Trace flipped open the cover. There was an inscription in large, flowing script on the inside:

To my son, Benjamin, on this most happy day of your life— may the words you write within tell a tale of service and honor. Love Mother. 12 June 1930.

"Hooker, you asshole," Trace muttered. The effort it had taken to open up the case had exhausted her. She put the diary back inside and slumped back against the seat. After a few minutes she passed into an uneasy slumber.

Trace started awake. For a few brief seconds her mind consoled her with the illusion that she was someplace else. Then she saw the crumpled cockpit surrounding her and felt the throb of pain from her legs and she returned to reality.

She knew she was close to hypothermia. The lower half of her body was in especially bad shape. Besides the broken leg, she was damp, having been forced to urinate where she sat.

Trace wrapped her arms tighter around herself and tried to keep her teeth from chattering so loudly. This time of year the training area was deserted and Trace knew the odds of someone stumbling across her location were slim. Looking at the grim side of the equation, she also knew that if no one came before nightfall, she didn't think she could make it through another night.

Even though it was only three in the afternoon according to the clock on the dashboard, the sun was already low in the western sky. The temperature was also dropping in preparation for nightfall. Trace coughed, trying to clear her throat, but it was no use. The chill had settled into her lungs and the coughing only made it worse.

There was no feeling in her left leg now, and that worried Trace more than the pain she had felt the past twenty-four hours. Whatever was happening in her lower limbs was bad. She was parched but didn't feel hungry. She leaned her head back against the hard metal of the seat and wished for unconsciousness, but even that desire worried her because she was concerned about waking up in the middle of the coming night. She just wanted it to pass, so that she would be able to wake and see the sun come up the next morning, but the logical, trained part of her mind told her she might not see the next morning.

Trace frowned through the negative thoughts swirling in her mind. Something was different. She froze, turning her head from side to side and peering about, listening carefully.

Trace cocked her head. There was no doubt about it now, as the sound grew stronger. A helicopter was heading this way.

In the cockpit of the OH-58 observation helicopter Captain Isaac had the controls while Major Quincy was scanning the terrain below with binoculars. They'd waited all night, checking in with local airports and the state police, waiting, for a report of the stolen helicopter, but nothing had come in.

"She could have gone anywhere," Isaac said, keeping Route 293 directly below.

"She had to land somewhere," Quincy said. "You can't hide the helicopter on the ground."

Isaac shook his head. "We're looking for a needle in a haystack. She could have gone anywhere," he repeated.

Quincy pulled away from the rubber eyepiece. "You want to tell the general that?"

"No, sir."

"Then fly."

Trace reached into the shoulder pocket of the survival vest and pulled out the small pen flare that was standard equipment. She leaned over as far as she could, gritting her teeth as pain exploded anew in her left leg, and pointed the end of the flare up and out the hole in the windshield. She popped it and watched it arc up through the trees.

"There!" Quincy yelled over the intercom. "To the right. See it?"

Isaac looked in the indicated direction and caught the tail end of the small flare as it went back down among the trees. "I got it." He banked hard right.

Quincy pressed the send button for the radio. "Gray Six, this is Gray Four. Over."

Inside Building 600—the Academy Administration Building—the radio call was picked up by a hastily rigged antenna on the roof of the 160-foot tower—the tallest all-stonemasonry building in the world. On the floor just below the roof, General Hooker grabbed the handset. "This is Gray Six. Go ahead. Over."

"We've spotted a flare. Going to investigate. Vicinity south end of Bull Pond. Over."

"Roger," Hooker responded. "I'll have a ground unit en route. Out." He put down the handset and turned to two young captains dressed in fatigues and wearing 9mm pistols on their hips. They had flown up with him from Alexandria. "You heard. Get going."

"Yes, sir."

At the MP station, Sergeant Taylor smiled as the radio went dead. Stupid sons of a bitches were using the frequency listed as reserved for the superintendent in the West Point CEOI—communications electronics operating instructions. Taylor had been asked to monitor both that frequency and the phone lines, and it sounded like he had hit paydirt. He grabbed the phone and dialed the number of a local motel he'd been given.

"Harry! Things are moving."

Major Quincy looked down through the Plexiglas pedals at the wreckage below. "Surprised she's still alive," he commented.

"How are they going to account for the chopper?" Isaac asked as he held the OH-58 in a hover.

Quincy laughed. "Shit, captain, you haven't seen anything yet. I remember back in 'eighty-eight we took out a Blackhawk full of Rangers just to get rid of the 1st Ranger battalion commander because he was making waves. One fucking Huey isn't going to be missed."

Captain Isaac's knuckles were white on the controls as he maintained a hover. Eight years ago when he'd been approached by The Line it had seemed a golden career opportunity. Now though, after seeing it in action, he was starting to question his decision. Unfortunately, it was too late for questioning. He was in.

"You might as well call Gray Six and tell them there's no rush. She must be trapped in the cockpit."

Isaac could see part of an arm moving about inside the wreckage. She was damn lucky to be alive, he thought as he took in the entire scene and the steel cable from the power lines. A pilot himself, he could well imagine what had happened: she'd been flying the lake surface, pinned down below the clouds when she hit the lines, always a pilot's nightmare.

"Maybe she'll die of natural causes," Quincy joked as he keyed the mike.

Trace peered up. An Army OH-58 was hovering about 100 feet up. They'd obviously seen her. She assumed they were radioing for help. "Thank God," she said out loud, leaning back in the pilot's seat to wait.

She thought of Boomer. First thing she would do when they got her to a hospital was call him. Her head snapped forward. How the hell did she know those people in the helicopter above were friendly? Boomer would tell her to assume they weren't.

Trace gathered up the diary. She opened it and randomly tore out some pages, stuffing them inside her jacket, pushing them through a hole she tore in the bottom of the inside pocket, then smoothing them out, hidden inside the liner. Then she began to look for a place within arm's reach to hide the book.

The white military van with the two captains rolled out Washington Gate and turned left onto 293.

A battered El Camino turned right out of the Mountain View Motel on Route 9W and headed north. Harry Franks checked the topographic map of the West Point Military Reservation laid out on the passenger seat. The map was held in place by the weight of a 9mm Heckler & Koch MP5SD5 submachine gun with silencer. His finger traced the route he needed to take. In three miles 9W intersected with 93. Turn left there and head west.

"Gray Four, this is Gray Five. Over."
Quincy keyed the mike. "This is Four. Go ahead. Over."
"We're passing Camp Natural Bridge. Over."
"Take a right onto Bull Pond road. You should be able to see us when you get up near the pond. Over."
"Roger. Out."

The helicopter was still up there, which left no doubt in Trace's mind that she had been spotted. Nothing to do now but wait. She'd jammed the diary up underneath the pilot's seat. Although she wasn't sure that was the greatest idea in the world, it was all she could think of.

The white van climbed up the steep incline as Bull Pond road went up the side of Blackcap Mountain. It hit a split— to the right to Bull Hill and the firetower, to the left the sign indicated Proctoria Road. Both captains had spent summers out here in training when they were cadets and knew where to go. They turned left, looping around the south end of Bull Pond. They could now see the helicopter above.

"Gray Four, this is Five. Over."

The captain in the passenger seat answered. "This is Four. Go ahead. Over."

"We've got you in sight. There's a small knoll off to your right. The crash site is on the other side of that knoll. Over."

"Roger." The van pulled to a halt and the two men got out. They circled to the left of the knoll. As they crested the shoulder of it, they could see the wreckage about 200 meters ahead on the bottom side of the high ground there. They dipped down as they continued and immediately struck swamp. They cursed as cold, mucky water seeped into their jungle boots and they had to beat their way through the thick, dead vegetation. The outlet for Bull Pond ran this way and meandered a bit, causing the swamp they were negotiating.

Back at the intersection of Bull Pond and Proctoria Road, the El Camino cruised to a halt. Harry could hear the helicopter ahead. He edged off under the thick cover of some pine trees and parked the car. He checked his map one last time, folded it and tucked it into the cargo pocket of his camouflage fatigue pants. Harry slipped on a combat vest bristling with killing tools and picked up the MP5. Keeping off the road, he began making his way to the west at a slow jog.

He hit the swamp closer to Bull Pond than the two officers. There the vegetation was thicker, but he had less trouble with it, slipping through the growth, rather than fighting it, years of hard-earned combat experience in a distant jungle coming back easily.

"Shit," the captain in the lead muttered as he splashed through the creek in the center of the swamp and started up the other side. He drew his 9mm Beretta Model 92 and chambered a round, his partner doing likewise.

Overhead, Isaac's concentration was focused on keeping his present position. Major Quincy was following the two officer's progress through the swamp and relaying that information back to Building 600.

"What a fucking mess," were the first words Trace heard. She watched the two men in fatigues come up out of the swamp, their boots layered in mud and their exposed skin covered with red scratches.

She didn't say anything, her attention focused on the pistols in their hands, the rank on their collar and the large rings glittering on each man's left hand. She felt her small reservoir of energy empty; the hope of rescue that had kept her going for over thirty hours snuffed out.

"Well, looks like you've got yourself in a pretty mess here," the lead officer said as he leaned into the hole in the front windshield. The nametag on his uniform identified him as Karlen. The second officer joined him—his nametag said Marks—and the two stared at her like she was an animal in the zoo.

"Hurt bad?" Karlen asked with a grin.

Trace tried to speak, but her mouth was bone dry. She worked around a little saliva and tried again. "My legs are pinned," she rasped.

"Hmm, too bad," Karlen said. He looked around, taking in the attitude of the crashed helicopter and the wreckage. "Seems like she should have at least broken her neck on impact, don't you think?" he said to Marks.

"At the very least. Maybe some internal damage also," Marks said as he clambered in the left cargo door and removed an emergency ax from its mooring on the left rear firewall. He climbed over the co-pilot's seat and squatted down next to Trace. "What did you take from the cemetery?"

"What are you talking about?" Trace said.

"What did you take from the cemetery?" Marks repeated.

"I don't know what you're talking about," Trace said. "I was doing a test flight and hit those wires and crashed. I've been trapped here and—"

"You stole this helicopter from Target Hill Field after digging up something at Custer's grave," Marks said. "What did you dig up?"

"I don't know—" Trace finished the sentence with a scream as Marks slammed the blunt end of the ax into her ribcage. She tried to control her breathing with short gasps as each breath caused the broken ribs to discharge mini-explosions of pain.

"What did you take from the cemetery?" Marks continued, the ax poised.

"I didn't take anything," Trace gasped.

Marks pulled back the ax for another blow. The left side of his head disintegrated as two 9mm rounds ripped through it, and his body was flung into the back cargo compartment.

Karlen whirled, bringing his pistol up to bear. He was still searching for a target as a line of 9mm subsonic rounds stitched a tight and neat pattern from his lower right stomach and up across his chest. The impact of the bullets slammed him against the Plexiglas in front of Trace, his blood forming a grotesque pattern as he slid down to ground, a look of surprise still on his face.

Trace watched, still trying to breath shallowly, as a large figure materialized out of the edge of the swamp like a ghost, his black skin glistening from the sweat of his efforts running here, after hearing the scream.

"You all right, missy?"

"Harry," Trace whispered.

Harry came up, letting the MP5 hang on its sling. He took the ax out of Mark's dead hand. "Let's get you out of here."

Overhead Major Quincy was still stunned at the rapid death of his two comrades. Isaac turned the helicopter, putting some distance between themselves and the large black madman with the submachine gun.

Quincy finally reacted, keying the mike. "Gray Six, this is Five. Over."

"This is Six. Go ahead. Over."

"They're dead. Gray Four is dead. There's some man down there, working in the wreckage. She's still alive. Over."

There was a long pause. "Keep them in sight. I'll get help to you ASAP. Out."

Harry ignored the helicopter. It was an unarmed OH-58, and there was no place close around to land. They could fly around up there all day and beat their meat as far as he was concerned. He figured he had about thirty minutes before they got someone new out here on the ground and whoever it was wouldn't be as cocky as these two assholes had been.

He levered the ax handle between the edge of the seat just to the left of Trace's leg and the panel. Leaning back he strained, watching the wood carefully, hoping the metal would move before the wood broke. With a slight noise, the panel moved a quarter of an inch. He heard Trace suck in her breath.

"Sorry, miss, but it's going to hurt getting this off you."

"Shit," Trace said. "Only hurts when I laugh."

Harry smiled. Biceps bulging, he exerted pressure and now the panel moved back, until a good four inches of space appeared above her legs. Harry did a quick primary medical survey of Trace, making sure that he wouldn't do any permanent or fatal damage by moving her.

"We need the diary," Trace said when he was done. She pointed out its hiding place and Harry tucked it into the back of his pants.

Tenderly, he scooped her up in his arms. Trying to be as smooth as possible her carried her out of the helicopter and headed back for his car, the helicopter buzzing overhead like an annoying mosquito.

Harry's internal clock was working, judging reaction times versus road distances. It was going to be close. "Can you take a bit more pain?" he asked.

"Do whatever it takes," Trace replied.

Harry carefully shifted her to an over-the-shoulder carry,

then he began to jog. Despite his best efforts, every footfall was agony to Trace, jarring the broken bones in her leg and ribcage. She·squeezed her eyes closed and went into the suspended time mode she had learned as a plebe at West Point—you were somewhere you didn't want to be, doing something you didn't want to do, but since you had no choice, you learned to zone out from reality. Trace tried as best she could but she'd never experienced pain like this and was very grateful when Harry halted at the car and lowered her into the passenger seat. She wanted to lean over to ease the pain in her ribs, but Harry insisted on buckling the shoulder belt on her. He got in and briefly consulted the map.

"Gray Six, this is Four. Subjects are in a black El Camino open-bed wagon. Over."

"Stay with them, Four. Let me know which way they go. Out."

Spitting gravel, the tires of the El Camino spun onto the road. Harry turned the hood west along Proctoria Road. Trace watched the scenario and realized they were following the route used for the Recondo Run—a two.and half mile run in full gear with rucksack that occurred at the end of Recondo training, the last hurdle to getting the Recondo patch. Trace remembered finishing the run with blood oozing through the socks inside her boots, barely able to stand for the entire following week, but she'd finished it. She knew now some of the reason for such brutal training— because there would be times when you would have to ask your body to do things it normally did not want to do and the more you stressed it, the more you found out you could do so much more than you ever thought possible.

Harry stayed with Proctoria Road, passing the turnoff for OP Charlie and splitting the gap between the ridgelines. Central Valley was spread out below them with the New York Thruway bisecting it a mile and a half away. The ground dropped off, losing 500 feet of altitude down to the valley floor.

The helicopter was above, having an easy time tracking them. Harry roared past the open field next to Lake Frederic where Plebes camped out every year at the end of Beast Barracks and exited the military reservation onto Mineral Springs Road. He spun a right and drove through the small township of Woodbury, the helicopter gaining altitude but still following.

Clearing the built-up area, Harry floored it, knowing he couldn't beat the aircraft but hoping to put distance between himself and whatever ground elements the aircraft was directing. He knew there would be no local law enforcement officials. This was a private war.

He cut over to the road next to the thruway, following it for several miles. First chance he got, he crossed over a bridge to the north side of the thruway. The entire western horizon was filled up with the bulk of Schunemunk Mountain, an eight-mile ridge that crested out over 1,700 feet high. The Erie Lackawanna Railroad curved around the north side of the ridge, and Harry followed the hardtop pavement that did the same loop.

"They're going north." Major Quincy was fumbling with the pilot chart—the only map they had. "Toward Washingtonville. Over."

"What road? Over."

"Shit," Quincy muttered. It wasn't marked on the map. "Around to the north of this big mountain," he replied, knowing that answer was insufficient.

"Stay with them. I've got a unit leaving post right now." The radio went silent.

"They'll never catch them," Isaac said to his partner. "They're too far behind—post is about twenty to thirty minutes back. We've only got another hour's worth of fuel, and it's going to be dark soon."

"Then we need to stop them," Quincy decided. "First open area they hit, try to get down and block the road."

Isaac glanced at his partner to see if he was serious. "That guy has got an automatic weapon, and he's willing to use it."

Quincy drew an M-16 from the backseat of the helicopter and pulled back the charging handle. "Then I guess I'd better shoot first."

*   *   *

Harry slammed on the brakes, expertly spun the steering wheel, and they were heading southeast, with the bulk of Schunemunk Mountain now off to the left.

"Where are we going?" Trace asked.

"We're trying to lose this helicopter," Harry replied. "Then we get going somewhere."

The roads had all been lined with trees, but now they suddenly burst out into an open stretch, about 800 meters long, and the helicopter swooped in. A man leaned out the left side, M-16 in hand.

Harry slammed on the brakes, then just as quickly punched the accelerator, causing Trace to yelp from the sudden pain of being slammed first against the seat belt, then back against the seat.

"Sorry, missy," Harry said as they shot underneath the helicopter, the skids barely five feet over the roof of the car, the pilot reacting too late. They were back in the shelter of the trees.

"Get down, right above those fuckers," Quincy ordered. "I'll stop them." He leaned out the left door, hooking his arm through the seat belt to steady himself as he tried to get aim on the car.

Isaac brought the helicopter down as low as he could, concentrating on the trees whirring up toward them and by below.

Quincy fired a three-round burst. It was impossible to see where the bullets had gone, but he knew for sure that he had missed. "Lower!" he ordered.

Trace looked out ahead, then twisted her head. The man was leaning out, looking like he was firing at them. She looked ahead again. "Oh my God," she whispered.

Harry grinned, seeing what she saw.

Isaac never saw it until it was too late. He was concentrating on the immediate danger of the trees just below.

"Jesus!" Isaac screamed. He hesitated for the briefest of seconds, not sure whether to try to go over or if he could make it between two of the massive steel girder supports of the New York City Aqueduct which loomed across the valley floor, blocking the entire way up over 200 feet.

It really didn't matter that he froze. He could have never made it over and there wasn't room to pass between. The blades struck first, a fraction of a second before the nose of the helicopter impacted with a steel girder.

From a forward speed of over seventy miles an hour to zero, the helicopter compressed into the unyielding steel girder, the shattered pieces flying about, littering the valley floor for hundreds of feet.

"Now we go," Harry said, not bothering to stop to admire the wreckage.

"Where?" Trace asked, no longer capable of being surprised by anything.

He drove hard. "Colonel Rison's place, missy."

After putting a dozen miles between them and the crash site, he pulled over. Pulling a military-issue first aid kit from behind his seat, he quickly bandaged Trace up as best he could. "The ribs will have to heal on their own. Try not to laugh too much, eh, missy?"

"I'll try," Trace said.

"We got a long ride. Let me give you a shot for the pain."

Trace was in no mood to object.

Harry smoothly slid the needle in and pushed the plunger. "This will help you sleep."

Trace was too tired to ask again and too tired to be irritated at the lack of a clear answer as to the destination. She could already feel the effects of whatever was in the needle. She leaned her head back against the headrest and was unconscious within seconds.

In the superintendent's office back at the Academy, Hooker put down the now-silent radio. He sat still for a few moments, then looked up at his aide. "You take charge here. Try to track them down. I need to go to Hawaii immediately."

CHAPTER ☆ 20

A day had passed, and Boomer was ready to explode on all fronts. No word from Trace—Skibicki had checked with Maggie. They had taken no action here, which meant the whatever The Line had planned was going along quite well without their interference.

"I'm worried about Trace," Boomer said. "She would have checked in by now. Something must have gone wrong."

"I'm worried, too," Skibicki said. "There's a hell of a lot at stake here. More than just the safety of Major Trace. She's got the proof and with Colonel Rison dead, we're up shit's creek."

"Is there any other information you have that might be helpful?" Boomer asked. Skibicki had gone over to Fort Shafter the previous evening and, without going to the tunnel, had checked in with some friends to see what was going on.

"A DDS from Special Warfare Group One is missing along with a Mark IX Swimmer Delivery Vehicle. No one knows who's got it," Skibicki said.

"You mean the SEALs who own it don't know where it went?" Boomer asked increduously.

"Roger that," Skibicki said. "Someone from Pacific Fleet came in and loaded it up on a cargo truck and wheeled it away. They could have taken it anywhere and mounted it on the *Sam Houston*."

273

''But isn't the *Sam Houston* controlled by Navy Special Ops?'' Boomer asked.

Skibicki shook his head. ''Negative. All those ships are under control of Fleet Headquarters. My buddies in Navy Spec Ops have no idea where the *Sam Houston* is.''

''So it looks like your idea about the DDS and SDV is correct,'' Boomer said.

''We got to go to someone,'' Vasquez said.

''There's an advance security detail from the Secret Service here already,'' Boomer said. ''I suggest we go to them and tell them what has happened so far.''

''We might as well pack our bags for a prison stay, then,'' Skibicki said. ''Or are you forgetting those two men we killed out at Kaena Point?''

''Like you said—this is bigger than Trace; this is also bigger than us,'' Boomer replied. ''We know something's going on. Let's turn it over to people who can handle it better than we can. We agreed last night that if we didn't hear from Trace we would act.''

''But if they don't believe us, we end up in prison, and that leaves no one out here in the real world who knows about the plot and can try to do something about it,'' Skibicki countered.

''What can someone do by themselves?'' Boomer asked.

''Well, we could have fucked up their jump into the island,'' Skibicki said. ''Maybe with a little better idea of what we're up against, we can do a better job. We can't go out to sea to check out these subs, but if they're planning anything in Pearl Harbor we can go down there and check things out.''

Skibicki closed his eyes in contemplation. When he opened them his mind was made up. ''All right. I agree someone has to go to the Secret Service, but only if someone stays out here in the real world and does the best they can to stop this thing if the Secret Service doesn't react in time.''

Boomer could read between the lines. ''I guess that means this 'someone' ''—he pointed at himself—''goes to the Secret Service, and that 'someone' '' he—pointed at Skibicki—''stays out here.''

"Pretty good figuring for a West Pointer," Skibicki said, slapping him on the back.

"Take me downtown," Boomer said.

OAHU, HAWAIIAN ISLANDS
4 December
11:00 A.M. LOCAL / 2100 ZULU

"Excuse me, the lady at the front desk said you were with the Secret Service, and I need to talk to you."

Stewart looked over the man who had approached him from across the lobby and decided he didn't like what he saw. Whoever he was, this man spelled trouble—the eyes that were flickering around the lobby, taking in everything, the untucked shirt with slight bulge underneath the right shoulder that suggested a concealed weapon and, most importantly, the uneasy feeling Stewart picked up, an instinct that he'd learned to trust.

"I'm Agent Stewart. How can I help you?" Stewart edged sideways, looking over the man's shoulder. The rest of the lobby was clear, and Stewart could see two of his men watching them carefully, so he felt somewhat more at ease.

Boomer dug out his special Federal ID and showed it to Stewart. "Major Boomer Watson, Delta Force."

Oh shit, Stewart thought. Not a gunslinger from Bragg. He'd dealt with Delta before and had not enjoyed the experience. He hadn't been told that any of them were going to be involved here.

"Special Agent Mike Stewart. Presidential security detail. What can I do for you?"

"Is there somewhere we can talk?" Boomer asked.

Stewart checked his watch. He had an appointment with his counterpart in the Honolulu PD in thirty minutes. "Reference?"

"Reference security for the President's trip," Boomer replied.

"I've got a meeting in thirty minutes," Stewart said. "You need to be more specific. I wasn't briefed that your unit had any jurisdiction or responsibility here on the island."

"We don't," Boomer acknowledged. "I'm not here in an official capacity. I showed you my ID to let you know I am legitimate."

"What can I do for you?" Stewart asked, weary of the roundabout conversation.

"You don't remember me, do you?" Boomer asked.

Stewart frowned. There was something familar about the man.

"I roomed with your second detail Beast squad leader," Boomer said.

"You're class of 'eighty-one?" Stewart asked. "Third company in Beast?"

"Right."

"So—I repeat my question—what can I do for you?"

"Can we talk somewhere private?" Boomer repeated.

"You just told me you're not here in an official function," Stewart said. "I *am* here on official business and I don't have time for games. You got something for me, lay it out."

"I think there's a military plot against the President," Boomer said in an even voice.

Two hours later, Boomer was exhausted. He was seated with Agent Stewart in a room on the floor below that reserved for the President. He'd laid out the story from the beginning, including his part in the killing of the two men found at Kaena Point—leaving out Skibicki's name. Stewart had made several phone calls to check on their story. Boomer wasn't certain how well his theory had been received but he knew one thing—he had crossed his Rubicon and he could not recross. The fact that Stewart was a West Pointer had worried him when he'd first spotted him from the hillside in Waiwa, but the more he thought about it, the more Boomer realized this might be a good break. He very much doubted that Stewart was in the employ of The Line. If he was, Boomer would find out very shortly.

"You've heard nothing from this Major Trace who supposedly has evidence of the existence of this organization called The Line?" Stewart asked.

"Nothing since she called after leaving the stadium," Boomer said.

"Philadelphia PD has no report of a shooting at the Army-Navy game," Stewart said, giving him the results of at least one of his phone calls. "The only confirmation I have of your story is that two bodies were found up at Kaena Point and that they were killed with 9mm rounds." He looked hard at the man across from him. "But that does little other than make your confession of murder legitimate. It says nothing of a plot against the President."

Boomer had said all he could.

Stewart leaned back in his chair, then picked up his special Satcom phone. He punched in a special code and accessed the special link with Air Force One.

"This is Agent Stewart. Is General Maxwell on board?"

There was a brief pause, then Stewart continued.

"General, this is Secret Service Agent Mike Stewart in Honolulu. We talked at Fort Myer at General Faulkner's funeral. I have a rather strange situation here that I'd like to run by you." Stewart proceeded to succinctly relay what Boomer had told him in about five minutes, with a few interruptions as he was obviously asked a question. When he got done, he listened for several minutes then put the phone down.

"What now?" Boomer asked.

Stewart held two fingers a fraction apart. "You were this close to having me call Honolulu PD and you being taken into custody."

"Were?" Boomer asked.

"Were," Stewart confirmed. "Now we wait. Air Force One will be here and the Man will have to decide what to do."

AIRSPACE, WEST COAST, UNITED STATES
4 December
1:30 P.M. LOCAL/ 2130 ZULU

Air Force One was cruising at 34,000 feet, heading west toward Hawaii. The airspace for 100 miles around the plane was kept clear by air traffic controllers. Inside that space, besides the large 747, two F-16 Fighting Falcons flew escort, shadowing the bulky plane like two sleek watchdogs, their radars scanning the skies all around, their missiles armed and ready for firing.

Inside Air Force One, General Maxwell slowly put the phone down. He glanced up as Senator Jordan walked down the aisle. Jordan had been spending more time with Maxwell over the course of the past month, feeling him out on his views. Maxwell knew that Jordan was a key player between the White House and Congress. Most importantly, though, was the fact that Jordan had the President's ear and Maxwell knew the best way to approach the President was through the senator.

"What's wrong, general?" Jordan asked, taking the deep seat across the way from Maxwell.

"We might have trouble in Hawaii."

Jordan waited silently. Maxwell began with the phone call from Agent Stewart, then worked backwards, telling the story he'd just been told. When he got done, Senator Jordan made no comment.

"What do you think?" he asked.

Maxwell took a deep breath. "I'm not sure. I don't know this Major Watson who came to Agent Stewart. However, I don't think we can afford not to believe that the story may be true, particularly with all that has been happening between this administration and the Pentagon. Before he departed on advance security I told Agent Stewart to be on the lookout because I've been concerned about the strained relationship between the President and the military."

Jordan shook his head. "This is ridiculous. This country has never been concerned about its military doing something like this. What you're talking about here—the plot this man has come to Agent Stewart with—it's unthinkable."

Maxwell thought that was a rather simplistic approach. "We have to consider it as possible, sir."

Jordan frowned. "This Major Trace. She supposedly has some sort of proof that this organization exists?"

"Yes," Maxwell said. "Unfortunately she has not been heard from in the last twenty-four hours. She was last seen at West Point."

"Is there anything we can do to track her down?"

Maxwell nodded. "I'll make some calls."

"And the soldier?" the senator asked. "What is his status?"

"I've asked Agent Stewart to hold him until we arrive. Technically speaking, of course, Stewart should be turning him over to the local police for questioning on homicide charges."

"You did right holding him," Jordan said. He paused in thought. "Have you ever heard of this Line?"

"No, I haven't."

"And you've been in the military for over thirty years. Don't you think you would have run into it? Especially when you were in command over in Yugoslavia? If you've never heard of it, I doubt that it exists."

Maxwell considered his thoughts carefully. "I have never heard of an organization called The Line, that is true. But I also could not swear to you that such an organization does *not* exist. I have seen and heard too much in my years of active service in uniform to discount the possibility. There has always been a closing of ranks among senior officers from the service academies."

"That's not a stand, general. I can't go to the President with that." Jordan pressed home. "Do you believe—yes or no—that an organization called The Line exists?"

Maxwell thought for a few moments, then startled himself, never mind the senator, with his next words. "Yes, I do believe it exists."

"Oh shit," Senator Jordan said, losing his composure. "Do you believe that there's a plot against the President in Hawaii?" he demanded.

Maxwell's forehead furrowed. "I think something is going to happen. I've felt all along that at the very least the President was going to be confronted by General Martin and the Joint Chiefs in Hawaii over some of the issues."

"Confrontation and assassination are two radically different words," Jordan said.

"I know that. But this information is disturbing, the Special Operations Forces parachuting off the north shore and the Vice President just happening to be vacationing up there. The movement of the Special Ops sub toward the SHARCC—the President was scheduled to participate in a highly classified exercise on board there, yet these people know about it—that meant others knew about it.''

''I want you to check on that, general,'' Jordan said.
''Find out who authorized those troops to move and what
their mission is. If there is a mission.''

''I'll check on it.''

Jordan pushed the call button and a steward appeared.
Jordan raised a finger and glanced at Maxwell.

''Coffee,'' the retired general said.

The steward returned with a drink for the senator and
the coffee. Jordan took a sip. ''Maxwell, you were one of
them.'' He held up a finger as the general started to protest.
''No, listen to me. The President has no ties to the military,'' Jordan chuckled. ''That may be the understatement
of the year. So talk to me. What's going on in the Pentagon?''

Maxwell cradled the coffee mug in his hands. ''They
want the President to back down on the MRA and allow it
to die in the Senate. They also want him to allow full funding of the Hard Glass system and cut all support for the
Ukraine.''

''What are they going to offer in return?'' Senator Jordan
asked.

''I think they'll endorse the recommendations of the
Fortney Commission,'' Maxwell said. The Fortney report
had been done by a group hired by the Pentagon in response to the administration's MRA research. Its recommendations, mollified by the fact that the Pentagon
controlled the commission's budget, had been mild to say
the least, and bore little resemblance to the sweeping
changes in the MRA.

''And?'' Jordan asked.

Maxwell shrugged. ''That's all.''

Jordan blinked. ''You're joking.''

Maxwell's face didn't betray any emotion. ''No, I'm
not.''

''And if the President refuses?''

Maxwell shifted his steel rimmed glasses toward the senator. ''We have a problem. Now you understand why I'm
inclined to believe Agent Stewart's report.''

Jordan stirred the ice in his drink. ''General Martin is
political. He has the support of the opposition in Congress.

The Joint Chiefs could embarrass the President with some incident if they so desired. But a military coup is a far cry from political embarrassment. It surprises me that you believe the situation could be this critical." Jordan looked at the folders piled on the seat next to Maxwell. "Have you seen a draft of the President's speech?"

Maxwell nodded.

"How do you think the military audience at Pearl will react?"

Maxwell remembered all too well the chilly, almost insubordinate, reception the President had received at a military post early in his campaign several years ago. "In a military manner," he said.

"What's that mean?" Jordan asked.

"It means," Maxwell said, a bit of exasperation in his voice, "that they will be exceedingly polite to his face and say 'yes, sir yes, sir, three bags full.' If he orders the Navy band to jump off the memorial into the Harbor, they will jump off into the water in perfect step. But he cannot control what they think or feel, and I don't think he should try."

"Is there something you aren't telling me, general?" Jordan asked quietly.

Maxwell's composure cracked slightly. "I don't know."

"You don't know what?" Jordan pursued.

The mask returned to Maxwell's face. "Nothing."

Jordan leaned forward. "General Maxwell, I deal with half a dozen to a dozen crises a day. I have to be able to trust the people close to me to not only tell me the facts, but I have to trust their instincts. I haven't been able to think about this trip to Pearl for more than a few minutes amid all my other duties. You've been across the river at the Pentagon and focused on it for several days. You seem a bit agitated about something. You just told me you believe this Line organization exists, yet you offer no proof. If there's something I need to know and bring to the attention of the President—even if it's just speculation on your part—I need for you to tell me."

Maxwell was ill at ease. "I really don't know. But I've had a strange feeling about this whole trip to Pearl ever since it was announced. Something's not quite right. I used to be able to go anywhere in the Pentagon, but the JCS war room is now off limits to me.''

"That could simply be because you are no longer on active duty,'' Jordan noted.

"No,'' Maxwell replied. "I had access until last week. Now, though, they're enforcing a new access roster—one that excludes me.''

"And?'' the senator prompted. "Is there anything else bothering you?''

Maxwell's eyes were fixed on the bulkhead over Jordan's left shoulder. "I did my first tour in Vietnam as a lieutenant assigned to advise a Vietnamese Ranger company. They had an old Vietnamese sergeant that always walked point for them on patrol, and he'd never once led them into an ambush. He'd been fighting almost all his life. First with the French, then with us. One day I talked to him through an interpreter and I asked how come he never had been ambushed. He told me the spirits warned him of danger on the trail.''

Jordan took another sip of his drink, waiting for Maxwell to make his point.

"Later, on my third tour, I met some of the men we sent across the border into North Vietnam and Laos. Members of our best recon teams and I talked to them, and they told me the same thing—the ones that managed to survive dozens of trips into enemy territory—except they called it something different. They told me there was a sixth sense that they paid very close attention to—that they trusted their lives to. I felt it occasionally too in combat. Once before my infantry company got attacked, I could feel something was wrong—that something bad was about to happen. And it did.''

Maxwell shrugged. "I've had the same feeling about this trip. I can't put my finger on anything specific, but I have had a bad feeling about this trip from the beginning.'' He picked up a folder from the seat next to him. "I looked at the itinerary. I see that the President is to participate in a national command and control exercise on the night of the sixth. I assume that will be aboard the SHARCC.''

"Yes, that's been scheduled for months,'' Jordan replied. "I don't know the details of the exercise. It's required by memorandum of agreement between the Office of the President and the Department of Defense that he participate in one C&C exercise every six months. Been in effect for over forty years.''

''I would say that is the opportune time for General Martin and the Joint Chiefs to confront him. Just before he gives the speech at Pearl,'' Maxwell said.

Jordan smiled. ''Then we can cancel the exercise, which will solve that problem. We'll make Martin and his cronies come to us.''

Maxwell nodded. ''That will help minimize the potential for problems. But don't underestimate General Martin. In Vietnam he won the Distinguished Service Cross—the second highest award, just below the Medal of Honor. He also has a Purple Heart with three oak leaf clusters, which means he was wounded three times—and he didn't get those wounds sitting on his ass in the rear. He walks with that limp because a large-caliber machine gun bullet took away most his right thigh. I disagree with some of his philosophies, but he is one hell of a soldier.''

''I served my country in World War II, so don't be trying to pull the wool over my eyes because of Martin's background,'' Jordan said sharply. ''He's not the only one who was shot at in the service of his country.''

''Senator, I say that merely as his due, because there are some nagging doubts about the general that even his record can't remove.''

''For example?''

Maxwell held up a binder with TOP SECRET stamped on the cover. ''The Backfire incident.''

''I've read the report,'' Jordan replied.

''I don't think it's complete.''

Jordan waited. Maxwell took a deep breath. He felt out of his league. ''I question how they knew that Ukrainian aircraft would be making that particular flight with this particular payload.''

''According to that report the military didn't know,'' Jordan replied. ''It was coincidence. They picked it up on AWACS as it crossed the Black Sea. The two F-16s were participating in a NATO exercise and were able to be diverted to intercept the Backfire.''

Maxwell nodded. "But the report states that while this was believed to be the first attempt by the Ukrainians to smuggle out a nuclear weapon, there were previous flights of the same sort, carrying conventional arms. How could General Martin and his people know that?"

"That information did not originate from General Martin," Jordan said. "It came from the CIA."

"I know that," Maxwell said. "But when did the CIA report that to Martin? Before or after the Backfire incident?"

Jordan didn't have an answer to that.

"If the CIA informed Martin *before*, then it should have been brought to the President's attention, and he could have tried diplomatic means to stop the shipments, instead of ending up with a nuclear incident over a friendly country and the loss of two pilots."

Maxwell flipped a few pages in the report. "It says right here that Martin specifically ordered U.S. forces in Turkey on alert for *three* days prior to the incident looking for such shipments."

"So you're saying Martin allowed it to happen?" Jordan asked. "Why?"

Maxwell ticked off reasons on his hand. "To support his own agenda. Hard Glass. Shooting down the MRA. To reduce confidence in the President." Maxwell picked up another folder. "And then the incident in the Ukraine," he continued.

Jordan finished his drink. "What are you trying to say, General?"

"I don't really—"

"If you have some facts, then you put them down on paper and you give them to me," Jordan snapped. "The President has a lot on his mind and until you have something solid, I'm not going to worry him with speculation." He stood up and left the cabin.

HICKAM AIRFIELD, HAWAII
4 December
1:00 P.M. LOCAL/ 2300 ZULU

The head air policeman for Hickam Field threw a couple of extra-strength Tylenol into his mouth and washed them down with a swig of orange juice. "Who the hell is that?" he asked irritably, as the chief air traffic controller acknowledged an inbound flight. "We're shut down for all but emergencies and specifically authorized flights until we get Air Force One in and out of here." The two men were standing in the control tower, both exhausted from the extra preparations for the high-level flights that were coming in.

"I don't know," the head ATC said. "Some VIP from the mainland. I got a personal call from General Dublois telling me to give this flight top treatment and direct clearance. It's not on the list of authorized flights, but I'll take General Dublois's word that it's authorized."

Given that General Dublois was the Air Force Chief of Staff, the head security man for the airfield knew he wasn't going to argue. He watched as the unmarked Lear jet rolled to a halt and a large limousine with darkened windows pulled up next to it. An old man was escorted down the short flight of stairs and into the waiting car, which immediately took off, heading for the gate to adjacent Pearl Harbor.

"Are there any other authorized unauthorized flights coming in?" the security man asked sarcastically. He wondered who the old man was to rate such high-class treatment and why the Lear didn't come into the international airport, which would have been just as easy.

"That's the only one I know of," the head ATC said. "I think I'm going to go home and get a couple of hours of sleep. Tomorrow's going to be a busy day."

CHAPTER ☆ 21

"It's a damn zoo out there," Stewart said as he carried in a pizza that had just been delivered downstairs. "The President is arriving soon and everyone is going crazy."

"Can I make a call?" Boomer asked.

"To whom?"

"To the person who got me the information on the submarines and the inflight refuel of the combat Talon."

"Go ahead, but put it on speakerphone so I can hear," Stewart ordered.

Boomer punched in the number for Maggie's car phone, and Skibicki answered on the first ring with a gruff hello.

"This is the Boomer. You got anything new?"

Skibicki knew when to be direct and to the point. "The *Sam Houston*, the Special Ops sub, just turned away from the *Glomar Explorer* and the SHARCC. It's heading for Pearl and it's moving fast. If it keeps up its present speed it will be off shore by this evening."

"What are you up to?" Boomer asked.

"I'm going to check out Pearl tonight," Skibicki said.

"Are you safe where you are?"

"So far. I keep moving and I haven't been to the places they'd expect me."

"Anything else?"

"No. Maggie's worried about you, and she hasn't heard anything from Major Trace."

287

"All right. Tell Maggie I'm fine. Out here." Boomer hung up.

"What does that mean—the sub coming toward Pearl?" Stewart asked.

Boomer grabbed a slice of pizza and devoured half the piece, thinking as he chewed. "I don't know. Maybe The Line is afraid their plan for the C&C exercise has been uncovered and they're going to backup plan B, which involves Pearl itself. Maybe stand off with the SDV, swimmer delivery vehicle, and pop off a Mark 32 Standoff Weapons Assembly—which is fancy Navy talk for blowing the shit out of the *Arizona* Memorial with a big-ass torpedo while the President is on board, or maybe hit the launch carrying him out there—even The Line might think twice about destroying the memorial." As he spoke, Boomer realized he had stopped adding modifiers such as "if" to his speech. Since he had come to Stewart he had to believe in this plot until he was proved wrong.

"They think they can get away with that?" Stewart asked, shocked at the concept.

"The only thing these people care about is not getting caught," Boomer said. "They can blame it on the Ukrainians, the North Koreans, or the Chinese—hell any shit-ass terrorist organization." He pointed at the newspaper lying on the coffee table. "You've seen the article in there about the Iraqis protesting our downing that Ukrainian bomber. They do have a few submarines. I wouldn't be surprised if the damn Navy doesn't have one or two Iraqi subs captured in the Gulf War that they've stashed to use as a blind for some sort of operation like this."

"Pearl's secure," Stewart said obstinately. "I was just out there."

Boomer laughed sarcastically. "Hell, Pearl's the most unsecure place you could think of right now. You don't get the picture do you?" He didn't wait for an answer. "You're not dealing with some psycho writing threatening letters here. You're dealing with professionals trained in these kind of operations. Infiltrating Pearl and taking out the launch with the President on it, with the equipment these people have, is a piece of cake. And you can be damn sure they know every single security measure you have planned, since you probably briefed the chief of security at Pearl. Correct?''

Stewart didn't answer, and his pizza grew cold on the paper plate in front of him. He'd be glad when the President and General Maxwell arrived. This soldier was correct. He was way out of his league and he didn't like it one bit. He'd received word a little while ago that the two bodies discovered at Kaena Point had still not been identified, and not only that, but that someone had tried to claim them using government ID. Only the fact that Stewart had called earlier had kept the officer in charge of the case from turning them over. The men who had shown up for the corpses had disappeared. That made the threat of a plot all the more real.

"The President will be here within the hour," he said. "We'll figure out what to do then."

HICKHAM FIELD, HAWAII
4 December
4:27 P.M. LOCAL/ 0227 ZULU

At Hickam Field, as soon as the President and his party debarked, Air Force One was rolled off the tarmac into a secure hangar. An outside security cordon of Air Force police moved in around the building while the normal four-man Secret Service detail set up shop inside, securing the interior doors of the hangar with sensors—they themselves were the final line of security on board the plane itself.

In the sky above the airfield, another specially equipped plane circled once before making a final approach. The modified Boeing E-4B was one of four in the Air Force inventory—specially designed as a post-attack command and control system code-named Looking Glass.

Right now, it was serving as a ride for the chairman of the Joint Chiefs of Staff. It touched down and was immediately met upon stopping by a limousine. The chairman and the rest of the service chiefs exited and were driven to their quarters at Pearl Harbor where they would be staying for the duration of the ceremonies.

The E-4B was directed to a parking place adjacent to the hangar holding Air Force One. Another security blanket of

Air Force police was unfolded and placed over the E-4B. The chief of security at Hickam, an Air Force full colonel, breathed a sigh of relief. It wasn't often they received two VIP flights in one day. He was glad that they were all safe.

BENSON, NEW YORK
4 December
9:30 P.M. LOCAL/ 0230 ZULU

Trace heard the words as if from a great distance, echoing through her skull. "You've got a fever. I've put you on antibiotics. Your leg has also been set. Just take it easy and rest."

She tried to blink to clear away the film of haze that covered her eyes but had no success. A large dark figure— she assumed it was Harry; the voice sounded like his—was leaning over her.

She felt something on her arm, then the prick of a needle. "You'll be all right. You're going back to sleep now."

"The diary," she managed to rasp out.

"I've got it. As soon as you're better, we'll be able to call Hawaii again. Sleep tonight. Tomorrow's soon enough."

With those encouraging words, Trace gave up the fight. She lapsed into a deep sleep, her body sinking into the comfort of a large bed.

Leaving the room, Harry went into the living room. He glanced at the memorabilia on the wall—all Colonel Rison's—a legacy of years of service. Harry picked up the phone and dialed long distance.

"She's out again."

He listened to the voice on the other end.

"She's in no shape right now to do anything. She's got two broken ribs, she was hypothermic when I found her and severely dehydrated."

A pause.

"Sometime tomorrow. Probably late morning." Harry looked about. "I'm going to need help with transportation." He nodded. "All right." He hung up the phone, then glanced at a picture of Colonel Rison in camouflage fatigues and nodded. "I'll see it through, sir."

HONOLULU, HAWAII
4 December
5:00 P.M. LOCAL/ 0300 ZULU

"Senator Jordan, General Maxwell, this is Major Watson."

Boomer noted that Jordan didn't shake hands, although Maxwell did. He stood at attention as the senator moved directly to the desk dominating the room. He gestured for the others in the room to be seated. "I wish I could be more cordial but I'm afraid I have neither the time nor the inclination. From what I have been told, you could well be facing charges for your recent actions."

Boomer sat motionless, waiting.

Jordan continued. "I must also tell you that I am not predisposed to believe that there is a coup or assassination plot in the works."

Now Boomer reacted, but the senator held up a hand, forestalling any spoken response.

"However, I am predisposed to believe that there are actions taking place that are prejudicial to the welfare of this country. Actions that may be initiated by some members of the military. Perhaps they are being organized by such a group as this Line you have briefed Agent Stewart about. Perhaps it is simply members of the Joint Chiefs acting in what they believe to be the best interests of the country. But it appears those actions may be crossing the line into areas, that while not directly illegal, are harmful."

Jordan paused and Boomer jumped into the gap. "Senator, with all due respect, I firmly believe that this is more than just the Joint Chiefs making a political play. There are military forces at this minute maneuvering in a manner that are clearly a threat to the President's welfare."

"We have only your word on that," Senator Jordan said.

"You can check on it," Boomer said.

"I can assure you that we are," Jordan replied.

Boomer tried to keep the initiative, something he'd been trained to do. "There is something I have not told Agent Stewart. I thought it was best to present it personally."

Boomer reached into his pocket and pulled out Colonel Stubbs's ID card. He placed it on the desk. Jordan picked it and glanced at it curiously. "And this is?"

"That is the ID card of one of the members of the NATO inspection team killed in the Ukraine."

"And how did you get a hold of it?" Jordan asked.

"A team of Delta Force soldiers under my command conducted that ambush."

Senator Jordan sat up straight. "You'd better hold on one minute, young man. Do you realize what you're saying?" General Maxwell was nodding slightly, as if his suspicions were confirmed.

Boomer kept his eyes on the senator. "I know exactly what I am saying. I was sent on a military mission into the Ukraine on the night of the twenty-eighth of November. At the time we were told the target was a group of the radical Ukrainian parliament. The same group that was behind the shipment of that intercepted nuclear weapon."

Boomer told the story of the mission from planning through the confrontation with Colonel Decker and his banishment to Hawaii.

General Maxwell spoke for the first time, summing up Boomer's account. "So you believe that the mission was not a mistake but deliberately planned to embarrass this administration?"

"Yes, sir, I do."

"That's a pretty strong statement," Senator Jordan said. "You're accusing people of murder, including yourself."

"I was misled—" Boomer began.

"That didn't work for the Nazis," Jordan countered.

"Those who worked for the Nazis knew what they were doing. They knew they were following illegal orders," Boomer replied. "I was following orders, but they were not illegal orders as far as I knew. And what actually happened was not at all what I was ordered to do. I would never have gone on that mission if I had known what it really was. Once I realized what was happening I did everything in my power to stop it. The blood on that ID card is the blood of a friend."

Boomer fixed the senator with his eyes. "Sir, there's dirty work out there needing to be done all the time and somebody does it for this country. I'm one of those people. During Desert Storm I went into Iraq with three other men several weeks before the start of the ground war to try and get a shot at Saddam Hussein on direct orders from the National Command Authority. And if I'd gotten the shot, I would have taken it, regardless of the fact that there's a law against that in this country. I figure that one shot would have saved hundreds of Americans, and thousands of Iraqis. But beyond what I figured, those were my orders.''

Senator Jordan wasn't swayed and met Boomer's gaze. '' 'Following orders?' So if the other guy is dirty, we get dirty too? Then who is right? We? Because we believe right is on our side? But doesn't the other guy think right is on his side? And if we use the same tactics and techniques, then don't we intrinsically sabotage the rightness of our cause by the wrongness of our methods?''

"I don't know," Boomer said. "I don't have the leisure of philosophical discourse before I act. Because of the nature of covert operations, I often don't have the opportunity to find out all the information I would like to have in order to make an informed decision. I trust that the orders I am given are legitimate. That's the way it works.

"But I do know the same man in Turkey who ordered me on the mission into the Ukraine, Colonel Decker, was involved in the parachute drop off the north shore of this island. And that same Colonel Decker is somewhere on this island right now. And I believe those same people are involved in the movement of a Special Operations submarine, first toward the site of the C&C exercise, and now toward Pearl Harbor.''

"The sub has changed course?" Maxwell interrupted.

"Last report I received—yes, sir," Boomer replied.

"That's strange," Maxwell said.

"All right," Jordan said in a flat voice, cutting through the discussion. "I think we all understand the ethics involved here, but the major does have a point—all the ethics and moral arguing in the world are not going to do us a damn bit of good if what he says is true. The problem is, Major Watson, that even with this''—he held up the ID card—''you really have no proof.

"I just find it hard to believe that a secret military organization has been in existence for what—seventy years—

yet we've never heard of it. That's stretching my credibility quite a bit.''

"Major Trace has proof," Boomer said.

"Major Trace isn't here, nor is her proof," Senator Jordan pointed out. Before Boomer could say anything, he swiveled his seat and looked at General Maxwell. "Again, I want you to check out this submarine and those paratroopers.''

"All right.''

"You might want to try and find Colonel Decker," Boomer added.

Jordan turned back to Boomer. "Major, I think you will understand if I want you kept close at hand. I'm turning you back to the custody of Agent Stewart. We have two days before the seventh. Let's hope we find something more solid before then.''

"Let's hope we don't," General Maxwell said as Boomer and Agent Stewart left the room.

"General, is there anything more you can tell me about this?" Senator Jordan asked. "I find it very difficult to believe that this Line exists. You told me earlier that you do believe it. Give me your reasons, no matter how vague.''

"All I've ever heard are rumors," Maxwell said. "Every officer in the Army has heard of the WPPA, the West Point Protective Association. We know that most of the ring-knockers scratch each other's back." Maxwell sighed. "However, like the problem we have now—I have no proof but I've heard things. Things that I never cared to report because I didn't want to believe them.''

"Things like what?''

"Let me give you an example," Maxwell said. "For the last thirty years, ever since Vietnam, there's been a big rift in the Army between the conventional forces and the Special Operations forces. The Special Operations forces have conducted over ninety percent of the real-world missions since the close of Vietnam yet receive less than one percent of the budget. The conventional folks who run the Army have always been preparing for the big war, yet the trend in the latter half of this century has been the little war. Anyway, I won't go into the details or the positions of all the players, but suffice it to say that there are two opposing camps, and that the camp with all the firepower and the money and the pull is the conventional camp.''

"Hell, yeah, I know about that," Senator Jordan said. "I was on the committee that drafted a law over the Joint Chiefs protests to get the Special Operations Command designated a separate entity."

Maxwell nodded. "Anyway, there are rumors. About seven or eight years ago, one of the Ranger battalion commanders was causing a lot of trouble. The Rangers were under the Special Operations Command, but they were the darling of the regular Army guys. The Ranger has always been viewed as the ultimate infantryman.

"The Army made a big push to get the Ranger regiment out from underneath the Special Operations Command and back into the regular Army fold, under the 18th Airborne Corps.

"The problem was that the battalion commander of the 1st Ranger Battalion at Hunter Army Airfield in Georgia thought they should stay under 1st SOCOM command. And he was quite vocal about it despite warnings from his chain of command. He even went so far as to agree to testify before a congressional committee investigating the controversy.

"Two weeks before he was scheduled to testify, he was participating in a joint exercise at Hurlburt Field in Florida. During a night operation, his helicopter crashed. He and twelve other Rangers were killed. The safety board at Fort Rucker investigated the case as they are required to do. I talked to one of the members of that board. He told me that they couldn't get access to some of the information they needed to determine cause of crash. They ended up labeling it, like so many other unexplained crashes, as pilot error. But he told me that what he did see of the crash site showed signs of a midair explosion.''

"You're saying the battalion commander was killed?" Jordan demanded.

"It certainly was convenient," was Maxwell's summary. "There have been other incidents over the years. Other accidents. Hell, no one has yet figured out exactly what happened at Desert One, but that certainly cost Carter the presidency. I talked to Charlie Beckwith before he died, and he was bitter. There was something he wouldn't tell even me. He had those Marine helicopters forced on him by the Joint Chiefs and he indicated there were other things that occurred at the behest of the Joint Chiefs that were not conducive to the success of the mission.''

Maxwell shrugged. ''I can't prove anything, but there have just been too many coincidences. And there are too many right now.''

Jordan drummed his fingers on the desktop for a few minutes. ''All right, you've convinced me that doing nothing isn't a good idea. The possibility of a real threat here is just too high. I'll go to the President with this and inform him of the situation.''

Maxwell had been thinking about this ever since landing. ''Let's bring General Martin in for a meeting,'' he suggested.

''For what purpose?''

''Let's let him square off with Major Watson. See what happens,'' Maxwell said. ''It might be interesting.''

CHAPTER ☆ 22

It was a perfect night for lovers on Waikiki but a terrible night for covert operations. The sea was smooth and flat. The moon was three-quarters full and reflected off the mirror surface, giving forty-two percent illumination. The sound of the minimal surf on the sandy beach was surprisingly loud.

The submarine lay off shore, due south of Fort Kamehameha, over the horizon so the lights on shore couldn't be seen. It was submerged, lying dead in the water 100 feet down, ten kilometers from the coast. On the back deck, a hastily welded hatch opened in the hull, leading into the pressurized compartment—the dry deck shelter (DDS)—bolted to the deck. The two men climbing into the DDS wore wet suits and carried their gear in black mesh bags.

They ran through the pre-operations checks on the vehicle cocooned inside the DDS—the Mark IX Swimmer Delivery Vehicle (SDV). The batteries were at full charge, everything was functioning properly. The Mark IX was a long, flattened rectangle with propellers and dive fins at the rear. A little over nineteen feet long, it was only slightly more than six feet wide and drew less than three feet.

The two divers slid inside, closing the hatches behind them. For the trip in they would breathe off air from the tanks on the vehicle and they hooked their breathing gear up appropriately.

The man on the right spoke into the radiophone which

was connected by umbilical to the sub. "Mother, this is Little Bird. We are clear to proceed. Over."

"Roger, Little Bird. We read all green in here. Over."

"Flood and release. Over."

"We'll be waiting for you. Good hunting. Umbilicals cut and flooding and releasing. Out."

The radiophone went dead. With a hiss, water began pouring into the DDS. The pilot worked at keeping the SDV at neutral buoyancy as the chamber flooded. Water also flooded into the chambers inside the SDV where the two divers lay on their stomachs peering out the front glass canopy.

Once the chamber was full, the large hatch on the end swung open. The pilot goosed the twin propellers, and the SDV was free of the submarine, clearing the DDS. The pilot controlled the Mark IX using stabilizers, both horizontal and vertical, added to the rear of the propellers.

The second diver was the navigator and he was currently punching in on the waterproof panel in front of him.

"Fixing Doppler," he announced over the commo link between him and his cohort. The computerized Doppler navigation system was now updated with their current location and would guide them on their journey, greatly simplifying a task that previously was a nightmare in pitch-black seas. The SDV also boasted an obstacle-avoidance sonar subsystem (OAS), which provided automatic warning to the pilot of any obstacles in the sub's path—essential given that they could see little more than an inch out the front window and would be "flying" blind, trusting to the Doppler and their charts for navigation.

"Course set. All clear," the navigator announced.

The pilot increased power to the propellers and they were moving, heading due north.

"It's like a shot in the dark, sergeant major," Vasquez said. "They're not going to come paddling through in a canoe."

"No, they aren't," Skibicki agreed. "But that's why we got this, Vasquez," he said slapping the small black box between his legs. They were seated on the breakwater, just to the west of Fort Kamehameha, facing toward the channel leading into Pearl Harbor. A housing area for Hickam Air Force base was just behind them, but all was quiet, the two having crept in just after dark and taking up their position, easily hiding among the rocks whenever the rare Air Patrol car rolled by.

"According to my buddy in Navy Special Ops we can pick up an octopus farting with this bad boy," Skibicki continued. "If they come in, we'll hear them and we'll be able to track them. We still up with the commander?" he asked, referring to the Satcom radio in the backpack she had carried.

"I got them six by." Vasquez considered the situation. "But why tonight? The ceremony isn't until—"

"Recon," Skibicki interrupted. "No man worth his salt would hit a target without taking a look first." He glanced out at the dark strip of water through which generations of fighting ships had passed. "They'll come."

"Running clear," the navigator said. "I put us at three klicks off coast. Change heading to three-four-five degrees."

"Three-four-five degrees," the pilot confirmed, as he manipulated the controls.

"ETA, forty minutes."

"Roger."

The SDV slid through the water, the propellers leaving no trace, fifty feet below the surface. As they got closer the navigator directed the pilot up closer to the surface, at the same time being aware they were getting closer to the coral reefs lying off the shore.

"We have one hundred feet under us," the navigator announced. Since Oahu was a volcanic island, the hydrography dictated rapid loss of water depth due to the steep slopes.

"Eighty feet."

"Sixty. We're near the reefs."

The pilot slowed their forward speed.

"Forty. I've got contact off to the right front. Path still clear."

The pilot slowed until they were at a crawl.

* * *

"Hey, why does the commander—"

"Shh," Skibicki said, slicing his across his throat. "I've got something." He listened hard into the headphones. "Something's coming underwater. Something small."

"I've got solid contact," the navigator said. "Shoreline," he confirmed. "New heading, one-one-zero degrees."

"One-one-zero degrees." The SDV turned hard right, paralleling the shore to the east.

"What the fuck?" Skibicki muttered. He turned the hydrophone in the water, tracking. "They're going *east!*"

"Not the harbor?" Vasquez asked, shifting her gaze in the indicated direction, even though she knew the vehicle that they were looking for was under water.

"Come on," Skibicki said, pulling up the cord for the phone. "We've got to follow. Call it in."

As Skibicki packed up the hydrophone, Vasquez called in the change to their higher commander.

"Easy, easy," the navigator muttered. "On my mark. Hold."

The pilot brought the SDV to a halt, then slowly let them sink down until they rested on the bottom, in forty feet of water, inside the coral reef off of the edge of Hickam Field, 200 meters off shore. To their front, due east, was the reef runway for Honolulu International Airport.

"Switch to personal air," the pilot ordered before he shut down the vehicle system.

The two men quickly turned off all the equipment on the SDV. They pushed open their hatches and slid out, pulling their equipment bags with them. Leaving the Mark IX resting on the bottom, they swam forward, toward the shore.

"I've lost them," Skibicki cursed, throwing the headphones down. "They must have stopped. They'll be coming in somewhere around here. Keep your eyes open," he ordered, pulling out his own set of night vision goggles. Putting them on, he then checked his MP-5 submachine gun, insuring the safety was on and a round was in the chamber.

He looked over his shoulder. The hangars for the Hawaii

Air National Guard abutted the shore, and in the distance the runways of the Air Force base lay straight ahead and those of the international airport were off to the right.

The two swimmers cut smoothly through the warm water, their fins flickering back and forth. The lead man held his computer nav board in his hands, directly under his mask, reading the data off it. There was no visibility and they dared not use lights. He followed the indications on the small glowing screen in front of his face and turned slightly right, his buddy close on his fins.

Skibicki and Vasquez walked past the Hickam Marina, weapons at the ready, eyes open for both the infiltrators and the Air Police. Skibicki saw a dark line ahead, cutting in from the shore—the Kumumau canal and, although he didn't know the destination, he now knew the route. It was what he would do. "Let's go," he ordered, sprinting toward the canal.

The two swimmers found the entrance of the canal. It was very shallow, less than eight feet, and they swam just above the bottom. They put their navigation devices away now. There was only one way to go. They followed the narrow waterway until it ended, then carefully popped to the surface. They were inside the perimeter of Hickam Air Force Base and the large hangar that housed Air Force One was less than forty feet away.

Caching their swim fins and nav devices, the two men slithered out of the water and began making their way through the six-inch grass toward the back of the hangar.

"There," Skibicki hissed, spotting the two forms edging over the lip of the canal and melding into the earth. He watched them move toward the hangar, then tapped Vasquez on the shoulder. "Stay here and keep in commo with the CO."

He went to his knees, then his stomach and began following the two men. They were very good, taking their time in the approach, but Ski had done this many times before during his years in Vietnam, and he was better. By the time the two men had reached the dark wall of the hangar, he was less than forty feet behind them.

He paused and watched as they began climbing up the outside wall, using rungs that were welded onto the metal. Like two dark insects they crept up, then disappeared over the edge of the roof.

Skibicki gave it two minutes, then he followed, grabbing the first rung and scaling the 100-foot wall. When he reached the top rung, he carefully peered over the edge. The roof of the large hangar was flat, with ventilation ducts spaced every thirty feet. The men were a little over halfway across the roof at one of the ducts.

Skibicki crept over the edge of the roof and made his way to the cover of another duct where he could watch them from a concealed position. Taking great care, the two men removed the top of the duct noiselessly. They then took something small and square out of one of the packs they had carried and attached it to the end of a rope. They lowered the object into the duct and Skibicki watched as they maneuvered whatever it was for several minutes, until they seemed satisfied. When the rope came back up, whatever had been on the end was no longer there.

The two men replaced the top of the duct and retraced their steps. Skibicki held perfectly still in the dark shadows as they passed within ten feet and slipped over the edge of the roof and disappeared. Skibicki gave it another ten minutes, then moved forward and peered into the duct where they had worked. Directly below was the front end of Air Force One. On the top of the plane lay the intake for inflight refueling. Skibicki nodded, satisfied that he knew what had happened and made his way back to Vasquez.

"They went back into the canal," Vasquez reported.

"Give me the handset," Skibicki ordered.

HONOLULU, HAWAII
5 December
8:00 A.M. LOCAL/ 1800 ZULU

"The *Sam Houston* is supposed to be out at sea on maneuvers. It's under radio silence as per normal operating procedure so we're not exactly sure where it is," General Maxwell said.

"So in other words, it could be doing what Major Watson says it's doing?" Senator Jordan asked.

"Yes, it could," Maxwell said.

"What about the soldiers parachuting in?"

"The information about the refueling is correct, but I can find no record of a parachute drop or of any missions to this island by a Combat Talon aircraft. The battalion commander for 1st Battalion, 1st Special Forces Group in Okinawa says all his troops are accounted for."

"What else?" Jordan asked.

"General Martin is waiting down the hall," Maxwell said.

"And we still have nothing solid," Jordan said. "All right, bring General Martin in first and see what he has to say, then we'll bring the major in and see what they come up with between the two of them"

Boomer had spent a restless night—no word on Trace, no word from Skibicki, and he didn't feel like he had made the best impression yesterday. In fact, somewhere around three in the morning he had seriously begun to believe that he was insane. It was only the hard plastic of Stubbs's ID card in his pocket that kept him from going over the edge.

He started as the door to the hotel room swung open and Agent Stewart appeared. "Senator Jordan wants to see you."

Boomer followed Stewart down the hallway and into the large office suite occupied by the senator. General Maxwell was also there, but Boomer was surprised to see General Martin sitting stiffly in a chair across from the Senator's desk.

"Major Watson, I believe you know General Martin."

Boomer snapped to attention and threw a salute in Martin's direction. He was irritated to note that Martin didn't stand up to return the salute, a severe breach of military protocol that only the three military men in the room were aware of. Boomer knew he was in the shit now and following the senator's gesture, took a seat at the corner of the desk, closest to Martin but facing both men.

"Major Watson, I've been telling General Martin that

we seem to have a problem with some military maneuvers going on around this island. I've had General Maxwell check things out and he has only been able to discover some limited information. I've also discussed with General Martin your allegations about your mission into the Ukraine. General Martin denies knowledge of any of these activities.

"I also informed him of your allegation that there is a secret military organization, which you call The Line, which has been active in the politics of this country for over half a century. General Martin says he has no knowledge of such an organization."

Boomer felt his irritation deepen with the senator's lawyerly diction. You didn't read people their rights on the battlefield—you fought. He kept his peace, waiting to find out where he was in the engagement being sparred in this room.

"I only felt it proper," Jordan continued, "to have General Martin here to discuss this situation." The senator looked down at his desktop. "I have an appointment with the President in an hour and a half. I hope we can resolve this situation now."

"There is nothing to resolve," Martin snapped. "I do not appreciate being called in here and having to listen to some insane story, which—"

"General," Jordan gently interrupted, "I appreciate your situation, but I do not have the time to follow proper format at the present, and I would like to get this over with." He shifted his gaze to Boomer. "Is there anything you would like to ask General Martin?"

Boomer could see Martin's face go red at the thought of answering questions from some lowly major. He didn't understand this setup—why tip your hand to the enemy, even if you're not sure they're the enemy? Having served in the military for half his life, Boomer was amazed sometimes at the different perspective civilians used to face problems.

"Sir," he said, addressing Jordan, "I'm sure you have already asked all the pertinent questions."

"Young man," Senator Jordan said, "you have confessed to us that you have committed two acts that would be viewed as criminal in nature: your actions in the

Ukraine, and here on this island in the death of two men. I would suggest you take a bit more interest in the situation.''

''What do you think he's going to tell me?'' Boomer asked, the irritation plain in his voice. He knew he was so far gone over the line now that nothing mattered. ''Do you think General Martin is going to say, 'Well, certainly, I was aware that the Delta Force mission into the Ukraine was designed to kill the NATO inspectors and embarrass this administration's policy in that matter?' ''

''Major, you'd better watch your tone,'' Martin said. He looked at Jordan. ''As you just said, this man is the one with the problem. He's the one who has apparently confessed to breaking the law and committing murder—''

As Martin ranted, Boomer suddenly realized what was going on. It wasn't at all what a military man would do. But Jordan didn't view this as a military situation—he apparently thought it was a political one. The modern soldier rarely saw his opponent face-to-face. The fight was conducted from a distance. Even if you were in a foxhole four feet from your foe, you didn't exactly stand up and look him in the eyes. But in politics you always looked the people you dealt with in the eye. It was the way the battle was waged. He realized that Jordan was watching the two of them and evaluating.

All that was fine and well inside this room, Boomer thought, but when the President went out to Pearl on the morning of the seventh they were going to be on very different turf with a very different set of rules. Bullets didn't argue niceties. They were final.

General Martin had finished and stood to leave.

''Do you know General Benjamin Hooker, class of 'thirty, sir?'' Boomer asked suddenly. ''He was head of the history department at the Academy for quite a few years.''

Martin paused and looked at Boomer. ''What does that have to do with anything we've discussed in this room, Major?''

''I believe General Hooker is a member of The Line, and I want to know if you are in communication with him.''

''*You* want to know?'' Martin asked incredulously. He turned to Jordan. ''I don't have to put up with this. I have always paid you the utmost respect, Senator, but I do not need to sit here and listen to this crap."

"I want your word that none of what Major Watson said is true," Senator Jordan said.

"I said it wasn't true," Martin said.

"I want your word," Jordan repeated.

"As an officer in the United States Army, you have my word," Martin said.

"I want the *Sam Houston* to immediately be ordered into port. I want any Army units participating in exercises on Oahu to return to their barracks. You will place all records of Delta Force operations for the past three months on my desk before close of business today. Is that clear?"

"You don't have the authority—" Martin began, but Jordan cut him off.

"Do you want me to go to the President and get him to order it?"

Martin changed tack. "Sir, those Delta Force records are—"

"Close of business today," Jordan said.

Martin nodded. "Certainly, sir." He leaned forward and put his hands on Jordan's desk. "But I want something in return."

"And that is?"

The chairman of the Joint Chiefs pointed at Boomer. "I want him to go with me now. I don't want him running around here causing trouble. He's probably AWOL, and I want him under the custody of the military."

Jordan nodded. "All right."

"Wait a second!" General Maxwell exclaimed. "You can't do that."

Jordan blinked. "I can do any damn thing I want. Major Watson is military and as such is subject to the uniform code of military justice. We have to turn him over to the authorities sooner or later. I believe this issue has been resolved. I believe it will be best for all involved if we forget about everything that has happened the last several days."

Boomer was numb. He felt like a detached observer watching everything play out like he wasn't involved at all. But when Martin escorted him to the door and two men in civilian clothes and military haircuts slapped handcuffs on him, he knew it wasn't a dream.

BENSON, NEW YORK
5 December
1:30 P.M. LOCAL/ 1830 ZULU

Consciousness returned to Trace on a tide of pain. Her leg throbbed uncontrollably. The pain in her chest was dependent on her breathing, but that being an essential bodily function, it was inevitable. She was flat on her back, and as her eyes slowly came into focus she saw a white ceiling above her head. She carefully turned her head. The room was painted off-white and the cheap dresser and small desk indicated that it had once been occupied by a child. The blinds on the window were closed, and she could see gray light all around the edges. The door opened, and Trace smiled as Harry walked into the room holding a glass of orange juice.

"Glad to see you're awake," Harry said, setting the glass down on the small table next to the bed. "How do you feel?"

"Lousy," Trace said.

"More specifically?" Harry asked as he lifted the sheet and looked at the large white cast. Trace was glad to see that someone had cut open the leg on her jeans, cleaned them and put them back on her. "Your leg?"

"Hurts like hell."

"It's been set. Should heal fine," Harry said. "Your ribs?"

"Same. They hurt." Trace remembered the captain with the ax, and suddenly tears came to her eyes and she sobbed, the movement causing pain to explode and leading directly into a gasp.

"Easy now, easy," Harry said, cradling her head in a massive hand. "You been through a rough time, missy, and you done damn well, but we got some more work to do. The tears and the feeling got to be held off for a while yet. I know what you're going through. First time I came back from a mission it hit me hard, but I only let it hit me when I was back, and we ain't back yet."

"The diary?" Trace asked.

"Yeah, the diary," Harry said. "I got it, and we need to get it in the right hands."

"I know who needs to see it," she said. She told him about Boomer and Skibicki and the entire situation in Hawaii and he nodded when she was done.

"Yeah, I know Ski. We served together, and I've been talking with him about this." He rubbed his chin. "They ain't got much time. Today's the fifth."

"What about Colonel Rison?" Trace asked.

"The colonel's gone, miss. We got to do this ourselves." He stood up. "Wait a second." He left the room and was gone for a while before reappearing with a phone in his hand. He plugged it into a jack in the wall. "I got us a way to get to Hawaii, but we won't get there until tomorrow. Do you think you're up to traveling."

"I made it this far," Trace said.

Harry handed her the phone. "I think you ought to call Hawaii."

Trace dialed and talked to Skibicki. She was surprised but relieved when he told her Boomer had gone to the authorities. At least it was out in the open now. She told Skibicki about what had happened at West Point and where she was, then handed the phone to Harry, who walked out of the room, still talking to the sergeant major.

There was no packing to be done. Trace had only the clothes she'd had on when Harry had rescued her, with the addition of the cast on her leg and a tight bandage around her ribs. Harry had pulled up the blinds. The snow-covered hills of the Adirondacks beckoned outside. It was as abrupt a change from the green of Hawaii as possible and Trace stared out at it, as her mind tried to work over all that had happened in the past few days.

She looked up as Harry came back in the room. "How did you find me?" she abruptly asked, one of many questions that were flitting about her brain like unsettled demons.

"Find you?" he asked as he handed her the diary.

"At West Point," she clarified.

"I got back in contact with Skibicki," he said. "He told me to put the word out on the NCO network to look for you. The MPs at West Point spotted you and I got a call. I came there as quickly as possible and waited until you got uncovered."

Trace wasn't satisfied. "Why didn't *you* recover the diary?"

"I didn't know where it was," Harry said, checking her cast and adjusting a set of crutches for her height.

"Why not?"

Harry paused and looked at her. "Because I was with the colonel and they knew that. All they'd have to do is snatch me, and one thing I learned a long time ago: everyone talks, all you have to do is apply the right pressure, physical or mental."

After her recent experience, Trace could most certainly agree with that.

Harry continued. "I didn't know where the letter was that the colonel gave you, but I imagine it was someplace that if anything happened to him, it would get into the right hands. Maybe there were copies of that letter."

"Where's the colonel?" Trace asked.

"I took him out of Philly and brought him back here." Harry pointed out the window at the snow covered hills. "He's buried where he always wanted to be buried. All I know now is we got the diary, and we got to get it to Hawaii."

"You haven't been very specific on how we are going to do that," Trace said.

Harry cocked his head. Trace paused to listen. Even though the walls of the house she could hear a plane's engine coming closer. "How are they going to land?" she asked, pointing out at the snow-covered hills and trees.

Harry held out a hand, helping her to her feet. "You'll see. Let's be getting outside." Trace fumbled with the crutches, but Harry made it easier, tucking them under one arm and lifting her with the other. He'd given her a down vest to put on and she was grateful for it as they stepped outside into the front yard.

A twin-engine plane swooped in suddenly from over the hills to the south. Trace stared in amazement as it slowed and came to a hover directly overhead as the wings themselves rotated up, pointing the massive propeller blades up into the sky. She'd seen pictures of the V-22 Osprey but never been near one in person. It was much larger than she had imagined, and she was impressed with the way it slowly settled down into the driveway, the blades kicking up snow and causing her to duck her head and shield her eyes. The plane had no markings identifying it and Trace wondered who owned it—the last she had heard the military had opted not to purchase the multipurpose craft, a move violently opposed by the Special Operations community.

A ramp in the rear came down, and Harry carried her on board. As he settled her down in the cargo web seating around the inside of the cargo bay, the ramp closed. The ramp swung shut and the pilots increased power, lifting the Osprey out of the snow and into the sky. As the wings rotated forward, the plane's velocity increased, and it roared off to the west.

FORT DeRUSSY
5 December
1:00 P.M. LOCAL/ 2300 ZULU

"We're moving you up to Schofield Barracks," the agent said as he slapped the cuffs back on Boomer's wrist. "We don't want your friends to get any strange ideas about breaking you out." Boomer had heard him called Lucas by one of the other men who had been guarding him, and he filed that information for possible later use.

After being brought out of the Royal Hawaiian, Boomer had been taken to a secure room at the small MP station on Fort DeRussy for safekeeping. From what he had heard so far, these men knew about him, Skibicki, and Vasquez. He'd even heard one of the agents say something about Trace in New York.

Boomer had no doubt now that The Line existed. He couldn't believe Senator Jordan simply taking General Martin's word. They were all insane with their complacency. These diplomats were too sure that the wheels of justice and normalcy would turn properly and everything would stay in its correct place, but Boomer knew better. He'd been there on that hillside in the Ukraine. He knew the men of

The Line were willing to sacrifice innocent lives to achieve their goals.

Of course, Boomer reminded himself, he'd been too complacent also. Waiting a day for Trace to surface with the diary, if that's what she'd gone to West Point for. Expecting someone else to do something about The Line.

Boomer twisted his hands inside the cuffs as Lucas led him to a waiting unmarked car. He pushed Boomer into the back seat and slid in beside him. Another man in civilian clothes was at the wheel. They didn't look like cops, military or not, to Boomer. Both men had the hard set to their face that said they were professional soldiers who had seen action. Lucas took a pair of cuffs that had a foot-long chain in the middle and snapped one around each ankle, ensuring that Boomer could not run.

"Let's go, Mike," Lucas ordered.

As the car rolled out the main gate to Fort DeRussy and turned west, Boomer tumbled the pieces in his mind: Keyes and the team from 1st Group probably hiding on the north shore; Colonel Decker in the tunnel; the *Sam Houston* somewhere off shore; General Martin and the Joint Chiefs ensconced at Pearl. Skibicki and Vasquez were now alone against an organization that seemed to be everywhere and know everything. Boomer was afraid to even think what may have happened to Trace.

Boomer looked around. They couldn't allow him to live. The thought made more sense than anything that had happened so far on this confused day.

They were on H1 and shortly made the turn onto H2, which ran up the center of the Hawaii to Schofield Barracks, home to the Army's 25th Infantry Division. Boomer knew he didn't have much time to act.

He was surprised when they pulled off the highway well short of the exit for Schofield Barracks. They were on a dirt road that descended off the shoulder of H1, then looped underneath it next to a stream. An old rusted sign read WAIKAKALAUA AMMO STORAGE TUNNELS SITE. The road was on low ground following the small stream, and the terrain rose steeply on either side.

They passed a long-abandoned guard shack and entered the site. Row upon row of steel doors were cut into both hillsides. A few of the doors were askew, opening into dark tunnels. Others were padlocked. The entire area looked deserted.

"No one's going to find you for a long time," Lucas said as he pulled up to one of the open tunnels.

Boomer didn't bother to reply. Days of frustration snapped as he realized the depth of his predicament. He twisted and slammed both hands into Lucas's face, stunning him. Before he could recover, Boomer looped the cuffs over Lucas's head and pulled him in, increasing pressure on his throat.

As Mike slammed on the brakes, Boomer used Lucas to anchor him as he lifted his feet up over the driver's seat headrest, splitting them to the maximum allowed by the chain, and then dropping his feet down on either side of Mike's head. He flexed his hamstrings, and the chain grabbed hold of Mike's neck and pulled him up against the headrest.

Boomer tightened every muscle in his body, contracting like a snake as both men desperately struggled against the chains around their necks. He felt blows in his chest from Lucas while the driver tore at his ankles.

The driver was the smarter of the two as it finally occurred to him after almost twenty seconds of getting choked to pull his gun. The problem was he had his back to Boomer and he couldn't move because of the pressure against his neck. Mike twisted his arm and fired blindly.

Boomer felt the bullet speed by his face, hearing it impact with flesh. His face was splattered with blood. Lucas went slack and Boomer maintained his pressure on Mike as he spared a glance to the other side of the back seat. The bullet had hit Lucas in the jaw and taken off most of the top of his head.

Another shot and the bullet shattered the right rear passenger window. The gun finally fell from unconscious fingers, but Boomer maintained the pressure for another minute against the possibility of a ruse. Finally, he lifted his legs and brought them back into the back seat. He went through Lucas's pockets, ignoring the blood that was soaking his clothes and retrieved the keys for the cuffs. Boomer unlocked himself. He took the gun out of Lucas's shoulder holster, then the holster itself. A Berretta 92, military-issue. He strapped it on under his shirt. He checked just to verify—Lucas was carrying a DIA ID card just like the others had.

Boomer got out of the backseat and opened the driver's door. He checked for a pulse: none. Pushing the body over, Boomer took the wheel. He drove into the ammunition storage bunker between the open steel doors. The car narrowly fit through and he parked inside. He took the leg cuffs with him as he went back out. Shutting the doors, Boomer locked them with the leg cuffs, then threw the key into the stream.

Orienting himself, Boomer began walking back east, toward the mountains and Waiwa where he hoped to find at least Vasquez, maybe Skibicki. If not—Boomer didn't even pause in his terrain-eating stride—if not, well then he'd continue on and do whatever needed to be done to stop The Line.

CHAPTER ☆ 23

AIRSPACE, UNITA MOUNTAINS, UTAH
5 DECEMBER
6:00 P.M. LOCAL/ 0100 ZULU

Trace noticed a slight change in the Osprey's speed and twisted on the web seating, peering out the window. Below, she spied the snow-covered mountains of Utah. The V-22's propellers were laboring in the thin air to keep it going. They were heading into the sun, which was low on the horizon.

Trace had slept quite a bit. Harry stayed at her side, only occasionally going up to the cockpit. Trace had settled her leg up on the web seat as comfortably as possible while at the same time trying to avoid twisting her ribs into a painful position. Harry had helped by placing two kit bags on the seat to give her some support.

Trace noticed a reflection to her right and tried to focus in the dwindling sunlight. Soon she didn't have to squint as the object came closer on an interception vector. Trace wondered what a twin-bladed Chinook was doing here. The answer wasn't long in coming. The Chinook swung out in front of the Osprey, the reason the V-22 had slowed down. The back ramp of the helicopter came down and she saw the refueling nozzle.

Trace had heard about Special Operations Chinooks being modified to accomplish inflight refueling of other helicopters and she had no doubt that this particular helicopter—coming from the Nightstalkers of Task Force 160, the secret Army helicopter unit—was a specially modified MH-47. The Chinooks own refueling probe in front, not standard equipment on regular CH-47s, reinforced that identification.

Harry came back from the cockpit. "Doing all right?"

Trace nodded. "As well as can be expected. My leg is starting to itch." She pointed out the window. "Where'd that come from?

"We can't make it on one tank of gas, and we don't want to be landing, so I asked Skibicki if he could get us some help."

"Is that how we got this plane?" she asked.

"Yes."

Trace wondered. Skibicki might be a sergeant major, but he certainly did not have the power to order an experimental aircraft to fly such a mission or to get the inflight refueling. She felt a tremor of unease in her gut that Harry believed that.

Harry stood. "We'll be in Hawaii in about eight hours. Try to get some more rest. You won't be getting much when we land." He went back to the cockpit.

Trace looked about at the interior of the Osprey, then out the window again at the Special Operations Chinook. The plastic box with the diary in it was on the seat next to her. She opened the box and pulled it out. Trace turned to the first page. The words were written in very neat, block letters and Trace read the initial entry:

12 June 1930

I will indeed miss my "rockbound highland home" above the Hudson, but I must admit to a certain degree of anticipation for the assignments that await me. I have become a man at West Point, and as a man I will take my allotted place in the Long Gray Line.

I thought my heart would burst today as we sat on the Plain and listened to Secretary Hurley give the graduation address. I find it difficult to believe four years have gone so quickly, yet looking at the faces of my classmates on either side I can see the changes wrought in us by the years. We came here as boys——we leave as warriors. And I have been fortunate enough to be the first of the chosen ones. I have received my instructions and training beyond that of my peers for the past two years. Now I am finally ready to go out into the Army as one of The Line.

Trace scanned slowly, reading Hooker's account of his graduation. She paused and leaned back in the seat, feeling the throbbing from her legs. This was real. She was almost afraid to continue. Hooker was part of The Line. It was no longer a fanciful idea for a novel. Indeed, she could see that she had had it wrong in her own writing. Hooker had not been approached the night before graduation. He'd been part of The Line for two years prior. It made sense. They'd want to draw the cadets in and make them feel something even more special than being part of the Corps. Trace wondered when The Line approached cadets. Maybe Ring Weekend, when the new third-year cadets received their band of gold marrying them to the Academy and the Army.

She wished Hooker's diary had started at the beginning of his association with The Line, but she realized it made little difference. The important question was what had The Line done over the years. The part of her that was afraid to know grew stronger. Then she remembered Mrs. Howard lying in her bed in Maryland, telling her story of Patton and his death. Trace turned the page.

She scanned Hooker's account of fulfilling his Rhodes Scholarship. There was no further reference to The Line.

Impatient, Trace flipped the pages. Where was Mrs. Howard's story? The story that had started all this. She found it a quarter of the way in:

18 Dec 1945

Only that damn fool Patton could break his neck and stay alive. If only George could have kept his mouth shut. If only he could have handled the Task Force Baum mishap better.

I told the staff eight months ago that George was a liability and that the best thing to do was to have him die "honorably." Perhaps a plane crash. We've done it before, and that would have been that. He would have had a great funeral, everyone would have said great things, and he would be remembered as a hero. Now we have this mess. He's caused us grief for a half a year now and he's still alive, damn it! Bernie and his complicated schemes. Just kill the son of a bitch——that's what George himself would have said.

Now I have to go over there and do damage control, and there's so much to do here. The chief has got some really great plans to get Europe on its feet and to counter-weight the Russians. I need to be here, not making sure some old fool doesn't open his mouth.

21 Dec 1945

I'm exhausted. The flight over with Mrs. Patton and the doctor certainly wasn't the most enjoyable experience. Went in to see General Patton right away. He's in bad shape, and the doctor assures me he won't see Christmas alive. Bernie did a good job isolating him. We've kept anyone he might want to talk to away.

I had to talk to him about Baum. He wasn't happy. He doesn't give a damn about the gold or the men killed. All he cares about is his reputation. Christ——some of these prima donnas. He got to lead the 3rd Army. I had to stay in D.C. and do the chief's and the staff's dirty work all those years.

I feel confident, though, that all is secure here.

21 Dec 1945

It is done. Time to get back to work. I've got to go to London and talk to Ike about the chief's plan. The staff approved it after a long argument——there is quite a bit of *fear about the Continent. After all we've already fought two wars here this century. Some wanted to let it rot. But those with a little more vision can see the threat in the Soviet Union, and we need Europe as a buffer. As long as we have the bomb and bases in Europe we are safe.*

Mrs. Patton wanted to return the body to the States. I was willing to do it, but Ike was quite upset when I talked to him on the land line. He was adamant——SHAEF policy is all who die here get buried here and making one exception would open the floodgates. So George gets to rest overseas. Glad to be done with it. I chewed Bernie's ass. Told him next time he needed a job done, pick someone who knew how to do it right.

Mrs. Howard's story was true. And fifty years later she died because she repeated it. Trace knew there would be time later to go through the diary in detail. Now she just wanted a feel for what they were up against. Trace turned a chunk of pages, jumping several years. Her eye caught an entry on the bottom of the page, dated 1951:

April 1951

Truman relieved MacArthur. The "Generalisimo" always was a damn prima donna and would never listen. We tried to help him, but he was always too bitter about losing the Phillipines and that we supported Ike first and not him in the war. Of course, behind it all was MacArthur's simple resistance to taking advice or even listening to those who graduated after him. The last time I saw the "Generalissimo" I warned him both of the Chinese and of Truman; to keep the balance in that pisspot country and remember Europe was the main scene; and he reminded me that he was superintendent of the Academy while I was still in grade school. As if that mattered. Our original decision to go with

Ike certainly is justified now beyond any reasonable doubt.

Will have to throw a bone to the general though—will have to meet with the staff to see what to do. Terry knows the Generalissimo well from the war, he'll know what to do. The good thing is that Truman has torpedoed himself with this. Couldn't have planned it more perfectly. It's all rolling for Ike in '52.

Such casual references about events that preceded her life and were written about in history texts astounded Trace. Obviously the staff was the ruling council of The Line. She turned several more pages, this time halting at a section that mentioned Eisenhower again.

2 May 1960

Ike is furious about Powers and the whole U-2 incident. CJ tells me that Ike somehow knows we gave Powers to the Russians. Hell, what does he expect? CJ warned him to back off with Khrushchev.

Ike still thinks he can pull off the summit. I think not and the staff agrees. However, we still have a few back-up plans in case Khrushchev does not act as expected in response to the U-2 shootdown. CJ has persuaded Ike to go with the cover story. It's all going as planned.

As Trace read on, the U-2 crisis unfolded, but with a vastly different tint than that laid out in history books. CJ was Eisenhower's top aide—a West Point graduate who had temporarily put aside his Army green uniform for a suit and tie and the role of National Security Adviser. Trace remembered him as a three-star general in charge of the III Corps at Fort Hood, Texas, while she was at West Point. But in reality, CJ was the link between The Line and Eisenhower. The cover story that CJ persuaded the President to issue—that the U-2 had wandered off course—was the key to destroying the summit when Khrushchev trotted out

Gary Powers and another version of what had happened days after the cover story was issued.

Despite these later deceptions, it was clear from Hooker's writings that Eisenhower had had the complete support of The Line from the early days of World War II. They had groomed him after the end of the war for the Presidency, and his election was perhaps their greatest coup.

But somewhere along the way, Eisenhower had begun to disregard the advice of The Line. Trace could well imagine the difference for the former general. As commander of Allied forces in Europe during World War II, his and The Line's goals had been in congruence. But as President of a country at peace, Eisenhower's vision must have shifted and become larger. No longer was having a strong military the number one priority. He had the entire welfare of the country to think of.

Trace flipped back several pages. The Line had strongly opposed any attempt at contact with the Russians and most particularly objected to the summit in Paris. Hooker's diary didn't exactly say how they had set up the U-2 incident, but there was a later mention of the CIA getting Powers back from the Soviets and taking care of him in order to keep him quiet.

Trace closed her eyes briefly in weariness. The Line had put forward one of their own and gotten him elected President and then when he failed to heed their wishes, they had sabotaged him repeatedly. She remembered reading about Eisenhower's final speech as President where he had warned of the military-industrial complex. It was as blunt as he could get without directly exposing the machinations that had been behind his own rise to power. And after reading what The Line had done to Patton after he stepped out of cadence with their plans, Trace had no doubt that Eisenhower had been aware of his predicament.

If The Line could threaten and coerce presidents, what chance do we have? Trace thought to herself. She turned a few more pages. Eisenhower had two terms. She noted Hooker's shock at Kennedy's election. The Line had sunk its claws into Nixon and backed him with a lot of help from Howard Hughes, who certainly had a stake in the military-industrial complex.

Trace kept reading. She read how The Line had helped the CIA mislead Kennedy about the invasion of Cuba and how they had assisted bringing about the disastrous events in the Bay of Pigs. After that Kennedy had paid more attention to his instructions from Langley and the Pentagon.

Trace found a diversion in the diary. Hooker had been at West Point, heading up the history department, but in early 1961 he went to Vietnam. There had been a U.S. military presence in that country since 1951, but it was a minor one. No one had really heard of Vietnam up to that point, despite the French debacle at Dien Bien Phu.

23 October 1961

The Staff wanted me to go to Vietnam and take a look. With Europe frozen and Korea gone cold, we need a new hot field. After a few weeks poking around, I think we've got one. Just like Korea except we don't have to worry about a big neighbor like China since the two are also at each other's throats. The North is isolated and we can take them at our pace. I envision five or six good years. A chance to check out the triangle division concept and this newfangled "airmobile" tactic that Gerry has managed to get approved by the chief for his 1st Cavalry Division.

Most particularly, we can blood our junior leaders. The last of the Korean War vets are all now at least majors. Our captains and lieutenants are green. We have good solid leadership at the highest levels, all of whom saw action in World War II, but we must look to the future. Even though running around the jungles of Vietnam might not be the best preparation for the coming war in Europe it is the best opportunity we have. I am going to recommend to the staff that we approve and implement OPLAN Burning Field. I think we have Kennedy's attention now. We can roll this thing up a notch or two so that in a few years we can get regular troops on the ground.

Trace closed the diary. In a way she was surprised that it really didn't surprise her. She'd already considered this idea when she was planning her novel. When people studied history, they often overlooked the obvious in search of reasons they considered valid historically, instead of reasons that were valid realistically. The two were often different. Trace knew that Vietnam had been fought in an illogical manner. Never mind all the military complaints about civilian interference, it had not been the civilians who had invented the one-year rotation plan for all troops and the six-month rotation plans for officers to field leadership positions. The Army *had* known better. Its own studies from World War II had stated conclusively that the average junior officer lasted less than a month in combat. If they survived longer than that, they got much better and their survival rate, and that of their men, was considerably higher than average.

In its haste to ''blood'' as many officers as possible, the Army—The Line, Trace amended—had not only gotten the country involved in an unnecessary war, it had implemented procedures that had killed over 50,000 young Americans.

Trace knew that Hooker and his cronies would not decry that cost. They would point to the fact that the Cold War in Europe had been won. If Europe had gone hot, 50,000 dead could have occurred in one day, never mind over the course of a decade and a half.

But it *was* wrong. Dead wrong. Trace flipped the pages, jumping a couple of years ahead. 1963. The Line was not happy with Kennedy, as they had not been with his predecessor. He had not pushed the missile crisis to the conclusion they had desired, that was evident from Hooker's tone. Trace paused. She ran her finger down the center of the book—there were pages missing. Between September, 1963, and December there was a gap. Why would that be? Trace turned back to the beginning of the diary. If she was stuck here, she might as well read it from beginning to end.

A few hours later, somewhere over the Pacific Ocean she was done. Trace glanced up at the cockpit then reached into her coat and pulled out the pages she had torn out of the diary. She borrowed a pen from the plane's crew chief and wrote a brief note on top of the front page, and then pushed it back into her jacket.

PACIFIC PALISADES, HAWAII
5 December
5:30 P.M. LOCAL/ 0330 ZULU

Boomer followed the edge of the jungle until he was directly behind Maggie's house. He hoped no nosey neighbor was watching as he strode directly across her back yard, grabbed a hold of the deck and pulled himself up. The sliding glass door was unlocked as he had hoped, and he let himself in.

There had been no sign of Skibicki or Vasquez in their camp site in Waiwi, so Boomer had continued south. He needed to get a hold of Skibicki and figure out what to do next. Maybe Vasquez could come up with some new information.

Boomer walked through the living room, glancing at the phone. He went down the hall, and the half-open door to Maggie's bedroom beckoned. Boomer glanced in and saw a silver-framed picture among several on the table next to the bed. He stepped into the room for a closer look. A much younger Maggie, dressed in a bright sundress was standing with a young man in a Navy uniform, his two stripes of gold braid indicating he was a relatively low-ranking officer. There was something vaguely familiar about the officer but the man's eyes were shielded by the visor of his dress hat.

Maggie had a stroller in front of her with a baby in it and she was looking at the camera. In the backdrop, Boomer could see the hills of Oahu and Pearl Harbor. Something caught Boomer's eyes and he peered at the background more closely. He could make out Ford Island and numerous cranes on the island, dipping down into the water. There was a metal object poking out of the water and Boomer could swear it was—

"Find something interesting?" Maggie asked from the doorway.

Boomer spun, embarrassed to have been caught snooping, the picture in his hand. Maggie glanced down at it, then pulled a cigarette out of her purse and lit it.

Boomer handed her the picture. "I thought your daughter was killed in the raid on Pearl." He pointed at the picture. "There's a child here, and it looks like the *Arizona* is sunk in the background of this picture and—"

"It is," Maggie said. She walked over and took it from him. "That's Jimmie, my lover. Or more appropriately at the time of that picture, my former lover. George was at sea as usual when that was taken. And the child is Peter. Jimmie's son," she added. "Ski's older brother, half-brother to be more exact."

Boomer blinked, and Maggie gave a sad smile.

"Oh, I ended the affair after the seventh when Grace died. But Peter, he was my answer to all that happened that day. I knew as soon as I found out I was pregnant that it had happened the night of the sixth. George knew it wasn't his—the timing and all. But he never said a word and raised Peter as his own."

She tapped the photo. "That's the last day I ever talked to Jimmie. It was about a year and a half after the attack and he was doing something with his new job. We decided it was best if he moved on and we both forgot. Jimmie's done real well with himself. I guess a lot of people are attracted to him. He had me under his spell for a long time. But he forgot and so did I, and I don't want Ski to know, and, well, now I guess I'm just rambling.

"Peter died in Vietnam in 1966 with the 1st Cavalry Division in the Ia Drang valley. Like I told you—I lost one generation each way."

Boomer wanted to know more about Jimmie and Pearl Harbor, but her mood told him it would have to be later.

Maggie took the picture and put it back next to the others on her nightstand. "All I've known is military men, and I'm tired of it." She led Boomer out of the bedroom. "It's just death and more death." She stubbed out her cigarette and lit another. "You want to find Ski, right?"

"Yes."

"He's not here, and he won't be back. If you look out the front window you'll see a van parked down the street, keeping an eye on the house. I assume you came the back way since I was on the front porch watching the watchers.

Your best bet is to go out that way and go to the campsite in Waiwa.''

''I've already been there,'' Boomer said.

''Last I spoke to him,'' Maggie said, ''Ski said he'll be in and out of there sometime tonight.''

''What's he doing?'' Boomer asked.

Maggie sighed. ''Everything he can to stop these people, son, everything he can. Now you'd better get going too, before they come looking for you here.''

An hour later, Boomer was settled into the vegetation next to the campsite. With night coming, Boomer settled down for a long wait, praying that Skibicki would turn up sooner rather than later.

HONOLULU, HAWAII
5 December
5:45 P.M. LOCAL/ 0345 ZULU

Senator Jordan rubbed a hand across his forehead. ''So what are you trying to tell me, General Maxwell?'' he demanded.

Maxwell was not in the best of moods either. ''I have not been able to find where they took Major Watson. I've checked his file and talked to his commander at Bragg. He's got an excellent record. I've checked on the information he gave us and as I told you earlier, I can neither confirm or negate it. I'd like to talk to him again.''

''Why don't you just drop this whole thing?'' Jordan asked.

''Because we finally heard something. I received a phone call a little while ago from a Sergeant Major Skibicki. He said that a plane with Major Trace and proof will be arriving sometime after midnight,'' General Maxwell said.

Jordan leaned back in his chair. ''All right. I'll arrange for Major Trace to be met at the airport and for her evidence to be brought here. As for Major Watson, he's in the hands of the military. He's not our problem any more.''

HICKAM FIELD, HAWAII
6 December
2:00 A.M. LOCAL/ 1200 ZULU

Skibicki glanced at the glowing hands on his watch and steadied his breathing. Another ten seconds. He checked the rope one last time, even though he had tied the knots himself and was confident they were secure. He looked down into the hangar. The large bulk of Air Force One loomed in the bright lights illuminating the inside of the hangar.

Vasquez tapped him on the shoulder and held up ten fingers. "Ten seconds, sergeant major."

Those lights went off exactly on schedule, as did all of Hickam Field and half of Pearl Harbor. Skibicki pulled up the night vision goggles that had been hanging on a string around his neck. He stood, climbed over the edge and carefully lowered himself into the vent, allowing the rest of the rope running from the snap link in the front of his waist harness to fall onto the top of the plane. He leaned back and extended his right arm, releasing the friction brake of the snap link pressure, and he slid down the rope. He'd rappeled hundreds of time, and even with the distorted depth perception of the goggles, he slid all the way, braking in perfect timing, just five feet above the top of the aircraft fuselage. He slowly dropped the remaining distance and landed just in front of the intake for inflight refueling.

Skibicki knelt and looked into the intake. He saw a small, plastic-wrapped package. He pulled off the leather gloves he'd worn for rappeling and carefully felt around the package. It was covered in adhesive, but there seemed to be no obvious external anti-handling devices. Of course, Skibicki knew, that didn't mean it might not have some sophisticated device on the inside, but he doubted that. They wanted it to go off once the plane was in the air, which meant the bomb had to be able to survive take off. He figured the odds were that the detonator was set to go off at a predetermined altitude. It was the way he would have designed it.

Using a knife, Skibicki carefully pried the bomb loose, then tucked it into a small backpack, which he threw across his shoulders. He pulled two chumars off a snap link on the side of his harness and hooked them into the rope. The chumars locked into place, one-way metal devices that he could push up, but then they would hold against downward pressure. Nylon straps were attached to the chumars with loops on the end that he stuck his feet through. He slid the left hand one up as far as he could reach, then stepped up, levering himself up with a leg. He did the same with the right and began his ascent. A mental clock was counting down in his head. His worst case estimate was that he had ten minutes before the post engineers would find the junction box with the "electrocuted" snake jammed into it. It was a rare accident but one that was known to happen. Once they found that, the power would be back on.

Halfway up, Skibicki had to halt, out of breath. He could hear the Secret Service agents down below, yelling to each other, not overly concerned from the tone of their voices. They could see out the hangar door that the rest of the post was in darkness. Skibicki would have cursed if he had the breath; he was getting old. He was surprised when he felt the rope jerk and then move upward a couple of feet. He looked up and in the goggles he could see Vasquez reach over the edge, grab a fistful of rope, and pull him up a few more feet.

Skibicki grinned, took a few deep breaths, then resumed climbing. He reached the top and and with Vasquez's help pulled himself over the edge. Quickly they pulled the rope up and resecured the vent top.

They made their way to the edge of the roof and began the climb back down to the ground on the metal rungs bolted into the side of the building. The outside lights flickered on for a second then went off. Three-quarters of the way down, the lights went back on for almost ten seconds, and Skibicki and Vasquez froze until the lights went out again.

Reaching the grass at the back of the hangar Skibicki paused, Vasquez bumping into him. Off to the left was the safety of the canal, to the right the E4-B the Joint Chiefs had arrived in sat on the tarmac. Skibicki hefted the backpack and paused. The lights for the airfield came back on and stayed on. Then he made his decision; he still had time before he had to make the rendezvous.

"Wait here," he whispered to Vasquez.

CHAPTER ☆ 24

"They had some problems at the airfield with the lights, but they're back up," Harry reported.

Trace watched the beach along Waikiki glide past as the pilot descended into his glide path. The hotels lining the shore were well lighted despite the late hour. Trace was startled as the plane banked hard left, further out over the water.

"What's going on?" she asked.

Harry didn't answer. He was busy buckling on a parachute that he'd pulled off it's place on the wall of the cabin.

"What are you doing?"

"Can't be landing with you, missy," Harry said. "The Secret Service and all those type folks will be waiting, and I killed a few people back there in New York. My job is done. It's up to you now." He stepped over to her and grabbed the seat belt, buckling it in around her. "You be safe now."

Trace thought for a second, then reached inside her jacket. She pulled out the pages she'd torn from the diary and thrust them into Harry's hand. "Just in case something goes wrong on my end," she said, "here's part of the diary. I hope to see Boomer soon, but if I don't, you get this to him."

Harry nodded an acknowledgement and stuffed the pages inside his flight suit and zipped it shut. With a roar the back ramp opened, and Harry stepped close to the opening.

331

When it was fully open, Harry stepped out into the darkness and was gone. The back ramp immediately began to close, and the pilot turned them back on a heading for Hickam Field.

Trace felt like she was in a vacuum as the plane descended, all alone in the back of the aircraft except for the crew chief who had remained quiet for the entire trip. The velocity of the Osprey slowed considerably. Trace remembered reading that the plane had to land in the helicopter mode as the blades were too big to allow landing with them in the forward position. She glanced out the window as the ground came up. She could make out military aircraft parked along the runway and several Air Police cars with lights flashing waiting to meet them. There were also two unmarked cars with darkened windows there.

The V-22 touched down and the engines immediately began rotating down. The back ramp opened, and Trace unbuckled her seat belt. Two men in three-piece suits stepped up in, stopping briefly in surprise at her condition. "Major Trace?" the lead man asked.

"Yes."

"I'm Special Agent Fielder," he said holding out his ID card. "I'm to escort you." He paused. "I understand you have a document."

Trace held up the diary, but pulled it back when Fielder reached for it. "I'd prefer to keep my hands on it until I see the President," she said.

Fielder kept his hand out. "What you prefer is not important right now. Give me the document."

WAIWA, HAWAII
6 December
5:00 A.M. LOCAL/ 1500 ZULU

A pair of headlights swept up the trail and raked across the open area. Boomer waited until Skibicki got out before moving. Skibicki must have heard Boomer coming because he knelt and pulled out a pistol, pointing it in his direction. "Hold it right there."

"It's Boomer Watson, sergeant major," Boomer called out.

Skibicki slowly stood. "What the hell are you doing here?"

Boomer twisted his head as he heard someone getting out of the other side of the jeep. The newcomer was a tall, massively built black man with a completely shaven head.

Skibicki did the introductions. "Major Boomer Watson, meet Harry Franks."

Boomer shook hands. "I've heard about you," he said. "Thank you for what you did for Trace."

"My privilege," Harry said.

"Is she all right?"

"I jumped off the plane before we landed," Harry said. "Ski picked me up off shore a few hours ago. Last I saw the lady was fine. She suffered some injuries but she's in good hands now."

Boomer looked at both of them. "We need to do something. The Secret Service and those close to the President aren't going to act. They've been infiltrated by these fake DIA people."

Skibicki grabbed his arm. "You ran away from them? They don't know you're gone?" he asked.

"Oh, they know I'm gone," Boomer said, remembering the car he'd left in the tunnel.

"You were supposed to warn the President!" Skibicki yelled at him.

"I couldn't even get close to him!" Boomer said angrily.

Skibicki had no reply to that.

"Have you heard anything new?" Boomer asked in a calmer voice.

"The *Sam Houston* is lying off-coast. I think they'll infil tonight sometime. Nothing from the north shore. Trace landed a little while ago, and your friends in the Secret Service have her in tow along with the diary. Hopefully that will make the President act. If not . . ." He slapped the dive knife he was throwing into a mesh bag.

"There's a good chance whoever met her isn't Secret Service," Boomer said. "She's might be in the hands of The Line right now."

Skibicki shook his head. "I talked to General Maxwell. He said he'd make sure she's safe. Tell me what happened from the time I dropped you off at the hotel."

"Maxwell was there when they took me away to kill me," Boomer said. Boomer laid out the events of the past twenty-four hours starting with meeting Stewart in the lobby through killing the two men at the abandoned ammo depot.

"I don't think Maxwell's with them," Skibicki said.

"I don't think so either," Boomer said, "but that doesn't mean Trace is safe."

"That's why we're here," Skibicki said.

"So what now?" Boomer asked, looking from Skibicki to Harry.

Skibicki pointed down to the harbor. "My guess is that they'll sneak into the harbor probably around four or five in the morning," Skibicki said. "Hooker's on the island," he added. "He's staying at the VIP quarters at Pearl."

"How do you know that?" Boomer asked.

"I have sources," Skibicki answered as he sat down in the passenger seat of the jeep. Harry sat on the hood.

"What sources?" Boomer asked.

"Listen," Skibicki said. "You opened this can of worms. I'm doing the best I can to deal with it."

"What's the plan?" Boomer asked. "Can you at least tell me that—*our* plan, that is."

Skibicki had a long, double-edged knife out and was sharpening it on a whetstone. Skibicki checked the edge against the hair on his forearm. "We go down to the channel entrance around midnight. I've got a sonar device that can listen for them coming in on their SDV. We hear them, we go into the water and meet 'em." The hair curled up as the blade slid up his arm. "Winner walks away. Loser's shark bait."

"Did Trace tell you anything about the contents of the diary?" Boomer asked Harry.

Harry shook his head, but then suddenly remembered something. He reached into his inside pocket and pulled out some pages. "She said to give you this—it's part of the diary."

Boomer took the pages and looked down at them. His heart skipped a beat when he saw the note in Trace's handwriting on the first page.

Boomer: The "fist" doesn't sound right. Trace.

Boomer remembered telling Trace the story of the radio operators jumping into France and how they were betrayed. Boomer looked over at Skibicki who was still sharpening his knife. Boomer could clearly see the depression on the side of Skibicki's head—from the wound he had received serving with Boomer's dad. "What about the Vice President?" Boomer asked suddenly.

"It's taken care of," Skibicki said shortly, without lifting his eyes.

"It's taken care of?" Boomer repeated. "How?"

"Trace got the diary to Maxwell, who will get it to the President," Skibicki said.

Boomer wasn't so sure about that given what had just happened to him. "Then why are we here?" Boomer asked. "Why not let the Secret Service take care of everything."

"Insurance," Skibicki said. "I don't think the Secret Service could handle what's happening. As you say, these fake DIA guys are all over the place. For all we know Major Trace won't get the diary to the President."

Boomer glanced at Harry, then back at Skibicki. "What's going on?"

Skibicki kept sharpening the knife.

"Something's not right with all of this," Boomer said, tucking the pages into the breast pocket of his fatigues. He leaned forward, looking Skibicki directly in the eyes. "I want your word, as someone whose life my dad saved, that you're being straight with me."

Skibicki's eyes flickered away for the shortest of moments, then came back to lock into Boomer's. He pointed down at the harbor. "To the best of my knowledge there's going to be an attempt to kill the President tomorrow morning. We're going to stop that attempt. I give you my word on that."

Boomer was not satisfied at all. The answer was well short of what he had hoped for. He thought again of Trace's short message, but there wasn't anything he could do about it right now except ride this thing out.

HONOLULU, HAWAII
6 December
9:00 A.M. LOCAL/ 1900 ZULU

Jordan stared at the diary as if it were a rattlesnake someone had placed on his desk. He looked at General Maxwell.
Trace was seated in the corner of the room in a wheelchair,
forgotten once she'd briefed the senator on her experiences
of the past several days.

"If one-tenth of what's in here is true, we have a crisis
of unprecedented magnitude on our hands," Jordan said.
"This, this . . ." He shook his head at a loss for words.
"My God, if any of this is true, we . . ."

"People tried to kill me to keep you from getting that,"
Trace said. "It all fits with what—" She halted as Jordan
held up a hand.

He tapped the diary. "But some of the things here are
just unbelievable. These people are crazy." Jordan leaned
back in his chair. "This could all be an elaborate plot designed to embarrass the President into going public with
this and then looking very stupid."

Jordan rubbed his forehead. "This diary ends in 1968.
We have no idea if this Line still exists and if they have
anything plotted for tomorrow. We've canceled the C&C
exercise aboard the SHARCC, which was the most likely
place and time for them to try something. This document
gives me nothing the President can use on General Martin
or any of the service chiefs."

General Maxwell cleared his throat. "Senator, I believe
you are still underestimating the situation here. In the military we always try to worst-case things. All the evidence
we have points to the fact that The Line exists and that
there is a plot. We alerted General Martin to that yesterday
and they've had time to deal with the cancellation of the
C&C exercise. If they did have a plot you can be sure that
they had backup plans. This is more than just a political
situation."

"But I'm a politician, general," Jordan replied. "I'm not
being facetious," he explained. "I'm being realistic. I can
not move to their playing field and expect to compete. I

have to deal with them on my playing field, and that is the field of politics.''

Trace twisted in her seat and caught General Maxwell's eye. He raised his eyebrows as if to say he understood what she was thinking but that he had made the best case he could. She was very confused. She'd asked about Boomer, and Maxwell had told her that he was in custody, although he couldn't tell her *where* he was in custody.

Jordan caught the look. "Let me ask you two something. In the over 200 years this country has been in existence, we have never had a military coup or even come close to having had one. Why are you both so willing to believe that one is occurring now?"

"We have *had* one, senator," Trace replied. She felt curiously calm, cast adrift from all known anchors, all her old allegiances gone, but now that she was here, it didn't bother her. She would worry about tomorrow, tomorrow. "If you believe that diary, the military, in the form of The Line, has been acting against the elected officials of this country for over fifty years. If that's not a coup, I don't know the definition of the word very well then. Just because they don't pull up to the front of the White House in tanks with guns pointed at the front door, doesn't mean they haven't been controlling things. Hell, Eisenhower himself warned us against the military-industrial complex when he left office.

"I find it very disturbing that all entries for the last three months of 1963 are missing. That was when President Kennedy was assassinated and—''

"Let's not get into that," Senator Jordan cut in. "That is something we don't dare get into. That could tear this country apart."

"But, sir," Trace said, "we need to get into it. We need to understand what we are up against here."

"It does not matter what we are up against," Senator Jordan said. He leaned back in his chair and gazed out the window at the bright sun coming up over Diamond Head. "There's a big picture here that no one seems to be considering, but we have to consider it. What if this''—he pointed at the diary—"is true? Do we release it to the media? Tell everyone that the past fifty or sixty years our country has been unduly influenced by a military junta? That we fought wars, and American citizens died and were maimed and wounded, because some generals sitting in a room somewhere decided we needed to test weapon systems and keep our forces in fighting trim? We can not let that information out!

"This is an abomination that has festered and grown in the shadows. And it is weak now—" He shook his head as General Maxwell tried to protest. "No, general, it is weak. Weaker than it has ever been. The world is changing, and many don't want it to change, but it is. The Wall did come down. We won the greatest war in history without a shot being fired. People are not going to stand for going back to the old ways, with nuclear missiles pointed at each other."

Jordan stood. "I'll brief the President. He will have to make the decision." He tucked the diary under his arm and left the room.

General Maxwell stood and wheeled Trace out of the room, the door shutting behind them.

"Do you know a Sergeant Major Skibicki?" Maxwell asked.

"Yes." Trace looked over her shoulder at the general. "Why, sir?"

"He called a little while back and asked me to look after you."

Trace smiled, but it quickly disappeared. "Do you think the President will believe Senator Jordan?"

Maxwell's lined face was worried. "I think the President is an excellent politician, but he'd make a crappy second lieutenant in the Infantry. Let's hope Jordan's right and The Line can be dealt with politically."

CHAPTER ☆ 25

The *Antietam* turned broadside to the *Arizona* Memorial, its crew on deck saluting in unison as the bosun's whistle signaled. The only difference between their actions in this rehearsal and what they would be doing tomorrow was that today they were dressed in work blues; tomorrow it would be dress whites.

Overhead, a thundering that had been approaching from the north reached a crescendo as a flight of Navy F-16s roared by, one plane on the wing missing. Mike Stewart stepped up to podium where the President would speak in the morning and stood there, taking the place of the Commander-in-Chief for this practice. He looked around at the harbor, watching the guided missile cruiser slipping by, the jets overhead, and the Navy security police cruising about in launches, and it all looked so much different than it had forty-eight hours ago.

Stewart watched it all with very different feelings. Everything that had looked comforting before now seemed threatening. Who could he trust here? Was Major Watson's story true? If it was, why had he disappeared? And why was the Secret Service doing nothing as far as Stewart could tell. There was no additional security being laid on, and there was still time to fly agents in from LA. Staring at the large gray bulk of the *Antietam* though, Stewart wasn't sure fifty more agents would do much good if the Joint Chiefs were in on this plot.

339

"Time for the wreath laying," the Navy protocol officer said, looking at her stopwatch. Stewart obediently stepped away from the podium and walked over to the naval honor guard standing at the railing. He simulated taking a wreath from them and throwing it over the edge. As he did so he looked down at the water. The rusting ring that had once held one of the large guns on the *Arizona* lay just below the surface. A small bead of oil, still leaking from the hull after all these years drifted to the surface and broke into a rainbow of colors. Stewart shivered, thinking of all the bodies just below, then he thought of what he could be facing in the morning at the President's side and the chill deepened.

WAIAWA, HAWAII
6 December
11:20 A.M. LOCAL/ 2120 ZULU

From the hillside Boomer could clearly see the rehearsal taking place on the memorial. He lowered the binoculars as the participants broke apart, boarding launches to take them back to the mainland.

Boomer frowned. There was too much going on at once. He wished he could sit down with Trace and talk. And Skibicki certainly didn't seem too pleased to have him here. Ski seemed sure that The Line was going to infiltrate Pearl and destroy the memorial with the President on it.

He had seen Stewart in the rehearsal. Who was who? Who could he trust? Skibicki wasn't being totally honest with him any more, Boomer knew. And Trace's warning on the manuscript pages. What did that mean? And the most important question for Boomer was where was she and who had the diary?

HONOLULU, HAWAII
6 December
1:30 P.M. LOCAL/ 2330 ZULU

"What's going on, sir?" Trace asked General Maxwell. They were seated in a room the floor below the President's.

They had not heard from Senator Jordan since he'd left with the diary.

Maxwell shook his head. "I don't know. According to Army records there have been no Delta Force operations in the Ukraine in the past twelve months. The *Sam Houston* is under the command of Navy Special Warfare Group One and is currently conducting training missions off the coast of California on radio listening silence, and this Colonel Decker does not exist."

Maxwell had come by the room she was "staying" a little while ago and told her about last seeing Boomer and his attempts to find out where he was being held. In the short time she'd been here, she'd begun to like the old general. She could tell he was very uncomfortable with everything that was going on.

"The Joint Chiefs are at Pearl Harbor," Maxwell said. "If one-tenth of what you said Hooker wrote in his diary is true, it is the most shocking document ever to surface in this country." They both looked over as the door to the room opened and Senator Jordan stood there.

"Major Trace," Jordan said, "there are some pages in the diary missing."

"Yes, sir. In 1963."

Jordan nodded. "Yes, I noticed that. But it also looks like someone tore out pages from an earlier time. I was wondering if you knew anything about that."

"I did that after the crash when I was afraid the diary might be taken from me. I gave them to a friend."

"A friend?" Jordan asked.

"The man who rescued me," Trace replied. "I gave them to him just in case things didn't work out here."

"So those missing pages are here on the island?"

"Yes, sir."

"What's your friend's name?"

"Harry Franks," Trace said. "He worked with Colonel Rison."

"Where is he now? How come he didn't land with you?"

"I believe he's with Sergeant Major Skibicki," Trace answered.

"Who no one can find either," Jordan said. "All right.

Thank you." Jordan shut the door before Maxwell or she could ask any questions.

"Well, at least it sounds like he's doing something," Maxwell said.

"I hope it's enough," Trace said.

WAIAWA, HAWAII
6 December
10:00 P.M. LOCAL/ 0600 ZULU

"Fifty-four years ago this evening the Japanese fleet turned to the southeast in order to be in position to launch their first wave at 0600 Sunday morning," Skibicki said. He was smoking a cigarette, his years of training showing in the way he kept the glowing tip hidden in the cup of his hand.

Boomer looked down at the lights of Pearl Harbor and thought of all those men so many years ago, going to sleep at Taps in ignorance of their approaching doom. He had no doubt that Skibicki was almost as much an expert on the events here as his mother.

"The Jap fleet was bearing down on the island at twenty-four knots. In Washington—at exactly 0238 local time, early evening here—the fourteenth part of the Japanese reply to the latest American peace proposal was received. The message ended by saying that the Japanese government found it impossible to reach an agreement through further negotiations."

Skibicki's voice was bitter in the darkness. "Maggie told you that Marshall relayed a warning to the fleet. Of course it arrived over fifteen hours after Washington received the fourteenth part of the message. It did the men dying down there little good, but the message did manage to cover Marshall's ass."

Skibicki field-stripped the cigarette, putting the remains into his pocket. "There was a battle of the naval bands that night in Honolulu. The *Arizona* band won."

Skibicki suddenly stood. "Time to be going." He grabbed one of the scuba tanks to load it onto his jeep, but paused, his eyes focused on the spotlit memorial. "It's been a long time coming, but the men who were responsible for that morning are finally going to pay.''

OFF SHORE, OAHU, HAWAII
6 December
11:00 P.M. LOCAL/ 0700 ZULU

The diver held his breath, kicked his legs up into the air, and slid under the waves. His right hand was on the thin nylon line that led down from the small buoy. The cord ran through his palm as he descended. The far end of the line was tied off on the bow of the deflated Zodiac twenty feet below the surface. Reaching the boat and gripping the line with one hand, the diver reached around in the dark water, searching by feel along the inside of the boat.

His fingers touched a canister. Quickly, his breath running out, he found the lanyard and pulled. The CO_2 canister immediately began filling the five chambers. The diver held on as the boat rose and broke the surface. He scrambled aboard, sealing off the valves between the chambers. He checked the engine—the watertight seals still held. Pumping the primer, he gave a pull. The engine started on the second try.

The man looked around. Off the port side a second boat popped to the surface with his comrade on board. Once that boat was ready, the two turned toward shore. They beached the noses lightly and twelve men materialized out of the jungle abutting the shoreline, their faces darkened with camouflage paint and their weapons locked and loaded. Six men got on each boat and they pushed off. They had a long ride to their destination, and they had to be there long before the sun rose.

CHAPTER ☆ 26

The location of the submarine was not that far from where a Japanese mini-sub had anchored exactly fifty-four years ago awaiting an early morning mission against the Pacific Fleet.

The routine was the same as that of forty-eight hours ago. The SDV cleared the dry dock shelter and headed in, maneuvering very slowly. This time though, the submarine followed at an agonizingly slow pace in an attempt to get as close as possible to the mouth of the harbor by dawn.

Eighty miles to the south, another submarine lay in wait, the control room crew shadowing their target. In the special compartment behind the control room, grim-faced men checked their weapons, loading the magazines round by round. Knives were sharpened, honing the razor-sharp edges even further. Breathing gear was tested one last time, and wet suits were slid on over muscled bodies.

WAIPIO POINT, HAWAII
7 December
2:30 A.M. LOCAL/ 1230 ZULU

"What is that thing?" Boomer asked.

"A listening device," Skibicki answered. "If they come in on a submersible I'll be able to pick them up with this." He lowered the microphone into the dark water and settled the headphones onto his ears. They were on the west side of the final entrance to Pearl Harbor proper, just north of Waipio Point. The channel was less than 500 yards wide here and any traffic coming in would have to go right by them.

They were both ready for entry into the water, wearing cutoff fatigue shorts, weight belts, and tanks, with masks and fins at the ready. Skibicki had given Boomer a double-edged Fairbarn commando knife. It would rust after being exposed to the water unless cleaned, but as Skibicki had noted, he would only have to use it this evening and the edge was razor-sharp. Boomer had placed the diary pages inside a plastic Ziploc bag and tucked it into his shorts pocket. Harry was inland, providing security against the possibility of a police patrol stumbling on their position.

"You think they'll still come?" Boomer asked. "Trace has got to have gotten the diary to Maxwell by now."

"If she got to him and wasn't picked up by these DIA goons," Skibicki said. "We can't take any chances."

"What about the Joint Chiefs? They'll be out there with the President in the morning. They wouldn't be on the memorial if their plan was to blow it up."

"They'll come up with something," Skibicki said. He indicated for Boomer to be quiet now and they settled in to listen.

Along the coast of Oahu, the two Zodiacs planed through the water at twenty-five knots, the men lying on the inside of the rubber hull, keeping their silhouette to a minimum. A light machine gun rested on the prow of each boat, pointing forward, just in case.

The navigator in the lead boat checked his heading on his handheld GPR. They were on course and would arrive in plenty of time.

HICKAM AIRFIELD, HAWAII
7 December
3:20 A.M. LOCAL/ 1320 ZULU

The head air traffic controller for Hickam Field had been rudely awakened by a phone call fifteen minutes ago, but when he heard the voice on the other end identify himself all irritation fled. The E-4B Airborne Command Post was to be moved to the ready flight line and prepared for take off. The head ATC had "yes, sirred," General Dublois and now he was ready, along with the plane. There was no flight plan filed but the E-4B didn't need one. It could fly anywhere it pleased.

The plane was at the end of the runway, waiting, engines idling, surrounded by Air Police, their blue lights flashing. The head ATC had no idea what was going on but he assumed it had something to do with the ceremonies coming up in a few hours.

PEARL HARBOR, HAWAII
7 December
5:00 A.M. LOCAL/ 1500 ZULU

"Stick with the plan," Hooker said, and the four generals nodded. "Your country is depending on you to steer a straight course.

General Martin stood, the other Joint Chiefs, minus the Commandant of the Marine Corps, a non-Naval Academy graduate, joining him. They left the superbly furnished VIP quarters and got into two limousines for the short ride to Hickam Field.

Hooker remained behind with his aides and bodyguards, watching the taillights of the cars disappear into the darkness. There was no hint of dawn yet in the eastern sky. Upstairs in a large room, the other members of the staff waited by the radios which they would monitor.

"Take me up to the second-floor balcony," Hooker ordered. From there he would have an unobstructed view of the Harbor and the upcoming activities. It was an event he had dedicated a lifetime to and nothing could keep him from missing it.

OAHU, HAWAII
7 December
5:20 A.M. LOCAL/ 1520 ZULU

A light tapping on the door to her suite woke Trace out
of an uneasy slumber. "Come in," she called out. She was
surprised to see an agitated General Maxwell standing
there. "What's wrong?"

"The Joint Chiefs are boycotting the ceremony," he
said. "I heard that from a reliable source at Pearl."

"What does that mean?" Trace asked, pulling on a
sweatshirt underneath the covers.

"I don't know," Maxwell said. "I'm just feeling
jumpy." He walked over to the window and peered out
into the darkness as Trace finished getting dressed.

There was another knock on the door. Maxwell turned
and opened it. Two men stepped in. "Come with us, general. There's someone who wants to talk to you." They
looked at Trace, now in her wheelchair. One man looked
at the other, then the leader decided. "You too."

"Where are we going?"

One of the men pulled a gun out. "We can do this the
easy way or the hard way."

CHAPTER ☆ 27

OFFSHORE, OAHU
7 DECEMBER
5:30 A.M. LOCAL/ 1530 ZULU

Through his night vision goggles, the navigator on the lead Zodiac spotted the IR strobe on shore. He steered directly in, slowing as they approached the rocky shore. A soldier in the prow threw a line to the woman waiting on shore. The party scrambled ashore, the last man opening the boat's valves, letting it slip back under the water.

The second boat came in and unloaded. The team leader walked up to the guide. "Major Keyes," he said, identifying himself.

"Sergeant Vasquez," the guide replied, taking his hand and returning his grip squeeze for squeeze.

Keyes broke off first. "All accounted for."

"I've got a van to take you on the final leg to your target, sir," Sergeant Vasquez said, pointing inland.

"All right." Major Keyes turned and gave a hand signal. His team spread out and they moved forward.

Eighty miles to the south, men began loading out of the submarine. Their target was less than a half-mile away, but totally oblivious of their presence. The captain had crept up slowly, on silent running, taking the entire night to cover six miles underwater.

The men were experts at this task as they formed up on their SDVs and mini-sleds. In a V, their team leader at the head, they slowly began to traverse the last of the distance to their target.

PEARL HARBOR, HAWAII
7 December
7:30 A.M. LOCAL/ 1730 ZULU

Boomer felt exposed as the sun continued rising over the hills to the east and shone down on the harbor. They were hidden in tall grass right next to the water, but already two naval launches had gone by with security personnel on board. Boomer checked his watch again. It was getting close—too close. "Maybe they were already in when we got here," he suggested.

"If they are in, then we're going to see some good fireworks soon," Skibicki said, briefly pulling off one of the earpieces, then replacing it. "But I don't think they would have stayed in that long. They only have so much oxygen on the SDV. No, they're still coming.

Several minutes passed, then Skibicki suddenly smiled. "I've got a contact," he said. "Moving steadily at two knots." He took off the headset. "Time to get wet."

Boomer slipped on his fins and pulled his mask down. Together they slipped into the water, Skibicki in the lead. He had another piece of exotic equipment in hand that Boomer had never seen before. The sergeant major had briefly described its function when Boomer had asked how they would pinpoint the Mark IX if and when it came through the entrance. Five hundred meters of dark water was a pretty wide area for two men to cover. Skibicki had shown him a small handheld device and explained that it would lock in on the OAR, obstacle avoidance radar, that the SDVs used and bring them right up on the craft.

The exercise of swimming through the water felt good to Boomer. His ribs still ached but the soreness wasn't crippling. He breathed in air through his mouthpiece, slowly exhaling in rhythm with his finning. Skibicki was a dark bulk just in sight. Visibility was less than four feet at their current depth of ten feet.

7:40 A.M. LOCAL/ 1740 ZULU

Agent Stewart could tell that the protocol officer for Pearl Harbor was extremely flustered. The folding chairs set up for the Joint Chiefs of Staff were prominently empty, except for the Marine Corps Commandant, and the young officer didn't quite know how to handle such an unprecedented breach of etiquette.

Stewart glanced about. There were a group of survivors of the *Arizona* gathered together on the other side of the memorial beside the media. The surface of the harbor was perfectly still, looking like a dark sheet of glass. The distant chatter of security helicopters was the only noise breaking the tranquility of the moment.

"Even at this moment," Stewart could hear one of the network anchors speaking, "fifty-four years ago, the five wave of Japanese planes was making landfall on the north side of Oahu, breaking into their attack formations."

Since the fiftieth anniversary celebration in 1991, the memorial service had hardly made a blip on the major networks, but the President's presence and the promise of a major policy speech had drawn the media.

Stewart glanced northward at the lush green hills. It was all so beautiful and peaceful. Then he looked back at the empty chairs. To him they were a bad omen. Last night, he'd talked to Rameriz, his boss, and they had brought in extra agents from the second detail. He looked around the memorial and noted the additional security. If someone tried an attack, they were as ready as they could be.

7:43 A.M. LOCAL/ 1743 ZULU

All Trace knew was that they were in a van somewhere on the landward side of the Pearl Harbor Navy base. Their guards had told them to be quiet when Trace had tried asking General Maxwell what was going on. She knew they were on the Pearl Harbor Reservation because she could see through a crack in the curtains separating them from the driver up front and had recognized a few landmarks.

The van had tilted, as if going down a ramp just before stopping, and Trace and Maxwell had been hustled out, down a long corridor, and into a large room with concrete walls.

There were two officers manning radios in the room and another officer dressed in camouflage fatigues standing at a map board. He turned as they were brought in and nodded. "General Maxwell, Major Trace. I'm Colonel Decker. Sorry for the inconvenience, but we need to talk." He glanced at the clock on the wall. "Unfortunately, I don't have time right now. Please, have a seat."

"I demand to know why we were brought here," Maxwell said.

Decker shook his head. "I don't have time right now, general. All your questions will be answered very shortly." He pointed at a TV on the wall that showed the ceremony just across the water. "Watch and see."

7:45 A.M. LOCAL/ 1745 ZULU

The two limousines had emptied their passengers fifteen minutes earlier. The boarding ramp was pulled back and the E-4B taxied the last few yards to the ready line. The pilot increased throttle and the plane roared forward, increasing speed until the wheels slowly parted company with the ground.

7:47 A.M. LOCAL/ 1747 ZULU

On the balcony of the VIP quarters, Hooker could see the silhouette of the E-4B disappear into the early morning haze, then he returned his attention to the harbor. The dark gray bulk of the *Antietam* was just making its presence known, coming out of the East Loch toward Ford Island and the memorial.

7:48 A.M. LOCAL/ 1748 ZULU

"All systems read green," the navigator reported.

"Turn the beacon on," the pilot ordered as he brought the propellers to a halt, having negotiated the final turn in the harbor entrance that would give them a line to the *Arizona* Memorial. They were just off Hospital Point, almost 2,000 meters from the target. It would be threading a needle, but if they got in any closer they risked getting picked up by one of the security launches.

The navigator transmitted a signal on the designated frequency and the beacon that had been hidden on one of the legs of the *Arizona* monument was activated. It began sending out its own signal.

"I've got target lock," the navigator said.

With the lock, they were confident that they would not miss. The guidance system of the torpedo would home in on the transmitter.

"Five minutes," he announced.

7:50 A.M. LOCAL/ 1750 ZULU

Eighty miles to the south of Pearl Harbor, the captain of the SHARCC was gratified to see that they had a secure link with the E-4B now airborne and gaining altitude to the north. He was less than gratified though, when his executive officer suddenly swore from his position near the sonar operator.

"Sir, we've got multiple small contacts off the starboard bow."

"What is it? Dolphins?" the captain demanded, looking over the shoulder of the sonar operator.

"Negative, sir." The technician frowned. "They look like five or six small submersibles and they're close." He fiddled with the controls. "Sir! There's a large contact on silent running behind the smaller ones. I wouldn't have picked it up if I hadn't gotten the others on screen. It looks like a large sub—maybe a Los Angeles or Ethan Allen Class!"

7:51 A.M. LOCAL/ 1751 ZULU

On board the E-4B, General Martin had the crew run through their communications checklist for taking over all satellite transmissions one last time. The five-mile trailing wire antenna was slowly unreeling behind the aircraft as it passed 4,000 feet of altitude.

Martin also made last-minute contacts with various military forces standing by, awaiting his orders. The SHARCC had been the primary plan, so they hadn't had a chance to do a run-through with the E-4B crew. He had no doubt, though, that the men and women on board would perform

when the time came. They were all handpicked for their
professionalism and even more so for their unquestioning
loyalty. Especially since only a select few knew the exact
nature of their mission.

7:52 A.M. LOCAL/ 1752 ZULU

"Two minutes," the navigator said, caressing the launch
lever as he watched the red numbers turn over on his display.

7:52 A.M. LOCAL/ 1742 ZULU

Major Keyes checked his watch. Two minutes. His men
were gathered together on the roof, the three-foot edging
keeping them hidden from the ground below. They'd
climbed up the back side of the adjoining building in the
dark using collapsing aluminum ladders. Then they'd tra-
versed across the gap between the two buildings using a
line fired across from a crossbow.

They'd quietly manually drilled in anchor points for their
rappeling ropes and securely attached the lines. Keyes slid
the nylon rope through the snap link on the front of his
harness, making sure it looped once so he could break. He
edged up on his knees next to the wall. Three other men
on lines watched him for the word to go. Behind each of
them, four other men waited their turn. Vasquez was there
too, over the protests of Keyes, dressed in black with a
submachine-gun, ready to go.

Keyes flipped his MP-5 submachine-gun off safe.

7:53 A.M. LOCAL/ 1753 ZULU

"Ladies and gentlemen, the President of the United
States!"

The President walked to the podium and looked out at
the sea of faces and television cameras. "Let us bow our
heads in a minute of silence for those who died here in the
service of their country."

7:53 A.M. LOCAL/ 1753 ZULU

The torpedo was a large bulk on the top center of the Mark IX, dividing the pilot's hatch from the navigator's. Boomer looked over the torpedo at Skibicki bobbing in the water and nodded. At the same moment they twisted the latch on the respective hatch below them. Skibicki leaned in and levered his arm around the neck of the pilot of the Mark IX, jamming the point of his knife into the soft skin under the man's jaw, pushing it up into his brain, killing him instantly.

Boomer wasn't so fortunate. The point of his knife glanced off the air hose of the navigator, severing it and leaving a gash along the left side of the man's face. The navigator convulsed forward, sucking in a lungful of sea-water.

Boomer dropped the knife, letting it dangle on its lanyard, and grabbed the other man's arms with his own hands, pulling them away from the firing lever the man was desperately trying to reach.

It was a silent struggle in the surreal green glow of fifteen feet of water. Boomer was half in the hatch, upside down, pressed up against the open latch, his hands on the other man's forearms, holding them up and away.

Skibicki could only watch from the other side, unable to get in, blocked on the inside by the body of the pilot buckled into his harness and on the outside by the bulk of the torpedo. A steady spray of bubbles from the severed airline floated to the surface, the only sign of the battle going on underneath the placid harbor surface.

7:54 A.M. LOCAL/ 1754 ZULU

Keyes stood and hopped onto the edge of the building. He pushed off and dropped out of sight, one hand on the rope, the other holding out his submachine gun ready for use. The other three men went over at the same time.

As soon as the ropes went slack, the next men hooked in and followed. As the last one cleared, Vasquez followed.

7:54 A.M. LOCAL/ 1754 ZULU

The arms grew weaker and weaker and then Boomer felt no resistance. He looped one arm around the man's chin and slid the blade of his knife into the man's neck to make sure he was dead. A small burst of red clouded the water.

Skibicki leaned into the Mark IX and adjusted the controls, turning off the power and disarming the torpedo. The submersible slowly sank down toward the harbor bottom. Skibicki then tapped Boomer on the shoulder and indicated for him to follow. Boomer turned to the west, but Skibicki grabbed him, shook his head and pointed east.

7:54 A.M. LOCAL/ 1754 ZULU

"Damn it, what's going wrong?" General Martin demanded, staring at the television screen in the war room of the E-4B at the President who still stood at the podium.

"We don't have contact with the SDV," Admiral Hancock reminded him. "They might have been held up. The President will still be out there for another twenty minutes."

"And if the SDV mission has failed?" General Dublois asked.

"We still have the back up on Air Force One." Hancock said.

Martin nodded. "Contact the SHARCC and have them relay the order for our decoy to back out. Go to alternate plan Stingray."

"Yes, sir."

As Admiral Hancock turned to give the order, the E-4B reached 10,000 feet of altitude. The air pressure indicator on the detonator of the bomb Skibicki had relocated to the E-4B's inflight refueling inlet did what it was designed to do and exploded the dual blasting caps set into the ten pounds of C-4.

Those inside had a brief moment to wonder what the cause of the loud popping noise was before the explosion reached the auxiliary fuel tanks just above the main fuselage, and the entire aircraft became one large fireball.

7:54 A.M. LOCAL/ 1754 ZULU

"Our link is down with Looking Glass!" the SHARCC executive officer yelled. "She's gone!"

"What the hell?" the captain exclaimed. He tore his gaze from the sonar screen. Whatever the contacts had been, they were now too close to be picked up. The large contact was stationary off their starboard bow, about 1,000 meters away.

An alarm screeched. "Torpedo lock!" the counter-electronics officers yelled, indicating that the large contact had locked in a torpedo homing signal on their hull.

"Have they launched?" the captain demanded.

"Negative, just the lock."

The captain had no idea what was going on, but whatever it was, none of it was in the intricate plan he'd been briefed on.

The SHARCC shuddered as an explosion reverberated through the hull. "Status!" the captain screamed. "I thought you said they hadn't fired!

"We've got a breach in number three and four swim locks forward," the damage control officer reported. He looked up. "It wasn't a torpedo. Someone's at the hatches. We're being boarded."

The SHARCC captain drew his pistol and gazed at the corridor leading to the front of the submarine. There was a chatter of automatic fire, then dead silence. The captain pointed his weapon at the hatch.

He never got a chance to shoot as the first Navy SEAL came through the hatch firing.

7:54 A.M. LOCAL/ 1754 ZULU

Hooker leaned back in his wheelchair and sighed. The members of the staff were scurrying about, yelling into portable Satcom radios. Except nothing was happening, all communication with Looking Glass and the SHARCC was down. He could see for himself that the memorial was still intact and if he squinted, he could make out the figure of the President behind the podium, still speaking.

There was the sound of a shot on the first floor and all

the men froze, looking at one another in confusion. Hooker
was ignored as four men dressed in black swung down from
the roof on rappeling ropes, landing on the balcony. They
fired long sustained bursts from their silenced weapons into
the room, killing all inside. Over a hundred years of military experience died in those seconds. Hooker's bodyguards
fought back and two of the men went down, but a second
wave followed and the sheer number of the attackers overwhelmed Hooker's men.

It was over in twenty seconds. Three black-clad men and
one woman—Hooker could tell by her figure—were still
standing. Everyone else other than Hooker was dead.

The leader of the men turned to the old man and pulled
up his black balaclava. "General Hooker."

"Major Keyes," Hooker nodded in return. "We wondered where you had gone. We haven't heard from you in
six months." He looked beyond, at the bodies strewn about
the room and the shattered radios. His staff was now gone.
There was no one left but him.

Keyes shifted the lever on the side of his MP-5 to single
shot. "You've failed, you know that, don't you?"

"I did my duty to my country to the best of my ability,"
Hooker replied. "I lost this battle, but there is a bigger
picture." His right hand was under the blanket covering his
lap.

"Enough macho bullshitting," Vasquez called out.
"Let's finish it."

Hooker's blanket shredded as he pulled the trigger of the
silenced Ingram MAC-10 concealed there. At 1,100 rounds
a minute, the thirty-round magazine was completely emptied in under two seconds.

The shocked look on Keyes's face was gratifying to
Hooker as the major staggered back under the impact of
bullets. Hooker's right hand flicked a switch on the left arm
rest and Claymore mines that had been wired into the ceiling exploded, spraying the other side of the room with
thousands of tiny pellets. The rest of Keyes's team and
Vasquez died in the blast.

7:55 A.M. LOCAL/ 1755 ZULU

The roar of the F-16s built to a crescendo and the missing man formation flew by overhead. The bosun's whistle on the *Antietam* blew across the water and the crew saluted in unison.

A lone bugler standing on the end of the memorial put his instrument to his lips and began playing Taps, a tune written by Major General Butterfield, West Point class of 1839, the soulful sound echoing through the hearts of the men standing at rigid attention. On the faces of some of the survivors tears flowed despite all the years that had passed. Tears for their young comrades in arms who had not known the blessings of the past fifty-four years.

CHAPTER ☆ 28

**PEARL HARBOR, HAWAII
7 DECEMBER
8:40 A.M. LOCAL/ 1840 ZULU**

A dark hole beckoned in the bright blue water, and Skibicki's fins disappeared into it. Boomer hesitated for a second, then followed. His compass told him they were on the east side of the harbor, which meant they were near the sub pens at Pearl.

The hole narrowed to a tunnel six feet in diameter. Dim, underwater lights lit the way, showing pitted concrete walls, slowly sloping up. Boomer surfaced in a chamber about twenty feet square with a wooden dock on one side. He slipped off his fins and joined Skibicki on the deck.

"Where are we?" he asked as he took off his tanks and weight belt.

"This is the dive area for NAVSPWRGP One," the sergeant major replied, referring to the Navy special warfare group at Pearl. "We're right next to the sub pens. They use this to get out into the water without being seen, which they occasionally have to do for training. It was actually built in World War Two as a service duct for the sub pens, but since the pens were expanded in the other direction and upgraded, this whole area was given to the SEALs." Skibicki pointed at a metal door. "This way. There are some people I want you to meet."

Skibicki twisted the hatch and swung the door open. On the other side a large room beckoned lit by halogen lamps. Several radio sets were operational along one wall, and a

361

large table was in the center of the room with maps spread out on it.

There were numerous men in the room, but Boomer's eyes fastened on the lone woman with the large white cast on her leg seated at the conference table. He ran across the concrete floor and skidded to his knees, wrapping Trace in his arms.

For several minutes he simply held her, head buried in her shoulder. When he finally pulled back, he smiled as he looked into her eyes. "What the hell happened to you?"

"Just some minor problems. I'm all right." She looked over his shoulder. "You'll be surprised to see who's here."

Boomer followed her gaze and stiffened as he spotted the familiar figure of Colonel Decker. At the radios he recognized Lieutenant Colonel Falk and Colonel Coulder. Boomer turned to Sergeant Major Skibicki who had followed him over. "Who are these people?" Boomer asked. He pointed. "That's Decker. He's the one who ordered the mission into the Ukraine."

Skibicki laid a hand on Boomer's arm. "We're getting ready to brief General Maxwell. You and Trace need to hear this too, because it's the only time this story is going to be told other than when Maxwell relays it to the President. I really don't know all that's happened either, so bear with us."

Boomer looked back at Trace. "Are you all right?"

"Yes."

"Do you know what's going on?"

"Not yet." Trace ran her hand up his arm. "I missed you."

Boomer took her hand and wrapped his fingers tightly around hers. "I'm glad you're back."

Colonel Decker went straight to the head of the table. He didn't acknowledge Boomer's or Skibicki's presence other than with a curt nod. "What's our status?" he asked Falk, who had a headset held up to one ear.

"Looking Glass is down. SEAL Team Three has the SHARCC secure. We haven't heard from Task Force Reaper yet," Falk succinctly reported.

"Will someone tell me what is going on?" Boomer demanded.

"Major Watson," Decker said, holding up a hand. "Have some patience. All your questions will be answered in a few minutes. Right now I'm trying to get the information together so that I *can* answer them."

In confusion, Boomer slumped down in the chair next to Trace as General Maxwell was escorted to the chair next to him.

Decker spoke into the radio and seemed perturbed at the lack of answer. Reluctantly, he faced the senior ranking military man in the room and saluted. "General Maxwell, what you are about to hear must be relayed to the President and that is why we asked you to come here this morning," Decker said.

"No one asked me a damn thing," Maxwell said, returning the salute angrily.

"We apologize for some of our methods, but as we explain I think you will understand the reasoning behind our actions," Decker continued. "First, let me give a little background. The Line has been in existence for over seventy years. We," he said gesturing about the room, "have been fighting them for the last five of those years."

"Who is we?" Maxwell asked.

"Members of the Special Operations community," Decker answered vaguely.

"And who elected you to this job?" Maxwell asked.

"No one elected us," Decker said. "We have been trying to do what was right and—"

"The right thing would have been to expose The Line as soon as you were aware of its existence," Maxwell cut in. "That is what your oath of office and your sense of duty would have required."

"Yes, sir, you are correct," Decker said. "Unfortunately, I became aware of the existence of The Line over twenty years ago on Ring Weekend as a cadet at the Academy when I became a member of the organization. I only turned against it five years ago, and by then I was already too far involved to be able to walk away or expose it.

"For a long time, I thought I was doing the right thing. It was only in the late eighties, after a good friend of mine was killed by The Line, that I changed my convictions. It has taken years to gather together a few men that I could trust in order to accomplish what we did today.''

Decker then proceeded to relate the story of the fight between the Special Operations community and the regular Army for the past several decades.

''After the death of the 1st Ranger Battalion commander, Colonel Bob Kelly, one of my roommates from West Point,'' Decker continued, ''there were certain people in Special Operations who realized that The Line was a threat that went beyond intra-service animosity. I knew—because I was on the inside—that The Line had caused Bob's death and the cover-up of the crash of his Blackhawk at Eglin. I approached a few people, and we began watching and waiting.

''We didn't know about Colonel Rison having the diary, but we did know about the events at Nha Trang where he had been arrested and we knew that the war between the regular forces and our forces was continuing.

''Even then there was no consensus on action to be taken. That is until we discovered that The Line was plotting against the President. At that point, we no longer felt we had an option. We had to act.

''Since I was already on the inside it was felt that it was best if I continued to play my part. Major Keyes also was on the inside and turned against The Line when he heard what I had to say after I approached him at Fort Benning. In fighting The Line we had the support of many people within the Special Operations forces,'' Decker said. ''Otherwise today would have turned out much differently than it did.''

''I understand all that,'' General Maxwell said, ''and your story is very interesting, but please tell me what is going on right now.''

''General Martin and the Army, Air Force, and Navy Joint Chiefs of Staff are dead,'' Decker said. ''Their E-4B command and control aircraft was destroyed by a bomb less than an hour ago forty miles southeast of Oahu.''

''You're joking!'' Maxwell said.

''No, sir, I'm not.''

''You killed them,'' Maxwell said.

''We transferred a bomb they had placed on board Air Force One onto their E-4B. I prefer to think they killed themselves. They were preparing to take over all satellite media in the United States after the death of the President and declare martial law. It was thought best they not have that opportunity.''

He looked Maxwell in the eyes, and Maxwell nodded for him to continue. ''General Hooker, the man who has been in charge of The Line—and the members of his staff, the controlling committee of The Line—should be dead. That was Major Keyes—Task Force Reaper's—responsibility at the VIP quarters a quarter mile away from where we are right now. Unfortunately we haven't heard from Major Keyes yet.''

''What about The Line?'' Maxwell asked.

''It will wither and die,'' Decker said. ''Hooker has been the brain for The Line for the past fifty years. Without him and the influence he exerted through the Joint Chiefs, The Line is finished.''

''Wait a second,'' Boomer said. ''I don't understand what's going on. Why was I involved and—''

''We knew The Line had a plot against the President,'' Decker interrupted. ''So we had to come up with a plan to foil them.'' He rubbed his forehead, as if trying to figure out the best way to tell the story. ''All right—let me back up and tell you first what The Line had planned. Then you will see why we had to do what we did.

''Between the MRA, the recent budget cuts, the cancelling of Hard Glass, the events in the Ukraine and Turkey . . .'' Decker paused. ''Well, I could go on and on, but to cut to the chase, The Line—and many other people—have not been very happy about the direction the country is going in. The difference is that The Line does something about it when they don't like the way the country is going. And usually something illegal.

''There were many small incidents—the raid into the Ukraine that Major Watson participated in for example—that were done to embarrass this administration and try to manipulate policy. Unfortunately—or fortunately, depending on whose side you're on—those efforts didn't work.

''The MRA passing Congress was the final straw, so to speak. General Hooker didn't think it had a snowball's chance in hell of getting Congressional approval but the

President won that round. Hooker didn't want to wait around and take his chances with the Senate. He decided to take action and this trip by the President to Hawaii played right into his hands. As you could tell by Hooker's diary, The Line has a history of acting drastically against presidents if necessary.

"Their primary plan was to kidnap the President when he attended the command and control exercise aboard the SHARCC. When that was canceled, they went to their secondary plan which was to kill the President this morning on the *Arizona* Memorial with a torpedo fired from a Mark IX swimmer delivery vehicle."

"How did they think they could get away with that?" Maxwell demanded.

"The SDV that was to fire the torpedo was delivered off shore by a Barbel Class submarine that we captured from Iraq during the Gulf War back in—"

"Wait a second," Boomer said. "What about the *Sam Houston*?"

Skibicki answered that. "The *Sam Houston* is further off shore—but it is under our control. We had to be prepared to stop all The Line's plans. The SEALs on board the *Sam Houston* were ready to take over the SHARCC and save the President if he had gone through with the C&C exercise.

"For foiling the secondary plan, we were relying on Sergeant Skibicki, whom you assisted in doing just that this morning. The Barbel Class Iraqi sub was carried by the *Glomar Explorer*, which also does resupply for the SHARCC. The Line's plan was that they would let the wreckage of the Barbel sub be found after counter-submarine actions by the Navy. Thus the destruction of the memorial and death of the President could be laid at Iraq's doorstep, which would kill two birds with one torpedo so to speak."

"You deceived me," Boomer said, looking at Skibicki. "You told me the *Houston* was moving in to shore."

"I only found out about that yesterday," the sergeant major said. "And we had to stop the SDV off the Iraqi sub which *was* moving in. Vasquez found all that out. I didn't have time to get into all this. What I told you was essentially the truth.''

''Their third plan,'' Decker continued quickly, ''was to destroy Air Force One with an altitude-detonated bomb. This was a backup in case the other two plans failed and the President attempted to depart the island alive. We were not aware of this plan. It was just fortunate that Sergeant Major Skibicki discovered and followed the men from the Barbel Class sub who infiltrated Hickam and planted the bomb on board Air Force One two nights ago. He retrieved it and placed it aboard Looking Glass.

''We have since discovered that The Line's cover for that action was to be an attack by long-range Iraqi bombers. Again captured during the Gulf War. The two F-16s that fly security for the President were to be flown by pilots loyal to The Line. Not too hard to find after the events in the Ukraine last week. They would swear to the attack by Iraqi planes, which they would have destroyed, when in reality the bomb would have destroyed Air Force One.

''The Barbel sub is currently being tracked down by the *Sam Houston* and will be captured shortly. The SHARCC is under our control. It was boarded by Navy SEALs from the *Houston* at the same time Looking Glass was destroyed. The two pilots are also in custody and the two Iraqi bombers are also under our control.''

''My God,'' General Maxwell exclaimed. ''These people were insane.''

''No, sir,'' Decker said. ''They were desperate.'' He looked at Boomer. ''And we were desperate also.''

''You ordered me to kill Americans,'' Boomer said staring hard at the colonel.

''The mission you did into the Ukraine was done under direct orders from General Martin. I knew it was a setup designed to work against this administration. But I had to go along with it or else expose my role as a double-agent. Like I said, we knew they were planning to kill the President here in Hawaii, and I had to continue playing my part until we could directly attack and destroy The Line and save the President.''

''The Coventry excuse,'' Boomer said. His voice was bitter. ''For the greater good, right?''

Decker met his look. "I don't justify what I did. I did it, and it's done. I could have saved those men in the Ukraine and ordered you to abort, but that would have tipped our hand and the President and whole bunch of other people would be dead. I'm the one who has to live with it."

"No, I have to live with it too," Boomer said. "Why me?" he asked. "Why did you use me?"

"Because you were the right person in the right place at the right time." Decker explained. "We needed someone to go to the President. Someone who wasn't involved with us."

Boomer looked about the room. He could see it all now. "Keyes and his A Team—the jump into north shore?"

"We set that up. We needed Keyes and his men here. To take down Hooker."

"There never was a plot against the Vice President?"

"Not as far as we know," Decker said.

"What about the two men we killed that night?" Boomer asked Skibicki. "Were they more pawns to be sacrificed for the greater good?"

"That's something that doesn't have to be on your conscience," Skibicki said. "Remember those men we killed the previous evening outside Major Trace's house? How we couldn't find their bodies and show them to the cops? They were the ones who had broken in and were ready to kill her. They worked for The Line. I hauled the bodies up to the point and dumped them. The whole firefight we had was a staged event. We were firing blanks and so were the men—members of Keyes team—shooting back at us."

"So the message on the drop I broke out was a setup too," Boomer said.

"We needed to get you thinking—and relay that thinking to the President—that something was going to happen," Decker confirmed. "As you can see, Colonel Falk and Colonel Coulder were in on it." He looked at General Maxwell. "If one of us had come to you, you might not have believed us and you certainly would have stopped our counter-actions. But having Major Watson and Major Trace believe in the plot and trying to convince you allowed us to continue our counteractions without interference."

General Maxwell looked at Boomer and Trace. "Yes, I believed them."

"You can't use people like that," Boomer said.

"We had no choice," Decker replied.

"What about Colonel Rison being killed?" Trace asked. "Did you plan that too?"

"That was unexpected," Decker said. "The Line has always had its own sources of information, and they were ahead of us there."

"Damn right they were," Trace said. "They almost killed me."

For the first time Decker showed some ignorance of events. "We don't know how The Line got onto you so quickly. You should have been able to get in and out with the diary. I don't know what happened at West Point."

Trace had been doing a little bit of thinking on her own. "They must have gotten my license number when I went to visit Mrs. Howard—the woman who told me about The Line in the first place."

"That was foolish on your part," Decker said. "They would have had an alert out for you there. We know about them killing her. It was unfortunate. We didn't think they would be that vindictive."

"Vindictive? Foolish? Unfortunate?" Trace said, her voice rising. "This is all *insane*! You just killed the chairman of the Joint Chiefs of Staff and you're telling me I was foolish? You're calling the deaths of innocent people unfortunate?"

"I prefer to think of it as we just saved the President's life and prevented a coup which would have cost many more innocent people their lives," Decker calmly replied.

"I'm sure you would," Boomer joined in. "But others might see it differently. *I* see it differently. I was directly responsible for the death of a friend of mine in the Ukraine. You set me up to do that. You put our lives on the line—Trace and me. Who the hell do you think you are? God?"

"No," Decker said. "*You* put your lives on the line." He pointed at Trace. "No one said you had to write about what Mrs. Howard told you. That's what brought you into this. No one said you had to go to the mainland to see Colonel Rison." He shifted to Boomer. "You're the one

that came up with the theory that the President was threat-
ened. What if we had given you the real information?
Would it have made any difference? The plot was real. The
Line was real.''

"Gentlemen," General Maxwell interrupted. "We can
sit here all day and argue the finer moral points of what
has happened, but it has already happened. There are important issues that have to be decided very shortly, and I
need to go back to the President and inform him of that
has occurred.''

Decker nodded. "It *is* over.''

"What about Looking Glass?" Trace asked. "How are
you going to explain that?''

"The same way The Line got rid of so many of its enemies over the years. We will control the report issued by
the investigation board. They won't find much of the E-4B
to investigate anyway. It went down over deep water. We
regret the loss of the crew, but we had no choice. They
were preparing to cut in to the satellite media coverage of
the ceremony and broadcast a message from General Martin. It would have blown the lid off this country. We
couldn't allow that. We also couldn't allow the Joint Chiefs
to survive.

"Most of the people who were on board the SHARCC
and the Barbel submarine didn't know what they were involved in." He looked at Boomer and Trace. "They were
simply following orders. They'll be quietly transferred.''

"The DIA men?" Boomer asked.

"They were The Line's agents," Skibicki answered.
"The rest of them will be taken care of.''

Decker pointed about the room. "This group of people
will go back to their lives and their careers, and that is why,
General Maxwell, you are here. You need to go to the President and tell him it is over. He has Hooker's diary. I assume he does not want that information made public.
Neither do we wish our activities made public. It's over.''

Lieutenant Colonel Falk suddenly spoke from where he
had been monitoring the radios. "Keyes and his team are
all dead.''

Boomer stood. "Playing God didn't work out too well,
did it?''

"What about Hooker?" Decker asked. "Did they get him?"

"I'm listening to the naval security frequency," Falk said. "I can't tell. There are a lot of bodies there. Sounds like it was a bloodbath. They probably got him."

CHAPTER ☆ 29

Boomer and Trace dropped General Maxwell off in the underground garage of the Royal Hawaiian. They watched as he went into the elevator to go to talk to the President. They knew that the men in the underground room at Pearl Harbor were scattering, covering their tracks.

Trace turned to Boomer in the car where they sat. "Since you've had time to consider this, what do you think?"

"I hate to say it," Boomer said, "but I have to agree with Colonel Decker's plan. We keep the lid on this whole incident. We mourn the loss of General Martin and the others on board the E-4B as a tragic accident. Then we move on. Quite frankly, there's no other option."

"And how do we stop this from occurring again?" Trace asked.

"I don't like the idea of a cover-up; even the word bothers me," Boomer agreed. "But if we expose what has just happened, then we will eventually be forced to reveal all that was in the diary, and that is unacceptable."

"Why?" The edge in Trace's voice surprised him. "It was secrecy that shrouded The Line for so many years and allowed it to grow and fester. Now we're doing the same thing."

"It would tear this country apart to find out what was in that diary," Boomer said.

Trace looked at him. "You were very big on expediency being no excuse, yet here we are talking about expediency

373

requiring . . ." Trace searched for the right words. . . . "requiring a bodyguard of lies."

"Secrecy was The Line's strength while it was alive," Boomer acknowledged. "But there are those who do know the truth," he continued. "You and I know what happened."

"Fat lot of good that will do," Trace said. "Colonel Rison knew the truth, and it didn't stop anything. And he eventually died because of this. How do we know The Line is finished? They haven't found Hooker's body. We don't even know if Hooker was the main man behind The Line. Maybe there are others in other places." Trace shivered. "To think this all started at West Point."

Boomer's face was drawn with exhaustion, but he had been doing some hard thinking in the past few hours. "It would be easy to say getting rid of the academies would prevent this from happening again, but I'm not sure they were the problem. There definitely need to be some changes made. An opening up of the curriculum and more interaction between the military and the civilian community. Right now we have two separate societies in our country and it's particularly pronounced in the officer corps. We need to get the people who guard our country more in tune with the country and out of their own separate existence.

"We need to remember something else," he said. "The people who stopped The Line were mostly Academy graduates also. Let's not condemn the system because, as the facts have shown, the system did indeed work."

Boomer shrugged. "But I don't know. I don't know what is going to happen." Boomer put his hand on Trace's shoulder. "How do you feel?"

Trace shook her head. "I don't feel like I helped save the country. I feel like a sponge that was dipped in dirty water and rung out a few times too many."

Boomer felt the same. "We don't have to wait here for Maxwell. He's probably going to be with the President quite a while."

"Just give me a couple of minutes," Trace said. "I don't feel too good. I didn't feel good listening to Decker in that underground bunker, and I still don't feel right."

Trace had touched on something that had bothered Boomer also. "There was too much explanation by Decker," Boomer said. "I agree with you: It doesn't feel right. I still don't understand why we got involved."

"They, the Special Op people, didn't involve us," Trace said. "The Line did when they found out about my book."

Boomer disagreed. "No, Decker set *me* up for a reason even before that." He remembered something he'd forgotten to ask her in the excitement of the morning. "Why did you write that note on the pages you gave Harry?"

"Things didn't seem right," Trace said. "The inflight refueling seemed a bit much for Skibicki to arrange, but after hearing Decker's explanation, I guess that part fits together now. Plus, what was on those pages made me nervous."

"What do you mean?" Boomer asked.

"The whole Pearl Harbor thing," Trace said.

"What are you talking about?" Boomer was lost.

"You didn't read the pages themselves?" Trace asked.

"No, just your note."

"You need to read them," Trace said.

Boomer pulled the Ziploc bag out of his pocket. He opened it and pulled out the wrinkled pages.

15 November 1941

Getting Roosevelt to act is like trying to lead a stubborn mule. The State Department still thinks we can do things the old way, with nicely worded telegraphs. Tell that to the people of Nanking in China. When will the fools in this country see reality?

18 November 1941

With or without the President, war is coming. The consensus of the staff is that we must enter it as prepared as possible, but more importantly, the country must enter it wholeheartedly. It is obvious from the Magic intercepts what is going to happen. The chief can't believe the audacity of the

Japanese——to strike directly at Pearl is daring, but ultimately stupid.

20 November 1941

The chief wants to hold the Magic intercepts. Keep Kimmel and Short out in Oahu in the dark. I told him that we couldn't hold them all. In fact, we have to make sure that the paper trail doesn't lead back to us. He assigned me to find a better means of doing it. I'll be leaving for Hawaii shortly.

26 November 1941

I found the perfect way. I've made a connection with the Navy lieutenant who picks up the classified telegrams and transports them to the Navy G-2 at Pearl who forwards a copy to Army G-2. I have let him in on what we are trying to do and he sees the wisdom of it and has agreed to help us. We'll keep Admiral Kimmel in the dark, although, as agreed by the staff, I did brief Admiral Halsey, and he will keep the carrier fleet safe out at sea. Now we have the added bonus of getting rid of Kimmel and replacing him with one of our own after the Japanese strike.

"Oh my God," Boomer said looking at Hooker's handwriting.

"I can't believe they knew about the attack and allowed it to happen," Trace said.

"No," Boomer said. "That's not it. This Navy lieutenant. I know who he is." Boomer paused as a limousine pulled into the underground garage and came to a halt on the far side. The doors swung open and a man got out. He leaned over and talked to someone still in the car through a lowered window.

It all came together for Boomer then. Trace followed his eyes. "What's the matter?"

"I correct my last statement," Boomer said. "I know

who the lieutenant is *now*." He pointed.

"Senator Jordan?" Trace asked incredulously. "He's the lieutenant who withheld the Magic intercepts?"

"Not only is he responsible for that," Boomer said, "but he's also the one who got you and I involved in this. He's been running everyone." Boomer remember the abandoned ammo depot. "The son of a bitch! He ordered me killed."

"What?" Trace asked. "What are you talking about? How do you know he was that lieutenant, and why would he want us involved?"

"To get his hands on the diary," Boomer replied. He watched as Jordan shut the limousine door and got onto the elevator. The large car swung around and headed for the exit. As the window Jordan had talked through powered up, Boomer was not all surprised to see Colonel Decker seated in the back of the limousine, smoking a large cigar.

CHAPTER ☆ 30

OAHU, HAWAII
7 DECEMBER
12:15 P.M. LOCAL/ 2215 ZULU

"It all makes sense now," Boomer said as he swung onto Kalakau Avenue and headed west. "The diary is the key to all this."

"It doesn't make sense to me," Trace replied. "This whole thing was just to get that diary? Killing the Joint Chiefs? The plot against the President? All of it was a setup to get us to get Rison to give up the diary?"

Boomer shook his head. "No. All that was real. The Line was real too. And they did have a plot against the President. But you and I. We were brought into it to get the diary. That's what made me feel uncomfortable down in that briefing room. I didn't buy Decker's explanation that I was involved just to go to the President with a warning. They could have picked anyone for that."

"But how could they have found out about you and me?" Trace asked.

"They did it backwards," Boomer said. "Skibicki wasn't in on it either. Not in the beginning. In fact, he was the key, and they used him too. Jordan must have known about the diary, and he knew it would destroy him if it was ever made public." Boomer tapped his pocket. "Obviously, according to Hooker, Jordan also knew about The Line way back in 1941."

"Back up," Trace demanded. "How do you know Jordan is this lieutenant?"

Boomer quickly related the story that Maggie had told

him about her lover and the picture in her bedroom of a young Jimmie Jordan. "I thought I recognized the face. Now I know for sure."

"So Jordan was the father of Skibicki's half-brother?" Trace asked.

"Right. And not only that," Boomer said, "but he was directly responsible for the death of Ski's sister."

Boomer sorted it all out in his mind and spoke slowly, fitting the pieces together. "Jordan knew the only way to get the diary was through Rison. Everyone who knew about the diary knew that. The Line was willing to have a truce with Rison as long as he kept quiet. But Jordan couldn't. Maybe Hooker was even blackmailing him about his previous collaboration with The Line in allowing the attack on Pearl to occur so long ago. Trying to pressure Jordan to get to the President. In fact, if Jordan refused to accede to The Line, it could have precipitated the drastic action here in Hawaii.

"The diary was a huge threat to Jordan. And he knew about Rison. And the best way to get to Rison was through Skibicki. But Skibicki wouldn't just let anyone go to Rison. He had to have a reason. So Jordan must have had Skibicki checked, and they found out about my dad and then me. And then when they checked me out, they found out about you."

"Don't you think that's a bit much?" Trace asked.

"Not for a man with the power that Senator Jordan wields. I'll bet you every dime I have that he had you set up with Mrs. Howard and the letter and interview. He was trying to kill two birds with one stone. Flush out the diary through you and me, and also try to fight The Line, because now that he's in the position he's in, he's on the other side, working with the President. Look at what The Line did to Eisenhower with the U-2 incident. I think Jordan was in bed with The Line until his close friend got elected President, then things got sticky for him, and he had to decide which side he was on."

"So many people have died," Trace said. "I don't know any more who the good guys are and who the bad guys are. You're telling me that The Line did plot to kill the President, right?"

Boomer remembered the struggle in the water just a few hours ago. "Correct."

"But you're also saying that Senator Jordan, the President's right-hand man, was working to get back evidence that he had collaborated with The Line in allowing the attack on Pearl Harbor fifty-four years ago."

"Right." Boomer took the turn off to head into Pacific Palisades.

"So what are you going to do about this?" Trace asked.

"I don't know quite yet. But I do know someone who has some decisions to make and is entitled to this information right now."

PACIFIC PALISADES
7 December
12:30 P.M. LOCAL/ 2230 ZULU

Skibicki looked at his mother. "Is it true? You told me the man in the picture was just an old friend of dad's."

In reply, Maggie went to her bedroom and returned with the photo that Boomer had seen and handed it to her son. "I let go of my memories of Jimmie Jordan until I saw his name in the paper years ago when he was first elected to the Senate. And then I simply avoided thinking about it." She looked at Boomer. "Let me see those pages." Maggie took the papers and read them, tears forming in her eyes. "So Jimmie really did know about the attack?" she asked, handing them back.

"Yes." Boomer said.

"And he allowed me to spend the night with him and leave my daughter home, knowing we were going to be attacked December seventh?"

Boomer didn't answer. Trace took Maggie in her arms as she surrendered to the anguish of fifty-four years of lies.

Skibicki stood, putting the picture down on the coffee table and began pacing the room. "That means they set me up too. When Falk told me about the planned attack on the President, right before you showed me the message about the drop," he added, looking at Boomer. "I thought that it was all above-board. At least from our end."

"It was," Boomer said. "You just didn't know that Senator Jordan was pulling the strings through Decker for his own motives.''

"Son of a bitch," Skibicki muttered. "Son of a bitch."

Maggie pulled herself out of Trace's arms and wiped her eyes with a tissue. "Will it ever end?"

"General Maxwell, and through him, the President believe it's over now," Boomer said. "They've closed the book on this."

"Who has the diary?" Skibicki asked.

"Senator Jordan," Trace replied.

"No shit," Skibicki said. "It worked just like he wanted."

Boomer stood. "Any word on what happened at Hooker's quarters?"

"Keyes and his men were killed," Skibicki said. "Vasquez was killed too."

"I'm sorry," Boomer said.

"I'm responsible for her," Skibicki said. "I got her involved. They found her body in there, along with a whole bunch of people at Hooker's VIP quarters. The people in the tunnel have broken everything down. Security folks at Pearl and Hickam are going crazy, what with the attack on the quarters and Looking Glass going down."

"Maxwell will cover all that," Boomer said. "Hooker?" he asked again.

"His body hasn't been found yet. His jet's at Hickam."

"I think they closed the book too fast," Boomer said. "If Keyes and his men are all dead, who do they think fired the last shot?"

"If Hooker's still alive, I want him," Skibicki said.

"He'll want to get out of here," Boomer said.

"Hickam," Skibicki said, standing.

HICKAM AIR FORCE BASE
7 December
12:47 P.M. LOCAL/ 2247 ZULU

"Hooker and Jordan," Skibicki said, glaring out the windshield of his jeep at the Learjet. "Like you said in the tunnel, they think they're fucking God. That they can use people, kill them, just to fit whatever plans they dream up."

The jet appeared to be deserted. They were parked off the end of the runway, about 200 feet from it. Boomer didn't know what to say to Skibicki. He himself was overwhelmed with all he had learned and experienced over the past several days. He couldn't imagine how Skibicki felt after learning about Jordan and hearing about Vasquez's death.

"He knew about Pearl. Hell, they both knew about it," Skibicki said. "Hooker and his pals might as well have been in Tokyo working with the Japanese Imperial staff. Then Jordan—fucking Jordan—allowed it to happen. He killed my sister!" Skibicki pounded the dashboard with his fist. Plastic splintered and blood seeped out where the skin tore. Boomer remained silent, watching the jet. Trace was in the back seat, but she'd been quiet ever since they'd left Maggie's.

Boomer tapped the sergeant major as a bus pulled up to the plane and two pilots stepped off. The bus pulled away as the two men began pre-flighting the aircraft.

"Someone's going somewhere," Boomer said.

"No they ain't," Skibicki vowed. He reached under his seat and pulled out the Calico.

"There's air police all around," Boomer warned. "We'll have to take him quietly."

Skibicki didn't answer. His eyes were two black beads, peering straight at the jet. One of the pilots climbed in. The other removed the chocks from the wheels.

Boomer looked around. A van was coming down the flight line. It stopped to the side of the jet. The driver hopped out and opened the side door. He offered his arm and an old man gingerly stepped out.

"That's Hooker," Skibicki said. He started to get out of the jeep.

"Hold it," Boomer said, grabbing his arm. "What are you going to do?"

"End it." Skibicki pulled back the bolt on the Calico.

"This won't end it," Boomer said.

"I'll end part of it." He looked at Boomer. "The rest is on you." He shrugged off Boomer's hand. He began jogging toward the jet.

"Stop him!" Trace slapped Boomer on the back.

"No one can stop him," Boomer said. They watched helplessly as Skibicki got closer to the plane.

The driver saw Skibicki first. He had Hooker in his arms. He pushed the old man toward the stairs leading into the plane, and one of the pilots grabbed Hooker. The driver reached under his jacket for a weapon, but Skibicki, who was now only fifty meters away fired a burst. The rounds caught the driver in the chest, flipping him backwards.

Boomer looked to his right. An Air Police vehicle was racing toward the scene. At the jet, the pilot was lifting Hooker inside. Boomer could hear the jet engines running. The other pilot was at the controls.

Skibicki was in an all-out sprint now. He fired at the cockpit and Plexiglas shattered. He was only ten meters away and must have been out of ammunition because he threw down the Calico.

The police car screeched to a halt at the wingtip and the two cops leaped out, weapons at the ready. "Freeze!" they both screamed.

Skibicki ignored them. The co-pilot jumped between him and Hooker, who was leaning against the stairs. Skibicki went through him like he wasn't there, his fists flailing, the man falling to the ground.

A knife appeared in Skibicki's hand and he grabbed Hooker drawing him toward him.

"Drop the knife!" the cops yelled, edging closer.

"Shoot him!" Hooker called out. "I am General Hooker, and I order you to shoot him!"

Skibicki smiled. He drew the knife across Hooker's throat, and blood gushed forth. The police shot, the rounds knocking Skibicki back against the skin of the plane. He slid down, his body on top of Hooker's.

Boomer slumped back in the seat. Other Air Police cars were arriving, surrounding the jet.

"We need to get out of here," Trace said gently. "Boomer?"

"Yeah." Boomer pressed the starter for the jeep, put it into gear, and slowly drove away.

They were silent for a while, until Trace spoke. "Skibicki was right."

"About what?" Boomer wearily asked.

"About not letting it go. About not letting this disappear into the blackness of secrecy again."

"Hooker's dead," Boomer said. "It's over."

"No, it's not over," Trace said.

"What are we going to do?" Boomer asked.

"Whatever we can," Trace said. "Whatever we can."

CHAPTER ☆ 31

Having gained sufficient altitude, Senator James Jordan turned on the autopilot of his Learjet 25B and leaned back in the pilot's seat. He was on his way back to Washington after Christmas break in Vermont. He had returned home to Vermont for Christmas for the past forty-two years.

The jet was his pride and joy and had almost cost him the election four years ago. His opponent had pointed to it as a sign that Jordan had lost touch with the common man of Vermont. Jordan had been forced to retaliate by trotting out the trip logs for the aircraft proving that his ownership of the plane had actually saved the taxpayers money because he used it for much of his professional traveling at his own expense.

Jordan looked out the right window of the cockpit at the Green Mountains. There was a fresh covering of snow, and he could see skiers sliding down the slopes of Sugarbush.

There was a scraping noise from the back of the plane and Jordan's head snapped around, staring at the door leading to the main cabin. He frowned as he stood up. Some of his baggage must have fallen over. He hadn't used the cargo compartment since he had the entire plane to himself. He'd simply dumped his bags in the first row of seats. The FAA wouldn't approve, he knew, but the FAA didn't look in his plane.

387

Jordan slid the door open, stepped into the main cabin, and froze at the sight of a man pointing a pistol at him. He recognized the face and he staggered back a step.

"Subsonic dum-dum bullets," Boomer said, waggling the pistol slightly. "It'll make a big hole in you but won't go through the skin of the plane and depressurize us."

"What are you doing here?" Jordan demanded.

"I was in the cargo compartment. You really ought to stow your gear," Boomer said.

"What do you want?"

"Did you know Earl Skibicki? I think you knew his mother, Maggie. Pearl Harbor? 1941?"

Jordan didn't say anything.

"You knew her, right?" Boomer insisted. He cocked the pistol.

"Yes." Jordan swallowed. "What do you want?"

"Did you know about her daughter getting killed?"

"What do you want?" Jordan repeated, his eyes casting about, searching for anything he could use as a weapon.

"Did you know about her daughter, Earl Skibicki's sister, being strafed by Japanese planes and killed on the morning of December seventh, 1945?" Boomer asked.

"Yes."

"Did you know about Skibicki's half-brother—your son—being killed in Vietnam in the Ia Drang Valley?"

"What?" Jordan said, his eyes stopping their search and fixing on Boomer. "What did you say?"

"You didn't even keep track of your own son, did you?" Boomer said. "Maggie told me you didn't, but I couldn't believe that. That a man wouldn't even give a shit about his own flesh and blood. You just don't give a shit about anyone, do you?"

Boomer shook his head. "All the things you've done over the years. All the bodies. All the pain and suffering. You are a sorry sack of shit, Mr. Senator."

"What do you want?" Jordan said.

"The diary," Boomer snapped. He smiled as Jordan's eyes flickered toward his snakeskin briefcase. "You're stupider than I thought. You should have destroyed it, but I knew you'd still have it. You wanted to keep it because you never know, right? Might need it some day?"

Boomer grabbed the briefcase with his free hand and set it down on a seat next to him. He pulled out a knife and cut through the locked flap, pulling out Hooker's diary. He stuffed it inside his parka. "But that's not really why I came here," he said. "I really wanted you."

"We can work this out," Jordan said. "The Line is finished. I did the right thing. I helped the President and General Maxwell too—"

"Spare me the bullshit. You don't have much time left. Better use it to pray. You tried to kill me once. Now I'm returning the favor."

"I beg of you—I can make it right—I can—"

"You can't make the dead come back to life," Boomer said. He tucked the gun into his belt, and Jordan breathed a sigh of relief.

Boomer took one step closer to the senator, then spun, his right leg lashing out and the boot slamming into Jordan's chest, forcefully expelling the air Jordan had just so gratefully inhaled.

Jordan crumpled down the floor, gasping in pain as the jagged edges of his broken ribs cut into his lungs. "Please," he gasped. "Please."

"Shut up," Boomer snapped. He pulled a parachute out of the cargo bay and buckled it on over his parka, making sure all the straps were tight. Then he turned back to Jordan lying on the floor.

"Come on, senator. You've got a plane to fly," Boomer said, grabbing the other man by the lapels and pulling him into the cockpit.

Jordan tried to scream as Boomer threw him into the pilot's seat, but the act of screaming hurt as much as the movement. Boomer carefully buckled up the senator's shoulder straps, making sure he was securely fastened to the seat.

"What are—you—doing?" Jordan managed to say, his hands gripping the armrests of his seat so hard the whites of his knuckles showed.

In response, Boomer knifed down with the outer edge of his right hand onto the senator's left wrist. Bones cracked with an audible snap. Before Jordan fully realized what had happened, Boomer did the same to the senator's right wrist.

"Oh God!" Jordan screamed, his hands dangling helplessly. "Please, please, don't do this!"

"Have a good flight," Boomer said. He reached over and flipped off the autopilot. Then he jammed the yoke all the way forward and the plane nosed over. Grabbing a hold of the doorjamb, Boomer pulled himself into the main cabin, where he hit the emergency opening on the crew door. It swung open and slammed tight against the outside of the plane. He could hear the senator screaming in the cockpit, and as he pulled himself out of the plane, Boomer idly wondered if the man had the guts to try and use his broken limbs to regain control.

Boomer was out into the windstream, and he spread his arms and legs until he stopped tumbling and was stable. He pulled his ripcord and gained positive control of his canopy. He looked about and spotted the Learjet 2,000 feet below him, still in a steep dive. It hit into the snow-covered slopes of the Green Mountains and exploded.

"No fucking guts," Boomer said as he turned his chute away from the mountains toward his landing zone and waiting jeep.

☆ EPILOGUE

Eisenhower Hall is the West Point equivalent of a student center. It houses several restaurants and meeting areas and it is there dances for underclass cadets are held on weekends. It also houses a 4,500-seat auditorium and for the past twenty minutes the Corps of Cadets all 4,200 strong—had been filing in with military efficiency, filling the seats from front to rear.

General Maxwell, the recently confirmed chairman of the Joint Chiefs of Staff settled into a back row seat and watched the process. By protocol he shouldn't be in the auditorium. He should wait until all others were seated, then make an entrance, requiring all inside to pop to their feet at attention and hold it until he gave them at ease. But he wasn't the reason the cadets were here this evening. He was neglecting protocol, because he wanted the young men and women in front of him to realize the seriousness of this evening.

Down the back aisle from him were several members of the press corps from New York City. They were a bit confused by the lack of protocol also, but for a different reason. They were here because Maxwell was here. A short press release issued by the public affairs officer at West Point earlier in the day had simply stated that the chairman of the Joint Chiefs of Staff would be giving a lecture to the Corps of Cadets. With the MRA still a hot issue, even in

391

modified form, in the Senate, the reporters were hoping for a good quote or two from Maxwell.

The previous superintendent had surprisingly resigned for "health" reasons just after the new year. The new superintendent was a hard-charging young two-star direct from command of the 101st Airborne Division—General Turnbull. And it was Turnbull who took the stage as the last of the cadets took his or her place exactly on time.

"Ladies and gentlemen, the Superintendent of the United States Military Academy," the cadet adjutant announced.

A sea of gray dutifully rose in front of Maxwell and remained at rigid attention.

"At ease," Turnbull boomed out, disdaining the microphone. He looked toward the rear, where he knew Maxwell was in the shadows. "The chairman of the Joint Chiefs of Staff, General Maxwell."

As the cadets rose, Maxwell yelled out in his best parade field voice. "Stay seated!"

This perplexed many of the cadets—a basic conflict between their protocol training and their obedience to orders. Which was exactly what Maxwell wanted. He strode down the center aisle as the cadets confusedly regained their seats. Bypassing the orchestra pit, he took the stairs up onto the stage and walked to the center.

"Good evening," he said, his deep voice carrying out as far as that of the best trained stage actor.

"Good evening, sir!" the Corps chorused back.

"You think you're here to listen to me," Maxwell said. "But you're not. You're here to listen to a couple of officers who have sat where you are sitting and who have gone through trials that you will go through after you graduate. Who have been forced to examine their sense of duty very deeply and who have done the right thing, even when it was the most difficult thing to do.

"Major Boomer Watson"—Maxwell pointed to his left where a spotlight went on, highlighting Boomer at a lectern—"and Major Benita Trace." A similar light went on to his right. "I want you to listen very carefully to what they have to say." Without another word, Maxwell strode off the stage, back up the center aisle.

There was a rustling of seats as people shifted position,

settling in for whatever lay ahead. The Corps was more than used to getting lectures on any sort of subject and since the chairman wasn't speaking, there was a lessening of interest.

Maxwell sat down and his aide handed him a copy of the speech that his newly formed Academy advisory board had worked out in conjunction with the two majors over the past three weeks. He felt it was a powerful wake-up call to the Corps that things were going to be changing a bit around the Academy, with a shift from the hard sciences to the humanities—and a good dose of ethics instructions. As much as the message was to be delivered to the Corps, Maxwell wanted it out in the press. Thus the news release earlier in the day. Good press never hurt, and the President needed all the good press he could get.

Boomer was first to speak. "Good evening. My name is Boomer Watson, class of 'eighty-one."

"And I'm Major Benita Trace, class of 'eighty-two." Trace left her microphone and walked across the stage to join Boomer on the right side.

"What are they doing?" Maxwell's aide asked. "They're not supposed to do that."

Boomer held up a piece of paper. "This is the speech we are supposed to give." He put it down on the stage and pulled something from inside his dress green jacket. "This is what we are going to read to you from. It is the diary of Brigadier General Benjamin Hooker, West Point class of 1930. We will allow you to draw your own conclusions about the contents."

Down the aisle from Maxwell the reporters looked at each other and the speech transcripts they had been given in confusion, but turned on their microphones and recording equipment anyway.

Boomer looked down at the leather clad book in front of him and read. *"12 June 1930. I will indeed miss my rock-bound highland home above the Hudson, but I must admit to a certain degree of anticipation for the assignments that await me. I have become a man at West Point, and as a man I will take my allotted place in the Long Gray Line.*

"I thought my heart would burst today as we sat on the Plain and listened to Secretary Hurley give the graduation

address. I find it difficult to believe four years have gone so quickly, yet looking at the faces of my classmates on either side I can see the changes wrought in us by the years. We came here as boys—we leave as warriors. And I have been fortunate enough to be one of the chosen ones. I have received my instructions and training beyond that of my peers for the past two years—now I am finally ready to go out into the Army as one of the The Line.''

"I'll stop him, sir," Maxwell's aide said, starting to stand up.

"Sit down," Maxwell quietly ordered.

Trace took the diary from Boomer and began reading the next entry.

The aide looked at Maxwell. "But, sir—they're—they're—"

"I can see and hear what they're doing," Maxwell said. He put down the prepared speech and gave a sad smile. "It's something someone had to have the guts to do. I wish I had done it."